AURTHORA
CELTIC PRINCE

THE EXPLOITS OF
A CELTIC WARRIOR.

AURTHORA
CELTIC PRINCE

R W Hughes

Matador
5 Weir Road
Kibworth Beauchamp
Leicester LE8 0LQ, UK
Tel: (+44) 116 279 2299
Fax: (+44) 116 279 2277
Email: books@troubador.co.uk
Web: www.troubador.co.uk/matador

ISBN 978 1848765 542

British Library Cataloguing in Publication Data.
A catalogue record for this book is available from the British Library.

Front Cover Photo: Lud Church. Gradbach. Staffs.

Typeset in 11pt Adobe Casion Pro by Troubador Publishing Ltd, Leicester, UK
Printed and bound in the UK by TJ International, Padstow, Cornwall

Matador is an imprint of Troubador Publishing Ltd

MIX
Paper from
responsible sources
FSC® C013056

Acknowledgments

I would like to thank Susan, my wife of forty six years, for her love-patience and understanding. Our friends in Italy Richard and Susan Kent for their help and advice in the early stages of this book. Our good friend Peter Robinson of Swythamley UK for his professional help and assistance especially in obtaining this book's front cover, which captures the Celtic mystery and mythology we were looking for in this historic adventure novel.

The road to fulfilment of ones dreams is always under construction. RWH.

In memory of Vera.

Prologue

When the Roman legions, the occupying force and administrators of a large area of the island of Britannia for over four hundred years, were departing its shores and returning to their lands on the Mediterranean to defend the borders against the barbarian hordes threatening their massive Empire, Britannia was left with a power vacuum.

Part of the Celtic tribes that would not submit to Roman control had been forced onto the fringes of the occupied lands from where they kept up a guerrilla war. These tribes were based in what is now Wales in the South West, Northumbria in the North West, Cornwall, and the fierce Caledonian Picti tribes in the wild, inhospitable areas of the far North, Albran, now Scotland, along with the tribes of Diariada, now Ireland.

With the departure of the Roman legions, the Celtic tribal leaders with their supporters returned to the lands of their forefathers to reclaim their birthright. The most successful leader among these tribes was Erion, the one they called the Great King. He had amalgamated several of the smaller tribes with his own by convincing them they would have a much better chance of survival by operating as one force, rather than as small independent kingdoms.

It was rumoured that the king was a descendant of the daughter of Queen Boudicca, the leader of an ancient people called the Iceni. She had continued the fight against the invaders long after her husband had been killed while leading his warriors in battle against the Roman legions.

The storytellers told how Queen Boudicca had taken up her husband's great sword and rallied the tribes after the Roman general Paulinus had savaged and plundered her kingdom, robbed her nobles, raped her daughter, then carried on to destroy Snetisham, the capital of their kingdom.

She had defeated the legions on many occasions, proving herself as a great general and master tactician. After winning several major battles against the invaders and reclaiming a number of important cities in the name of the Celtic tribes, the Celtic War Council, [under the influence of the Druid religious leaders who did not want a woman as head of their victorious army] replaced her with a braggart and hot-headed king of a neighbouring tribe. Although this man was a fearless warrior, he did not possess the tactical skills of Queen Boudicca.

The history of the final battle against the Roman army was well known from the tales told by the storytellers. Outnumbering the Roman army six to one, the impetuous young king had led his Celtic army in a great charge against the formations of the legions.

The well-trained Roman army stood firm, their rectangular metal shields forming an impenetrable barrier against the brave but wild attack of the combined tribesmen. The Celtic army was so tightly packed against the line of Roman shields they were unable to wield their long swords, swing their great two-handed battleaxes, or use their long spears effectively.

The Roman soldiers, however, could stab with their short swords from behind their wall of steel. It was a terrible carnage. The War Council watched in dismay as their army was destroyed before their very eyes. The Roman cavalry came behind the beleaguered army and, catching them unawares, put them to the sword. Attacked from both front and rear, the Celtic army was destroyed along with most of the leaders of the uprising. Queen Boudicca, who had watched this disaster from a hill overlooking the battlefield, turned her war chariot and, along with her two daughters – one pregnant from her rape by the Roman general Paulinus – plus her small band of followers, fled the scene. Using secret paths and trails they eventually managed to reach the distant mountains. There, on the island the Celts called Mona, Queen Boudicca's daughter gave birth to a son. The Queen and her followers and after them their descendants, continued her tribe's guerrilla campaign against the occupying Roman legions for hundreds of years.

King Erion realised when he was a young man and his father was still king that the only way to reclaim their ancestral lands and to retain them against any future army of plunderers or invaders was to emulate the success of the Roman legions.

With the eventual death of his father, Erion was duly appointed king and leader of the small mountain kingdom. It was then that he began to put his ideas into practice, against much opposition from his father's warlords and chiefs. He refused to attack the retreating Roman legions: his argument was that the Romans were leaving and so were no longer a threat. He was certain the young men of his army would be put to better use reclaiming their lands and defending them against any outsiders who might try to fill the vacuum left by the Roman retreat. It was only when his tactics proved successful, and his small, well-trained army won many battles and skirmishes in the process of retaking their ancestral lands, building a formable reputation, that the mutterings amongst the older chiefs and advisors subsided.

The Great King's lands covered what is now North Wales; when the

Roman legions left, King Erion laid claim to part of what are now the counties of Cheshire, Staffordshire, Derbyshire and South Yorkshire.

The borders of the kingdom were defined, and apart from some minor disputes with the adjoining kingdoms, which were usually resolved by a high level meeting between the king and his neighbours, within this domain twenty years of peace and great prosperity followed.

King Erion was seen as fair and honourable in his dealings over border disputes, the shedding of blood was usually unnecessary. Loyal chiefs and followers of the king were granted land and buildings from the areas they had occupied and reclaimed. The former Roman owners who stayed behind when the legions departed were given the choice of being amalgamated into the kingdom if they so wished, but only on condition that they and their servants were prepared to swear an oath of loyalty and allegiance to the king. Any man living and working within the boundaries of the kingdom who refused to swear such allegiance was sent to work in the gold, silver, lead or copper mines alongside criminals and thieves.

Some of the remaining Roman owners of farms and small estates who had served in the Roman army or in its administration, being well versed in the training and manoeuvres that had proved so successful for the legions, were employed by King Erion to train his warriors, being well paid for these services in grants of land.

He followed this course in order to discipline and train his small army in the manoeuvres and battle plans used by the Roman legions, in the ways and use of Roman weaponry, their method of warfare. When this had been accomplished, the men returned to their own towns and villages continuing to train the young men in their area. King Erion had decreed that all men under the age of fifty summers should attend the training sessions. Failure to do so, unless by special exemption, could lead to being sent to work in the mines. This law was rigidly enforced by the king's appointed officers. This far sightedness was soon to be put to the test: the peace that King Erion had maintained in the country for such a long period was about to end. The dark clouds of war were gathering on the horizon. A vast invasion force had landed in the far North and already beaten the armies the northern kingdoms had sent against them. Now they were occupying and colonising vast tracts of land on the island of Britannia. These newcomers were an alliance of foreign peoples called Angles, Jutes and Saxons. They were tall and fair and formidable warriors. They were the most serious threat to the Celtic way of life and the Kingdom of Elmet that Great King Erion had ever had to face.

Aurthora: Celtic Prince

Author's Introduction

The seeds of this story were first formed twenty years ago when I moved to the parish of Wincle, a Cheshire village on the edge of the Peak District National Park near the town of Macclesfield. This village dates back to Celtic times and the Roman period of occupation and influence from 55 BC – 410 AD. On one corner of my land were the remains of a Roman checkpoint. This was beside the old salt trail which was where the merchants passed with their line of pack ponies, carrying salt from the salt mines at Northwich and other trade goods to barter in the rest of the north of Britannia as they had done for many hundreds of years. It was here they would be stopped by the Roman soldiers to check if they had the stamp of the local governor to show they had paid their taxes.

It was a period in Britain's distant past when Druid priests and wizards still practised their mystic professions. When fairies were said to dance in the Black Forest on the night of the full moon, brave soldiers in highly polished chain mail rode out to do battle against the disciples of evil with their false gods…The invading barbarians.

R W Hughes

Chapter 1

As the swirling mist lifted and thinned from the Whistling Moor – so-called because of the sound of strange music, as if from a damaged flute, that could be heard when high winds blew through the bare branches of the stunted trees – a tall figure could be seen striding purposefully along, draped in a thick woollen cloak in an attempt to keep out the bitter, biting east wind that was sweeping across this exposed stretch of moorland.

He was leading a horse laden with his belongings; this animal was no ordinary pack pony, it was much taller than the local breed, with a deep chest that indicated stamina and powerful hindquarters for speed. Now as dusk fast approached, even though the horse was heavily laden and been travelling since dawn, there was still a spring in its step as both man and animal followed a faint path that wound its way across this high moor.

They had spent the previous night in lodgings in the village of Blujon, whose inhabitants earned their living by mining a rare coloured stone which they turned into prized jewellery, much sought throughout the Kingdom of Elmet and even further afield for its beauty and supposedly magical properties. Legend was that if a piece of such jewellery was given by a true love when the ground was white with a full moon as far as the eye could see, then their wishes would be granted.

Aurthora, for that was the traveller's name, pulled his cloak tighter around his shoulders. There had been an occasional flurry of snow in the cold east wind, and by the sky's colour there would be more to come before the day was over. It was hardly fitting for man or beast to be about in such weather and wild country. Several days earlier he had started on this journey from Great King Erion's army encampment, which was based within the walls of the High Town of Buxonana. Speed was essential if he was to honour the mission he'd promised his old friend and tutor before returning to his duties as protector of the Great King. He was surprised to find the track so faint and wondered why more travellers had not used it to trade with the village of Blujon and other hamlets nearby. Before leaving the village that morning he had memorised his map for the day's journey. The map had been drawn on the finest material, a rare and beautiful silk traded by merchants who came from distant lands who spoke languages no Celt could understand. When opened it was a full square yard, showing in detail the trail and written instructions he needed to follow in order for him to reach the place where his tutor had hidden the treasure twenty or so years before.

As he strode the faint path, his mind wandered back to when his father Prassatt Ambrosius who, in spite of his sickness, had gathered his noblemen and men-at-arms and placed Aurthora, his only son, in charge of them. He instructed him to answer the call-to-arms and ride in support of Great King Erion and the Celtic Round Council.

So much had happened since leaving his father's fortified house, which stood majestic on a hill overlooking the bustling town of Macefield. It was the house from which his family administered the area for many years on behalf of the king. He smiled to himself recalling the scene: townspeople cheering as he left at the head of the great body of armed men, chain mail glittering in the morning sun, leather work oiled and shining as they sat high on battle saddles astride their sturdy horses. He felt so proud and privileged to be in charge of such a loyal group of warriors...

As the head of the line travelling along the stone paved road reached the crest of the hills to the east of Macefield, he pulled his horse aside from the group and looked back.

His gaze first fell on the twelve noblemen following him, each with two men-at-arms and ten soldiers from his father's house. There were also the lesser nobles from the surrounding area, each with a man-at-arms, and about thirty free men whom Aurthora's father provided with arms and equipment from the town's armoury.

Following the main body of mounted noblemen came thirty-eight bowmen, jogging at a pace they could maintain all day. They wore loose woollen trouser-like garments, and shirts under long leather waistcoats; some had long daggers hanging from their brass-studded leather belts, but most carried short axes combining a highly sharpened blade on one side with a hardened, pointed spike on the other. They were led by Roderick Tristan, a tall man, taller than Aurthora, with enormous shoulders developed through years of vigorous training in drawing his great bow. He walked with a slight limp: constant use of the longbow since his youth had overdeveloped his right shoulder and twisted his spine. This man with his mop of black unruly hair and snow-white beard was a legend in his own lifetime: his speed and accuracy with the longbow were renowned throughout the Kingdom of Elmet, wherever people gathered, the travelling bards would entertain the children and their parents with tales of his exploits.

His father and grandfather before him had both been excellent archers and had served the family of the Great King in the past. Throngs of people turned out if it was known that Roderick the Bowman was to display his exceptional skills with the longbow in any of the archery competitions.

The bow was usually taller than its handler, a full six feet, with shafts three feet long and goose feather flights to guide the arrow. This weapon had struck fear into the Roman soldiers, who could be killed from a great distance by an assassin they would never see. All the victim heard was the *swoosh* of the arrow before its hardened iron point impacted with enough force to penetrate the heavy Roman metal-covered shields and body armour of the soldier sheltering beneath. Many arrows could be fired within moments: six shafts fired by one man could be in the air before the first found its target. It was said that a group of archers could have so many arrows in the air at one time they could blacken the sun, and turn day to dusk.

This powerful weapon had been written of and recorded in the Ogham script, the tree writing of the Druids. When the remains of the Celtic army and the retreating Celtic tribes with all the remaining Druid priests of that great civilisation had gathered on the sacred island of Mona for a Great Summer Solace. At this important religious ceremony of prayer and chanting which lasted for three days and included many sacrifices to honour the animal gods of the Celtic religion and the warriors who had fallen on behalf of their people, there had been the final blessing to the yew tree, the great Tree of Life. The High Priest who had visited the Second Kingdom of this god Cerrunnos, lord of all the Druid gods. Who then returned to the Kingdom of Earth with a message from this god, which the gathered religious leaders then interpreted.

All the craftsmen in the tribes were instructed to take the sacred branches of the yew tree that were as thick as a man's wrist; they were to use both the heart and body of this great tree and from it make a bow taller than a man, which would be more powerful than any ever seen before. With this weapon they would defend themselves against the Roman legions, and strike fear into the Roman soldiers. All this was seen in the vision of the leading Druid Priest.

And so a pattern of guerrilla-type, hit and run warfare against the occupying forces had been developed by the various, remaining tribes. Only once had the tribes forgotten their differences and mounted an attack in force, ambushing the Roman Ninth legion based in the city of York and inflicting such a great number of casualties that the remnants of the legion were cashiered and the Ninth Roman legion was never reformed.

Behind the archers came the baggage train of twenty pack ponies linked together, bridle to tail, in groups of four, supervised by their five handlers. These animals bore spare armour, weapons, tents, food, and all the paraphernalia required to support a large body of men away from their homes for a long period. Behind them came two carts, each one drawn by a pair of oxen and driven by the two cooks travelling with the body of men. It was their job to prepare a hot meal in the morning to break the night's fast, and then another in the evening. Forming the rearguard was a group of six men armed with smaller bows for use on horseback, but just as powerful at short range as the longbow. These were local farmers' sons, who were mounted on smaller, stockier local horses.

Aurthora turned his horse back into the flow of mounted men wondering if he would ever again see his town of Macefield or the large timber dwelling where he had been born. His mother had been the youngest of Togi Dumis's four daughters. Her father had been the leader of a small tribe that joined the alliance formed by Great King Erion, but he had been killed in battle many years before while fighting to reclaim their lands.

Like those in his alliance who belonged to the new Christian faith, Great King Erion had taken up the practice of adopting godchildren, and he'd taken a serious interest in their upbringing and wellbeing. Thus, at the ceremony to celebrate Aurthora's birth, held in his father's house in the presence of many assembled clan chiefs and leaders of high-ranking families, Great King Erion had announced to all the gathered guests that he would stand as godfather to this child, the firstborn son of his old and trusted friend, Prassat Ambrosius.

Aurthora's father had supported the Great King's cause and fought alongside him in many battles. When the king had been wounded he recuperated at the fortified house of his friend, Prassat Ambrosius, who had continued the campaign in his name. But this had all taken place before Aurthora was born.

At the celebration for Aurthora's birth the king had presented Prassat Ambrosius with a suit of highly polished, black chain-link armour, manufactured by the famed Celtic smiths of the Royal Armoury. The leather straps had been oiled, smoothed, then tanned using the bark from the wild mountain oak. This suit of armour had been kept in trust for Aurthora until he came of age and could take vows of allegiance to King Erion and the Kingdom of Elmet.

At the age of twenty-one, again at a celebration in his father's house. Aurthora had sworn allegiance to Great King Erion. Promising to uphold the laws of the kingdom as decreed by the Great Council, and to defend the kingdom and its people unto death.

His godfather accepted Aurthora's pledge presenting him with the suit of chain mail that had been waiting for him for over twenty years.

That same morning the Druid priests held a religious ceremony, and many believers of the old religion followed them in praising Cerrunnos, Lord of the Gods. The ceremony began at daybreak with the blowing of great horns to summon the gods to the gathering of their worshippers. A large procession formed, led by Druid priests dressed in long white robes, followed by a group of young novitiates, behind them a group of musicians playing a variety of string and wind instruments, most notably harps and pipes. In the rear came all those who kept the old religion, although many amongst them also appeared at the Christian service later that day. This was common practice since the people wished to appease as many gods as possible.

The place chosen for Aurthora's Druid blessing was the centre of a large meadow selected by Zanton, the high priest. It was said to be a point where the earth's great power lines met, a place where animal gods worshipped by followers of the Druid religion would feel comfortable and welcome. Which would bode well for Aurthora. A young lamb was slaughtered; during the chanting and blowing of the great ceremonial horns, carved in the shape of boar heads, the blood of the lamb was mixed with woad. Zanton supported by his wooden staff came close to Aurthora, while the priest painted the dark blue mixture onto his face. Aurthora could not help but be impressed by the intricately carved boar's head on the staff's handle, as Zanton announced to the crowd: "This will protect Aurthora against injury in battle, as long as he believes in and follows the old and true religion. If he does so, the gift of greatness will be passed on to him by Camulos, the Celtic god of war."

It was while this high priest was painting the blue woad on his forehead and cheeks that Aurthora managed to look at the face that was covered and hidden from the rest of the gathering by a large hood. He knew this priest was of a great age by the deep wrinkled skin on the back of the man's hands. The face in the shadow of the hood was gaunt, and as wrinkled as the owner's hands. But most striking were the old man's eyes. Aurthora had never seen eyes like these before: bright, penetrating and alive, as black as polished pieces of ebony.

Aurthora had then been offered a potion; to the blowing of the pipes and horns, with much chanting of charms, he drank some of the evil-tasting liquid as a spell was cast to protect him. The day was a Sabbath, the Christian monks also held a service for their followers later. This ceremony was in great contrast to the one the Druid priests conducted earlier that morning. Aurthora had been impressed by the simple ceremony held by the priests of the new religion, who called themselves monks and friars, proclaiming they were the disciples of the true Christian God. These men wore a long, plain, hooded garment made from wool, which they fastened at the waist with a length of twine. They and their followers worshipped only one God. Everyone who attended their services simply knelt down where they were while the friar chanted prayers.

With water taken from a simple clay bowl the friar had marked the sign of a cross on Aurthora's forehead proclaiming him a soldier of good against evil, a protector of the truth and defender of the kingdom.

At both of these separate ceremonies a prayer had been offered on behalf of Aurthora that he be victorious in the battle against evil and be given a long and fruitful life. His father had arranged these prayers and blessings; as was expected on these occasions, he presented the leaders of both religions with a large donation in return for this favour.

A great feast then followed to celebrate Aurthora's coming of age, also the King's visit to the town which was packed with people from the surrounding countryside, as well as visitors from much further afield, all eager to take part in the festivities. Aurthora's father was well known for his generosity when it came to family celebrations. Oxen and pigs were roasted in the town square, and mead and ale was available for everyone who cared to partake.

Zanton, the Druid high priest, was selected for the priesthood as a young boy, mainly because of his accurate memory when writing the Ogham script. These tree writings the Druid priests performed on the stretched bark of the beech tree. Later, with his knowledge and interest in the planets and stars in the night sky, also being taught by many clever tutors the innermost secrets of their cult, he quickly progressed within the hierarchy of the Druid religion. Later, when he rose to the position of chief priest, he remembered how difficult it had been at times to maintain the spirit of the Celtic tribesmen and encourage them to continue their guerrilla fight against the occupying Roman army.

He had participated in many human sacrifices, where captured Roman soldiers had been garrotted in ceremonies to propitiate the Druid animal gods.

He also observed the slow progress of this new Christian religion that was creeping across his domain; on many occasions he made arrangements for the preachers of these blasphemous teachings to disappear without trace, their bodies weighted down with rocks and deposited in one of the many peat bogs or marshes that covered the country.

He secretly cursed the new king Erion and his decree that forbade human sacrifice and allowed his subjects the freedom to worship any god of their choosing on the sole condition that they first swore their allegiance to him and to the Celtic cause.

King Erion had no male heir, only a daughter, Elemar. Zanton had observed the interest King Erion had shown in Aurthora since his birth. He had himself spoken to Aurthora's father, offering to be responsible for his son's education, but much to Zanton's frustration and annoyance Prassat Ambrosius had politely refused the offer. Zanton was also frustrated when he was unable to influence the decisions taken by King Erion— leader of the Celtic alliance.

The king was a tall, slim, elegant man with the typical characteristics of the western Celtic tribes – deeply set, striking blue eyes and jet-black hair.

It was these tribes, the Deceangli, the Ordovices and the Cornovii, who had been the backbone of the resistance in that part of the country, the Roman army had only been able to maintain a presence there by sheltering within their highly fortified and well-defended towns.

Aurthora, on the other hand, was much fairer, taller and heavier boned, but he too had deep, striking blue eyes like the King. Aurthora's father's family were from a Celtic tribe called the Brigantes who, before the Roman occupation, ruled an area in the far north of the country. They had been driven from their own lands by the brutality of the Roman legions, and been forced to flee to the mountainous lands governed by King Erion's Celtic ancestors. Aurthora heard many tales of these events from the itinerant storytellers who wandered the land.

The warriors of these tribes who had fought against Roman domination were the great Celtic heroes, and though many had been injured in previous battles, they volunteered to a man to stay behind to defend the passes through the mountains in order to delay the pursuing Roman cavalry thus allow the women and children to escape to freedom. The Roman general issued instructions to slaughter everyone in the tribes who had participated in the revolt against the Roman Empire. Many Celtic children were still named after those Celtic warrior heroes.

The column was now travelling through thick forests. Aurthora remembered this area well; as a youth he hunted in these forests for deer, wolves and wild boar with many of the men now accompanying him.

Aurthora's father, Prassat Ambrosius, encouraged this as he felt it built up a sense of comradeship amongst the young men under his stewardship.

King Erion initiated many significant changes in the training of his warriors. By his decree, the traditional powerful, two-handed broadsword and the heavy battleaxe was discarded. For many years now the Celts had been training hard with the gladius, which was the favoured Roman short sword, and the pilum, the six-foot-long throwing spear that was used against an advancing foe, and with the long, ornately embossed, metal covered Celtic shield used during close formation manoeuvres.

The instructors made the men repeat the same manoeuvres time and time again until Aurthora and his companions performed the movements almost instinctively on command. Their instructors were under orders to teach them how to use the longbow, the traditional weapon of the Celts for many generations, although the latest weapon introduced by King Erion had been the long spear, used when mounted on a heavy horse, a breed of animal introduced from abroad and purchased by King Erion's agents many years before when he took over as leader of the kingdom on the death of his father, King Eldgar.

The foreign traders in these fine animals were paid in silver and gold to encourage them to obtain many more. It was the ambition of all the noblemen to own and ride one of these splendid mounts. Most of the other armed men rode horses that were a cross between the local, short-legged, nimble-footed mountain breed, characteristic of that part of the country, and the large horses ridden by the armoured noblemen, but there were still a large number of the smaller farmers-turned-warriors who still rode the sturdy local horses.

King Erion had decreed that all his followers and supporters should rally to his call to arms and meet at Buxonana or, as it was known locally, 'the High Town'. All were to bring supplies to sustain them in the way to which they were accustomed, without needing to beg, borrow or steal from their neighbours. Any person who could not provide for himself was to be fed by the Great King from the royal supplies and granaries.

Buxonana was a place renowned for its naturally hot, healing springs, and was surrounded for miles by desolate, bog-ridden moor. A settlement had existed there long before the Roman legions had occupied the area. The Druid priests had used the hot springs as part of their healing methods for centuries.

The Romans had developed the small settlement into a spa town with many fine stone buildings. It was here that soldiers on leave, or recovering from illness or injury, could spend their wages in the many taverns, or bathe in the covered, hot spring pools.

Because the Romans considered the town important, they quarried stone from the hillsides and laid out a road across the high ground of the moor. The road travelled all the way back to their main garrison town Ceastra, which was many days' ride away.

The Celtic armies' gathering point had been well chosen since it could be easily defended: there were only three ways across the surrounding deep marsh and moors, the most important of which was the Roman paved road; the other two were simple tracks that were practically impassable in the winter months, or even during the summer after heavy rain.

The stone paved Roman road entered the township, then carried on through the town and out to a small village called Castford. Here, at the northern entrance to the town and standing guard at the foot of the pass that continued through the mountains, was a fortified stone keep built by the Roman legions.

Progress for such a large column was painfully slow, since speed was dictated by the slowest mule-drawn cart, it was obvious it would take several days to reach their destination. All the time the column was being joined by additional, smaller groups of armed men wearing a varied collection of armour and carrying a wide range of weapons.

"Will you be able to swing that meat cleaver you carry, youth?" Aurthora called out to a young slip of a lad, no more than fourteen, who had a leather bound shield strapped on his back and a great two-handed, double-headed axe across his shoulder.

"I carry this for my grandfather, sire. My weapon is the sling," answered the boy, tapping a leather thong strapped to his belt, next to a pouch that would carry the shot for use in the sling. The boy's jaunty answer brought a cheer from the men walking within earshot.

The camaraderie is excellent thought Aurthora to himself.

"What distance can you sling your shot, my man?" continued Aurthora to the youth.

"Three hundred long steps, sire, but I am deadly accurate and can hit a fly at one hundred," came the confident reply.

"And what name does this terror of the Anglo-Saxons answer to?"

"My name is Ammianus, sire, Ammianus Camulos," came the prompt, proud reply, the name indicating to Aurthora a common practice: the lad was the product of the intermarriage of a Roman and a native Celtic woman, and so the boy had been given his father's family name as his first name and a Celtic name for his second – in this case that of the Celtic god of war.

These men who answered the call to arms had never lost a battle under the leadership of Great King Erion, but the opposition had never been as formidable as the foe now gathering. Would this enthusiastic band of men with their hotchpotch collection of armour and weapons be able to match the seasoned, well-trained, combined force of the Angles and Saxons? Especially if the rumours that were circulating proved true and they far outnumbered the small Celtic alliance.

Aurthora pondered these and other questions in silence as he rode along. The noblemen were well trained and well armed, they were mounted on good horses, their chain mail armour was the finest to be had. Man for man, on foot or in the saddle, they could match any soldier in the known world. The same could be said for the men-at-arms who, with the sponsorship and encouragement of the king, had trained at regular intervals in the manner of a disciplined army, practising manoeuvres and observing a strict code of discipline, rigidly enforced by their lieutenants. The archers had always been proud freemen, King Erion encouraged their art by donating valuable prizes of gold coins at the archery tournaments. This farsightedness in encouraging the archers had paid rich dividends: there were not many men or boys in the kingdom who were unable draw a bow and fire a shaft with a respectable degree of accuracy. So it was that many men who would otherwise not have answered the call to arms issued now joined the growing force of armed men, carrying their yew longbows and their varied collection of assorted iron-tipped arrows.

He realised the bulk of King Erion's army was made up of men who worked the land. If they had been ploughing, planting or harvesting, or if the winter snow had been too deep for travel, they were unable to attend the training sessions. So many of these men had never been tested. They had never before been together in such great numbers, thus their ability to manoeuvre had never been established. Aurthora wondered what tactics the Great King would use with so many untried men, how many of those he now rode with would leave the coming battle alive or unharmed. If discipline collapsed and they broke ranks and ran, they would be left to the mercy of the invading army and slaughtered like sheep set upon by a pack of hungry wolves.

He was woken from his reverie by a shout: "Aurthora!" He turned in his saddle and saw, amongst a group of armed men joining the column, a young, broad-shouldered man mounted on a fine, jet-black stallion of the newly-introduced breed. His face was instantly familiar but otherwise his appearance had changed dramatically since the days when they had trained together at Aurthora's home. Back then they had both been young, beardless, skinny boys. He could not fail to recognise the bright red, flowing hair of Ethellro. "Ethellro!" he exclaimed, "Ethellro!"

They dismounted and clasped wrists, then hugged each other warmly. It had been almost five years since Aurthora had last seen his closest friend. King Erion decreed that from the age of twelve all sons of nobles should be taught the skills of warfare, that they should practise until they were capable of earning their right to be called noblemen.

The two boys had begun their training together in the art of war and weaponry.

Ethellro had been billeted at Aurthora's house since his small family estate was many days' ride from the lands of Aurthora's father. But after five years of training and on the death of his father, Ethellro had been allowed to return home to administer the estate, which specialised in the breeding of the new large warhorse. Ethellro himself had introduced an addition: a simple hanging leather loop attached to each side of the saddle. This bore the weight of the horseman making it easier for the rider to keep his balance and control the horse's movements, especially when travelling at speed.

"Aurthora, I am sorry to hear your father is not in good health and cannot join you on this expedition, but you are an excellent choice as a lieutenant in his place. You have changed, you're no longer the skinny youth I remember," said Ethellro. This was very true. Under the regime of training and exercises imposed by his tutor Orius, Aurthora had turned into a young man with an exceptionally fine physique.

"Let me introduce you to my sister," said Ethellro, turning to a young woman mounted on one of the smaller local ponies who stopped beside him. "Katrina, this is my good friend Aurthora. Aurthora, may I present my sister Katrina."

Aurthora's gaze fell on a woman wearing a cloak of patterned wool with its hood turned down over her shoulders, and loose trousers that were the fashion and worn by both men and women. They had leather patches on the inside of the knee to provide a degree of extra comfort when riding for long distances. Her shirt was of soft, brushed deerskin, tucked into trousers and tightened with a leather belt held in place with a brightly polished bronze buckle. On her feet she wore leather sandals with thongs that were fastened around a shapely, exposed ankle. She had the same bright red hair as her brother, her skin was pale, her eyes, green like jade, sparkled with life and laughter. Aurthora took in all this at a glance, and found what he saw very pleasing.

"Salute!" said Katrina to Aurthora, showing perfect white teeth in the process.

"It is so good to meet you at last; my brother can never tell me enough about the good times you had when you were training together at your father's house."

Aurthora remained stunned by this woman's beauty, and in reply muttered something about them having indeed shared good times. Then nimbly mounting his horse he turned away to join Ethellro, embarrassed by his own shyness.

Katrina spotted Aurthora before her brother called out his name. She had been impressed by the way he sat on his great horse, by his broad shoulders and his frank open smile as he greeted her brother. Now, as she rode behind the two men, she noticed how his strong thighs clamped the ribcage of his mount. She also noticed and was pleased by the way he kept glancing in her direction, pretending to check the column of men behind them.

Chapter Two

The column was growing longer by the hour as it continued to be joined by more and more small groups of armed men, carts and horses. Aurthora and Ethellro found many things to discuss as they travelled along. They reminisced about fishing in the river that ran through the valley below Aurthora's father's house, about snaring rabbits in the woods at the edge of the great forest that stretched as far as the eye could see, and of training their dogs to flush out the ducks and geese from the marshes at the side of the river in order to test their new-found skills with the longbow. They recalled collecting crab-apples, juicy blackberries and other fruit that grew wild in the surrounding woods.

They talked well after the army of tired men had been fed and settled down for the night, leaving awake only the sentries, who were changed every two hours, patrolling the outskirts of the camp. It was nearly dawn by the time both men dozed off, wrapped in their thick woollen blankets near the dying embers of the cooking fire.

Aurthora was awakened by noise of the morning hustle and bustle as the men rose to another day. Their first meal was simple but robust: rough barley ground between flat stones, soaked in water overnight then brought to the boil with a little salt and allowed to simmer in great iron cooking pots over the campfires. All men carried their own basic utensils, consisting of a wooden bowl, a wooden spoon, and a small dagger for cutting meat.

The meal was free: the barley had been provided from the king's granary and the men simply helped themselves from the nearest large cooking pot. When evening came, the same travelling cooks would provide an evening meal of hot stew, usually consisting of root vegetables that had been dried in the summer sun, together with salted beef, pork, horse, or whatever meat the cooks had on their wagons.

It was very simple fare, but for any man who had no supplies of his own, it provided basic sustenance. This was another indication to Aurthora that the campaign had been well planned by King Erion and his advisors: not only had the Crown granaries been opened for supplies to feed the large groups of men that were joining together to form the Great King's army, but the king cleverly dragged out negotiations for peace with the Saxon warlords and their allies, constantly asking for more time to consider their demands for an annual tribute in gold and silver bullion. Eventually the Saxons ran out of patience giving King Erion a deadline to either pay the tribute of gold and silver they demanded, or be invaded and suffer the consequences of having the population slaughtered – or worse still, captured and sold into slavery.

Like all the younger men of the kingdom, Aurthora had been disillusioned by the Great King even considering any form of negotiation with this foreign enemy; Authora only wanted to test his mettle and new-found battle skills against the invaders. But now he understood the Great King's ploy. He bought time with his protracted negotiations, while his subjects, who were all free men, had time to gather in their harvest of barley and root crops. Many animal sacrifices had been made by the Druid priests at ceremonies in various sacred places around the country to thank their gods for such a bountiful harvest, these ceremonies had always been well attended by the populace. The farmers paid their one-fifth dues in barley livestock to their lord and also their one-fifth dues to their king, and yet their own granaries were also well stocked.

Their families would sell any surplus in the nearby towns after the men left in response to the king's call to arms. The men left their hamlets and villages knowing that if this turned out to be a long campaign, at least their families would not go hungry during the winter.

This is indeed good for the men's morale, thought Aurthora. *This Great King, my own godfather, is most certainly a very clever man.*

Since being proclaimed king more than twenty years before, Erion had foreseen this moment, knowing it would only be a matter of time before his kingdom and the ways of the Celtic civilisation would once again be threatened. He formed the alliance of the Celtic tribes and been proclaimed their king. In their domination of the Celtic world, the Romans had virtually succeeded in destroying the fabric of a fifth of the old tribes. In only a small section of these isles the Romans named Britannica, had the Celts survived with their culture and religion intact.

Aurthora busied himself gathering personal belongings together. The bulk of these were carried on a small pack pony under the care of his ex-tutor and manservant, a man named Orius Tomase. This man, in addition to many other duties, would help him to fit on his armour ready for battle when the time came.

Aurthora could not remember a time when Orius had not been involved in his life. He was there when Aurthora was born, he helped and showed him how to ride his first pony, had also been there when he'd taken his first fall from the very same pony. He'd seen the boy gritting his teeth in order not to cry in pain as a Druid priest set the broken wrist in splints. He had been the first to show the boy how to string the longbow, and the correct way to stand and release long arrows with their goose-feather flights.

He'd also been the first to teach Aurthora how to snare, skin, prepare and cook a rabbit, had also been there to comfort the youth when his mother died of consumption, watched as the lad tried, but had not been able to hold back the tears. He witnessed Aurthora catch his first trout in the river, seen the boy lose his footing and be swept away by the fast flowing current for a hundred yards or more, buffeted and banged against the projecting rocks in the process before Orius found a place where he could reach down and grab the top of the boy's leather jerkin. It had been he who noted, as he yanked the semi-conscious youth out of the river, that he was still tightly clinging to a large brown trout.

Orius rarely praised the boy but smiled to himself in satisfaction on many occasions, feeling proud to have been involved in the instruction of this outstanding young man.

Orius was not a Celt. He joined the household of Aurthora's father when the Roman legions had departed the region. He'd been a young infantry soldier in the Roman army of occupation but was not himself a Roman.

He and his younger brother Mattos volunteered for the Roman army when the Roman forces came recruiting in his village. They occupied his native land and renamed that conquered province Romana, after their own capital city of Rome.

After their training Orius and Mattos had been posted along with a cohort of young, newly-trained recruits and their Roman officers to the distant city the Romans called Nova Roma.

There he fought against a dark-skinned race of people who were threatening the borders of that part of the Roman Empire. Later, when the revolt had been brutally crushed by the legions, they had been posted to the island of Britannia. It was here that Mattos and Orius had been separated.

Orius served in the legion for five years and reached the rank of *dieci corpi*, a soldier in charge of ten men. He had seen the Roman army struggle to guard its borders as more and more soldiers were sent back to protect Rome, and also to defend the Empire against barbaric Germanic tribes that were forever probing and testing the Roman legions' border defences in the country of Gaul. Then orders had been received for all remaining troops on the island of Britannia to prepare to leave and return to the continent.

Like many of his companions Orius had discussed the options available to them, with two fellow legionnaires. He had decided – if and when the opportunity arose – to take up King Erion's offer of amnesty to any Roman soldier who wished to desert the legion, join this king's army, and stay on the island of Britannia.

There were now rumours circulating among the Roman forces that Roman armies were fighting one another for control of Rome, that barbarian tribes were crossing the Empire's borders, attacking and laying siege to some of the cities in Roman provinces. The thought of the legion's long march through many hostile countries, of the many battles they might have to fight on the way, the uncertainty of what would become of them, made up their minds. Orius and his two companions decided they preferred to settle for the Celts' simple life. So when one night Orius and his two companions had been posted on sentry duty to guard the outskirts of the camp, they had taken the opportunity to slip quietly away.

But things had not gone well for them after abandoning their post that night. Because of the many desertions the retreating army suffered, the officers were under orders to check their sentries every half hour, within ten minutes of Orius and his two friends clearing the Roman picket lines, the alarm was sounded. The guard was called out and a pack of hunting hounds released. These large, savage dogs, trained by the Romans to hunt escaped slaves, criminals, or in this case, three deserters, began to bay loudly as they quickly picked up the scent.

Orius shivered with fear as he heard their cries: he had been with the hounds many times when they hunted runaway slaves, and more recently deserters.

The officers and men in the legion considered this a great sport, a diversion from the boring duties of garrison life. Bets were placed on the length of time it would take for the hounds to claim their victim. If there were several runaways, as in this case, the bets would be placed on the time it took the pack to hunt down each individual, the closest guess took all the money in the pot.

The ordinary soldier's pay had been very inconsistent over the years, the men received no stipend in over twelve moons. There had been many floggings to try and retain discipline, as the months went by, the men had become more and more insolent towards their officers. In these circumstances any soldier winning a bet could live exceptionally well for some considerable time.

Once the hounds picked up their quarry's scent, they hunted him down relentlessly; by the time the hounds' master and the pursuing soldiers reached the spot where the hounds had caught up with their prey, the pack had usually torn their victim to pieces.

Orius hoped they would have had longer before the alarm was raised; he also hoped they would have been able to reach the ford in the river the army had crossed earlier that afternoon which he had crossed on a previous occasion with the army many years before. His intention had been that he and his companions would separate at the river ford: one headed upstream and the other two headed downstream. By travelling through water he hoped to throw the pack off the scent and thus make good their escape.

Once clear of the Roman camp they started to jog along the stone paved road the legion had followed the previous day. But on hearing the alarm they left the road – the hounds could travel faster on the hard surface.

Now they were travelling through light brushwood, at one time the nearby forest had edged the road, but over time the trees had gradually been cut down and carted away to supply the nearby towns and villages with building materials, charcoal and firewood.

One of Orius's companions was a tall, thin, athletic type whose name was Ballsi. Orius knew Ballsi well it was even possible that he might outrun the hounds. Orius had seen this man perform in games held in the Roman encampment every two years. One of the events was a race of stamina over a distance of 25 miles, open to all comers. Ballsi had come third in this race on the last two occasions, with only a matter of yards separating him from the eventual winners.

Orius's second companion was Marcus, a much older man. He had been an engineer with the legion and in charge of a section of five scorpios, but recently he'd been demoted. However, his previous position allowed him to put on a lot of excess weight, he was not really suited for the exertions required by a desertion attempt. It had taken considerable persuasion before he agreed to accompany his fellow legionnaires on this dangerous escapade.

The scorpio was a large crossbow fitted on a wheeled cart; it fired short bolts with long iron tips, had a range of three hundred yards and a self-loading device. It was deadly accurate. This machine was lethal when used against an advancing close-packed formation of men since one bolt was so powerful it could pass through two men's bodies. But it was inefficient and overly cumbersome against the Celtic tactics of hit and run. Therefore Marcus had been removed from his easy position of sitting on his supply wagon overseeing his five, mule-drawn scorpios. He had been placed instead in the undermanned infantry.

Marcus's position as engineer in charge of the scorpios and their carts had been taken by another Roman engineer, Aidas Corrilus, who was still recovering from the loss of an arm, amputated by the surgeon after an accident with a ballista. The weapon snapped under tension and mangled his arm up to the elbow so badly it could not be saved. Rejected as unfit for service by his division officer, he had been retired on a small pension and spent most of his time in and around the army barracks doing small jobs for the legionnaires or the officers and their families.

Upon hearing that the Roman army in Britannia was moving back to its homeland, and that his pension, like the army's pay, had finished, he requested to rejoin the legion that was the only way he had any hope to see his beloved, warm and sunny country again.

And even though he was still weak from loss of blood, and still suffering from the shock of the crude operation, the legion relented and reinstated him in his former position, at the expense of Marcus. Aidas Corrilus's expertise and knowledge of both the scorpio and the ballista (a large wheeled catapult that could hurl fifteen pounds of rocks for many hundreds of yards) was well known to the officers, and this influenced their decision.

Now Marcus was struggling. As much as he tried to force his short, fat legs to go faster, they would not respond and he was dropping further behind; Ballsi was a hundred yards in front, running loosely and easily, Orius was twenty yards in front of Marcus. When Orius heard Marcus fall for the second time in almost as many seconds, he turned and quickly retraced his steps to where, on hands and knees, Marcus was vainly trying to push his weary body upright again.

"Here my friend, let me help you," said Orius as he placed his hands on both of Marcus's trembling shoulders and helped him to his feet. "Keep going my friend, not far now to reach the river, then you will be safe."

He left Marcus standing upright and shivering with fatigue then he jogged off in the direction of Ballsi's faint outline, opening as he ran the large pouch he had just removed from Marcus. He took his own smaller leather bag from around his neck and stuffed it into the larger one, which he then slung over his shoulder and across his chest.

He was quite pleased with himself. He had taken the leather bag from Marcus as he helped the distraught man to his feet. *By the feel of it there are plenty of coins in that pouch*, thought Orius to himself, *also a small, plain drinking goblet that seemed to have great significance for some of the other legionnaires.*

But was it worth all the trouble and loss of time, especially with the hounds so close? Making sure his pouch was secure he increased his pace, trying to close the distance between himself and Ballsi.

From behind Marcus could now hear the leading dogs as they pushed their way through the loose brush, and many yards behind them the faint shouts of the pursuing guards and dog handlers as they struggled to keep within earshot of the baying hounds.

When they left their post, all three deserters abandoned their armour and heavy leather jerkins, along with shields and short throwing spears. All they kept about them was a little purse containing any valuables or silver coins they possessed – except for Marcus, who had a leather pouch strapped across his chest.

Several days earlier Marcus had been involved in a heavy game of gambling. One of the players was a drunkard called Carsius Magon who always seemed to have plenty of money to throw around. The dice had fallen well for Marcus all day and he had taken all of Carsius Magon's money, including a drinking goblet that Carsius claimed he had taken from one of the Druid priests that a Roman pack of hounds had hunted down many years before. This priest had supposedly taken the goblet from one of the friars of the new Christian religion. It was said the goblet was a sacred relic and the religious centrepiece of the new Christian Church that was trying to establish itself on the island of Britannia. This relic was supposed to have been used by the one they called their Son of God at a last meal with his friends before he had been dragged off and crucified as a blasphemer. It was a tale that Orius found hard to believe.

The three deserters each started out carrying a gladius, a short stabbing sword that was standard issue to all Roman soldiers. Marcus abandoned his as soon as they entered the scrub because he found it cumbersome. He now wished he had kept this weapon, it might have been able to keep the dogs at bay until their handlers and the guards caught up and he could plead with the officers for his life. After all, he was a trained ballista operator and been a cinque ballista commander in charge of five machines.

He was, in fact, nearly an officer; they might well have spared him. He would say the other two forced him to join them on pain of death. He had never before been on a chase with the guards and dog handlers, but he had placed bets and won money on the eventual outcome.

He too had cheered with the rest of the camp as bloody carcasses of deserters or slaves had returned with the hunting party, their remains spread out for all to see as a warning to anyone who might be contemplating his own attempt at deserting.

All these thoughts flashed through Marcus's tired brain. He could run no further. His eyes desperately searched the landscape. In the faint light of approaching dawn he could see the outline of the beginning of a forest about one hundred yards away. *If I could reach those trees*, he thought.

Staggering and stumbling over clumps of grass, he forced himself in the direction of the tall trees now taking shape in the dawn light. He was taking in great gulps of air and felt quite dizzy; the pain in his chest was now severe, but he had to keep going. The leading hound did not need to follow the scent of the men any longer; he could see one of his victims clearly outlined against the dawn light. The man was struggling to stay upright, he staggered as if blind towards the edge of the forest. The dog's senses told him this would be an easy kill, the prey was weak and exhausted and not carrying any of the sharp, shiny objects that were capable of injuring him. Its fine hearing also picked up a soft, sobbing sound from the direction of the man; he heard this sound many times before from these humans as the pack closed in for the kill.

Marcus reached the first tree, but there were no low branches he could reach. He moved on in a daze to a second tree, a large, mature yew tree. His mouth was full of blood; he had bitten his tongue at his last fall, and was now choking and finding it difficult to breathe. He reached up with his right hand to a branch just above his head, but when he tried to raise his left arm, there was no feeling or movement in that limb. The pain in his chest spread throughout his body; his head felt as if it exploded from within. The hound reached the man just as he reached for the branch of the tree.

The dog's great teeth sank into the back of Marcus's neck and both animal and man collapsed onto the damp ground. Only the dog was moving as it dragged the body of the inert ex-scorpio engineer along the forest floor. The hound had hunted many of these humans since he joined the pack, more so within the last few months. He enjoyed the chase and the sport at the end, but this human was not struggling like the rest, and that lessened the enjoyment.

Within seconds the other hounds arrived, barking and baying as they fought one another in an effort to attack the bloody corpse at the base of the large tree.

The hound that caught the man was the pack leader not merely because of his speed, stamina and acute sense of smell; it was his intelligence that made him superior.

Now he recalled that just before he had seen this man staggering toward the forest of trees, he smelt two other humans heading in another direction, their scents the same as those he had been following since leaving the human encampment several miles back.

The dog left the carcass of the dead man and backtracked, passing his handlers as they made their way towards the pack gathered around Marcus's remains at the base of the large tree. When the handlers saw their lead hound heading in the opposite direction they paid no heed, they knew their dog. There were three fugitives; the pack had probably caught only one. There were two more to find and their lead hound was exceptional. He was on their trail and would give sound as soon as he picked up their scent.

If things worked out, there was a good bonus to be had for the three dog handlers for this night's work.

The lead hound did not disappoint them. Soon his deep baying informed all that he had found the scent. The pack handlers had driven the rest of the dogs from the mutilated corpse; hearing the call of their leader, the pack bolted in that direction. They had tasted blood and wanted more. A quick search of the corpse and surrounding area did not reveal the heavy pouch the dog handlers knew Marcus was carrying. The likelihood it was still in the possession of one of the two other deserters gave them the added incentive to make their hunt successful. The dog handlers returning from the edge of the forest in pursuit of their hounds met with the soldiers who had been on duty when the alarm had been raised. These men were wearing full armour, heavy leather jerkins, were armed with shields and spears, which meant they could not keep pace with the lightly clad handlers. All the towns and villages along the legion's route were now deserted. Roman soldiers, or indeed anyone travelling with the main Roman army who ended up a straggler, was likely to be quickly disposed of by the enraged former inhabitants of the towns and villages.

The legion's policy was for their men not to stray far from the main column, and if they were obliged to do so, then only in large numbers. Meanwhile, the two remaining deserters were still jogging through the light brush at the edge of the forest.

The going was easier now, they could see where they were running in the early morning light and were no longer constantly stumbling over tussocks of grass and partly buried tree roots. Both men heard the baying of the lead hound and realised that it had picked up their trail again. Both knew the fate that had befallen their companion, they had both been on hunting parties many times before. They had seen at first hand what a pack of half-wild hounds crazed with blood lust could do to a human body before the handlers could whip them clear.

The river was about a mile away. They knew they had to reach it, separate, and be out of sight before the hounds arrived on the scene. If they could manage, there was a good chance that the pursuing guards and dog handlers would abandon the chase.

They were a long way from the main force's night encampment, it was fast becoming light. Also, they were few in number and knew there were bands of mounted Celts following the Roman army. The destiny of anyone lagging behind the legion's heavily armoured rearguard was indeed perilous.

Chapter Three

Ballsti increased his pace, intending to reach the river first. He knew he could outrun Orius, who was beginning to pant loudly. *Orius is badly out of condition,* thought Ballsti, *the hounds will have him before he reaches the river. He will put up a good fight. He is a good swordsman, and that will give me all the time I'll need to move upriver and out of sight before the guard can resume the hunt, if they decide to do so.* Ballsti was feeling quite confident. He and Orius had persuaded Marcus to join them in their desertion attempt. At first he had been reluctant, but they eventually convinced him that there was no future for him on the long journey back to Rome through hostile countries, constantly under the threat of ambush, always desperately short of food and supplies. On the other hand here in Britannia, a scorpio engineer such as himself would be in great demand, would be offered a high well-paid rank in the new army being formed by the Celtic king. So Marcus eventually succumbed to the persuasive talk, and in so doing had sealed his grisly fate. The two younger men had known if the alarm were raised and the hounds were released, Marcus would be the first to be caught, giving them more time in their attempt to flee.

Ballsti was not liked by the rest of the company of Roman soldiers with whom he served, being a Macedonian and a mercenary. He joined the legion when they were recruiting in his native land and had received very little training before being posted with several of his countrymen to the island of Britannia. He never stopped bragging about how his ancestor, Alexander the Great, had ruled an empire as large, if not larger, than the Romans.

Ballsti was an excellent soldier and a great athlete, the only one left of the ten Macedonian soldiers who arrived on the island seven years before. When the guard was called out to chase deserters he had always been ready to volunteer, consistently been the first on the scene when the hounds had run their prey to ground, refusing to share with the rest of the guard the money or valuables he took from the victim, which they usually carried in a little pouch around their neck.

Orius put on a spurt even though his lungs were bursting he was having dizzy spells. He drew level with Ballsti who, aware of Orius alongside him, decided to increase his pace. They had run a few miles since leaving the camp and Ballsti now had his second wind, and was feeling good, it was all working to plan.

As Ballsti began to pull away from him, Orius drew and swung his short sword. The blade was razor sharp. Ballsti felt no pain as his left leg collapsed from under him. Orius slashed the ligaments at the back of Ballsti's knee, and as the athlete collapsed, struck him a blow with the hilt of his sword to the side of the head, not hard enough to render him unconscious, just enough to daze him. Bending quickly he grabbed the money belt from around Ballsti's waist. A quick movement of the sword and the sharp blade sliced through the leather strap and the belt was free.

Ballsti was on his hands and knees, slightly dazed, but still aware that the money belt he kept around his waist was being torn from his person, it all happened in seconds. Orius was pleasantly surprised at the weight of coins and valuables in the belt; throwing it over his shoulder, he continued jogging through the undergrowth at a much slower pace than before. With every step the heavy weight of the money belt bouncing on his shoulder, and the heavy pouch around his neck, gave him a wonderful feeling of wellbeing.

Ballsti shook his head, trying to clear the dizziness. He could hear the sound of Orius fading in the distance and was overcome with rage. He knew that he had stolen his money belt after hitting him on the side of the head when he stumbled. He would catch the thieving son of a dog, slit his stomach and leave his innards to feed the hounds he could hear approaching. Ballsti tried to rise but his left leg would not carry his weight. He felt with his hand behind his knee, and his fingers touched the warm blood running down his calf. There was no pain, just a dull ache. Ballsti now realised what Orius had done: he left him wounded in order to slow up the pack. "I will be waiting for you when you try and enter the next world, you son of swine," screamed Ballsti in the direction of Orius.

Ballsti was trapped. Should he fight the hounds, delay them as Orius was hoping he would, or should he allow the hounds to rip him to pieces without putting up a fight, so they would quickly continue the hunt and catch that traitorous thief? Or should he commit suicide before the hounds reached him? Ballsti was a fighter; he came from a long line of warriors. He was proud of the name the other legionnaires scornfully gave him: 'Ballsti of Alexandria'. He was also an optimist. He would slaughter each of the dogs as they attacked him; he would destroy these puppy dogs and leave them as food for the crows. The Roman officers would regret they had used their hounds to hunt him— Ballsti of Alexandria.

The leading hound could smell blood: one of his prey was injured.

Warning bells rang in the brain of the pack leader as he came within sight of the man. He was off the track, leaning against a small tree that could barely support his weight. He held a shiny object in his hand. The experienced pack leader approached slowly, beginning a wide, wary circle around the man, he in turn followed the dog keeping the shiny metal object, which the dog knew could inflict great pain, pointing in his direction. The second hound who arrived on the scene several seconds behind the pack leader had always been a brash youngster. Some days before at the army camp he had made a challenge to become pack leader, but had been savagely subdued by the present leader, who sent the upstart scurrying off with his tail between his legs. This second hound now charged straight towards the injured human; he too had smelt the blood of the wounded legionnaire and was full of confidence after the easy kill a short while ago.

He jumped for the man's throat from six feet away. Ballsti's short sword entered the dog's heart while he was still in the air, killing it instantly; its momentum carried its great frame forward hitting the man hard in the chest. The small tree supporting the injured soldier snapped under the combined weight of man and dog so that both crashed to the ground.

Ballsti struggled to push off the carcass of the dead hound, at the same time attempting to withdraw his sword which was embedded deep in the dead animal's chest. It was then that the pack leader seized his opportunity. He pounced, grabbing Ballsti's forearm and wrenching it free from the sword hilt. Seconds later the rest of the pack was on the scene thirsting for blood. Ballsti's terrified screams were heard by the dog handlers, who were only a short distance behind. Within minutes it was over.

The handlers arrived on the scene quickly whipping the dogs clear of the bloody remains that lay amongst the clumps of grass. "This one is Ballsti of Alexandria," shouted one of the handlers in surprise, "I did not think we would have caught him of all people."

"His money belt has gone!" shouted another of the handlers as they searched Ballsti's inert body. The senior dog handler, Maddoc, was watching intently as the men searched the surrounding area, looking in vain for the missing money belt. "Get those hounds back on the trail," he yelled. "Of all the Gods!" he spat, knowing Ballsti had been carrying a small fortune in his money belt.

He lashed at the hounds with his leather-thonged whip in sheer frustration, sending the dogs yelping and scattering out of his reach. Two of the soldiers arrived panting on the scene. "The rest of the guard has decided to return to camp," gasped the younger of the two, first to regain his breath. "They have taken our heavy armour so that we could keep up with the hounds."

It was obvious to Maddoc that the other two dog handlers were not very happy with their situation. They stood shuffling their feet and muttering together.

"What's the matter with you two?" growled Maddoc, glaring at his uncomfortable juniors.

"We don't have enough armed support," replied the taller of the two men. "It's now broad daylight, we risk being ambushed?"

All the members of the small party knew the Celts were following the main column and understood the risk they were running. Even though the Celtic king had offered amnesty to any Roman soldier who was prepared to desert and join his Celtic forces, the local Celtic chieftain was ignoring this order.

Maddoc, the senior dog handler, started to reply to his underlings, but he was interrupted by the retching of Agricola, the youngest auxiliary guard who had just noticed the disembowelled bloody remains of Ballsti. Maddoc watched in disgust as the auxiliary, hands on knees, continued to be sick.

"We should rejoin the main force at once," continued the other soldier.

"In the name of all the gods, am I surrounded by cowards?" muttered Maddoc under his breath. He looked at the small group who were glancing furtively around them. "Listen," he began, "if the Celts were anywhere near us they would have been here by now. Orius is carrying a fortune in valuables and coins and is just a short distance away. Catch him and we can buy ourselves out of this army of lost souls. We'll all live in luxury; we'll travel back to our homelands in style.

"If we miss this opportunity we'll continue to be the dregs of the army, at every one's beck and call: Do this! Do that! Kicked here! Kicked there! Being half starved most of the time, and no wages for the rest." Maddoc stopped to catch his breath. His words were having an effect on the men. The young soldier had stopped his retching and was deep in thought, as were all the small group of men.

What Maddoc had said to the group was the truth: there was no future in their army, only the risk of death on their long march back to Rome, as they travelled through the lands of an occupied people, who were now in open revolt against Rome's weakened authority.

If they captured Orius, the money he carried would buy them out of their contract with the army, and they would still have the funds to buy their passage by sea to their homeland, thus bypassing the long march back to Rome. This was every soldier's dream and it lay within their grasp. It was worth the risk. Maddoc was right! If the Celts were in this area they would have made their presence felt, and they would surely have been attacked by now.

"Let's carry on as far as the river; if the hounds do not pick up the scent we will make all haste returning back to the main column. Are we all agreed?" continued Maddoc, sensing that he was winning the men over to his way of thinking. "Are we all agreed?" he repeated, but did not wait for a reply. "Get those hounds back on the trail," he ordered. "We've lost enough time already." His whip scattered the hounds who had returned to Ballsti's body, with his two junior handlers, he began once more to drive the pack along the path in the direction of the river.

Orius had heard Ballsti's cursing following him as he continued down the faint path towards the river, and a short time later the screams of the injured legionnaire savaged by the hounds, but they were very faint. The sound had only travelled that distance because the morning was very still, and the light wind was blowing in his direction.

Orius had been pondering his plan since the army was first informed of their departure from Britannia. For many months he had closely scrutinised the other soldiers in his company, eventually selecting his two companions. He had gently quizzed them on their views over many weeks on the possibility of desertion; he had been very careful not to ask them directly if they would consider deserting with him. Had he done so and been reported, he would have risked instant arrest, torture and a painful death. He had no regrets about his actions. He had done what was necessary for him to survive. If his companions had thought of such a scheme they would have done the same.

As he jogged along he calculated he was roughly one mile in front of his pursuers; the river was only several hundred paces in front of him. It was possible they would now abandon their hunt and return to base. They would by now have realised that they were prime targets for the mounted Celts they knew were following the main column. They had all done their duty, their officers would be pleased; two of the three deserters had been caught the graphic details of the hunt and its outcome would spread through the retreating army. For a short while this would deter any more potential deserters.

Orius decided he would cross the river at the ford, then travel along the path on the opposite side for several hundred yards, double back to the river and travel upstream for a short while, then take cover where he could still see the ford. He needed to know if any of the soldiers would be foolish enough to continue following him. Stopping at the ford, which was in a small clearing, he knelt down to splash the cool, running water over his face and chest. When he came here many years before with an army patrol, they had come from the opposite direction. They had been pursuing Celtic raiders who had attacked a small Roman settlement driving off their livestock. He remembered the tall stone pillar embedded close to the path near the ford, with the strange markings carved on the face of the stone.

Three paths met at the ford: the one that he was travelling along, one that came from the opposite bank of the river and went upstream, another that was on his side of the river arriving from downstream. Their Celtic guide told them that this was the boundary where three of the old Celtic kingdoms met. The carved stone pillar was one of the special places where the Druid priests traditionally held their ceremonies. It was said that a maiden had been found dancing on the day of her wedding by travelling Druid priests. It was one of their sacred days and she should have been fasting. They were so angered by her gaiety that they turned her into a pillar of stone, thus she had remained to this day.

At this time Orius's patrol had been following the raiders for two days and they decided to go no further. He recalled how nervous the patrol had been; they were already far inside Celtic controlled territory. He remembered how he and his companions had tried to deface the carvings on the stone pillar with their spears, while their Celtic guide had looked on in disgust.

As Orius examined the carvings these faint, but by now weathered, attempts were still visible. The money belt and pouches he had taken from his companions, plus his own purse, were weighing him down. He made a decision: he would bury the money belt. He concluded that the ideal position would be at the rear of the stone pillar. "*The barbarian stone maiden will be useful once again*", he said aloud to himself.

He would now have to find somewhere to hide, although it needed to be a spot from where he could still observe the crossing. If his pursuers did not appear he would return and retrieve his money belt and proceed on his way. If the hounds arrived he would slip away while they followed the false trail; hopefully he would find a way to come back at some later date. If (the gods preserve him!) the hounds did catch him, at least their handlers would not have the satisfaction of finding his gold. This thought amused him and he laughed to himself, *all their sweat and toil for nothing*.

He finished digging a shallow hole with his sword, placed the money belt and pouches inside, covered them with the loose soil and finished by placing a large slab of stone he found lying in the surrounding grass over his treasure.

He was in no hurry. He was by now fairly confident that his pursuers had given up the chase. He even stopped to gather some of the small fruit of a wild apple tree just off the track and he settled down to hide in a dense clump of bushes close to the riverbank, before a bend in the river about five hundred yards from the ford.

He had just begun to breathe more easily after his exertions, and was eating his third small apple, when his heart missed a beat. The first of the hounds appeared at the edge of the ford and began to work the banks on that side of the river. This dog was quickly followed by the rest of the pack. Seconds later the dog handlers and auxiliaries arrived, panting and gasping for breath.

Meanwhile the lead hound, having found no scent on either of the paths on that side of the river, crossed to the opposite bank his baying brought the rest of the pack splashing across the ford to follow their leader, who was following the false scent that had been laid.

Orius was standing with his back to a great oak tree, stretching himself up to see the ford above the bushes and low undergrowth when the snort of a horse no more than six steps away made him freeze; he slowly pressed himself against the trunk, trying to become one with the great tree, the only parts of his body he moved were his eyes.

The horse was to his left and level with him. Its rider, a well-armed Celt, was steadily watching the small group of men at the edge of the ford, who were now deeply involved in a heated argument. Even Orius from his hiding place could hear their raised voices. A slight sound to his right caused him to swivel his eyes in that direction. There, another well-armed mounted Celt was also concentrating on the noisy group of Roman soldiers standing by the water's edge.

The two horsemen slowly passed his hiding place, their surefooted mounts making no noise as they threaded their way through the undergrowth. Orius slowly sank to his haunches so as to be hidden from view by the leafy bushes that surrounded him. In all, six horsemen passed on either side of him as he hid at the base of the oak tree. After several minutes and no further movement, he cautiously stretched to look above the foliage.

The horsemen had stopped several hundred yards in front of his hiding place and about the same distance from his pursuers, who were still arguing on the riverbank.

The mounted men were obviously waiting for a signal. The hounds had returned and were milling around their handlers and the two lightly armed auxiliaries, all except the lead hound, who was easily distinguished by his unusual markings: a light coloured body and a jet-black head. He was standing about twenty yards upriver from the rest of the group, facing in

Orius's direction. Orius gasped! Had he caught his scent, or had he just sensed the presence of the stationary Celtic warriors?

He slowly sank below the foliage once more, turned, and on his hands and knees crawled away from his hiding place. After fifty yards he rose to a crouch and ran, and when he thought he was well clear and out of sight of the ford, he stood upright, stopped, and listened intently.

There was no sound of pursuit, all he could hear was the merry sound of birds singing as the rays of bright, summer morning sunlight shone down between the gaps in the leaves and branches of the tall woodland trees.

A large bird of prey was gliding on the thermals high in the blue sky. Orius watched the bird for several minutes. *A bird of that size must be a buzzard,* he mused to himself, *if only I could converse with that bird, it has such a great aerial view over the woods, the river and paths. From its vantage point it can see everything happening below. It could guarantee my safe passage away from this dangerous area.* It occurred to Orius in a moment of reflection, if he had not been running for his life, what a wonderful morning it would have been.

It was the howling of the lead hound, quickly picked up by the rest of the pack that eventually stopped the argument among the small group of men standing at the head of the ford. The mounted Celts had moved from the shelter of the wood and were now grouped at the edge of the clearing, just twenty paces from the now very silent group of Roman soldiers. "Of all the saints in the sky!" exclaimed the young auxiliary as he turned to run. But blocking his path were another six, well-armed mounted warriors. The same applied to the other two paths: both were blocked by mounted men.

"Say your prayers my comrades," said Maddoc. "Pray to your gods for a quick, clean death."

"Let's rush the group that's on the path we came along," said the young auxiliary, "at least one or two of us may break clear and lose them in the forest. And even if we don't escape we will fight to the death and avoid being tortured by these barbarians."

"That statement is stupid," replied the second auxiliary, whose name was Nicolas. He was forty years old and all his twenty years' army career had been spent in Britannia.

"Stupid and reckless," joined in Maddoc. "You two are the only ones with swords, and we have only short daggers," he said, indicating his two junior handlers. "There are five of us on foot, and there are over twenty of the mounted barbarians. They will cut us to pieces before you have time to draw your second breath."

"Why don't they attack?" asked Agricola, the younger auxiliary. He was from one of the Greek islands and had only received basic training before being sent to the island of Britannica six months before. The Celts were sitting on their stationary mounts watching the huddled group of legionnaires, who were now standing back to back in a loose, defensive circle. The dogs were silent rather than their usual noisy selves: they too sensed that everything was not as it should be.

"They're waiting for a signal to attack," voiced Maddoc.

"Or waiting for someone else to appear," suggested Nicolas.

Fifteen minutes passed and there was no movement from either side. "Your lead dog is wandering off," said Nicolas, breaking the silence. Maddoc turned in the direction Nicolas was indicating.

The leader of the pack of hounds with his distinguishing markings had moved past the mounted Celts and, nose sniffing the air, was loping off down the path that followed the river upstream. "Hadrian! Come back here," yelled Maddoc after the fast disappearing dog. If the dog heard his master's command he chose to ignore it, continuing to move along the path by the side of the river.

"I wish I were a dog!" exclaimed Agricola. Even though the small group was in such dire circumstances, this dry statement brought a chuckle from the encircled legionnaires.

It was now mid-morning and the sun was quite strong. The group of men in the centre of the small clearing had tried to edge into the shade of a nearby tall chestnut tree, where the pack of hounds had settled, but an arrow from one of the feared Celtic bows had stopped their progress, by quivering in the ground inches from the foot of the leading soldier. All the men in the small group were desperately thirsty, the sound and sight of the clear running water of the nearby river was an added torture.

Chapter Four

The Celts had withdrawn their mounts into the shade of the trees on the edge of the clearing, they sat motionless on their horses, quietly watching the five Roman soldiers.

"Have any of you any water left in your carrier?" Maddoc asked the other four men. But his question went unanswered, all eyes in the small group turned in the direction of a slight commotion at the edge of the clearing. Six more mounted Celts had joined the group already there.

Amongst them could be seen a man of noteworthy bearing, and even though he rode a taller horse than those of the other warriors, it was clear that he himself was a tall man with a powerful physique. After a short conversation amongst the mounted men, one of the riders left the group and approached the Roman soldiers in the clearing.

"I speak your language," he said. "You will throw down your weapons and surrender to my Lord Prasatt Ambrosius, otherwise you Romans will die here in this clearing on Celtic soil, far from your own lands." He leant down from the saddle of his horse and placed a sand timer on the ground. "When the sand runs out we require your reply." He turned his mount and joined his other companions at the edge of the clearing.

"It's a trick to disarm us," said Agricola, "let's make a run for the woods."

"No!" Shouted Maddoc in frustration. "If they intended to kill us they'd have done so before now. I vote we surrender," he added.

"I vote with Maddoc," said Nicolas.

"Me too," said Maro, one of the junior dog handlers. The final decision was taken out of their hands as Agricola made a dramatic dash for the trees at the edge of the small clearing. He had travelled about eight strides when the first arrow entered his shoulder; the force of the projectile spun him around as the second arrow entered his chest, smashing through his chest bone and flinging him onto his back on the clearing floor. His body quivered for a few seconds, made two or three violent jerks, then lay still.

During the few seconds it took for life to slip away from Agricola, the memory of his short time on earth passed before his mind's eye: from playing with his elder brother and two sisters in front of his parents' small farmhouse, holding his mother's hand as she collected the eggs from the little shed in the compound where their small flock of hens were kept. He felt again the pride he had experienced as an older boy when being made responsible for looking after the flock of goats without any adult supervision, the sorrow he had shared with his family when both his father uncle, and several other menfolk from his village, did not return after being caught in a freak storm while out fishing along their coast.

Agricola had always been fascinated by soldiers based in the stone fortress at the entrance to the island's small harbour. Admiring their smart attire, polished leather and shining armour; the way they marched in step when they were changing guard at the gate to the fortress. So when the Roman Army held a recruiting drive on the island, Agricola had taken the small purse of coins offered, and signed his name for twenty years' service in the Roman legion.

He had not told any of his family of his decision, it was several days before he could speak to his mother through the gaps in the wooden stockade that surrounded the camp where he was billeted. He told her not to worry, that he would soon make his fortune and return.

He passed her the small bag of coins through the slats of the wooden stockade; the vision of his mother sobbing, her shoulders hunched as she walked away, stayed with him for many years.

A garrison supply ship arrived at the island several days later, and when it sailed away, Agricola and his companions were on board. After a wretched journey during which the ship was battered by storms and lashed by gales of sleet and snow, he'd arrived at this damp, cold, soggy island they called Brittanica. During this trip Agricola made the acquaintance of one of the sailors who had been born in a village near to his own, from this well-travelled fellow islander Agricola was made aware of the serious situation facing the Roman Empire.

In defending the borders of its vast empire, the Roman army was losing more soldiers than it could replace with new recruits; how they were only given the minimum of basic training before being sent to their new commands, with little hope that they would live to return to their homeland.

Agricola was finding it very difficult to breathe, the world was blurring, his arms and legs refused to move. Yet in the distance he could hear his mother calling his name. Agricola smiled: he was going home to his mother…

Agricola's four companions watched as if in slow motion as the young auxiliary sprinted towards the nearby trees. It had seemed he was going to make it until the two arrows entered his body in quick succession. Agricola's flailing arms released his short sword, which went spinning into the air. It came to rest a foot behind his head, its sharp point penetrating the grass and earth at an oblique angle behind his inert body, like the cross of the new Christian religion.

Maddoc was the first to throw down his weapon, quickly followed by the other three men. He cursed his luck, he had only been promoted to head handler only two weeks before. After a heavy session of cider drinking, his predecessor Jomas Magon had staggered off to his tent, only to be found mauled to death in the hounds' compound the following morning.

Jomas Magon's death had caused suspicion since his money pouch was missing. A pouch that was known to contain a sizeable number of coins taken over many previous months from the deserters he had hunted down. His mistake had been not to share the proceeds with his assistant handlers, especially Maddoc, who had bitterly resented this.

Periodically the Legion stopped for several days to allow all the stragglers to catch up; it was during these stops that Jomas Magon took the opportunity to indulge in his passion for gambling.

One of Maddoc's duties had been to feed and look after the hounds, but he had been so intent on watching Jomas Magon's heavy gambling, buying drinks for his cronies with the money that Maddoc considered to be his, that he had neglected this duty. The already half-starved hounds had gone hungry for two days. As Jomas Magon bought drinks for all and sundry, the more bitter Maddoc became. When, as the sun set on the second day, Jomas Magon eventually left the entertainment tent, Maddoc was waiting with a plan in mind.

As the shadows lengthened, Jomas Magon began to make his way in the general direction of his quarters, staggering and stumbling drunkenly through the line of busy tents and shelters that the large group of camp followers quickly erected at every stop, to provide all the home comforts that were otherwise unavailable under the strictly disciplined army regime. Once he had cleared the hustle and bustle, Maddoc appeared beside him to help him along, slipping a fresh pig's liver into the drunken man's pocket and guiding him all the time in the direction of the hounds' compound.

When Maddoc was promoted to chief dog handler the following day, he resolved he would not make the same mistake as Jomas Magon. He had always given a small percentage to his assistants, while keeping the bulk for himself. Between the coins taken from his predecessor and those he had since accumulated, he owned a tidy sum. But now all his rosy prospects had come to a disastrous end. Their fate lay in the hands of the leader of the Celtic warriors surrounding them: Prassat Ambrosius.

As Orius jogged slowly along the path beside the river, his thoughts were still on his pursuers and their pack of hounds, and how they had fared with the Celtic horsemen. *But that is a problem I need not concern myself with any longer,* he decided. He stopped for a short while to regain his breath at a point where the main path was joined at right angles by another fainter, narrower track.

He debated with himself whether to continue along the main path that disappeared from sight at a bend in the river some three hundred yards further on, or to take the much fainter, less used trail. A heron feeding at the banks of the river just before the bend took off in startled flight, its feet paddling the water in its haste to depart. Orius did not miss the sign and scrambled quickly off the path and into the undergrowth, drawing his sword as he did so. He had no sooner thrown himself behind a thick gorse bush than he heard the dull thunder of many horses' hooves on the hard ground and the sound of jingling horse brass coming towards him along the river path. For the moment he knew he was quite safe and out of sight from anyone travelling along the track.

Through the thick foliage he could see about twenty horsemen travelling two abreast like the group he had seen earlier. These were also well-armed Celts, their bodies armoured in chain mail were seated on high, pommelled saddles, which supported them front and rear so that they could turn in the saddle and use their short bows to fire behind them while riding forwards. He had seen at first hand the Celtic cavalry use this method with devastating effect against the mounted Roman light cavalry.

The group of horsemen came slowly to a stop where the two paths joined. The leader of the men dismounted and passed his horse's reins to his nearest companion, while he walked a short distance along the adjoining path: he had obviously made arrangements for a meeting at this point. He was only a few yards from where Orius was hiding. Orius could see the man's face quite clearly. The left-hand side was badly scarred and the short growth of beard on the right-hand side did nothing to enhance his features. He was wearing a gold torque around his neck, which indicated he was of noble blood. He was extremely frustrated and in a foul mood, barking orders and instructions to his riders, sending horsemen galloping along the two adjoining paths, also back along the track from which they had just come. "In the name of Taranis, god of thunder, where are they?" he shouted to his companions. Some of the other men had also taken this opportunity to dismount, and were relieving themselves at the side of the path. Orius froze, not even blinking, as the scar-faced man himself came within two yards of the thick gorse bush that was hiding him, and urinated. As he did so he seemed to be looking straight at him, but it was obvious his thoughts were elsewhere.

Refastening his breeches he turned at the sound of horses' hooves coming down the track. With a shouted command to his men, they quickly remounted their horses, while he nimbly vaulted onto his own as it was brought level with him. Orius could feel the tension rise amongst the group of men as they fanned out behind their leader.

About fifteen mounted warriors came cantering down the narrow path. They pulled their horses to a stop as they confronted the men who were spread three deep across the main track, blocking their passage. The leading horseman came a few yards further and saluted the leader of the waiting group and the tension eased. As the two men carried on a deep conversation, the two groups of horsemen dismounted and the men spread into the undergrowth on either side of the main track, talking in small groups, the horses grazing the course woodland grass.

The scar-faced warrior's horse was only several feet away from Orius; he could smell the sweet odour of its breath as it grazed the coarse grass at the foot of the thick gorse behind which he remained frozen and hidden. He had pressed himself so hard against the gorse that it had penetrated his skin like a mass of needles, but he did not feel any pain.

He noticed a Roman shield fastened to one flank of the Celt's horse, and several pilums, the Roman metal throwing spears. The markings on the shield told him that it was from his own company; they had been on guard duty the previous night, and some of them would have been sent in pursuit of him and the other two deserters, along with the hounds and their handlers. It would seem that not all his previous comrades-in-arms had managed to return safely to the main Roman column.

He was debating with himself whether he could mount the horse nearest to him and bolt clear before the Celts realised what was happening, but as they had not seen him up to now, if he stayed hidden there was a fair chance that they would mount their horses and ride on about their business, leaving him free to carry on with his journey. He also noticed that several of the warriors carried the short cavalry bow, while others had the dreaded longbow that he had seen used in action.

From a distance of over 1,300 yards the effect of this weapon had been devastating. The Roman soldiers had nothing to match this deadly tool of war. What was more, the Celts were also expert horsemen and much better in the saddle than he, so that even if he did manage to mount one of their horses and break clear they would be on him within minutes. No, he would have to put up with the discomfort of the gorse bush until this group of Celts and their horses had moved on.

It was while he was in this quandary that one of the horsemen who had been sent back down the path that Orius had travelled a short while ago, came galloping up to the junction, shouting to the scar-faced leader of the group. Orius raised his head and looked through the branches of the bush at the scene that was unfolding in front of his hiding place. He did not understand all that was being said to the leader, but recognised the words "mounted" and "warrior". There was a scurry of activity shouting of orders as men grabbed their loose mounts, while those men with the bows moved into the trees at the side of the track. Their horses were being led out of sight down the track from where they had originally come, the rest of the mounted warriors spread themselves four lines deep across the narrow track, their scar-faced leader at their front.

They had barely organised their positions when Orius heard the sound of a large group of horsemen moving along the track towards the waiting Celts. He knew that it was not Roman cavalry since the approaching horsemen were riding horses with iron-shod hoofs, a practice particular to the Celtic tribes.

The group of horsemen came around the bend at a trot, but slowed to a walk when they came in sight of the armed warriors blocking their path. The leading horseman had the fair complexion and characteristics of a Celt from the northern tribes, with long, flowing, bright red hair, which was braided and hung over his shoulder down to his waist. Orius also noticed that fastened to his saddle was a great two-headed battleaxe. The man stopped his mount ten paces from the leader of the first group; he was very relaxed as he sat comfortably on his battle saddle.

For what seemed like several minutes the two mounted men stared at one another, as if it would be a sign of weakness to be the first to speak. Orius recognised the dress of several Roman auxiliaries who were on foot amongst the group of Celts, two of whom were struggling to keep in check a pack of hunting hounds that were straining at their leashes and pulling in different directions. The other two had their hands bound in front of them and a leash around their necks, held by one of the mounted warriors.

"I am Albion Egilos from the Parisii tribe, why do you obstruct our passage?" inquired the mounted red-haired Celt. "We are here on important business for Great King Erion, and I am the protector of the Celtic Round Council of Elders." He did not direct his message to the scar-faced man confronting him, but to all the mounted men blocking the track.

There was an uneasy stir amongst the men. Great King Erion was the elected leader of the amalgamation of Celtic tribes, the Council of Elders were the leaders of the different tribes, or a person whom a tribe leader had nominated to speak and act on his behalf. They were the supreme power in the Celtic world, now that the Roman army was marching to the coast to be evacuated, the Celtic Round Council controlled the only organised armed force left on the island of Britannia. To disobey or obstruct their orders was considered an act of treason, for which the penalty for the culprit was garrotting; also their family would be banished from their tribe, with no one allowed to raise a hand to help them on pain of losing that hand.

From his hiding place Orius could see what was happening, with his limited knowledge of the language he understood that a serious confrontation was about to take place. 'Scarface' was obviously uncomfortable and kept fidgeting in his saddle. The Council had proclaimed that any deserters from the retreating Roman army should be disarmed and given safe passage under escort to the Great King's encampment. Petrov Joma, the scar-faced man, had cause to be concerned. He and his band of warriors had ignored the order of the Round Council of Elders, and slaughtered any stragglers or deserters they came upon while patrolling this sector designated to them by the Council.

Petrov Joma hated everything Roman or Romanised. He had been a small child when a Roman patrol surprised his village, burned their thatched roof huts, driven off their white, long-horned cattle, small flock of sheep and goats, and loaded the villagers' own carts with their sacks of wheat and oats. When the survivors of the village crept back from the forest to where they had fled, they found a blackened pile of smouldering ash and the burnt skeleton frames of their huts. Amongst one of the piles of ash they found Petrov Joma, his body badly burnt and scarred. He teetered between life and death in a coma for fourteen days. He did not speak a word for a further four years. Both of his parents had been killed, when he had recovered sufficiently to travel he was sent to be cared for by a distant relative.

Orius decided he would crawl away from his present position; the bowmen from the first party of armed men had positioned themselves opposite his hiding place on the other side of the track. In the event of a skirmish any arrows not finding their target would be landing around him – or in him! So while the Celts' attention was focused on the two mounted men facing each other, he slowly detached himself from the gorse bush, turning slowly on his stomach, began to crawl away from the shelter it had provided him and into a large clump of tall stinging nettles. He could hear the conversation of the two leaders as he made his slow painful way forward.

He crawled six yards through the nettle bed and had just reached the tall grass at the edge of the riverbank, when a slight rustling in front of him caused him to freeze.

Sniffing the air and the ground alternately, but all the time moving slowly in his direction, was a great hound with a massive head and unusual black facial markings, great slobbering jaws and a large, brass-studded collar. It was the lead hound of the Roman hunting pack.

"Why do you pass through my lands without the courtesy to first inform me?" Petrov Joma was shouting. He felt insulted that Albion Egilos had virtually ignored him by speaking directly to the entire group of men.

"This land you claim for your own," replied Albion Egilos, "belongs to the Round Council and the Great King. You were only appointed a guardian by them to look after this area in the interests of the Celtic kingdom and its people."

Petrov Joma realised he had overstepped the mark and was losing the argument, but what he also realised was that amongst the mounted group behind this redheaded northern tribesman was a member of the Round Council itself. They would not have sent such a high-ranking official to check on rumours that the Council's orders were not been carried out by a local group leader like himself.

This was a relief to him and meant that they were in this area on much more serious and secret business. He knew he could not obstruct the group in front of him, but at the same time he did not want to lose face with his followers. "I humbly apologise to the member of the Round Council for obstructing his passage," said Petrov Joma loud and clear, deliberately ignoring Albion Egilos himself, directing his words to the group of men behind in order to return the insult he believed he'd received, "but we have heard reports of a large group of mounted armed warriors in the area and we came to investigate, as are my orders."

"Indeed, I would have been concerned if I had been able to ride through your area without being challenged," came a voice from within the group of mounted men, which parted to allow the speaker to show himself. Prassat Ambrosius walked his horse until it was level with Albion Egilos. He was well aware of Petrov Joma's brutal actions, there had been many rumours about this ruthless Roman hater who blatantly disregarded the orders of the king and the Round Council, but now was not the time or place to reprimand or change the leadership of this band of warriors.

There were much more important things at stake and it was necessary for him to make the fastest time possible back to Great King Erion's encampment to report to him and the Celtic Round Council. But Prassat Ambrosius also had more personal reasons for returning to the king's encampment as soon as was possible: after fifteen years of marriage his wife was expecting their first child.

Petrov Joma raised his hand in salute as the member of the Round

Council emerged from the group of mounted warriors. He also noticed the Roman soldiers in the group, his dark eyes glittered, his scarred face twitching uncontrollably, but his attention was centred on the pack of hounds that were being restrained by their handlers; *now there's a prize worth having*, he thought to himself. What sport he could have hunting down Roman stragglers and deserters with such a pack of savage dogs!

It was at this point that the proceedings were interrupted by a series of deep barks and a great howl from the direction of the riverbank – the howling was quickly taken up by the rest of the pack of hounds, who frantically began to pull on their leads, dragging their Roman handlers in a multitude of directions. Orius, startled by the sudden appearance of the hound, had pushed himself onto his knees and drawn his gladius. At the sight of the short sword the dog jumped two paces backwards and begun to bark and then howl at the kneeling man.

Orius slowly rose to his feet holding his sword high in the air. Had he been able to swim, he would have contemplated jumping into the river, which was quite deep and fast flowing at that point and may have provided an avenue of escape. He was trying to watch the reaction of the two groups of Celtic warriors on the track, at the same time keep close track of the great hound as it pranced about in front him, just out of reach of his short sword, its great jaws slobbering as it barked and howled. Orius was finding this difficult: his face and back were a mass of red blotches from the gorse bush and stinging nettles. His body had reacted violently to them and his right eye was also badly swollen, reducing his vision on that side to just a blur.

The sudden eruption of this figure from the long grass, along with the frenzied barking and howling of the pack of hounds who were dragging their handlers among the mounted men, unnerved several of the horses who in turn reared and stamped, kicking out wildly, causing further confusion and panic amongst the tightly-packed group of warriors.

Albion Egilos was one of the first to react. One swift movement and his great battleaxe was in his hand as he wheeled his horse between the stationary, upright figure of Orius, and Prassat Ambrosius, the man whose life he had taken an oath to protect. On the other side of the path, the archers Petrov Joma had placed there moved out of the cover of the trees to obtain a better view of the proceedings slightly below them. A shout of "ambush!" by one of the group around Prassat Ambrosius caused Albion Egilos to swing his horse in that direction, yelling, "Protect the Councillor!" which caused several of the mounted Celts to raise their shields and place themselves between the archers and the Council member.

Petrov Joma raised one of the short throwing spears he had taken from the Roman soldiers he had slaughtered, and with a shout of "assassin!" threw it in the direction of the solitary figure with the raised gladius. It appealed to the killing lust of Petrov Joma to destroy a Roman soldier with a Roman weapon, and this was an ideal situation.

Orius, standing in the long grass, and aware that he was the cause of all the confusion, that the shouts of ambush and assassin were directed at him, threw down his sword and raised both his hands above his head to show them all he was no threat, that he had surrendered. The great hound, seizing its opportunity, jumped, its front paws hitting Orius in the chest and sending him crashing backwards into the nettle bed while the metal pilum thrown by Petrov Joma passed harmlessly over both the horizontal bodies of the man and dog struggling on the ground.

Orius landed on his back with the dog on top of him. As he fell he managed to grab the thick leather collar around the hound's neck, a quick reaction that probably saved his life, as he was able to keep the great fangs from sinking into his neck. This situation did not unduly bother the hound; he had been in this position on several occasions in the past he knew that as long as he remained on top of the man and used his great weight, the victim would eventually weaken. At the opportune moment he would slash right and left at the man's forearms, his hold would give way, and the dog could attack his neck or throat.

A serious situation was prevented from spiralling out of control by Prassat Ambrosius, who realised it only needed one over-eager warrior to release an arrow, throw a battleaxe or spear, for a savage battle to begin. Waving his armed bodyguard back, he rode into the small clearing and, with both hands raised in the air, shouted as loud as he could, "Hold fast you Celtic warriors! Do not strike down your brothers, there is no ambush, there is no assassin, that man is a Roman deserter. Drag that hound off him," he shouted in excellent Latin to Maddoc, pointing in the direction of Orius.

Petrov Joma watched as the metal spear passed through the air where a second earlier the man had stood upright; now he was on the ground with the great dog on top of him. But even though the spear had missed its target, Petrov Joma was not disappointed; he was immensely impressed by the actions of the great hound.

Maddoc quickly passed the leads of the hounds he was holding to one of his assistants and ran swiftly to carry out Prassat Ambrosius's orders. He recognised the voice of authority and did not want to offend anyone of such high rank. The hound on top of Orius could feel his victim's struggles becoming weaker, the time was right to savage the forearms, then the way would be clear to attack the throat.

Chapter Five

Maddoc was shouting at the dog, but there was no reaction: the dog was enveloped in a killing lust. Grabbing the dog's heavy leather collar, he forced the handle of his whip between the collar and the dog's thick, muscular neck then twisted the collar savagely, using it as a tourniquet to cut off the dog's air supply. "I will teach you to disobey me!" Maddoc muttered to the dog as he struggled to drag its weight off Orius. Maddoc was quick to notice there was no money belt on Orius, or on the ground nearby, just a handful of small wild apples that had been squashed in the struggles. He was certain Orius would not have hidden the money at night when no landmarks could be seen to mark the spot. So somewhere in the close vicinity a small fortune was hidden, and he, Maddoc, if he were given half a chance, was going to be the one to find it.

The dog was gasping for air and dizzy from the lack of oxygen, the man under him was forgotten. He could feel himself being dragged off the human and remembered who had done this to him once before, the previous handler, who had then proceeded to thrash him with the heavy whip that all the handlers carried. But he had taken his revenge: one night that same handler staggered into the dogs' compound stinking from the evil-smelling liquid the humans drank that made them strange and unpredictable.

The pack was always kept hungry, but during that particular time they had not been fed and were starving. The handler came into their compound alone with raw meat stuffed in his jerkin; moments later he collapsed onto his belly. The dog had led the rest of the pack in savaging the intoxicated man. He would bide his time, given the opportunity he would do the same to this handler too.

The situation between the two groups of armed Celts had calmed as Orius rose to his feet in the trampled grass to find a mounted warrior positioned on either side of him, Maddoc dragging the dazed dog off to join the rest of the pack. Orius tore a strip of fabric from his tunic and proceeded to wrap it around the bleeding gash in his forearm, at the same time taking the opportunity to look around him.

The rest of the horses were being brought back for the archers, who had now left the shelter of the trees and joined their comrades in the centre of the track. Prassat Ambrosius and Petrov Joma dismounted and were in deep conversation. Albion Egilos, still mounted, was several yards away, his great battleaxe once again fastened to his saddle. The rest of his group also dismounted, some were in several smaller groups while others strolled about stretching their legs; it was obvious they had been riding for a great length of time.

The late morning sun was shining on Orius's face; he could feel its warmth despite its throbbing from his recent encounter with the stinging nettles. It was good to still be alive after the trauma of the last hour, he turned his face further in the direction of the warming sun. With the sight of his one good eye he could see that the sky was very blue with no clouds in sight – and there was the buzzard again, gliding on the warm currents of air! If only it could talk, what a tale it could tell as it looked down on the squabbling human race below.

"It is obvious you are in a great hurry, my lord," said Petrov Joma, scratching his beard on the good side of his face, a habit he had acquired when his mind was working overtime. "If I may suggest, those hounds are slowing you down. In order for you to make better time, leave them and their handlers and this other wretch" – indicating Orius – "in my safe keeping, I will return them to you at a later time."

Prassat Ambrosius considered what the man before him was saying; the hounds and their handlers were indeed slowing his party down and time was of the essence.

The dog handlers, even though they were Romans, would be safe with Petrov Joma for they would be needed to look after the pack of hounds, which it was clear Petrov Joma would love to own for the prestige and standing it would give him in his community.

The other Roman soldiers he would take with him. Their lives would be in jeopardy if they were left in the custody of this bloodthirsty killer. He would take horses for the other Roman auxiliaries if they could ride, if not they could travel on foot with a mounted armed guard. The Roman army and all its train would be out of Petrov Joma's designated area by the following day; they would then be monitored by the chief of the Coritani tribe Calgacus, whom Prassat Ambrosius knew, who, unlike Petrov Joma and his followers, would follow the king and Council's directives to the letter.

The problem was that these minor chiefs neither saw nor understood the larger picture, nor the dangers that were forming on the distant horizon, even as the Romans departed, dangers that would eventually threaten the fledgling kingdom that Great King Erion had created. It was important that as many of the Roman deserters and stragglers as possible should be captured alive and delivered to the king's encampment. The more experienced the soldiers, the more valuable their services would be. If he took some of Petrov Joma's warriors' horses it would take several hours for him to replace them.

He decided that at that particular moment he could not afford to make an issue of Petrov Joma's failure to follow the Council's directives. The Council's position was fragile, held together by the personality of his friend, King Erion. He would not be the one to place the king and Council in jeopardy; many of the Council might agree with Petrov Joma's actions, it was imperative at this moment in time that the Council show a consolidated and unified front to the rest of the Celtic tribes.

Prassat Ambrosius decided to release the pack of hounds and their Roman handlers to Petrov Joma; by doing so the man would not lose face before his followers. He would then take the Roman soldiers and several extra horses back to the king's encampment, report to the king and Council the outcome of his meetings with the captains of the convoy of ships that had been designated to carry the Roman army and their equipment and stores across the sea to the mainland of Gaul.

Orius listened to the bartering between the scarfaced Celt and the older man who was obviously of high authority, but his knowledge of the Celtic language was insufficient for him to understand the outcome of the exchange. He had already decided that if he were to be left in the hands of Joma, he would attempt to escape. He could neither outrun the mounted Celts nor the pack of hounds that they would turn on him, he would merely be more sport for them and would be back in the same position as before, but with different and fresh pursuers. Plus he was weary. He would therefore have to try and mount one of the horses and make his break for freedom on horseback. Better to take that risk and die in the attempt than be slowly tortured to death by the leader of this local Celtic tribe.

Prassat Ambrosius walked his horse to a position close to Orius and observed the man in front of him for several moments. He saw he was not a Roman, he was like so many in the occupying army, a native from one of the many lands that formed the Roman Empire, recruited and given some basic training and then sent to serve in countries far from his homeland, according to Roman army policy. This meant the legionnaire would feel no loyalty to the country he was sent to control, and would carry out his orders no matter how distasteful they might be, or how they might affect the local population.

The man before him seemed quite unconcerned, he was rubbing the nettle stings with some large leaves that were growing nearby; the reaction to the nettle stings had been quite severe his face and shoulders were very badly swollen. He also had rags wrapped around his forearm where the dark stain of blood was slowly seeping through. In the struggle the dog had drawn blood with its great fangs.

"What is your name, soldier?" asked Prassat Ambrosius in Latin.

"My name is Orius Tomase," replied Orius. "I claim the sanctuary that has been offered by your king."

"Then you shall have it," replied Prassat Ambrosius instantly. "Can you ride a horse?"

"Yes!" replied Orius without hesitation. He had only been on horseback a few times, but he was not going to risk being left behind to the mercy of Petrov Joma and his band because of his lack of riding skill. "You speak the Roman tongue?" continued Orius.

"Yes. I have traded with your army on many occasions and for many years," replied the Council member, "but now we must make all haste to reach our destination. We have many hard leagues to travel. You will ride with my men if you so wish," then added with a smile, "or you can stay with Petrov Joma."

Prassett Ambrosius did not enlighten Orius that he had traded with the Roman army on many occasions in order to gauge their strength prior to attacking them when their outposts had encroached on the Celtic mountain stronghold. Yet despite having fought the occupying Roman force all his adult life to protect his Celtic heritage, he had to admit to himself that he rather admired the ordered way of life in the Roman settlements the luxuries that were made available from distant lands still under Roman influence and control.

Orius joined the group of Celtic warriors along with the other Roman auxiliary, whose name he found to be Nicolas of Mesopotamia. They travelled hard for several days and nights, stopping only to rest and feed their horses, until they eventually reached the encampment of Great King Erion.

It was during this journey that Prassat Ambrosius took a liking to this young man who had taken the trouble to learn some of the Celtic language, who only days before had been a conscript in the Roman army that occupied his homeland. He offered Orius a position in his household: he would be a free man, he would be clothed, fed and have his needs taken care of. In return he would swear loyalty to Prassat Ambrosius. This Orius readily agreed to, and over a period of time became a trusted member of Prassat Ambrosius's personal guard. He learned later that Nicolas of Mesopotamia, the man with whom he had struck up a friendship, also became a bodyguard, but to Boro Sigurd, one of the Celtic court's high officials.

"Come Orius!" said Aurthora, "snap out of your daydreaming, we have a lot of baggage to pack. At this rate we'll end up at the rear of the column eating all its dust. I've made arrangements to break my fast with my friend Ethellro Egilos and his sister Katrina."

Orius started at Aurthora's shout; it had been the sight of the red-haired Ethellro and the great battleaxe fastened to the young man's saddle that had started his recollections in the first place. "You go and enjoy your meal, my friend," replied Orius, "I will collect and pack the rest of our equipment." He'd observed the previous day the sly looks Aurthora had directed towards Ethellro's sister Katrina. He was obviously attracted to her, Orius was pleased for his young companion. Katrina was indeed a beautiful young woman, she rode a horse well, and he had seen her at the end of the previous day's journey, busying herself preparing the evening meal for her brother and their party. She was obviously not afraid of hard work. Orius concluded she would make a suitable partner for his young lord.

His thoughts again wandered back to when he buried the money belt behind the stone pillar near the river ford. He had not given it much thought during the years, even though on many occasions he had been back to that area during his duties as protector to Prassat Ambrosius. While in his employer's household, he had never gone hungry, if his garments were ripped or damaged they had been repaired or replaced. He had held a good position as the personal attendant and guard to the man who had saved him from what would have been a painful death at the hands of Petrov Joma and his band.

Aurthora set off across the meadow where the column had camped for the night, groups of men were busy packing away their belongings on small, two-wheeled carts pulled by mules or small ponies, while others were strapping their possessions onto their horses.

He passed the kitchen tent where some of the soldiers were helping themselves to the pottage that had been prepared by the column's cooks. It was their first meal of the day, the next would be when the column stopped and camped for the night. He had eaten the pottage on many occasions, it was always hot and always very lumpy. It consisted of crushed oats that had been mixed with water and some salt, then brought to the boil and allowed to simmer. It was plain food, quick and easy to prepare but nutritious and warming, sustaining the men until their evening meal.

There were several smaller shelters near the main food tent where some of the camp followers had set up their own cooking fires. Here you could purchase a tastier meal if you did not wish to take advantage of the free pottage on offer from the king's granary.

He was warmly greeted by Ethellro, who came to meet him as he neared their small encampment. "It is good to see you again my friend," placing his arm around Aurthora's shoulders as both men walked back to the small fire where Katrina was spooning pottage into polished wooden bowls from a cooking pot hanging over the small fire.

Oh well, thought Aurthora, *more pottage, nothing changes.*

Ethellro moved to a leather square that was suspended from its corners on a light, triangular timber frame, proceeded to pour water from a clay jug onto the leather which formed a bowl. Aurthora copied Ethellro and washed his hands in the leather bowl then dried them on the cloth Ethellro handed him. *A Roman practice,* he mused to himself. Katrina smiled her bright smile at Aurthora handing him a bowl of the pottage and a wooden spoon. She indicated a short tree trunk where he could sit with her brother while she made herself comfortable on a low stool opposite them.

Aurthora had never tasted pottage like this prepared by Katrina: it was smoother than any he had ever eaten, sweetened with honey and cooled with goat's milk, having crushed nuts and wild berries scattered over the surface. During their meal he made light conversation about the weather with Ethellro. He was desperately trying to think of something witty to say to Katrina, but his mind was blank. When he glanced in her direction during the lulls in his conversation with Ethellro, she smiled sweetly at him, embarrassing him still further.

He scraped the bowl clean with his wooden spoon and passed it to Katrina's outstretched hand saying, "That was the most wonderful pottage I've ever tasted."

"You must join us for an evening meal Aurthora," said Ethellro.

"Yes, please do," joined in Katrina quickly. She liked this well-built, shy friend of her brother's, and she could tell her brother felt a great affection for him too, so arrangements were made on dining together the following day.

Orius arrived with the pack pony loaded and both horses saddled. "Have you broken your fast, Orius?" asked Katrina as Orius stood holding the reins of the three animals. Orius shook his head, and so Katrina proceeded to spoon the last of the pottage simmering in the pot over the fire into a clean wooden bowl. She poured the rest of the goat's milk, sprinkled wild berries and crushed nuts onto the surface then handed the full bowl to Orius.

Orius passed the reins of the three horses to Aurthora, and as he proceeded to spoon the pottage into his mouth, he looked at Aurthora and rolled his eyes. Aurthora smiled back at his friend; he knew exactly what he was feeling. Orius finished his meal and handed the empty bowl back to Katrina complimenting her on her cooking. "I have eaten pottage on more occasions than I care to remember," he said, "but never have I tasted it so well-prepared and delicious. You must have been tutored by the handmaidens to the gods."

"Oh Orius, you're too kind!" laughed Katrina in reply.

Aurthora looked at Orius in amazement. Where had he learnt to be such a flatterer? He was always a man of such few words. Orius took the reins from Aurthora's limp wrist and began to walk the three horses away, smiling as he went.

"Can I help you to pack your camp?" Aurthora asked Katrina. He was desperately trying to think of a reason for staying in her presence, he felt so content and happy in her company. Orius, who was only a few yards away, stopped so abruptly the horses bumped into his back. *Have I heard correctly?* he wondered. *Aurthora has never packed away a camp in his life. It's me who does all the packing and clearing of the equipment.*

"No, it's no trouble," Katrina replied, "I've done it more times than I can count, and I have Emilia my handmaiden to assist me. You join Orius, he's waiting for you." She smiled at Aurthora, then turned and continued to pack the equipment. At the sight of Katrina's smile, Aurthora's heart missed a beat, but he quickly caught up with Orius, who had a broad grin on his face; together they joined the column of men and animals that was now travelling along the old Roman road. He began whistling a tuneless melody, much to the annoyance of Orius, who dropped behind out of earshot.

Aurthora seemed unaware of this. All he was thinking about was how much he was looking forward to his dinner the next day in the company of Katrina.

Restricted as it was to travelling at the pace of the slowest cart, the column was not making good progress. In addition, groups of armed men, some mounted, some on foot, as well as several small groups of camp followers, were joining the long, straggling line at every junction, adding to the congestion on the overcrowded paved road.

Orius was looking out for someone he had recognised the previous day, and after a short time moved into the slow-moving column alongside a much older, one-armed man who was riding on one of the compact two-wheeled Celtic carts, pulled by one of the small mountain ponies – much smaller than the mount Orius was riding. "Aidas!" Orius shouted as the older man turned in his direction. "Aidas Corrilus! It must be twenty summers since we were together in the 5th cohort. So you did not leave with the legion and the rest of your comrades?" Orius inquired.

"Orius! Orius Tomase!" replied the man, looking at Orius in amazement. He was so startled he had to hold on to his seat to stop himself from slipping off his cart. "Well I don't believe my eyes! In the names of all the gods, Roman, Celtic and Christian, what are you doing with this mob of Britanculi?"

"Careful with your choice of words, Aidas," interrupted Orius, "some of these Celts understand Latin. They would not take kindly to you calling them 'wretched little Brits'."

"You're still alive! Everyone thought you were dead," continued Aidas. "None of the soldiers or the hounds and their handlers returned the night that you three deserted. A much larger, well-armed force was sent out to make a search the following day. All they found were the remains of Ballsti and Marcus. I don't think they were unduly concerned about the loss of the men, I think they were really searching for that pack of man-hunting hounds. I did see the one they called Maddoc many years later, he was the one who was in charge of that pack of dogs. He was at one of the Celtic fairs several summers ago, travelling with an evil looking, scar-faced Celtic chief, the one they call Petrov Joma."

The sound of Petrov Joma's name sent a cold shiver down Orius's spine. He had realised on many occasions that his gods had been looking down upon him with great favour that particular day more than twenty years ago. He was certain it was only the appearance of Aurthora's father Prassat Ambrosius that had saved his life, for which Orius had been eternally grateful.

"There was also another Roman with Maddoc – Victor Aberuso," continued Aidas. "Does that name ring any bells with you, Orius?"

"The name sounds familiar," replied Orius, "wasn't he a gladiator at one time?"

"Yes," continued Aidas, "he was a slave turned gladiator, he won the wooden sword of freedom in the arena, but still continued as a gladiator to quench his thirst for killing. At the last games, held where the Roman army was congregating before its departure, Victor Aberuso's opponent put up a tremendous fight. I was there. The contest lasted for over two hours, the crowd was in uproar. They had never seen two gladiators so evenly matched. Eventually Aberuso gained the upper hand, he ended up astride his unarmed opponent, his gladius poised to strike the fatal blow.

"The crowd was shouting for mercy, and the General also gave Aberuso the sign for clemency, he ignored them all and cut off his opponent's head. There was uproar amongst the legionnaires in the crowd: most of them knew Aberuso's opponent personally. Also, his action had been a direct affront to the General, and in front of all the high-ranking officials present. The General was a representative of Caesar, so it was also a direct insult to Caesar. Aberuso was taken by the guard for his own safety and thrown into the dungeons, otherwise the crowd would have ripped him apart with their bare hands. As I recall, when the army departed he was left chained there, left to the mercy of the Celts. After that, I don't know what became of him."

"Well then Aidus, tell me what became of you," said Orius.

"I applied to re-enlist and was accepted, even though I only had one arm. The legion were desperately short of experienced soldiers. After you des…" Aidas paused for a second and then continued, "…after you left the legion we had no more trouble with the Celts, things went smoothly until we reached the coast and the fortified port, which was to be our port of embarkation…"

Aidas stopped for breath and reached for a leather water bottle. Drawing the stopper with his teeth, he took a swig then offered the leather bottle to Orius, who declined. "It's not water Orius, this is the best Celtic cider." Aidas again offered the bottle to Orius, who took a great gulp of the liquid.

"It is indeed fine cider," he said, handing back the leather bottle to the older man, who hooked it by its short strap around the horn of his seat.

"Now where were we?" continued Aidas. "Ah yes, we had reached the port, we found there were not enough ships available to take the legion and all its equipment. So the General decided that the equipment would have to be left behind. He was not prepared to split his force, there were rumours that a large army of Celts was being formed to attack the legion while it was at the port. He decided that half the legion could not defend the port until the ships could return to evacuate them, and he was under orders to make all haste and deliver his forces back to Rome as quickly as possible. And I, Aidas Corrilus, master operator of the ballista, was left along with several hundred legionnaires who were too ill, injured, or too old to keep up the pace of the fast moving Roman army.

We were left behind along with a vast amount of field equipment, all of us surplus to the Roman army's requirements. I was forced to watch as the last legions of the Roman army of occupation sailed away from this damp, miserable island of Britannia, back to my sunny warm homeland."

Orius listened intently to Aidas's story; it was all beginning to fall into place. When he had been captured by Aurthora's father many years before, Prassat Ambrosius had been returning from an important meeting with the sea captains, Orius understood that much from the scraps of conversation he had overheard while travelling back with his Celtic capturers. These independent captains controlled the great fleets of cargo ships that operated between the island of Britannia and the mainland of Gaul they had obviously been paid by the Celtic officials to make fewer ships available.

Aidas had stopped talking, he was re-living the time the legion had sailed away leaving him behind, his opportunity to return to his beloved homeland gone forever.

"What happened then my friend?" asked Orius, breaking into Aidas's silent daydreaming. The man shook his head as if to shake off bad thoughts and continued.

"A large body of mounted Celtic warriors arrived. They had been riding to and fro across the skyline to create the impression of a greater force than they really were. This had been a ruse to force the Romans to evacuate their army quickly, and had given them little time to damage or destroy the siege and battlefield equipment they were forced to leave behind."

Aidas unhooked the water bottle with his good hand, pulled out the stopper with his teeth, and took another good swig of the sweet cider, leaning over and offering the leather container to Orius, who politely refused. *He'll be lucky to stay upright on the cart by the setting of the sun if he carries on like this,* thought Orius to himself, as Aidas took yet another drink before returning the bottle to its resting place, looped on his seat.

"What happened next?" prompted Orius eagerly.

"The Celts asked us if we wished to swear loyalty to their King Erion," continued Aidas. "We had nothing to lose, and to refuse would have been a quick passage to the next world, so to a man we all accepted. We were then taken under escort to the fortified town of Camulodunum along with all the equipment. No one tried to escape because there was nowhere to escape to. Since then I have spent twenty summers and twenty damp miserable winters showing groups of Celts how to build and maintain the roads and bridges in this kingdom of Elmet. I often wondered what it was all for, now I know. My old siege equipment is following on behind. I'm travelling ahead to try and organise the operators – if and when they arrive at our designated rendezvous."

Aidas stopped to regain his breath and proceeded to take another drink from his container, but this time when he had finished he did not offer it to Orius.

"And what happened to you, my friend, that dark night when you left the employ of the Grand Roman Army?" continued Aidas, smiling to himself at his witticism.

Orius told his story briefly, but withheld the part he had played in the capture and subsequent deaths of his fellow deserters Marcus and Ballsti. "I have done things in my past that I am not proud of, but circumstances were very different then compared with today. I was fortunate enough to be taken into the household of Lord Prasatt Ambrosius, who had been appointed law-enforcer by the king and the Celtic Round Council. Over the years, after several skirmishes with rebellious tribesmen and warlords, in which I was involved and showed my prowess as a fighter, as well as my loyalty to my benefactor, I was offered the position of Prassat Ambrosius's personal guard, which was my duty until several years ago, when he took to his sick bed with the consumption he has been there ever since.

It was only then that he relinquished his responsibilities to the king, and designating his son Aurthora to represent him and his people. I continued with my duties, so I am now personal guard to the son instead of the father."

Orius made it sound very matter of fact, but he was very proud of his position and of the way Aurthora had developed under his tuition. He had been a good student of warfare; he had a quick and active brain, was very nimble on his feet for such a well-built young man. Orius could teach him no more.

"Mm!" exclaimed Aidas, "I wondered why you stuck so close to that young man. You never let him out of your sight. I thought at first you were lovers!"

Obtaining no reaction from Orius, Aidas continued. "So, Orius, life has been good to you, too. But tell me, what do you think of the present situation and the capabilities of this king with his Celtic Round Council and mismatch of an army?"

Orius thought for many moments then dismounted his horse and looked along the straggling column of men, some mounted, some walking, some, like Aidas, travelling on a collection of wheeled carts. He could see Aurthora with a group of young men about fifty steps down the column, who were joking and laughing together. Orius grasped his horse's reins and fastened them to the rear and side of the old armourer's cart; on the other side he fastened the reins of the pack pony. He then joined the old man who had moved over to make room on the seat of his rickety, two-wheeled transport.

Chapter Six

Orius made himself as comfortable as was possible on the hard wooden plank, helped himself to a drink from Aidas's container, then passed the drinking vessel back to Aidas, who took another long draught of the cider before hooking it back onto his side of the seat.

"In the course of the last twenty summers I have travelled all over this small kingdom since the legions left its shores," Orius began. "I have seen this king bring together the barbaric, warlike Celtic mountain tribes with the Romanised plain-dwelling, villa-living Britons. He has persuaded, cajoled and threatened them into practising with the gladius and pilum, also to practise group manoeuvres in order to form the tortoise-like testudo using their rectangular Celtic shields. All this has been carried out under the supervision of the ex-Roman legionnaires, who, like me, deserted before the army left the shores of Britannia; or by retired Roman soldiers who decided to stay on in this country and are now employed like you by the king and the Round Council.

"These new training methods were completely against their natural Celtic way of warfare. But discipline has been vigorously enforced and they have practised without respite. There have been small skirmishes in which they have excelled, but they have never been tested in serious combat against a ruthless, experienced foe.

"It's one thing to train an army, it's another to see if they can maintain their discipline and their formations when under attack. I do not doubt their individual courage but it all remains to be seen. Neither they nor their officers have ever been tested in combat as an entire army; they are an unknown quantity. It is, as they say, in the lap of the gods."

"Do you know how all this is being financed?" inquired Aidas.

"Gold, silver, copper and lead from the mines scattered around the kingdom, beef cattle, hides, surplus wheat, all that could be traded, anything that would bring in revenue. All the mines are under the king and the Round Council's guardianship, all supervised by their nominees – their scribes check that the output is correctly recorded. The king's faithful supporters have licence to trade with the fleets of great ships from far-off lands.

"I know for a fact that for every one of the new breed of horses brought into the kingdom, the king and Council pay a high bonus to the traders. I have observed all this in my position as the personal guard to Prassat Ambrosius. The king and his Round Council have been preparing for this situation for over twenty years. They realised that as soon as the Roman Army departed these shores, other peoples from other lands would be trying to carve out a piece of this rich island for themselves. These Saxon pirates were already causing problems with their large raiding parties along the coasts even when the Roman army was still here, doubtless there will be many more confrontations. However, if these opportunist mercenary armies were soundly defeated from the beginning, word would spread that there was a strong, organised army in control in the island of Britannia. One prepared to defend its country." Orius stopped to regain his breath and then continued.

"The Celts are well organised, their army is well trained, although not to the standard of the old legion. Their army has not been blooded yet, but I think they could hold their own against these Anglo-Saxon invaders who, from what I gather and what I have seen, are a mad, all-out-charge type of army. If the Celts can maintain their discipline, even though they are only a small army and may well be vastly outnumbered by the Anglo-Saxons, they could still win the day."

"I agree they are well organised," replied Aidas, "many of the Romanised Britons have been allowed to carry on governing their areas as long as they swore allegiance to the king and the Great Round Council, enforced their laws, collected the appropriate taxes for the king and Council, making their able and fit male population available for training. I, too, have observed all this in my travels. I hope I am in a position to observe the battle, it will be interesting to see how it all develops, and still be here to see the final outcome."

"If the Anglo-Saxons are successful – and I pray to all the gods that they fail – you will not be treated by them the same way you were by the Celts under the guidance of King Erion," replied Orius drily.

The two men continued to exchange yarns and tales of when they were together many years before as legionnaires and soldiers of Rome in the army of occupation. Orius also told Aidas about the exploits of his student Aurthora.

"When he was a fifteen-year-old and under training with a group of other young men at the main Celtic camp at Camulodunum, the fire towers on the cliffs gave warning of a Saxon pirate raid further down the coast. Aurthora was left behind with the two cohorts of students, while all the senior warriors, officers, and instructors assembled and marched to meet the pirates.

"But it was a Saxon trick to draw the fighting men away, leaving it undefended and open to attack by their main body, which intended to plunder the area and sail away with their booty before the other Celts could return. Young Aurthora took charge, realising that this group of students, consisting only of young men and boys, could not hope to stop the main body of Saxons. First he sent a rider to bring back the main body of Celts, other riders were sent to warn the surrounding villages, telling them to drive their livestock and take their prized possessions and hide in the woods, away from the foraging main body of Saxons.

With twenty young men and boys, he attacked the six lightly guarded pirate ships. After a brief but fierce encounter, the young Celts eventually overpowered the few Anglo-Saxon guards. Fastening the six ships together they climbed on board and allowed them to drift back out to sea.

"They were about seventy steps from the shore where the water was about seven feet deep, when the main body of Anglo-Saxon pirates returned. They tried unsuccessfully to reclaim their ships; they were only able to swim if they removed their heavy armour, Aurthora and his few companions were able to fend them off and stop them boarding, until eventually the main Celtic force returned. The Anglo-Saxon soldiers were caught divided: half their force was on the beach while the other half were swimming around, trying to board the raft of six ships. It was a decisive victory for the returning Celtic forces. For his prompt action and decisive leadership, Aurthora was deservedly praised by Great King Erion, in the presence of the Round Council and many senior tribal leaders and elders."

There was a long silence between the two men, eventually broken by Aidas. "By what you say, and by the look in your eye, you have a lot of affection for this young man, Orius."

"Yes, that's true Aidas," replied Orius, looking away and down into the long coarse grass that grew at the side of the road. "If I'd ever had a son, I would have been proud if he'd been like Aurthora." Aidas looked across at his friend and smiled.

It was about an hour before dusk when the long column of men started to pull off the road and proceeded to make camp in a small valley with wooded slopes and a stream running through its centre. They were now travelling through the land of the Cornovii tribe and, as had been decreed by the king and the Celtic Round Council, it was the responsibility of the tribes to provide food and sustenance for the column as it passed through their area.

The tribal elders of the Cornovii had excelled: there were several pigs roasting on spits, waiting for the men to help themselves, and chunks of freshly baked bread on large wooden platters laid out on long wooden tables, with two barrels of coarse local cider set on wooden stilts close by.

Aidas pulled his cart off the road trying to avoid the deep ruts left by the larger, heavier wagons that had already passed. "Aidas my old friend," said Orius, "let me disembark to lighten your load." Orius climbed down from the small cart, rubbing his buttocks as he did so. It had been a very painful two hours of travel he was now beginning to understand why Aidas drank so much of the local cider. Orius untied his horse and pack pony from the rear of the cart and Aidas started to pull away.

"Salute Orius! Till the morning!" he shouted.

"Salute!" called Orius in reply as he watched his old friend bouncing over the ruts in the small, two-wheeled cart. Suddenly a thought occurred to him, "Aidas!" he shouted, "What was the name of the gladiator who fought against Victor Aberuso?"

Without turning round, Aidas shouted back, "Mattos! I will always remember the soldiers chanting his name: 'MATTOS! MATTOS!' And then that bastard Aberuso cut his throat."

The cart with Aidas aboard was by then out of earshot. Orius was left dazed by Aidas's words.

He stood motionless at the side of the stone-paved road as men, animals and carts passed by on either side of his stationary figure.

It was Aurthora who found Orius, after he had searched the encampment and the tail end of the column of men. "Are you well, my old friend?" he asked as he observed Orius's pale face in the fading evening light.

"Less of the old," replied Orius with a forced sense of joviality, "it is being in this column and in the company of so many armed men, it brings back memories of the old days in the legion."

Aurthora knew that there was more troubling his friend than the old memories of his time in the Roman army, but decided not to press the issue. If Orius wanted to tell him his problem then he would do so if and when it suited him.

"Give me your horse, I will bed it down with mine and the pack pony." Orius took Aurthora's horse and walked slowly away leading the three animals behind him. Aurthora watched his old tutor; he knew it would be a struggle to find a reasonable spot since all the best places had been claimed much earlier.

Aurthora made his way slowly across the clearing in the direction of the remains of the spit-roast pigs, where he helped himself. A large group of men had gathered around the barrels of cider and a bright campfire. Some of the men recognised him as he came into the light from the fire to take a drink. Some he had trained with at his father's house under Orius's supervision, and with others he'd practised manoeuvres several years earlier at the old Roman training camp at Camulodunum, which the Celts had taken over. When, under Aurthora's leadership, they had captured the six Saxon pirate ships, Aurthora Ambrosius, young as he was, had become a talking point amongst the warriors of the Celtic community. They felt honoured to know him, and indeed it was very prestigious to be seen in his company.

His action that day lifted the morale of the king and the Round Council, who until then had been fighting a losing battle against the ever-increasing number of pirate raids by the Saxons, who were getting bolder and bolder in their attacks on the south coast of Britannia. Not only had Aurthora's involvement lifted the morale of the Celtic tribes, the addition of the Saxon ships taken doubled overnight the number of ships available to the Celtic alliance to patrol the vulnerable coast of their island.

Aurthora stopped for a short while to renew some old acquaintances among the large group of men that had congregated there. He recognised several of the different tribes, the Demetae, the Silures, the Ordovices, and also the Dobunni. who came from the mountains to the west of Britannia and had very little contact with the Romans during the four hundred years of occupation. Whereas Aurthora found their pure Celtic language difficult to understand, he could communicate easily with the Coritani, the Cornovii, the Catuvellauni, the Iceni and many of the other smaller tribes who had been in constant contact with the Roman occupation forces and mixed in their towns and traded with them.

Then there were the warriors of the Novantae, Selgovae and Votadini tribes who had arrived from Alban, the far north of the island, in support of the appeal by King Erion, and whom the Roman legions had not been able to overcome and dominate. Aurthora found their tongue virtually incomprehensible, their accent was so strong. The same applied to the two large groups of warriors that had crossed the sea from the 'Green Island of Diariada', as it was known to the mainland Celtic tribes. They, too, had not been conquered or ruled by the Romans.

One of these groups was led by a Druid priest, and the other group was accompanied by a friar of the new Christian religion. Both groups spoke the very same language, and in some cases came from the very same tribe, but they could not agree with one another over their religious beliefs. Nonetheless, they had joined forces to fight against the invading, pagan Anglo-Saxons who posed a threat to their way of life.

Looking at the large group of men that gathered around the barrels of cider, it was obvious to him that it was going to be a long, noisy night, and that there would be many sore and heavy heads travelling in the column the following day. *But can you blame them?* thought Aurthora to himself. Some men released their tension by heavy drinking, high spirits, laughter and song, while others sat quietly around their small fires, deep in their own thoughts. It was inevitable that the Celtic and Anglo-Saxon armies would meet in battle shortly. In a few days' time a lot of these young and middle-aged men could well be dead, or maimed.

He made his way to where Orius had set up camp and pitched the two small shelters that were carried on the pack animal. These were simple affairs, but they kept the occupants dry and out of the worst of any bad weather, it also protected them from the heavy summer dew.

Orius swore it was this damp, plus sleeping on hard ground, that was causing the pains in his joints. "I'm getting too old for this type of campaigning, it's a young man's game," he'd complained to Aurthora on several occasions.

Aurthora sat down at the entrance to his shelter, listening to the sounds of joviality from the large group of men in the distance. Slowly the noise subsided as they drifted off to their own small shelters, until there remained only seven or eight men from the Deceangli tribe from the far west of the island. He was about to crawl into his shelter when the sound of one man singing in a deep and mellow voice drifted across the camp from the direction of the remaining group. The single voice was joined by several others, and accompanied by one of the men playing a harp. At first the singing seemed to drift at ground level, enveloping the shelters of the sleeping men, then it lifted to swirl around the trunks and linger in the branches of the mature trees on the campsite, eventually to rise with the smoke from the dying fires to disperse amongst the surrounding hills. It was a beautiful, haunting sound that would slip into Aurthora's mind every time he smelt the burning wood of a campfire.

Katrina was up at the crack of dawn the next day, intending to put into practice an old Celtic custom. Taking the hammer that Emilia had borrowed from Aidas, she made her way to the wood at the edge of the clearing, searching the fringes until she found what she was looking for. It was a large, mature oak tree. Taking the heavy hammer and a shiny new coin, she proceeded to drive the coin into a crack in the bark of the oak. The coin penetrated the bark without bending until the final blow, when the last fraction of coin bent over. Katrina studied her handiwork. *When the opportunity arises, I'll have to have the coin's behaviour interpreted by one of the Druid priests travelling with the column.*

Nevertheless – she was quite pleased with her efforts; she felt the omens were positive. As she made her way back across the clearing she did not notice a figure in the shadows at its edge watching her movements. Katrina left the borrowed hammer on the seat of Aidas's cart before returning to her camp.

Aurthora was also awake very early that morning, there was something he intended to do.

Making his way towards the woods at the edge of the clearing, he passed the small cart belonging to Orius's friend Aidas. He borrowed a hammer lying on the cart's seat; he would return it on his way back.

He eventually found what he was looking for: a tall, mature oak tree just inside the wood, but out of sight of the camp. He found a slender crack in the bark of the oak, and placing a shiny new coin on the crack, proceeded to drive the coin deep into the bark with well-directed blows from the hammer. The coin entered true until the last blow, when the edge of the coin bent over. *Hmm, I wonder what the Druid priest will have to say about that?* he mused.

He made his way back across the meadow as men were appearing from their shelters – some bleary-eyed and still unsteady from their over-indulgence in cider the night before. He placed the borrowed hammer back on the seat of Aidas's small cart, its owner still fast asleep, wrapped in his blankets beneath his rickety transport.

Orius appeared from the shadow of the wood. He had not slept well, constantly going over in his head the previous day's conversation with Aidas, concerning the fate of his brother. At first light had taken a short walk to try and clear his thoughts. He had seen Katrina hammer a coin into one side of an oak tree, then, a short time later, he had witnessed Aurthora do the same on the other side of the same tree. Orius thought it a little odd, but perhaps it was pure coincidence that of all the trees in the forest, Katrina and Aurthora had both selected the selfsame one.

Once Aurthora left and was walking back across the meadow to their camp, Orius went and inspected both coins. *Most unusual,* he thought, when he saw that both coins had bent at exactly the same place. He had heard of the old Celtic belief that if a coin hammered into a mature oak tree by two lovers entered without bending, a long and fruitful relationship would develop. Orius didn't believe in the practice himself, but then again, he wasn't a Celt.

Chapter Seven

With her brother Ethellro and Emllia's help Katrina packed and broke camp even before the cooks started to boil the oats they had left soaking in water all night for the pottage.

From his shelter under the cart, Aidas did not hear the small party as they quietly made their way back onto the old paved road before the rest of the camp had roused itself. At every junction they came to on the main road there were groups of armed men who had camped there that night, waiting to join the main column when it arrived.

It was midday when the three decided to stop, rest, and water the animals at a small spring that ran beside the road. Once the horses had been hobbled and began to graze the short grass at the roadside, Katrina, Ethellro and Emilia made themselves comfortable on a grassy bank at the road's edge. Emilia unwrapped the light snack that she had prepared earlier that morning: freshly baked oatmeal bread spread with soft goats' cheese, which they washed down with water from the spring. It had been a beautiful fresh morning, but now that the sun was high in the sky it was very hot and peaceful.

The conversation between the three was cleverly orchestrated by Katrina to centre on Aurthora as she quizzed her brother about the young man who had suddenly appeared in her life. Even though their acquaintance had been very brief, she began to feel a new and strange sense of wellbeing in his company. Ethellro was happy to talk about his friend Aurthora who, after all, was quite a celebrity amongst the Celtic tribes, and being his personal friend had also increased his standing in the community. Although Aurthora's reputation was mainly based on his exploits with the Anglo-Saxon pirates, it was also because his mother was a member of the Iceni, the same warlike tribe to which Great King Erion belonged. Even when the Roman legions had defeated the great Iceni Queen Boudicca and the remnants of the tribe had been divided and driven to the wild, far north and west of the island, the tribe had continued a guerrilla war against the Roman forces that occupied their land. Ethellro had told the tale of Aurthora and the Anglo-Saxon pirates on many occasions and was well versed in his friend's history.

The tale had provided him with many a free mug of cider over the years.

The conversation slowly faded as each one in turn dozed, then fell asleep in the hot sun, Katrina with a faint smile on her lips as she thought of the evening meal they had yet to share.

They had slept for about an hour when they were awakened by a shout from a group of mounted men. "Hello there! You three sleeping in the sun, awake! I require information,"

Ethellro was startled and embarrassed, he had fallen asleep when there were two women under his protection. Jumping up from the grassy bank, his hand instinctively reached for his sword handle. But it wasn't there – it was in its sheath, still fastened to the side of his saddle – and his horse was grazing a good ten steps away.

"I am Boro Sigurd," continued the spokesman of the group, "I am on the business of Great King Erion and the Celtic Round Council." Boro Sigurd chuckled to himself quietly, he had seen the panic in the young man's eyes when he had been rudely awakened from his doze with no weapon at hand to defend himself or his two female companions, who were obviously in his charge. Ethellro's panic subsided as he observed the plaque of authority hanging from a silver chain around the speaker's neck. "The day's greetings to you, Boro Sigurd. It is indeed a good day to be travelling," he replied.

"Good day to you Ethellro Egilos," continued Boro Sigurd.

"You know my name?" exclaimed a surprised Ethellro.

"Yes, I knew your father well," continued Boro Sigurd. You bear a strong likeness to him, whereas you my child," he said, turning to face Katrina, "you favour your mother, who was also very beautiful. Your father and I fought side by side in many skirmishes, he was a good friend and companion of mine. Your family's work of breeding the heavy war horses, and the way you have continued it since his death, is held in high regard by the king and the Round Council."

Ethellro was taken aback by such praise from someone who obviously held a high position in the king's court. "We ride to meet the column," continued Boro Sigurd.

"It is far behind us," replied Ethellro. At least several hours down the road. It travels very slowly."

"I thank you for this information, Ethellro," said Boro Sigurd. "Did you notice if there was a one-armed man in a small cart travelling with the column?"

"Yes there was," responded Katrina, "he was in the company of Orius Tomase, the one who attends the needs of Aurthora Ambrosius."

Boro Sigurd smiled at the mention of Aurthora. "I thank you for your information my friends," said Boro Sigurd as he pulled his horse's head around and the small group cantered off down the road in the direction of the column.

The three watched the group of horsemen until they were out of sight. "He was riding one of our horses," commented Katrina proudly, breaking the silence.

"Yes, and I wonder what they wanted with Orius's friend?" said Ethellro.

"His name is Aidas Corrilus," joined in Emilia. "He's a Roman, he was in the same infantry cohort as Orius before the legions departed."

"You seem to know a lot about this man, Orius," replied Ethellro, looking quizzically at his sister's handmaiden.

"I needed to borrow something from him," said Emilia, wishing she had not volunteered the information in the first place.

"And what did you need to borrow from this ex-Roman legionnaire?" pressed Ethellro, his curiosity aroused.

"She was on an errand for me," interrupted Katrina, seeing that her maid was becoming embarrassed.

"And what was this errand that had to be carried out with such stealth and secrecy?" persisted Ethellro, now extremely curious as to the reason for his sister and her maid's acute embarrassment.

"She went to borrow a hammer for me," blurted Katrina, and with that went over to the horses, followed at once by Emilia. Both women proceeded to remove the hobbles from the horses' front feet and repack the small items they had used for their meal. They then mounted quickly continuing their journey along the road, each wrapped in a thoughtful silence.

Within an hour's travelling in the opposite direction, Boro Sigurd and his three companion bodyguards met the head of the Celtic column. The leading group consisted of about twenty well-armed, mounted warriors from the Cornivii tribe, whose lands the column was presently traversing.

The first thing that Boro Sigurd noticed was the quality of the horses that all the Cornivii were riding: they were the same tall, heavy, well-muscled, deep-chested breed that he himself rode. He was also quick to notice they all carried the new, twelve-foot, iron-tipped spear, its end resting in a purpose-built socket hanging from a thick leather strap fastened to the saddle. Boro Sigurd was impressed. All the men were young, in their early twenties or thereabouts, straight-backed and comfortably seated on their large horses. He also noticed that lying across the back of each saddle was a suit of the Celtic chain mail armour, along with a rectangular-shaped shield that the Great King had introduced for use with the long spear, with which these warriors had been practising for many years.

As the two groups stopped, Boro Sigurd was the first to speak. "I am Boro Sigurd, a member of the Celtic Round Council. I am here on the instructions of King Erion and I require your assistance. There were several moments of silence while the Cornovii absorbed his words, then a swarthy, thickset youth edged his horse forward. "I am Cimbonda, the youngest son of Neila Gilberto, tribal leader of the Cornivii, whose land you are now travelling through. What do you and your companions require of us, Boro Sigurd?"

"We require your assistance in finding the whereabouts of a one-armed Roman who goes under the name of Aidas Corrilus. We believe he's travelling in this column."

Cimbonda turned in his saddle and addressed the group of horsemen behind him. "Has anyone seen or heard of this one-armed Roman that the Council member seeks?" There was a small discussion among the mounted warriors then one of them spoke out. "The man you seek was seen with another Roman, a man called Orius Tomase. They were last seen travelling together on a small cart in the middle of the column."

"I thank you," said Boro Sigurd, then continued, "the Great King and the Round Council wish to speak with this man. Do we have your permission to escort him to our king?" The protocol did not pass unnoticed by Cimbonda Gilberto. Here was a member of the Round Council on the business of the Great King asking him, a small sub-chief, for permission to approach a member of the column.

"You have my permission as leader of the column as it passes through the land of the Cornivii, to proceed and carry out the Great King and Round Council's wishes," Cimbonda replied, feeling ten feet tall. To be spoken to as an equal by a member of the Celtic Round Council and in front of his own men would raise his esteem in the tribe to previously unknown heights. Cimbonda shouted instructions to the group of men behind him and two of the mounted warriors peeled off to escort Boro Sigurd and his bodyguard back along the column to look for Aidas Corrilus. Boro Sigurd smiled to himself. He had found you achieved results much more quickly by lifting the standing of an individual than by degrading him with authority. His small group and the two escorts slowly travelled back down the long straggling column of walking and mounted armed men, heavily loaded carts, wagons, and strings of pack animals.

The weather was fine and sunny, Boro Sigurd could sense the feeling of confidence emanating from this large body of travellers. There were several of these columns around the country, all converging on the headquarters at Buxonana where Great King Erion and the tribal Round Council had made their camp, and which would be the meeting point for the army of the Celtic Alliance. After half a mile or so, the two guides halted beside a small, two-wheeled cart. Sitting on the narrow platform that formed a crude seat was a one-armed man, looking curiously at the group of mounted men that had stopped at the side of his cart.

"Aidas Corrilus, salute!" shouted Boro Sigurd. "It is good to see you again." Aidas looked at the mounted man who had edged his horse forward to the front of the group.

He recognised the voice, even though it had been several years since he had last seen the speaker, who had aged considerably in the interval.

"Salute!" he replied, also using the Roman expression for a greeting. "You look well my friend, life has been good to you. What brings such an eminent member of the Celtic Round Council to this ragbag mix of lost souls?" Aidas had lost all respect for anyone in authority ever since he lost his arm many years before, addressing all and sundry the same way, even the Great King. After all, what more could they do to him? He felt he was now only half a man anyway.

Boro Sigurd continued: "King Erion and the Council wish the company of your presence. I and my companions have come to escort you to them."

Aidas pondered for a moment. "For them to send for me means they must have serious problems." Boro Sigurd did not reply at once but turned in his saddle to look behind him. The two guides who had accompanied the group left to return to the front of the column after they had found Aidas Corrilus, and were now well out of earshot.

"Come, leave the column Aidas, I will discuss things with you on our way to King Erion's camp. Can you ride a horse if one of my men drives your cart?"

Aidas grimaced; it had been a long time since he had been on a horse, and never on a horse the size of those Boro Sigurd and his group were riding. "I can but try," he exclaimed, "but if I fall from that great height and break my neck, I hope your king punishes you accordingly."

Aidas mounted one of the large horses from his raised position on the cart, the rider in turn taking his place. They moved slowly at first as Aidas rediscovered his riding skills and balance, but by the time they drew level with Cimbonda Gilberto and his group of mounted warriors at the head of the slow-moving column, he had settled comfortably into the rhythm of the large horse.

Boro Sigurd returned Cimbonda's wave and soon the column was left far behind as the increased pace of the small group swallowed up the leagues. After some distance the horsemen left the main road and took a very faint, barely distinguishable track that led into heavy woodland, and soon they were out of sight of the road and travelling along a single path, manoeuvring around large oak, elm and sycamore trees, with dense undergrowth on either side, forming a narrow avenue where they were forced to travel in single file.

Ethellro and the two women made good progress for the next two hours. Ethellro reckoned they were about a mile from the river, which would be the next stop for the column that night. They had come to a junction in the road there were the usual group of men and the odd cart waiting for the main column. Sheltering in the shade of some trees set back a short distance from the side of the road was a group of about thirty horses, all of the type that Ethellro and his father had been encouraged by King Erion to breed. The owners of these fine animals were sitting about in small groups. They were the new column escort, waiting ready at the boundary dividing the two tribes to take over from the existing escort when the column reached them. It was the duty of these men to keep some semblance of law both in the camps and while the column was on the road.

As Ethellro stiffly dismounted a short distance from the nearest group, he recognised several of the horses that were tethered nearby as some he had sold quite recently. As he approached the group and a man stood and came to meet him. He was much shorter than Ethellro, clean-shaven, and his long brown hair was fastened in a ponytail. "Ethellro!" he exclaimed loudly. "How good it is to see you again so soon. Are you well?" Ethellro immediately remembered the man: he had purchased four of his horses several months before, bartering for four full hours until he had worn Ethellro down, a sale had then been agreed and finalised.

"Timus! How fare you? Have the animals I sold served you well?" replied Ethellro.

"The animals are excellent, even though you drove a hard bargain," responded Timus Calgacus. Both men laughed.

Ethellro could not help noticing that just like the present column escort, these men also carried the long spear. And glancing at their horses' harnesses he observed they also had the leather loops he had introduced to fit the foot of the rider and the leather socket to carry the spear in order to take its weight when the horsemen were travelling any great distance.

"I am the leader of the escort for the column as it passes through the territory of the Coritani tribe," continued Timus. "The camp site for the night is by the river one mile further down the road. It has been prepared as requested by King Erion and the Round Council. The latrines have been dug, wood for the cooking fires has been chopped and stacked, fresh bread has been baked and placed on long tables together with much cooked poultry and venison, and fresh drinking water – or cider if preferred – is available in wooden casks."

Timus was proud of his achievements; he and his men had worked hard to prepare the overnight campsite for the column and had only finished cutting the last of the tall stinging nettles that had covered the large, flat area at the side of the river an hour before they met Ethellro and his two companions.

"The column is still several hours behind us," replied Ethellro, "we set off early this morning to avoid the dust that so many men, horses and wagons are creating."

Timus was looking at Katrina when he replied. "That was very wise, it would not do for the complexions of two beautiful women to be tarnished by the grime of a hot, dusty journey."

Katrina was flattered by the young Celt's compliment, but her heartstrings had already been well and truly plucked by Aurthora. "I thank you Timus for your concern, but what of my brother's complexion?" she asked, and with a light-hearted laugh she spurred her horse down the road to the evening's camp, followed by her two chuckling companions.

Timus watched as the trio trotted away. He liked Ethellro's sister, she sat well in the saddle, upright and straight-backed, she also showed spirit and wit. He had admired her from the first moment he had seen her several months before, demonstrating the horses he eventually purchased from her brother. He had tried to impress her with his bargaining skills, trying desperately to keep her attention as he bartered with her brother for the four horses he eventually purchased. He resolved that after these troubles were over, if he came out of the imminent battle alive, he would approach her brother about courting his sister. She was indeed a beautiful woman and he would be a lucky man if she ever consented to be his wife.

A short while later the trio rounded a bend, and there before them was the river with a ford where the water barely came up to a man's knees. Alongside the river was the land Timus and his men had prepared for the column to spend the night. Several men were still stacking freshly chopped wood, while traders were assembling their few stalls at the entrance to the meadow, one of which was selling salt, most likely from the large mines nearby that provided salt for use throughout the kingdom. Another stall was selling a collection of various cooking utensils. These traders had arrived early in order to claim the best pitches for selling their merchandise.

Katrina and Emilia unloaded the pack animal, all four horses were hobbled and loosely tethered, allowing them to graze on the tall stinging nettles that had been cut down earlier by Timus and his group. Emilia prepared their camp while Ethellro went to collect wood from one of the great piles that were scattered over the meadow.

They had chosen a spot at the far end of the cleared area close to where it joined the woods, at the farthest point from the entrance to avoid being disturbed by the column as it entered the meadow. Emilia began preparing vegetables for the evening meal to which Aurthora and Orius had been invited. Katrina, meanwhile, spent half an hour catching fresh water shellfish in the shallows at the edge of the river. She would use these as a starter for the evening meal. She intended to do her utmost to impress Aurthora, and whatever chore she was engaged in, her thoughts kept returning to the tall, good-looking man she had met several days earlier. She then went into the woods and searched until she found some edible fungi growing at the base of some of the large trees. She intended using these to add flavour to their evening meal.

It was not long before the leading groups of the column entered the area, and in no time at all the quiet meadow had been transformed into a bustling town of tents and temporary shelters, wagons, carts, groups of tethered horses, and men and women busily preparing their evening meal before the light faded.

Aurthora had travelled with his own men that day; he had been having an interesting conversation with a young man who had joined their group. The man was a physician; he had been tutored by a master of medicine and herbal remedies who was attached to the Great King's court. This physician had sent one senior student and several junior assistants to each of the three columns that were converging from different directions of the kingdom towards the main meeting point at Buxonana. Their instructions were to attend to the ailments of anyone in the column, and during the coming battle they would be available to assist the injured Celtic soldiers.

Aurthora was also curious about the wicker baskets attached to the physician's pack animal, each of which held several pigeons. "I see you also carry readymade meals while you practise your profession," he joked, indicating the pigeons to the young man.

"No sir! Those are not for eating," replied the young physician. "Every morning I fasten a written report of our position and the approximate numbers in the column to the pigeon's leg, and when released, the bird flies straight back to my master, Myridyn the Physician, at the king's court. He in turn reports to the King and the Round Council."

"Your master is indeed a clever man," said Aurthora, making a mental note that he must make a point of meeting this unusual person. But then he added, "I think, however, that you should keep this information to yourself. As I'm sure you are aware, there are many prying eyes and wagging tongues in the column."

The young man blushed at this gentle rebuke, taking the opportunity of Orius's appearance at Aurthora's side to drop back further down the column. The more Aurthora saw and heard, the more he realised how organised and well planned this campaign was, and the presence of the physician and his assistants would act as a tremendous boost for the morale of the men travelling in the separate columns.

Orius had intended travelling with his old friend Aidas. He had always got on well with his old comrade, and even though old age had made the man more argumentative, Orius had been looking forward to spending the day in his company, exchanging tales and yarns about the old days when, as younger men, they had both been proud legionnaires in the service of Rome. Aidas had travelled widely and freely around the kingdom over the last twenty years, and if there were any of their old comrades still working, or indeed still living, then Aidas would be the man to know.

He had glimpsed the old cart used by Aidas, and the old man still wearing the old leather cloak he used to try and stave off the morning damp that he claimed caused the severe aches and pains in his joints. He'd seen it in the centre of the column, and now made his way slowly through the throng of men, carts, wagons, and animals that were packed along the narrow, stone-paved Roman road. He was surprised when he drew level with the cart to find the driver was not Aidas. The man refused to tell Orius where Aidas was. It was only when Orius threatened to report the man to the column's escort for the theft of the cart that he reluctantly disclosed that Aidas had been called urgently to the presence of the Great King and the Round Council, and had been escorted there by none other than Boro Sigurd, the high ranking court official.

Orius passed this information on to Aurthora when he joined him later that morning. "And what would that action signify to you, Orius?" Aurthora asked.

"As you are well aware, Aurthora," Orius began, "Aidas Corrilus is an expert on the capabilities of the ballista and the scorpio. The fact that such a high official of the king's court should come in person to collect him tells me that they require his knowledge to site their ballista and scorpio machines. I think your king is preparing his battle plan, and selecting the site of the coming battle to his advantage, which is prudent and thoughtful planning. The fact that Aidas's cart, and to all intents and purposes Aidas himself, his still with the column helps to mislead any prying or curious eyes," concluded Orius, pleased with his assessment.

Over the last few days in the column of armed men, the rough banter between the different tribes at their nightly stops, and the meeting and discussion with his old friend Aidas, had caused him to begin to feel the thrill of excitement he had known a full twenty years or more ago when he'd been marching with the Roman legions prior to battle.

Aurthora paid close attention to Orius's words. He respected his guardian's assessment; the old soldier was an experienced and seasoned campaigner and not prone to making rash statements. Aurthora knew the area they were travelling through quite well. As a youth, once the harvest was in, he and his friend Ethellro had spent many days away from home, camping out and living off the land, catching small game in the woods and fishing in the river for trout. They'd passed many happy summers, as only young boys can, exploring this very area. They probably knew the surrounding countryside as well, if not better, than most of the local inhabitants. It was with this knowledge in mind that he now racked his brain wondering where the Great King would stand and fight the advancing Anglo-Saxon army.

As Aurthora turned into the meadow he stopped at one of the many stalls and purchased a small bag of salt to take to his hosts that evening. It was a Celtic custom to take a small gift when being entertained, and salt was considered appropriate. "Orius, I wonder if the Saxon pirates we captured who were sent to work as slaves in the salt mines were the ones who produced this salt?" Orius merely answered his young friend with a smile.

Aurthora gazed over the meadow. It was a clear evening and in the distance he could see hills rising above the plain. On the other side of those hills King Erion had made his encampment, and it was there that they would complete their journey in several days.

His attention was drawn to the buzzard that had been following the column since early dawn. It was still circling high above, its great wings catching the warm thermals as it looked down on the long straggling line of men, women, animals, and the motley collection of heavily laden wagons and carts. He wondered what the attraction could be for the great bird of prey; perhaps the movement and noise created by the column was disturbing the small game, making it easier for the bird to catch its food.

When he lowered his gaze he was surprised at the size the column had grown in the last few days. It had become difficult for people to find their companions in the milling crowds at the nightly stops, so the different groups had begun the practice of fixing their tribal emblem, or the particular sign of the Celtic god they preferred, onto a large pole, or onto one of their long spears, positioning them in the centre of their encampment.

These could be seen above the heads of the animals and men, guiding any stragglers to their own group. Aurthora looked for Ethellro's family crest – a prancing black horse on a white background, in reverence to the Celtic goddess Epona. *Most appropriate*, mused Aurthora, *given that Ethellro's family are the largest horse breeders in the kingdom.*

Aurthora spotted the crest at the very end of the meadow, but first he and Orius needed to find a place to erect their shelters and make camp before joining Ethellro and his sister Katrina for their evening meal as had been arranged.

The column had swollen so much that day that Timus was having difficulty marshalling the camp and had to call on Cimbonda Gilberto and his men to assist him. The armed warriors, however, were not the problem, although any bickering or minor arguments were stopped before they got out of hand – no one wanted armed groups of the many different tribes confronting one another at this stage, they needed to keep their fighting for the Anglo-Saxons.

Moreover, the Celtic Round Council had decreed that during this period while the Celtic tribes were gathering, any Celt found fighting another was to be publicly whipped, and any Celt drawing steel against another was to be detained and sent to the mines. If blood was drawn, the guilty party was to be beheaded in public and his immediate family stripped of their goods, belongings and land, branded on the forehead and banished from their community. No one in the kingdom, on pain of the same penalty, was to assist or help these branded people. It was a severe deterrent, but it seemed to be having the desired effect. At every night's stop a man ringing a small brass handbell proclaimed the law as he walked through the encampment. There had been many disagreements, but these had been settled by the use of fists and feet, and it was very rare for steel to be drawn.

Chapter Eight

The real problem was all the column followers. The traders, tinkers and opportunistic thieves and gamblers that this large gathering had attracted, these were the ones who required the most watching. On first entering the meadow with his escort, Timus had noted where Ethellro and the two women had pitched their camp. He was hoping he would have the chance to call on them later in the evening, but his duties as Camp Marshal kept him very busy. There were minor skirmishes and disagreements that required his attention, as was inevitable when such a large group of armed men with different ideas and views were forced into close confinement with one another, and the opportunity for him to slip away never occurred.

Aurthora and Orius went to the riverside to wash away the grime of a day's travelling. They had found a small space to camp just inside the wood at one side of the meadow, and here they had erected their shelters, watered the horses and pack pony, fed them some grain and tethered them, before setting off in the direction of Ethellro's camp, leaving their animals contentedly grazing on clumps of coarse woodland grass.

The meal that Katrina and Emilia had prepared was one that Aurthora would never forget. They began with a small dish of fresh shellfish on a bed of boiled young tender nettle leaves, which was followed by pork sausage with a rosemary and sage dressing, lightly cooked cabbage and sliced turnip. There then followed a course of thin grilled slices of beef laid on a bed of lightly cooked young onions and fresh celery, with the option of a thick mint relish if desired. Next came a selection of olives, almonds and dates. The meal closed with stewed apple in an oatmeal casing, baked over hot ashes. They drank wine with their food instead of the rough cider or ale that Aurthora and Orius were used to. Aurthora was not a connoisseur of food or cooking, but he had always eaten well since Orius was an excellent cook. Indeed it was Orius who surprised Aurthora with his knowledge concerning the ingredients and origin of the spices used in the meal.

Orius had always enjoyed the preparation and cooking of food since he'd been a child and had helped his mother prepare ingredients for the family. Even after leaving home and joining the Roman army, during his travels to many different countries in the great Empire it was always he who volunteered to prepare and cook the evening meal for his fellow soldiers. There had never been any objections since most of Orius's companions detested the chore of preparing and cooking, and so Orius's efforts had always been much appreciated. His meals had been something for his comrades to look forward to; they represented a break in the monotony of soldiering or the boring daily routine of the barracks. Orius was always experimenting with the different local dishes that were characteristic of an area, and the use of local herbs and spices in the different countries in which he was posted.

That evening, food became the main topic of conversation since both Katrina and Emilia were also well versed in the culinary arts. This was why Aurthora ended up knowing so much about the meal he had eaten. Orius was not surprised to find that all the array of foreign produce could still be obtained. It appeared that even though the Romans had left the island, the trade routes were still open and operating as before. Ethellro's simple explanation was that as long as there was a profit to be made, merchants would continue to trade.

As the evening wore on, the conversation shifted away from various cultures and the preparation of their different national dishes to focus instead on Aurthora and Ethellro and their experiences as boys camping out in this very area of the country.

It was decided that the following day Aurthora and Ethellro would take Katrina and show her the hidden valley they had stumbled upon as boys many years before. They would walk across country and pick up the column at its evening stop later that same day. Aurthora felt strangely excited about the prospect, he enjoyed Katrina's company tremendously and had been placed next to her at the short table where they had eaten their meal. Because the space was rather cramped, their bodies occasionally touched and he felt with a thrill the warmth of her thigh next to his own. He was finding it increasingly difficult to take his eyes from her face. The others however did not seem to notice his infatuation, so engrossed were they in their own conversation.

It was in the early hours of the morning, and with some reluctance that Aurthora and Orius left their hosts to make their way back across the meadow, skirting around the various tents and shelters, carts and wagons, and the dying embers of the many campfires, to their own camp just inside the wood.

A wedding celebration was coming to a close and the party of well wishers were going their own separate ways in small noisy groups.

It had become a regular occurrence for a young warrior to be betrothed to his sweetheart and have their partnership blessed by one of the many Druid priests travelling with the column, or if they were of the new faith, by one of the several Christian friars who were also present. These ceremonies were much shorter than usual, the reason being that there were so many of them the friars and priests were finding it difficult to cope. Also, funds were not forthcoming from their parents; indeed it was unusual for either the bride or groom's parents to be present at the ceremonies since most of these marriages did not have their blessing. The groom's parents knew their son was going into battle shortly and could be killed or seriously maimed. Who would support his wife, and possibly a child as well? The same thoughts also applied to the bride's parents: they did not want their daughter to be left looking after a crippled ex-warrior, or to find herself a widow with a child. But these were the thoughts of old, experienced heads, not the thoughts of young people in love.

The two men checked their horses, crawled under their shelters, and wrapped themselves in their woollen blankets. On the edge of sleep, Aurthora's last thoughts were of Katrina. and the last thought of Orius, surprisingly, was of Emilia, Katrina's maid. He thought what a good and knowledgeable cook she was, what a pleasant and enjoyable evening it had been in her company, and how her talents were wasted as a mere handmaiden. It had been the first time in two days that Orius's thoughts had not been absorbed in plotting revenge for the death of his brother at the hands of the ex-gladiator, Victor Aberuso.

Katrina, too, slept soundly, she was happy with the way the evening had progressed and the meal had been a huge success. Orius had surprised her,. Who would have thought it possible that a rough, ex-Roman legionnaire, now employed as a bodyguard, could be interested in and have such a vast knowledge of the culinary arts? Or would feel such an obvious attraction to her maid, Emilia? But it was Aurthora who occupied her final thoughts as she drifted into a deep, contented sleep.

Emilia, on the other hand, did not sleep easily that night. She, too, had been surprised and impressed by the knowledge that Orius, a simple soldier, had shown in a field that was usually a woman's interest. As an orphaned child Emilia had learnt her skills of food preparation and cooking in the kitchens of a Roman centurion officer. His wife had taken a great interest in cooking and entertaining as a way of relieving the boredom of her life as an officer's wife in an isolated army barracks on the outermost edge of the Roman Empire. Emilia had been a quick and interested learner, had helped prepare the food for the well-attended parties that the officer and his wife regularly held. It was during her visits to purchase food for her kitchen in the local market that she came into contact with Katrina's family and in time Katrina. Both women found they shared a common interest in the preparation and presentation of good quality, simple, or at times exotic food, so it was that their friendship flourished.

When the officer received orders to return to Rome, his wife offered to take Emilia with them as part of their household, but she declined. Even though she had no family she knew of, she decided she still preferred to stay on the island of Britannia. Katrina's family, hearing of this, offered Emilia a position as a companion and maid to the young Katrina, which Emilia gladly accepted. Emilia had never been with a man, and had never had feelings for the opposite sex, now she was disturbed that she could not shake off thoughts of this rough soldier with his knowledge of cooking and the attention that he had paid to her. But eventually she, too, fell into a fitful sleep.

Aurthora and Orius rose early the following morning. They were among the first in the queue for the pottage that was being ladled out by the camp cooks. "This is not up to the standard of fare we are used to, is it Orius?" Aurthora commented, as the lumpy, steaming pottage was unceremoniously dumped onto his proffered wooden platter.

"It is warming and will do us no harm," replied Orius, pulling his thick woollen blanket further around his shoulders. The damp morning mist had not yet dispersed from the valley where the river twisted its way, but the sky was clear, and the signs indicated another fine, hot, midsummer's day. After eating their meal, both men proceeded with the dismantling of their small shelters and the packing of their camp, loading their few possessions onto the small pack pony.

The whole valley was a hustle and bustle, with men stowing various items onto pack animals, carts and wagons, making their way back onto the old paved Roman road for the start of what would be for them another day's hot and dusty journey. Aurthora and Orius, moving in the opposite direction to the stream of animals and men, led their horses and pack pony towards the far end of the meadow to where Katrina, Emilia and Ethellro had made camp the previous night. In the process they passed Cimonda Gilberto and several of his men, who had been kept busy into the early hours of the morning. There had been several weddings and a lot of joviality, which conflicted with men trying to sleep after a hard day's travel. This had led to several minor disturbances keeping the combined forces of Cimonda Gilberto and Timus Calgacus occupied in preventing these upsets from developing into more serious forms of conflict.

Aurthora and Orius reached Ethellro and the women just as they finished loading their pack animal. It was decided that Orius and Emilia were to travel with the animals and possessions in the main column, while Ethellro, Aurthora and Katrina would trek overland and see if the two men could find the hidden valley they had discovered as young boys many years before. They would then cut across country and join the main column much later that same day. Aurthora and Ethellro had filled their water containers while Katrina had packed the remains of the cooked meats from the previous night's meal. So as the rest of the main camp broke up and dispersed, heading down the meadow to the Roman road. Aurthora, Ethellro and Katrina began to walk upriver in the opposite direction.

When Aurthora turned and looked back before they entered the wood, the column already stretched far down the straight road, the final stragglers from the camp were streaming from the meadow onto the tail end of the column, shepherded by several of Timus Calgacus's armed men. Circling high above was the buzzard. *That bird seems to be a good omen*, he thought as he turned and followed Ethellro and Katrina.

Soon they were out of sight of the meadow as they made their way through the woods that came down to the water's edge. They followed the river for about three hours. Sometimes it would run fast as the waters raced over the shallows, other times it was placid and deep, with the odd rings of water as a trout took a fly that had settled on the surface.

They came across a family of otters and for a short while watched them playing on the riverbank; they saw the odd flash of bright blue followed by the sound of a small splash as birds hunting for fish dived into the quieter parts. Aurthora and Ethellro called excitedly to one another as they recognised different landmarks – an unusual shape of a rock here, a particular bend or deeper section in the river there – pointing them out to Katrina as they continued their journey along the bank.

At a point where the main river met a stream that came cascading down a cliff face to enter the river as a waterfall from a high ledge of rock, they decided to stop and eat the cooked meats that Katrina had packed. Aurthora refilled his water container from the waterfall; talking to Katrina for most of the journey had made him thirsty. He was surprised at his own behaviour since he was generally quite reserved, but he felt relaxed in Katrina's company finding himself unusually talkative. For her part, Katrina was interested in Aurthora and in what he had to say. He had told her about his boyhood and his mother who had died when he was small, and how his father had spent so much time away on the business of Great King Erion that Orius Tomase had more or less acted as his guardian. He made no mention of his role in the famous episode with the Saxon pirates, which impressed Katrina. Everyone in the Celtic community knew of Aurthora's exploits with the Saxon pirates, and how, as a reward the King and the Round Council had placed him in command of a cohort of Celtic troops, the youngest commander in the Celtic federation army. How proud Aurthora's father had been at the presentation, aware of the great honour that he had brought on the family and the name of Ambrosius.

After their meal they left the river and began to climb, following the stream that had produced the magnificent waterfall. The going was much harder now as they had to scramble up steep banks, pulling on the branches of the thick undergrowth at the side of the stream to assist them. After an hour of clambering up the steep hillside and struggling through the heavy growth of tall ferns and bracken, they came to a plateau of level ground. It had been here that, as boys, Aurthora and Ethellro had cooled off by swimming in the large pond that had formed at the top. From here the stream went tumbling on its way down the hillside to eventually join the river far below.

The two men decided to take a swim, Katrina decided she wanted to dive into the inviting water also, as she was damp and sticky with sweat after the hard climb up the steep hill on such a hot summer's day. In the Celtic community it was accepted for children of both sexes to play and swim together up to the age of ten summers, after that, unless they were betrothed, it was frowned upon. If they disobeyed, they risked serious chastisement by the elders of the community, and having their family publicly criticised for their laxity in allowing their offspring to flaunt the laws of the community. But now the temptation was too great, and anyway, as Katrina reasoned to herself, she was being chaperoned by her brother. So with the wild abandon of youth all three stripped to their underclothes and jumped into the refreshing mountain spring water. The water was so cold it took their breath away, as they laughed and giggled at the thought of how their tribe elders would react if they could see them.

They came out of the pool refreshed and shivering, grateful for the warmth of the hot summer sun. They removed their wet underclothes and dressed in their jerkins and loose breeches. They then made their way across the plateau, the wet underclothes hanging from tall staffs carried over their shoulders, hoping the strong sun and light breeze would dry the undergarments before they reached the main column later in the day.

It was pleasant walking on the plateau, the sun was hot but there was a cooling breeze blowing across the flat terrain. There were no large trees, only coarse clumps of grass with the occasional pool of brown water lying on a bed of peat. It was from one of these pools that they disturbed a small flock of wild ducks. With a clatter of wings the birds took to the air when the party was only several paces away from them, startling all three and causing the men to snatch at the small daggers they carried at their waist. They laughed at the incident and joked about how nervous they were.

It took two hours to cross the plateau and then began their slow descent, the long coarse grass changing to heather and stunted trees as they progressed downwards.

They eventually came to the edge of an almost vertical cliff, from which there seemed no apparent way down. Neither Aurthora nor Ethellro could recall with any certainty where, as boys, they used to descend into the heavily wooded valley they could see below. They remembered a narrow path they used to follow, but they could see no sign now of any such path.

They sat finishing their water while they decided what course of action to take. They concluded that previously they must have come to the edge of the cliff at a different point. They decided to separate: Ethellro would go in one direction for approximately half a league, Aurthora and Katrina would travel along the top of the cliff in the opposite direction for roughly the same distance. They would then return to the starting point and report their findings. If any.

After 600 paces or so, Aurthora and Katrina came across what he thought was the narrow ledge that led down into the valley. The many years of rain, wind, storms and hail appeared to have washed much of the path away, and he was unsure if it was a track down into the valley at all.

"It's hard to say, Katrina, it seems so different from when we were children."

He pondered for a while. "I wouldn't like to risk your safety on such a perilous narrow ledge, Katrina!" he said, aware of how protective he felt towards her, and how much he enjoyed saying her name out loud.

"If this path is the only way down from the plateau then it's the way we have to go," replied Katrina, continuing, "the alternative is to return to the river, and from there retrace our steps all that distance we've come."

This was a daunting task, even for Aurthora; he did not relish the thought of journeying all the way back to the previous night's encampment, followed by the long walk along the Roman road to the Great King's headquarters where the tribes were gathering. Apart from the fatigue of it all, it would make him look such a fool in Katrina's eyes.

"I'll follow this ledge for a short while, Katrina, to see if it's safe. If it is, we'll go back for Ethellro and discuss the situation." The decision made, he took his damp underclothes from the staff he was still carrying and stuffed them into the front of his jerkin. He would need the staff to test the condition on his descent. He then began to make his way along the ledge.

The descent was steep, had it not been very dry, there would have been no way a person could have travelled along such a crumbling, narrow path. He travelled about twenty paces before he realised that Katrina was following him, "Katrina!" he gasped, "It's not safe for you, I thought we'd agreed you would wait?" There was a hint of panic in his voice: it was a long drop to the bottom of the cliff. Katrina could sustain a serious injury if she slipped and they were many miles from assistance.

"There's no alternative, Aurthora," replied Katrina calmly. "I am lighter than you; if the ledge will hold you, it will definitely hold me."

There is definitely a woman's logic in that statement, thought Aurthora. "But what of Ethellro?" he said, "we were supposed to meet him."

"Don't worry about me, Aurthora," shouted a voice from above, "I've found a path further along." Aurthora groaned inwardly; he had taken the wrong path and was now risking both their lives.

By this point they had negotiated about a third of the descent, which was the steepest part of the cliff. Below him was loose shale – the incline was still steep but not as sheer as the part they had just traversed. "I'll take the other path," shouted Ethellro, "I'll meet you both at the bottom of the cliff. It'll be easier for you to go on rather than to try and climb back up again."

What Ethellro said made sense, they had already climbed down the worst part of the cliff. Now they just had to take it steadily, keep their nerve, and hopefully everything would be fine. If the gods were willing, they would reach the bottom unscathed. For several minutes more they continued their descent, both making slow but steady progress as they wound their way downwards.

It was a loud shout that startled them and broke their concentration. It came from the wooded area the path was leading to. "In the name of King Erion, what are you doing in this area?" boomed a deep voice. It was a voice of authority, and one that was obviously used to being obeyed. From behind Aurthora came a sharp cry as Katrina, surprised by the voice, lost her balance and slipped, sliding passed Aurthora down the cliff amongst a shower of loose shale, dust, and some larger stones she disturbed as she fell.

Aurthora froze for several seconds as he watched Katrina tumble, roll and somersault amongst the debris she had disturbed, the occasional flash of a white arm or calf glimpsed among the dust as she plunged down the cliff.

Without another thought he launched himself feet first from the narrow ledge; he was no longer thinking of his own safety, only of Katrina and the injuries she might sustain. He managed to stay upright for the first fifteen or so feet of his descent down the steep incline. He had jumped slightly to the side of Katrina's line of fall, so that any large stones or rubble that he disturbed would not endanger her further. He was now sliding as if on ice, as he had done in his youth. It was quite a thrill, a feeling that took him back to his childhood, sliding on the frozen pond in his village.

The slide, however, came to an abrupt halt when his foot struck a deep rock projecting a few inches from the surface of the cliff. The rock did not budge the impact launched him into a somersault, from which he landed on his back and continued his descent. Amongst all the dust and pebbles a sandal came into view, which he managed to grab, then he rolled several times more before landing in a clump of bushes at the foot of the cliff.

For several seconds he lay still and dazed as a cascade of small stones and dust continued to fall and envelop him. Slowly the dust cleared. Tentatively he moved his arms and legs: there were no broken bones. He had cuts and grazes all over his body and would be black and blue for days to come, but he was alive with no serious injury.

His immediate concern was for Katrina. He moved slowly through the undergrowth in the direction he thought she might have landed. He was still slightly dazed, he had only moved a few steps when suddenly he was confronted by a rider on a large grey horse bursting through the undergrowth and sliding to a stop in front of him. He could not tell who was the more surprised, himself or the man on the horse. He recognised the horse almost immediately, it was such a particularly beautiful animal, and he also knew the rider who sat so tall in the saddle of this magnificent creature for he had been in this man's company recently. The man on the horse was the single, most powerful man in the kingdom – he who had united all the Celtic peoples and organised them under the government of the Celtic Round Council into a formidable fighting force. It was Aurthora's godfather. It was Great King Erion.

Before either man could speak there was a flurry in the undergrowth, followed by a lot of squealing as five wild boar piglets burst into the small clearing, followed by a very large female boar with a set of short, vicious-looking tusks projecting from her jaws.

The piglets bolted in panic across the small clearing, passing under the forelegs of the large horse, which in turn reared, catching its rider unawares and throwing him to the ground. He landed on his back, motionless and badly winded. The sow stopped and looked at the fallen man, who was directly in the path between her and her piglets; they had now stopped running and were in a tight squealing group at the edge of the clearing, clearly not wanting to venture into the dark undergrowth beyond without the protection of their mother.

Aurthora desperately looked around for some form of weapon if the sow decided to charge; all he had in his hand was a leather sandal. The King's short hunting spear, lying between the King and the wild sow, was too far away for him to reach. The sow's beady-eyed attention was diverted from this human form on the ground, who had now pushed himself up onto one elbow, to the sudden appearance of two other humans entering the clearing from the undergrowth, just a short distance from the frightened group of piglets.

At a loud grunt from the sow, the frightened piglets scampered once again across the clearing, passing the stationary form on the floor to reach the protection of their mother, who turned and charged back into the brush, closely followed by all five of her offspring.

Aurthora's attention was now centred on the two men, each of whom carried short hunting daggers. One was definitely a Celt by his appearance and dress. Aurthora could not help but observe that one half of his face had been badly burned at some time. There were irregular tufts of hair growing on this side, on the other side of his face he had a full beard. His companion was a tall, heavily-muscled, deep-chested figure of a man dressed in a combination of Celtic and Roman attire, with a badge sewn onto the top right-hand side of his leather jerkin. This Aurthora recognised: it was the crest of the Roman legion that this man had served in before the Roman army had left the shores of Britannia.

It had always amazed Aurthora how these ex-legionnaires who deserted the Roman army many years before, whom many Celts considered nothing but paid mercenaries, should still carry with great pride the crest of the Roman legion in which they once served.

He observed all this in one quick glance. The two men were focused on the dazed figure still lying on the ground, his unprotected back towards them.

When Aurthora saw the look in both men's eyes, alarm bells rang. Their attitude was not that of concerned guards or servants: on the contrary, their body movements indicated sinister intentions. Both men were not aware of Aurthora, who now stepped out of the shadows into the clearing, several paces nearer to the short hunting spear that was partially hidden by the long grass. "Hold! What are your intentions?" he shouted in the most authoritative voice he could muster.

They stopped and looked in the direction of the voice, more startled by Aurthora's appearance than the attempt at authority in his voice. What the men saw suddenly appear from the shadows was a bedraggled character with a mass of unruly hair, covered in cuts and bruises, with several undergarments hanging from a tear in the front of his dust-covered leather jerkin, holding in his left hand what looked like a woman's leather sandal.

"A ready-made assassin," muttered Petrov Joma to his companion Victor Aberuso. Who was furtively looking around checking whether this stranger was alone.

Chapter Nine

After leaving Aurthora and his sister Katrina making their way slowly down the narrow ledge, Ethellro had quickly returned to the path he had found further along the cliff. *This is definitely the path Aurthora and I used all those years ago,* he thought as he made a speedy descent. A faint scream, which he recognised at once as his sister's, sent him crashing through the waist-high tangle of brush in the direction of the sound.

He had burst upon and surprised a family of wild pigs as they foraged below a stunted mountain oak. The pigs had bolted, Ethellro had continued to seek his sister, but hearing voices, he backtracked and entered the small clearing dagger in hand, close to where the pigs had departed only moments before.

He came to an abrupt halt. What he saw was a dust covered, dishevelled Aurthora standing on one side of a fallen man, two men with drawn daggers on the other side. The sudden appearance of Ethellro distracted the armed men's attention from Aurthora, who quietly stepped forward and picked up the short hunting spear. The odds were now even, and he knew that Ethellro would back him in whatever action he took.

The man on the ground had heard the muttered word "assassin" spoken by Petrov Joma, which Aurthora had been too far away to hear. "Hold!" called out the man as he struggled to his knees, "I know this man, he is no assassin," he said, directing his words at the two men facing Aurthora and Ethellro.

Whatever the intentions of Petrov Joma and Victor Aberuso had been, the opportunity to carry them out had vanished with Ethellro's arrival. Especially now that Aurthora had armed himself with the King's hunting spear. With a curtly muttered. "Now is not the time," from Petrov Joma, the two men quickly sheathed their short daggers and moved forward to assist the King to his feet, still shaky after his heavy fall.

Aurthora looked down at the sandal he was still clutching in his hand, then at Ethellro, and they both exclaimed together, "Katrina!" The events of the last few minutes had made them forget their female companion. As they both gasped her name in unison, almost magically Katrina entered the small clearing.

What Katrina saw as she painfully stepped from the bushes was the man responsible for her fall. He was being assisted and supported by two men since he was obviously very unsteady on his feet. Aurthora was standing with a short hunting spear in one hand, her missing leather sandal in the other, and his bundle of damp underwear hanging from a tear in his leather jerkin. He looked as she must look after her fall: covered in cuts, bruises and a fine layer of dust. Her brother standing several paces from Aurthora was just replacing his dagger in its sheath.

Katrina had not survived the fall down the cliff side as lightly as Aurthora, her shoulder was giving her a great deal of pain, it seemed to be at an odd angle.

Severe stabs of pain overwhelmed her every time she took a step, and by far outweighed the aches and pains from all the other minor cuts and bruises she'd received due to her fall. Worst of all as she fell, she'd lost her small bundle of underwear. At least Aurthora had found her missing sandal! The King had recovered quickly from his fall, and Petrov Joma with his guard, Victor Aberuso, were now standing sullenly behind him.

It had been Petrov Joma, second cousin to the King, who had persuaded him to go hunting that afternoon as a way of relaxing from the pressures of the headquarters and court officials. The King realised he was the cause of Aurthora and Katrina's present predicament: it had been his shout that had set events in motion, causing Katrina's fall and painful injury.

Meanwhile, the rest of the small hunting party had caught the Great King's riderless horse and, concerned for his safety, now arrived on the scene, most of whom were officials from his court. King Erion introduced Aurthora and Ethellro to the rest of these mounted men; both names were already well known in the Celtic community. For generations Ethellro's family name had been associated with the breeding of fine horses, Aurthora had become famous more recently for his exploits with the Saxon pirates.

King Erion insisted they travel back to his camp with him, where he claimed to have in his employ the best physician in the land, whom he would place at their disposal. They readily agreed as Katrina was very pale and in great pain, and both her companions were deeply concerned about her condition.

Even though it was only a short journey to the Great King's temporary hunting encampment, for Katrina it was a very painful one. She could not ride since the movement of even the quietest pony gave her tremendous pain. And while walking, even with the assistance of Ethellro and Aurthora she had lost consciousness on several occasions. Eventually Ethellro carried her as gently as he could, but even then she sobbed quietly, her head buried in his chest. Aurthora followed behind, the sound of Katrina's sobbing pulling at his heartstrings. He felt helpless, and guilty for being partly responsible for her plight.

The Great King's temporary camp was very basic. It was just an overnight stop for the hunting party and consisted of several large tents and two small groups of lesser shelters. A fire was burning in the centre of the camp and a string of small hunting ponies were tethered at one side; here they had access to leather buckets of water and small piles of fodder placed at regular intervals. An armed Celt was standing on guard outside the largest of the two tents, and there were several men busy doing various chores around the camp. It was a scene of order and tranquillity.

On their arrival, Katrina was placed in the second tent on the instructions of King Erion, a servant was sent to search for the King's personal physician, who was away collecting herbs in the nearby woods. Ethellro carried his sister through the opening of the tent, closely followed by Aurthora. Inside, a youth of about sixteen was standing at a simple workbench fastening leaves into bunches and hanging them onto a frame made from hazel sticks. He looked up as they entered and Ethellro blurted, "Where shall I put my sister?" The youth indicated a stool and a low couch. He sat Katrina on the small stool; she declined the couch since lying down was far too painful for her.

As their eyes became accustomed to the gloom, Aurthora looked around the tent, noticing the various bundles of plants hanging from the roughly-made hazel stick frames; a simple table on which several mortars stood, partly filled with crushed leaves and flowers; a couch with several heavy woollen blankets at its foot, neatly stacked on top of a wooden iron-bound chest. There were several long cloaks fastened to the centre pole of the tent, an empty wooden stand similar to those used as a perch for birds of prey and the small stool Katrina occupied, still supported in a sitting position by the strong arms of her brother.

Aurthora remembered his conversation with the young trainee physician the previous day; his wish to meet the young man's tutor was about to come true sooner than he had envisaged. The youth took one of the blankets from the top of the chest and, with Ethellro's help, gently wrapped it around the shivering girl. He then went back to his task of dividing and fastening into bundles the collection of plants and leaves that were scattered on the bench. Aurthora noticed that in all this time he had not uttered a sound or spoken a single word.

The man who entered the tent a short while later was tall and very slim, wearing a cloak that came to just below his knees, fastened around the waist by a simple piece of twisted twine, and at the rear was a deep hood hanging from the shoulders. It was a garment very similar to the ones Aurthora had seen worn by the Monks and Friars of the new Christian religion. In his hands he carried a wicker basket that was full of wild flowers, bulbs, leaves and various roots of plants. "I am Myridyn," he said, at the same time moving forward and placing the basket on the wooden table. "The Great King informs me that one of you requires my services?" He did not look like a Celt, but Aurthora noted that his pronunciation of the Celtic language was perfect.

As he moved to one side, Myridyn saw Katrina for the first time, sitting uncomfortably on the low stool, with Ethellro still kneeling beside and comforting her, holding her hand between both of his. Myridyn stood for several moments taking in the scene before him. "Which of you is Ethellro?" He said, breaking the silence, "I am!" exclaimed Ethellro, rising to his feet.

"I need hot water," said Myridyn.

"I will go," said Ethellro, stepping forward and taking the proffered leather bucket from the physician while Aurthora moved to take his place supporting Katrina.

There is an iron cauldron near the fire in the centre of the camp," explained Myridyn.

"Collect your water from the stream above the camp, make sure you take the water from the centre of the stream, where it finishes running over the pebbles and the gravel bed.

"Remove any other water from the cauldron and replace it with this, then place the cauldron over the fire and bring it back to me when the water starts to boil and steam."

Ethellro left to carry out these precise instructions, as Myridyn turned his attention to Aurthora. "If that was Ethellro, then you must be Aurthora, of whom we have all heard so much." There was no malice or sarcasm in Myridyn's statement, in fact Aurthora noticed a twinkle in the physician's eye. "There are no other females in this camp," continued Myridyn, "but I am a physician, and your betrothed is in safe hands." Myridyn had assumed that Katrina was promised to Aurthora, which was understandable given the circumstances, since he was now kneeling beside her, holding her hand in his own, his tender concern for her obvious in his demeanour.

Aurthora began to try and explain but Myridyn stopped him with a wave of his hand, and turning, reached into a leather pouch hanging from the hazelwood frame. "Take this tablet," he said, handing Aurthora a large tablet of what felt like wax, "go to the stream at the bottom of the camp, it is sheltered and private. Strip naked and scrub your body with it. Your cuts and grazes will sting at first, but that will ease and they will begin to feel soothed. You can use this cloth to dry yourself." Myridyn opened the chest, and handed Aurthora a clean cloth of soft fabric.

"But what of Katrina?" he exclaimed.

"Katrina has dislodged her shoulder joint from its socket. I must put it back in place, which will be a painful exercise, but the sooner it is done, the better. There should be no lasting or harmful effects. My assistant here is called Disaylann, he cannot respond to you for he is deaf and dumb. He will assist me. Myridyn then shooed Aurthora out of the tent and pointed him in the direction of the stream.

As Aurthora made his way through the camp he saw Ethellro at the main campfire, but he was too busy placing sticks and small logs in the fire around an iron cauldron to notice him. The guard was still outside the Great King's tent, leaning on his spear, another man was filling the water buckets for the string of ponies while a third was grooming the Great King's horse. Further off, sitting outside the group of shelters nearest the two large tents, were two men sharpening the tips of their short hunting spears; they waved back in response to Aurthora's salute.

Beside the other small group of shelters was the man whom he recognised as Victor Aberuso. He was tending a small fire and from what Aurthora could see and from the smell that drifted in his direction, he was cooking several small fish, probably trout from the stream, placed on skewers over the hot embers. He glanced up as he saw Aurthora approaching, then deliberately turned his back and concentrated on the preparation of his evening meal. Aurthora walked by and made a mental note that he must make enquiries about the man, possibly from Orius who knew most things that were happening in the Kingdom. If that failed, he would ask elsewhere and discover any information that was available.

When he reached the stream he stripped naked and, using the wax-like tablet as he had been instructed, proceeded to scrub his body. He'd used soap before – it had been introduced by the Romans when they first came to Britannia – but the soap he'd used had been grey and coarse and rather evil smelling, whereas this tablet created a rich, sweet-smelling lather. As the physician had warned, at first it stung his many cuts and grazes, but shortly afterwards the stinging and aches from the bruising seemed to fade away.

He finished his bathing as quickly as possible, putting on his dry underclothes, beating his jerkin and breeches against a nearby tree to remove some of the dust they had gathered in his fall. He felt much better and refreshed as he made his way back across the camp in the direction of the two large tents, where he found Ethellro standing with Disaylann at the entrance to Myridyn's tent.

Ethellro did as he had been instructed, Myridyn had taken the cauldron of hot water from him bidding him wait until he was called. Dusk had already fallen and the guards had lit several brush torches near the tents; the light from several oil lamps also gleamed from within Myridyn's tent, from whence came a short sharp scream of pain – and then silence.

When Myridyn eventually emerged to join Aurthora and Ethellro, he murmered in a low voice, "Ethellro, as I explained to Aurthora, your sister in her fall damaged her shoulder quite severely. I have managed to put the joint back in position. In the process your sister suffered much pain losing consciousness for a short while. Her shoulder is now strapped in place and will be best left like that for several days. The pain is now much less severe and it will decrease as the days go by. I have bathed and treated the cuts and bruises your sister received in her fall, I have also given her a potion to relieve the pain and help her to sleep. She is now resting on my couch, I suggest that this is where she should stay until the morning, if you both so wish you may spread these blankets on the floor of the tent and stay here for the night." Myridyn handed both men two heavy woollen blankets, putting his finger to his lips to indicate the need for silence, he beckoned them to follow him into the dimness of the tent's interior. Aurthora could make out the still form of Katrina lying on the couch, her slim figure covered with a woollen blanket.

Although she looked pale in the light of the oil lanterns, her breathing was regular, and both men were relieved to see that she was obviously no longer in severe pain.

They quietly spread their blankets on either side of the couch and prepared for their night's rest, but not before Myridyn had given Aurthora a paste-like substance to spread on the cuts and grazes on his chest and thighs while he, with the light of an oil lamp, did the same to Aurthora's back.

It was while Myridyn was covering a deep graze with the paste that he asked Aurthora if either of his parents had the same brown mark as the one he had on his shoulder.

Aurthora told Myridyn that he was born with the mark, but that as far as he was aware neither his mother nor father bore it. It was a question he thought no more about at the time, since a movement in the shadows and a rustle of feathers startled him. As he peered into the gloom he made out the silhouette of a large buzzard sitting on the wooden perch, the bird's sharp eyes focused unblinkingly on him. *This bird must have arrived while I was bathing in the stream.* He thought. *It was definitely not here previously.*

It had been a hectic day, and Ethellro, by the sound of his heavy breathing, was already fast asleep. Disaylann had already moved to one of the shelters in the small camp, and Aurthora was also having difficulty in keeping his eyes open. He was so tired that as soon as he lay between the rough woollen blankets he fell into a deep sleep, leaving Myridyn sitting on the low stool. What the physician had seen caused him some concern; he stayed deep in thought for most of the night. Indeed, it was only when the first glimmer of dawn appeared on the distant horizon that he pulled the blanket further around his shoulders and dozed, still perched on the low wooden stool.

Even though Aurthora and Ethellro rose at daybreak the following day, on leaving the tent they discovered that Petrov Joma and his group had already broken camp and departed, leaving the King and six guards provided by the local Coritani tribe, Myridyn, his young deaf and dumb assistant Disaylann, Aurthora, Ethellro and Katrina.

While Ethellro went to see if he could organise some food since both men were famished, having eaten very little the previous day, Aurthora went back inside the tent to check with Myridyn on Katrina's condition.

The physician was just stirring from his position on the stool as he entered the tent. "Good day to you," he greeted Aurthora, "I assume you've come to see the patient."

"You have Ethellro's and my deepest thanks for your attention to Katrina," replied Aurthora. "We sincerely apologise for not thanking you properly yesterday."

"Your thanks may be premature, my young friend," replied Myridyn, "we will have to assess the situation when the patient awakes." He rose from the stool, leant forward and gently slapped both sides of Katrina's face with the ends of his fingers. Katrina slowly opened her eyes, starting at the sight of Myridyn leaning over her. However, she quickly relaxed when she recognised Aurthora peering over the physician's shoulder. "Now sit up gently my child," said Myridyn, slowly helping Katrina to a sitting position, taking care not to place any pressure on the injured shoulder, or the side where Katrina's arm was strapped tightly across her chest.

Aurthora noticed that besides the thick woollen blanket that covered Katrina, there were also lengths of soft linen cloth, one below and one above. Furthermore, she was not wearing the rough spun jerkin and breeches that she had worn when they had brought her into the tent, but a long shirt of finely spun brightly coloured linen that was nearly transparent.

Katrina now had a healthier look to her complexion than when they had last seen her the night before by the dim light of the oil lanterns. He was greatly relieved and thought how beautiful she looked, and how he wished he was indeed betrothed to such a lovely, pleasant-natured young woman, just as Myridyn had mistakenly assumed the night before. He also realised how great their fortune had been to find such a gifted man as the Great King's physician, how another turn of fate could have led to dangerously different circumstances. Over the last few days the gods had indeed looked down on them with exceptional favour.

While Ethellro and Aurthora were catching brown trout for their breakfast in the deep pools of the nearby swift-flowing stream, King Erion inquired about the wellbeing of Katrina and his godson Aurthora from Myridyn, who was not only his physician, but also his friend and advisor. It was obvious that Katrina could not travel at the same speed as King Erion's party, so it was decided that they would follow at a more leisurely pace. King Erion informing Aurthora that he would see that Orius and Emilia were notified of their situation, and that they would be joining them as soon as was possible at the Celtic Alliance meeting point in Buxonana.

Katrina found that as long as the pace was very slow, she could now ride on the surefooted hunting pony. Myridyn's tent and equipment were sent on ahead along with the Great King's baggage, while Aurthora, Ethellro, Katrina, Myridyn and Disaylann followed. Myridyn and Katrina rode the small ponies, Aurthora walked leading Katrina's mount, with Disaylann ahead leading Myridyn's and Ethellro following.

It was during this long but pleasant journey that Myridyn questioned Aurthora about his upbringing, his mother, the role that Orius had played in his life, and how Great King Erion had come to take him as a godson. Aurthora in turn asked Myridyn how he had accumulated so much knowledge about healing, and how he became part of the King's Court. Myridyn was very frank in his discussion with Aurthora, he appeared to be glad to tell his fellow traveller his life story.

Myridyn's past had been both hectic and adventurous. His family had been wealthy merchants who had owned many ships in the port of Cadiz, one of the flourishing independent cities of the Mediterranean that had been forced to submit to Rome. Myridyn's father had indentured his youngest son at an early age to a physician, and there he had stayed, learning his profession, until he was about the age of his assistant Disaylann.

"I enjoyed my life in the city; there were so many different nationalities and so many different languages spoken. There were the various smells of all the commodities and spices that passed through the busy and prosperous port to the stalls and markets, where goods from all over the known world were sold and bartered. In a sense, the prosperity and wealth of the city were its downfall.

"The Roman Empire was struggling to find the money to pay for the vast army required to defend its borders against the increasingly aggressive barbarians. There had already been riots in some of the Empire's main cities against the heavy increases in taxes that had been imposed. The Roman authorities envied the wealth of these independent trading city-states and began a process of increasing the burden of taxation. When the merchants could no longer find the money to pay, their possessions were seized and sold at public auction. The local Roman military governor was under strict orders to meet the quota imposed by his superiors. If the traders and merchants like my father could not meet their demand, their families were taken, no matter their profession or their position in our society. When my father failed to pay, I was taken by the Roman tax collector's guards spending several weeks in a filthy compound, where I and my fellow companions were treated no better than animals. But little did we realise that worse was yet to come.

"Eventually we were all taken and sold in the slave market to the highest bidder. My father was devastated by this action and the incapacity of the city fathers and elders to oppose the Roman army's unlawful actions. Along with many other merchants he was left penniless and destitute by the Roman authorities. Several of my friends and I were chained together and taken to the port by the slave dealer's agent.

"There were many ships in the port that day as the auctions had been well advertised, with dealers present from all over the Roman Empire and beyond. It was not just a slave market, it was also a great sale of goods and possessions confiscated from the merchants' warehouses together with the personal belongings from their homes. We slaves – because that's what we were at that point – were forced to load great bales and boxes, containers and sacks of various commodities into the dark hold of a great cargo ship. When the jetty was finally cleared and everything had been placed on board, we were led down onto a galley and chained four abreast to benches, the long oars that propelled the ship stretching the full length of the bench.

"The ship also had a large square sail, but unless the wind was in the right direction this was of little help. The ship was quite low in the water as it was stacked high with the goods purchased by the dealer, we slaves, the oarsmen, were forced to row even when the sail was fully stretched with a strong wind. Many of the slaves were not used to the rolling of the ship, and so were constantly seasick, others contracted an illness in the filthy conditions of the holding camp and were compelled to relieve themselves where they were chained. The stench in the hot hold was overpowering. The condition of the men made no difference to the brutal overseer, he still thrashed our bare backs with his snakelike whip, and it was not long before our soft hands were sore and bleeding for we were not used to this hard, physical labour.

"I managed to wrap my hands in strips of cloth torn from my tunic this somewhat eased the pain in my palms, but after we had been at sea for several days my shoulders felt as if they had become detached from the rest of my body, I could feel the sting of the ugly weals across my back from when the overseer caught me slacking and used his long whip to stir me back into action. From the gossip and the partially overheard conversations of the crew, I learned that we were sailing in a small convoy of merchant ships, I presumed for safety, escorted by a heavily armed ship of the Roman navy.

"One midday when there was a strong breeze blowing and the large sail was fully stretched, we slaves manning the oars had stopped rowing to receive our midday ration of water – no food, that was only given in the morning and late in the evening. We were making good progress through the calm sea, we slaves had been allowed on deck in small groups to stretch our legs, and to sluice our stinking bodies down with buckets of sea water. It was while my group were on the deck that another flotilla of boats was spotted heading on a course that would soon intercept our own. These ships were of a different design from the large cargo boats that made up our small convoy. They were slim, sleek, and travelling at a much greater speed than the clumsy vessel beneath my feet. The sight of these other boats sent a wave of panic through the crews of the large cargo boats.

"I was taken to one side and sent to help on the large steering oar at the rear of the ship while the rest of our small group was quickly driven below to their positions at the oars and there was so much haste to start them rowing again that they were not fastened by the chains to their seats. The drumbeat they followed to keep their stroke was almost immediately increased to maximum, and the great overloaded hulk of a boat slowly began to increase its speed.

In order to save money, the traders' agent had not employed the experienced longshoremen to load the vast amount of cargo onto the boat, but used the slaves he had purchased instead: consequently the load was not evenly balanced, and as the speed increased so did the amount of water that splashed over the front prow of the boat. From my position with the steering oar I could glimpse the pirate boats – for that's what they were – gaining on the slow cargo boats with every pull of their oars. Our escort boat turned, and as fast as its two decks of oarsman could pull, sped towards the four advancing pirate vessels in a brave attempt to ram one, or possibly two, of the pursuers in order to delay them sufficiently to give the convoy time to escape.

"The pirate ships were approaching four abreast, when they were about three hundred paces from the much heavier Roman escort ship, I saw from my vantage point a smoking projectile about the size of a man's head leave each of the pirate ships in turn. Two landed in the sea in front of the speeding Roman escort ship, but one landed on the prow of the ship, which was immediately engulfed in a great sheet of yellow flame. The last hit the great square sail, dropped on to the deck below, and also burst into a great ball of fire.

"I was transfixed, I had never seen anything like it before. The escort ship's large sail quickly caught fire, the burning liquid must have run into the rowers' gallery below because the oars stopped on one side of the ship, I could see men leaping into the sea from the burning deck. The stricken Roman boat slewed around in the water while the nearest pirate boat pulled in its oars from that side, and the keel of the boat ran over the projecting oars of the burning escort vessel, smashing them like dry sticks. The action had taken but a few minutes and the pirates did not bother any further with the escort vessel. Instead they continued to chase the more lucrative, heavily laden prizes, our ship being among them, leaving the escort vessel ablaze and floundering with only half its complement of oars. I fear that unless the crew found some way of controlling the fire, they were all most certainly burnt alive or drowned.

"The oarsmen on the cargo ship could only maintain the accelerated pace for a short time, and slowly, one by one, suffering from acute fatigue, some of my fellows collapsed over their oars, hindering the men on either side of them who were still trying to propel the boat forward, no amount of thrashing with the whip was able to revive them or drive them back to work.

There were six cargo boats in the convoy, all heavily laden and low in the water. Our badly loaded boat was third in line and had been taking in water over the prow, but I had seen during our pause on deck that the other boats behind us were in an even worse condition, taking in water over the prow and through the rowlocks as well.

"From my position at the steering oar I saw a fast pirate vessel simply pull alongside the slowest vessel, crushing the oars in the process, iron grappling hooks fastened to heavy ropes were thrown, and as these held the two boats together, the pirates swarmed from their boat onto the cargo ship. Any resistance was quickly and ruthlessly eliminated. The crew of the cargo boat knew that to resist meant instant death, whereas to surrender would mean a life of slavery – perhaps, ironically, chained to the oars of some pirate ship. But at least they would still be alive.

"By the time the fourth pirate ship reached us, many of the oarsmen on my ship had collapsed, while several of the group I had been with on deck, who had not been re-chained to their bench at the beginning of the action, took the opportunity to strangle the bully of a whip master with his own whip. It was then that a pirate vessel ran over our oars.

"I was drawn below by the terrible screams that came from the rowers. I don't think I have ever seen so much devastation in a confined space before. The breaking of the oars had lifted some the oarsmen and crashed them against the roof of the deck, some of the oars had smashed into the men in front with such force they broke ribs, limbs and spines, others crashed into the oarsmen's chests, lifting them off their benches as far as their chains would stretch, before dropping them on their injured comrades, leaving a mangled mess of bloody bodies, most of them still chained to the wooden benches. The ship at this point was floundering in the water and was easy prey for the well-armed pirates who swarmed on board. As you can imagine they met little or no resistance."

Myridyn leant forward and tapped Disaylann lightly on the shoulder with his staff, and when the boy turned around, he indicated with finger signs for him to halt while he slowly dismounted from his pony; he required to stretch his legs and take a drink of water from his container fastened to the prow of his small pony's saddle. The rest of the group also sat for a moment to rest and drink, although Katrina preferred to stay on her pony to avoid the additional pain that dismounting and remounting would involve. Aurthora was enthralled by Myridyn's tale and felt privileged to be treated as an equal by this knowledgeable, well-travelled, and clearly very clever man.

Chapter Ten

After several minutes the group set off once more and Myridyn continued his story.

"Several of the pirates came to inspect us, but it was obvious we were of no threat to them, so for a short while we were left alone to our own devices. Those of us who were not chained or injured attempted to assist the many injured and maimed oarsmen. Their screams were heartrending, but at least we managed to remove their chains in order to relieve their suffering in some small way. Many had serious internal injuries and would not survive, some were bleeding to death, others were in great pain with broken limbs, but had they been able to receive proper treatment they might have survived.

"It was while I was helping the injured that the leader of the pirates, a short swarthy man with a black beard and heavy gold earrings, came to inspect the damage to the oars and to assess the number of oarsmen who were either dead or incapable of rowing. I had managed to organise the injured men by this time: the more seriously wounded were lain out on one side, whereas those that I thought might survive were opposite them. The pirate captain was impressed with my efficiency, and most surprised to find a physician among the galley slaves. He gave instructions for me to be taken to inspect the injured on the other cargo ships and to arrange them into two rows as I had done on my ship. At the time I was so naive I did not realise that I was in fact selecting those who would live and those who would die.

When I had finished assembling the row of seriously injured on each ship, I was horrified when they were thrown overboard on the orders of the pirate captain: The others who survived were probably destined to be sold at some distant slave market. My objections were met by a hail of blows that left me badly bruised, battered and left hunched in a corner of the deck. The rest of the able-bodied slaves and the members of the cargo ships' crews were fastened to the oars and we set sail on an unknown course, escorted by the pirate ships.

"During this voyage I was instructed to attend to the injured sailors and slaves, but as the facilities I required were unavailable: no herbs, no medicines, no clean linen to bind their wounds, several of these men inevitably deteriorated and eventually died, with their bodies being unceremoniously thrown overboard. Each time one of the sick men died, I was given a severe beating. I remember I was livid with resentment that the pirate captain should hold me responsible for the death of these men, since it was through his actions that they had been injured.

"We sailed for fourteen days, avoiding any sails seen on the horizon by the sharp-eyed lookouts perched high on top of the tallest mast. The weather was kind to us and I dread to think of the outcome of the badly loaded cargo ships had we encountered any severe storms. We eventually entered a port where many more of the same strange type of sailing ship as those of the pirates lay either at anchor in the harbour or were fastened to the quay.

This was the first time I saw the beast of burden they called a camel, an unusual animal with two great humps on its back. I later discovered they also called them the Ship of the Desert, for this unusual animal is able to carry heavy loads, travel for many days and cover great distances without food or water.

"I was not taken and sold in the slave market like the rest of the captives but retained by the pirate captain whose name was Sheikh Bageto Hur. His home was a great house with a high surrounding wall, built on a hill overlooking the town and port, well away from the stench, filth and flies of the harbour and nearby town. I was allowed to go to the local market and permitted to scour the surrounding countryside in my search for herbs and plants, but always under the supervision of a guard.

"Sheikh Bageto Hur had only sold the able-bodied captives at the slave market; there was no demand for injured or sick slaves, so it was my responsibility to return the injured oarsmen and crew from the cargo ships to health as quickly as possible. I was left under no illusion that if I attempted to escape, my several friends amongst the injured would be beheaded.

"As the injured slaves and crew slowly recovered, they were sold in the slave market, apart from two friends, Arsene Benitez and Cahill Sbragia, whom, like me, Sheikh Bageto Hur kept. They were given the same ultimatum: if either of them attempted to escape, we who remained would be instantly beheaded. You could say it consolidated our friendship!

"We were there for two years. Whereas they were given work in the Sheikh's extensive garden within the walls of his large house, I was Sheikh Bagato Hur's personal and family physician since I treated him and his children, but I was never allowed to attend any of his many wives. It was really quite interesting for me, and eventually I was allowed to roam more or less where I pleased. I met and conversed with other physicians in the town, exchanging ideas and cures, remedies and various methods of administering to the sick. But most interesting of all, I also acquired some of the secret knowledge in the preparation and mixing of chemicals that produced the frightening and devastating explosion I had seen from the cargo ship.

"I suppose I would have still been there now but for my two friends, who were not as happy as I, and did not want to spend the rest of their lives in the Sheikh's garden. They were also under the constant threat that if anything happened to me they too would be sold as slaves. Though already slaves to the Sheikh this thought terrified them. One of their duties was to take the surplus food produced in the garden to the local market, their route taking them past the harbour where they had seen the slaves working on the quay, loading and unloading the various ships that came and went. These poor souls were treated no better than the stray, flea-ridden and mangy dogs that inhabited the port. Sometimes they ended up chained to the oars in one of the many galleys that visited the harbour, since there were always spaces to be filled on these ships.

"After many months they eventually managed to persuade me to consider an escape attempt with them, for if they were ever sold as slaves they would never again get the freedom or opportunity we then had of escaping. So while they stole and dried small amounts of the fruits from the gardens where they worked, I wandered around the harbour and made a map of all the alleys and streets that surrounded the port.

"I also kept watch for a suitable small boat that the three of us would be able to manage, and one that would be easy to steal. The Sheikh always seemed to be very well informed, he never seemed to set sail with his crew and four ships without returning with a prize. It was decided at one of our many secret meetings that the best time to escape would be at night on the day the Sheikh left on one of his expeditions; we would set sail on the following early morning tide.

"The Sheikh and his men were usually away for a score of days or more, which in theory gave us ample time to make our escape, and it was unlikely that an intensive or prolonged search for us would be launched in his absence. It was several days later we noticed our opportunity had come sooner than we had anticipated; the Sheikh and his four ships had left early that morning.

"Our plans were delayed for one day as I had a very important meeting with an alchemist, whose young son I had been treating for a disease of the eyes. If I left without completing the cure, he would eventually become blind, a complaint that seemed to be prevalent in that part of the world. The following night my friends lit two incense candles to their gods, which they left smouldering in their small hut at the edge of the Sheikh's garden.

Loading ourselves with the bags of dried fruits and goatskins full of water, we left.

"We easily avoided the old man who was employed by the Sheikh as a night watchman, we quietly departed through a gate in the garden wall whose large bolts we had previously taken the precaution of greasing so that they slid open noiselessly, allowing us to slip out of the compound and make our way silently down the hill in the direction of the town. We had decided to avoid the town centre, so, keeping to the outskirts, we arrived at the beginning of the port.

It was too dangerous to go into the port itself, there were always too many armed men in the vicinity. Carrying our water and bags of food we would have looked suspicious and almost inevitably have been challenged.

"Our plan was to steal one of the small, punt-like boats belonging to the local fishermen who fished close to the shore, and use it to reach the larger, more seaworthy vessels that were anchored in the bay. Several of the punts were moored at the edge of the town and the beginning of the port, but the slight noise we made as we were launching one of these was heard by one of the local dogs, which started to bark loudly for several seconds. Fortunately for us, the dog must have been hit by its tired owner, for it suddenly yelped and stopped barking.

"We had all frozen when the dog began to bark, and Arsene was quietly sick with fear over the side of the small boat. When he stopped, we gently pushed the shallow punt into the water and, using our hands as paddles, slowly made our way to a much larger seagoing vessel moored in the centre of the harbour.

"There were many similar boats moored to the harbour wall which we had considered, but the risk of being observed was far greater, so we had decided to take one that would be partially hidden by the sea mist that usually settled just before dawn. We cut the larger vessel's moorings and slowly towed it out to sea. We then abandoned the small punt and boarded the larger boat. Once again luck was on our side since it was a dark night with a new moon whose light was regularly obscured by large clouds. We carefully and quietly raised the sail and made our escape without the alarm being raised."

Neither Aurthora nor his companions had made any sound or attempt to interrupt Myridyn as he spoke because they were deeply engrossed in his story. The physician told his tale so well, and in such great detail, they all felt that they too had been with the trio of escapees.

Myridyn continued with his tale: "We were blessed with reasonably fine weather, plus the odd minor squall that allowed us to funnel rain off the sail and into our water skins. We were also fortunate to have been born and brought up on the coast, which meant we all had some knowledge of sailing and, weather permitting, we constantly tried to sail westwards, towards the setting sun.

"A fairly constant wind allowed us to sail in this, our chosen direction, but we were quick to change course if we saw any oncoming sails on the horizon. Nevertheless, after many weeks at sea, and with our food and water exhausted, we were reduced to drinking our own urine filtered through a piece of the sail. Our bodies were covered in running sores and we were drifting in and out of consciousness.

"My older companion Arsene Benitez." continued Myridyn sadly, "came from a very old and proud family; he found it much harder than his younger friend Cahill Sbragia to adapt to being a slave, the beatings he had incurred when he slackened during a hard day's physical work in the gardens had gradually affected and weakened his resolve to survive. He refused to drink his own urine – even that meagre supply of fluid dried up as our bodies became more and more dehydrated – he lay curled up in a ball in the stern of the boat, mumbling to himself and constantly wringing his hands. One day we found him drinking seawater and were forced to bind his arms and legs for his own safety.

"We awoke from our fitful dozing one morning, by the light of the new day's dawn found that during the night we had drifted amongst a large convoy of merchant ships, with several large Roman navy escort vessels. Sadly, we also discovered that Arsene had passed away during the night, never knowing he had been so close to rescue.

"The story we told to the commander of the convoy was accepted. We claimed that while going about our lawful business we had been captured by pirates, from whom we eventually escaped. Obviously, we never mentioned that it was the Roman authorities that originally sold us as slaves. We then negotiated an agreement with the captain of the merchant ship: in exchange for our passage to the nearest safe port he could have the boat in which they had found us. After several weeks at sea with decent food and ample amount of liquids, we both recovered physically. My friend, even to when we parted, still had terrible nightmares of his ordeal.

Eventually we disembarked on the Roman fortress island of Malta. Cahill and I went our separate ways, I have never seen or heard of his whereabouts to this day. I obtained employment as the physician to the Roman army stationed on the island, and after several years of travelling in various distant countries with that legion, in which I was always free to do whatever I wished. Most fortunate in being able to study a wide variety of remedies used by many different cultures, and to learn the composition of a great many chemicals. Those were happy and interesting years for me. The legion was eventually posted to Britannia, and in the course of my duties with the Roman army I've travelled all over your island. When the legions were given their orders to leave and return to Rome, I decided to accept the generous offer made to me by your Great King Erion, and I have been in his service for the last twenty years."

Aurthora was the first to break the silence. "What a fascinating story!" he exclaimed in genuine amazement. "What sights you must have seen. Tell me, Myridyn," he continued, "did you ever discover the method those pirates used to hurl their balls of fire such great distances?"

Myridyn smiled and thought to himself, *What a tactician's brain this young man has, he's already sensed the advantage such a device would give in battle.*

"It was a closely guarded secret known only to very few," replied Myridyn, "and if anyone extraneous to that small group was thought to know it, he would be doggedly sought out and killed. I did, however, come away with one item from my time with the pirates." Taking a small, arrow-shaped pin from the collar of his cloak he passed it to Aurthora, who inspected it closely. It was too small to hold a cloak together, and was little different from the needles he had seen the womenfolk use when joining or repairing cloth, except it had no eye in one end through which to pass the thread, but instead a hole in the centre.

"And what would this be used for Myridyn?" asked Aurthora curiously, passing the pin back to the physician. Myridyn took the pin and placed it on a ring on his finger, which had a slight projection onto which the hole in the pin fitted. He gently spun the pin on the ring, and when the pin stopped the arrow pointed in the direction they were travelling. He did this several times, and each time the pin stopped, it pointed in exactly the same direction.

"Amazing!" exclaimed Ethellro, who had not uttered a sound during Myridyn's story.

"Is it a form of magic?" joined in his sister. She too had been listening keenly as Myridyn told of his past adventures.

"No, I can assure you it is no magic," replied Myridyn. "I acquired it for my medical services to the family of a retired sea captain in gratitude for the successful treatment I administered. I used it for navigating when the thick sea mists blocked the sun, for with its guidance we could sail in a straight line and eliminate the risk of travelling in circles."

The group travelled in silence for the next hour, and were on the outskirts of Buxonana and the Great King's headquarters when Ethellro stopped to tighten the girth on Katrina's pony. Aurthora and Myridyn moved on a few paces, and when there was no danger of them being overheard, he confided in Myridyn his observations and fears of the previous day concerning the suspicious behaviour of Victor Aberuso and Petrov Joma when the King had been thrown from his horse.

As Myridyn listened to him in silence, a thoughtful, worried look came over his face, *which is the same look he wore when he asked about the birthmark on my shoulder*, thought Aurthora for a split second, then the thought vanished.

"I will send for you later when you have made your camp and we will discuss your thoughts in more detail," said Myridyn. "In the meantime I implore you to say nothing of this to anyone."

It was decided that Katrina would be more comfortable that night if she stayed in Myridyn's quarters within the town, as there were several spare rooms. So Ethellro and Aurthora set about looking for the camp Orius and Emilia would have by now erected. It would be situated somewhere on the outskirts of the walled town and amongst all the other Celtic tribes who had answered the call to arms made by the Great King and the Celtic Round Council.

Aurthora had never before seen such a vast hive of activity, both in and around the town. It was as if all the Celtic fairs and religious ceremonies he had ever experienced had come together in this one large gathering. There were great transport wagons pulled by teams of oxen carrying various supplies for the Army, and drovers driving their flocks of sheep and goats amongst the carts of traders who were trying to set up stalls alongside the bustling, overcrowded Roman road. There were lines of pack animals loaded with heavy sacks, or wooden crates of ducks, geese and hens, all trying to either enter or leave this high walled settlement.

It was just before dusk when amongst all the other small encampments, Ethellro eventually spotted his family's flag on a tall pole fluttering in the evening breeze. Orius had erected the two small shelters for Aurthora and himself, then had helped Emilia to erect shelters for Ethellro and his sister. A messenger from the King's court had informed them of the minor accident that had caused their delay. While Orius began to prepare them a meal, Aurthora related their adventure, with Ethellro adding his part to the tale. He then waited for Emilia to gather together some of her mistress's belongings; he planned to escort her to the accommodation allocated to Myridyn within the relative safety of the walled town of Buxonana. This was an excuse to see Katrina again, but he was also looking forward to the promised talk with Myridyn. He was also feeling rather guilty: never before had he intentionally kept any secrets from his friend and tutor Orius. On arriving with Emilia at Myridyn's house, Katrina informed him that the physician had been called to the court of the Great King leaving in extreme haste, not even stopping for his evening meal.

After seeing that Katrina and Emilia were settled comfortably, Aurthora relaxed, especially since Disaylann seemed to be delighted with their company being quick to attend to their every needs. Since Aurthora could not have his planned conversation with Myridyn, he decided he would instead use the time to explored the walled town, and began by making his way through the narrow streets; he wanted to get a feel of this place that the Great King had chosen as headquarters for himself and the Celtic Round Council.

After an hour or so in the town he decided to leave through one of its guarded entrances. From there he threaded his way back through the multitude of small encampments, and by the time he reached the emblem on the tall flagpole, Orius was ready to serve their evening meal.

As they ate they told Orius more about their experiences, and also the story and adventures of Myridyn the Physician. But as Myridyn had requested, Aurthora said nothing about Petrov Joma and Victor Aberuso. Apart from the odd grunt, Orius listened in silence until Ethellro and Aurthora had finished their story. "I have heard of this physician," said Orius. "Even though Aidas Corrilus lost an arm, it was Myridyn who saved the life of my friend. It is also said that he has the gift of talking to the animals and birds."

The small group continued the conversation for a while, surrounded by the drifting smell of wood smoke that mingled with the odours of the many different meals being prepared around the hundreds of small cooking fires flickering in the dark as far as the eye could see. It had been a long day for all three, so they crawled into their shelters and were soon asleep. Aurthora was the last to relax, his brain too busy reliving the story that Myridyn had told them that day. He was also intrigued by Orius' comment that Myridyn could talk to the birds. His last thought before he fell asleep was of the great buzzard in Myridyn's tent watching his every move with its bright beady eyes, also the rumours that were everywhere in the camp of a serious disagreement amongst the hierarchy of the Celtic Alliance.

When Myridyn had left Ethellro and Aurthora at the gate of Buxonana earlier that evening, he had dismounted from his pony and bade Disaylann with a series of hand signs to guide the one carrying Katrina, while he led his own animal along the narrow cobbled streets between small dwellings crammed in on either side, leading to the house that he was occupying which had originally been a wealthy merchant's residence.

It was built of stone with a thick thatched roof and was much larger than its surrounding neighbours, which were of heavy, rough hewn solid timbers with external and internal walls of wattle and daub. It consisted of three bedrooms, a kitchen, a small room for bathing, a central room for meals, a small room for receiving guests, and a room that Myridyn used to prepare his herbal medicines. Each room had an external opening covered in stretched pigskin, which allowed some light to penetrate into the dark interior. In front was a small garden, surrounded by a high wall with a stout wooden gate. The garden was blossoming with a vast array of herbs and wild flowers, in one corner was a wooden cote from which came the cooing of pigeons. Myridyn took down a note written on birch bark that was fastened to the main entrance, then bade Disaylann to show Katrina to her room, instructing him to light the fires in the kitchen and to provide hot water so that she could bathe. He also provided more of the ointment for her grazes and bruises.

He studied the short note which simply bade him, on his return, to make his presence known to the Great King and the Round Council. Myridyn sensed the urgency even though there were no details: any details on open letters from the Royal Household only tended to cause speculation and rumour.

Having done all he could for the comfort of his guest, he hurried along the narrow streets to the large building that was the King's headquarters where the Celtic Round Council was already in session. Even before entering the meeting hall he heard raised voices and the name of Zanton mentioned.

The entrance to the hall was guarded by a young, clean-shaven man, his long brown hair fastened in a ponytail. "Ah! Timus Calgacus," said Myridyn to the young man, "so you and your men are on duty tonight?"

"Yes, Myridyn," responded Timus. "Both today and the morrow."

"That is good," replied Myridyn, relieved that the King and Round Council would be safe for several days at least, until he could come up with a solution for Petrov Joma, Victor Aberuso and any followers they might have. But for now he had to see what current crisis was unfolding to test the resolve of the council..

Taking a deep breath he stepped into the hall where the senior members and representatives of the tribes were seated at a large round table on which a dozen or so candles were burning, casting an eerie light in the fast approaching dusk. They were so involved in their heated debate that they remained unaware of his presence; he stood quietly in the shadows at the entrance, listening to the cause of their disagreement. During the hour he remained there, they were unable to arrive at any course of action that was satisfactory to them all.

When he finally stepped forward and made his presence known he was greeted warmly by some of the gathered chiefs, who appreciated his logic when called upon to give advice. Others, however, remained silent: they were jealous of his position and the favour the King showed towards this foreign physician. Myridyn waited, careful not to put forward a proposition until they had run out of ideas of their own and lapsed into silence. It was then they asked him for his views. He pondered for a few moments smiling to himself: a strategy had been forming in his mind as he had listened in the shadows. If implemented it would give him a few days' respite and time to think of a more permanent solution.

Chapter Eleven

Myridyn felt quite pleased with himself as he made his way back through the narrow streets of Buxonana to his quarters: it had been a good constructive day's work, but now he had to put into play the plan of action he decided to follow.

The next day, as the first rays of the morning sun appeared over the distant hills, the large camp was awakened by the blowing of the great Druid horns with their elaborate carved boars' heads. These were blown when a sacrifice was to be made to Taranis, the Celtic god of thunder, or to the great horned god Cerrunnos, the lord of all Druid gods. Today was also the Summer Solstice, the main day in the Druid religious calendar. When the time came these same horns would also be blown to lead the Celts into battle.

The procession made its way through the camp, with several Druid priests in long white shawls leading the column, four more junior priests blowing the great horns, and several women playing small, harp-like instruments. Following this small group came eight sturdy men carrying a tall chair fitted on long poles. Sitting on the chair Aurthora recognised the frail figure of Zanton, the Druid High Priest. Aurthora was curious. Orius had told him the previous night of a rumour circulating the camp about a serious disagreement between Zanton the High Priest and the leaders of the Celtic tribes who still worshipped the old Druid religion, and the tribal chiefs who supported and followed the new Christian teachings. Apparently, if the rumour was to be believed, Zanton wanted to publicly sacrifice a group of Saxon mercenaries, who had been captured while trying to loot a Celtic supply wagon.

The Christians had objected strongly, which had caused a serious confrontation between the two groups, the Celtic Round Council had been asked to intervene. But as there were supporters of both camps in the Round Council they were finding it hard to come to a decision. The wrangling had gone on for hours, all were aware that this could cause a split in the Alliance and weaken and divide their army before they had even set foot on the battlefield.

Most of the camp seemed to be awake early, a great throng of men was following behind the procession of Druid priests. Some were just curious hangers-on who wanted to see the eventual outcome, but there were also many Christians among the group. Aurthora and Orius were swept along by the crowd, to be joined a short while later by Ethellro. He had been attending to the horses when the throng of men had streamed past their small camp he stayed to calm the animals until the bulk of the crowd had passed.

The group of men following the Druid procession was now several thousand strong. When the horns stopped blowing the great mass of bodies shuffled to a halt. Aurthora observed that the atmosphere was not the light hearted, jovial mood that usually accompanied the carnivals and fairs he attended in the past; instead, a strained feeling of unease seemed to have gripped the large gathering of men. The group of Druid priests had moved to a large depression in the ground and the rest of the crowd of Celts had spread round in a great circle on the higher ground to obtain a good view. Zanton's chair had been placed on the edge of a circle of large, white, limestone blocks.

Zanton rose from his chair and stepped into the circle of stones, which was the signal for the horn blowers in unison to sound a long blast. The priest raised his hands to the sky as the rays of the early morning sun reached towards the circle of stones; as the first of these entered the circle, he lowered his arms as a signal for the horns to stop. The Druid High Priest now had the full attention of the several thousand men who had followed the Druids to this spot on the fringes of the vast army encampment.

For several moments not a sound was to be heard. Then came a slight disturbance on one side of the great circle of men as a group of guards made a passageway for six bound men who were led down into the depression and towards the circle of white stones. Aurthora recognised Petrov Joma and Victor Aberuso at the head of the guards.

There were gasps of disbelief from some of the men who had a good view of what was taking place, and cheers from several others. A friar standing close to Aurthora dressed in his simple, belted brown robe fell to his knees and began to pray. He was quickly joined by others as word spread through the crowds of what was about to happen. Aurthora looked around at the faces and recognised some of his own men in the milling throng of bodies.

Some groups were cheering and chanting Druid prayers. Others shouted the Celtic war cry of *AIIBRAA*, others fell to their knees and, following the example of several friars in the throng, began to pray aloud. Aurthora realised he was witnessing a wedge that was being driven deeper by the second into the Celtic Alliance, and could ultimately affect the resolve and morale, and fragment all the tribes and their warriors.

It was Orius who brought Aurthora's attention to another slight disturbance on the fringes of the crowd. A man on a large grey battle horse was trying without success to move through the body of tightly packed Druid supporters.

Aurthora quickly read the situation; shouting to Ethellro, they began to force their way in the direction of the mounted man, managing to collect four of his own men on the way. Reaching the horse he grabbed the bridle, with Orius on one side and Ethellro on the other, assisted by his other four men, they forced a path through the dense crowd with Ethellro shouting in his rich booming voice: "Make way for the Great King Erion! Stand aside! Make way I say!" Slowly, the sea of men parted and reluctantly allowed Aurthora through, leading the large grey carrying King Erion.

King Erion was in a full suit of the finest Celtic chain mail, which had been highly polished and was covered with a cloak of deep red, the colour of the Celtic Royal Household since the time of his ancestor, Queen Boudicca. Aurthora led the grey on which the Great King was mounted down the slight incline to a murmur of recognition from a large number in the surrounding crowd. The news passed through the crowd that the Great King himself had made a personal appearance at this, a Druid religious sacrifice, and his horse was being led by the hero Aurthora Ambrosius, the one who had defeated the Saxon pirates. Aurthora continued to lead the Great King's horse straight to the edge of the circle of large white limestones, bringing the animal to a halt directly opposite the Druid High Priest, Zanton. The appearance of the King in person together with Aurthora Ambrosius stunned the surrounding crowd into silence with a feeling of expectation and excitement.

Aurthora stroked the nose of the Great King's nervous horse while at the same time he observed Zanton the High Priest. The man was not wearing the hood as he had worn at their last meeting; Aurthora could see the weathered skin stretched over a shaven skull and skeletal features. Two penetrating dark eyes, glittering with outrage and anger, directed at these two ordinary mortals who had dared to encroach on this, a sacred Druid ceremony within the holy circle of stones. Zanton was convulsed with rage at this upstart king, who obviously favoured the foreign Christian religion and who sat looking down on him from his high vantage point: also this despicable youth, who had no respect for the ancient and the true ways! How dare they insult him, the High Priest of all the Druids and the religious leader of half the Celtic tribes on the island of Britannia!

King Erion, magnificent on his large grey, with his shining chain mail and draped in the royal red cloak did indeed look like a warrior king. He was the first to speak – not to Zanton, but to the multitude of people surrounding them.

"Celts!" he shouted, "My brothers in arms! We have all joined together and taken the oath to defend our country and our way of life against the Anglo-Saxon barbarians who have invaded our island. We have all seen our brother Celts and their families from the far North, the tribes of the Novantae, Selgovae, Votidini and Damnonii, being driven from their lands and farms by these invaders. Indeed many of these fellow Celts are here among you today." The King was referring to the hordes of refugees from lands occupied by the Anglo-Saxon armies who had sought shelter and refuge over the past few months and had flocked over the borders into King Erion's kingdom of Elmet.

"The High Priest Zanton is to offer a sacrifice for our victory in the forthcoming battle. He proposes to sacrifice the Saxon prisoners." There were cheers and the thumping of breastplates by Zanton's supporters at this statement.

King Erion waited until the shouting subsided before he continued. "I propose that we sacrifice this great white bull to the Great Horned God Cerrunnos, the lord of all Druid gods, and tonight we will all feast on its meat, blessed by the High Priest Zanton, which will give us all the great God's strength in the long conflict that is to come." The part of the crowd who could hear this statement cheered, and there were further, spasmodic bouts of cheering as word of what had been said filtered back amongst the packed crowd.

Those at the top of the incline parted and Myridyn's assistant Disaylann appeared leading the largest, pure white bull that Aurthora had ever seen, taller than the tallest of men there, and with horns wider than a man's outstretched arms. *This bull is exceptionally quiet considering he's surrounded by so many men and so many strange sounds and smells*, thought Aurthora, guessing that Myridyn had played a part in this and was observing the proceedings from somewhere close at hand.

Disaylann led the docile bull down the incline to the edge of the large circle of white stones. He too, like Aurthora and Erion, did not enter the sacred Druid circle. Zanton realised he was losing the initiative with the crowd, but was not prepared to give up quite so easily.

"And what will become of these Anglo-Saxon mercenaries who have Celtic blood on their swords? They too should be slaughtered along with the bull!" he shouted to the crowd. There was a murmur of approval from the men overlooking the circle of stones, and several cheers from Zanton's supporters.

"These mercenaries," shouted Great King Erion, "will spend the rest of their lives in the salt mines, and when each one of you men here today next takes salt with your meal, you can think of these Anglo-Saxons digging in the bowels of the earth, never to see daylight again as long as they live." This sense of rough justice appealed to the vast majority of the crowd, and a great cheer went up from the gathering. "Once we give these invaders half, they will want the whole. We will crush the bones of these Anglo Saxons until they are like hailstones under our horses' feet. So much Anglo-Saxon blood will be spilt on the battlefield it will be hard for a man to stand". There were great cheers from the crowd at this warlike speech from their king. Turning his horse he directed it up the incline. Aurthora, followed by Ethellro, Orius, and with his men in the rear, walked over to the prisoners, and looking Petrov Joma directly in the eye, took hold of the chains that bound them and turned to lead them up the incline.

Victor Aberuso moved as if to draw his sword, but he was stopped by Petrov Joma, who was well aware that this was neither the time nor place to cut down a hero of the people and a man with the support of a large section of the Celtic Alliance.

Aurthora and his group followed the King back towards the entrance gate to the town, the crowd chanting "Great King Erion! Great King Erion!" And mingled with this could also be heard the occasional chant of "Aurthora! Aurthora!" especially amongst some of the younger warriors, for in their eyes he was indeed a hero.

Zanton watched from the centre of the circle of white stones as the small group, led by the Great King on his magnificent grey horse, slowly climbed the slope and passed through the still chanting crowd of warriors. The High Priest had no choice but to continue the ceremony with the great white bull. After the due process of passing around the small cakes that had been baked using the first corn of the harvest and much blowing of the great war horns accompanied by chanting and the playing of harps and pipes, the white bull was duly slaughtered as an offering to the horned Lord of the Gods, Cerrunnos. Its blood was collected in several large silver bowls and offered to anyone who wanted to drink. The blood of such a magnificent animal that had been blessed by the High Priest was in great demand, and there was no shortage of participants amongst the large gathering of Celtic warriors.

Everyone with coins to spare would eat well that night from the meat of the slaughtered bull, which had been the pride bull of the Great King's herds of cattle; this was distributed amongst the vast throng that had gathered for the ceremony, many of whom had simply been attracted by the spectacle and had no deep commitment to the Druid religion. Aurthora and his men, together with Orius and Ethellro, escorted the King and the Saxon prisoners back to Buxonana, while Disaylann was left with enough coins to purchase several choice cuts of meat from the great beast.

As they passed through the town's guarded gates they were joined by Myridyn. Aurthora took the opportunity to enquire about Katrina's health and wellbeing. Myridyn smiled before replying, "The child is recovering and making excellent progress under the most capable and protective wings of both Emilia her maid, and my assistant Disaylann. Feel free to visit them while you are here, and instruct Disaylann when he arrives to prepare some food for when I return. With all this morning's excitement I missed my breakfast!"

Aurthora turned and followed the sound of the horse's hooves on the cobbles as the King negotiated the narrow streets on his way back to report the morning's events to the Celtic Council. The mention of food made himself, Orius and Ethellro all realise that they hadn't eaten anything either that day.

Aurthora sent his men with Orius to return the Anglo-Saxon prisoners to the guards at the stone jail in the centre of the town, with instructions for them to go back to their camp and prepare themselves a meal. Meanwhile he and Ethellro would pay a visit to Katrina at Myridyn's quarters.

Myridyn caught up with the Great King before he entered the hall where he would inform the Council of the outcome of the morning's confrontation with Zanton. "Sire!" exclaimed Myridyn attracting the Great King's attention, "I request a few minutes of your time after your meeting with the Great Council, I think we can resolve the problem we discussed at our last meeting."

"Very good, my friend," replied the Great King, placing his hand on Myridyn's shoulder. "Your solution to the little problem that arose this morning worked admirably, and for that, on behalf of myself and the Celtic Alliance, I thank you." King Erion then turned and entered the hall to meet the Council.

As Aurthora and Ethellro passed through the narrow streets of Buxonana all around them in small workshops men were preparing the weapons of war: willow bark was being stripped and boiled in a charcoal mash to turn it into twine for bow strings; bluebell bulbs were also being boiled and the residue used for glue to flight the yard-long arrows of ash and poplar wood that had been straightened out over open fires. These were then fitted with goose feather flights, coloured with a vegetable dye in order to show the type of arrowhead that was fitted. The smiths were busy working over their anvils while their assistants operated the bellows to increase the heat of their fires. They used the black rock that burnt and gave much more heat than ordinary charcoal, and so made the high quality metal for which the Celts had been renowned for generations.

Aurthora and Ethellro stopped at one of the forges. Aurthora was curious, he had seen the smith in his own village working the white-hot metal, cooling it quickly in water to make it brittle and then re-tempering it again. This particular forge was making the gladius, the short stabbing sword previously used so successfully by the Roman army, and with which Aurthora and many thousands of Celts had trained in obedience to the Great King's decree. The two men watched for a few minutes and marvelled at the skill of Master Cullan the Celtic blacksmith. The next forge was making arrowheads of hardened metal. When used with the power of the Celtic longbow they could penetrate even the highest quality armour.

When they arrived at Myridyn's house there was no one in the small garden. Ethellro banged the great iron doorknocker, sending the booming noise ringing through the house. *Loud enough to waken the dead*, thought Aurthora, wincing in anticipation as Ethellro, arm raised, was about to lift the knocker again – but just at that moment Emilia opened the iron-studded oak door so that he almost fell into her arms.

Orius followed Emilia to the kitchen where they began to prepare a meal while Aurthora and Ethellro went into an adjoining room where Katrina was resting on a low couch. *How beautiful she is*, thought Aurthora. Even though she was still quite pale, the walk through the wild countryside on the day of her accident had brought out the freckles on her face adding to her charm. She was dressed in clothes made of the same very fine material that he had seen her wear at the camp when Myridyn had reset her damaged shoulder. These, he noticed, were more tightly fitting, and accentuated what a fine figure Katrina had.

"Those clothes are very elegant, and of a very finely woven material," commented Ethellro to his sister. Katrina forced her gaze away from Aurthora's and replied to her brother rather sarcastically: "Why yes! I am recovering Ethellro, how kind of you to enquire? My shoulder is much better and the cuts and grazes are healing well. As for these fine clothes that Myridyn has allowed me to borrow, they are indeed made of the finest material. He collected them during his travels in far-off lands I wear them because they do not irritate or rub against my bruises and grazes as my own spun woollen garments would." Taken back by his sister's sharp comments, Ethellro retreated into the adjoining room to enjoy the more pleasant company of Orius and Emilia.

Aurthora walked across the room to Katrina taking her hand in both of his. He detected the sweet aroma of the scented soap Myridyn had also given him to use when bathing his cuts and grazes. "I'm glad you're recovering," he said, looking into her eyes. "There will be many turbulent days ahead of us," he stammered, "and many of us may not return. But if the gods are favourable to me, and this conflict with the Anglo-Saxon army is successful, I would like to ask your brother, as head of your family, if I can walk with you, but only if you, Katrina, are in agreement."

Katrina was pleased with Aurthora's approach: he had asked her first, and not gone over her head to seek her brother's permission to visit her, as was the usual custom. "That day cannot come soon enough for me," replied Katrina, and grabbing Aurthora by the hair she pulled his head down to hers and kissed him full on the lips.

It was while they were in this embrace that the great clang of the iron doorknocker vibrated through the house. Aurthora tried to pull away but Katrina held him to her by her grip on his hair. It was Orius who passed the doorway on his way to open the great oak door, and observing the couple in this embrace, smiled and thought to himself, *if only Emilia would grab me like that, it would be like flying in the heavens with the gods!*

It was Disaylann at the door. He had purchased the best cuts of meat that the coins he had been given would buy, and he handed them to Emilia. "This meat would be better if it were hung for several days in a cool place," said Emilia as she examined the fine cuts of beef, "but as time is of the essence, Orius and I will rub it in various herbs, seal the meat then it can be cooked for our evening meal and eaten with the newly baked wheat bread…"

"…and cooked peas and beans!" joined in Orius. Emilia and I have decided it will be followed by a pudding of red berries and dried apple set in a soft pastry and covered in a layer of goat's milk whipped into a fluffy cream." Having said their piece and taken charge of the evening meal, Emilia and Orius made their way back into the kitchen.

Several hours later, even though hours of daylight remained, Disaylann was busy lighting the many oil lamps and candles. The house was always rather dark: the pigskin-covered window openings in the building were few since the house had been built to provide warmth and cosiness during the severe winters that struck that part of the country. The live flames gave off a warm glow and sufficient light to move around the house.

The loud clang of the heavy doorknocker, sounding more like a gong from within, vibrated around the house to herald Myridyn's return. Disaylann went to open the door, for though he could not hear the doorknocker he could sense the vibrations it created.

The physician entered with a flourish. "The wonderful smell of roasting meat can be enjoyed by everyone in the street, and to complement such a fine meal I have been presented with a flagon of the best red wine, in recognition of our services today." His words were greeted by loud cheers from the occupants, and a broad smile from Disaylann.

Together Orius and Emilia prepared a wonderful meal and Myridyn's many compliments were directed at both of them. He even suggested recommending them to prepare a meal for the Great King when his busy schedule permitted. He then cleverly directed the conversation round to the day's events, listening intently as, one by one, his male companions gave their opinion of what they would have done in a similar situation. Ethellro was the first to give his views.

"I can understand the feelings of the Druid followers: after all, many of them have been driven from their lands by the Anglo-Saxons. Every day you can see Celts flocking over the border into this kingdom after being forced to leave their farms and dwellings, having lost everything. Some have seen their friends and relations slaughtered before their eyes for resisting. The sacrifice would have made our message quite clear to the Anglo-Saxons: expect no mercy if you enter our kingdom."

"I think they already know they will receive no mercy", commented Orius, "but the rewards for them are substantial. They haven't sailed across the sea with their families and chattels and settled in the northern kingdoms lightly; they've come this far and they don't intend to stop at any borders. They've met little resistance up until now, the two Celtic armies they have fought and beaten were badly organised. Now that they occupy and control those two kingdoms they are confident that they can deal with any force the Celtic Alliance can bring against them.

A battle is inevitable: for you Celts it will be a battle for the survival of your race and the continuation of your culture; for them, if they lose, it will just be a serious setback, and they will try again. It may not be soon, but in several years' time, when they have consolidated their gains and are under pressure to expand, I can assure you they will be back."

This statement by Orius left the group quiet and very sombre. Myridyn was impressed with Orius's sensible and logical assessment of the situation.

"And what are your views Aurthora?" he asked, interested to hear how this young man sitting quietly in front of him would asses the situation.

All eyes turned to Aurthora, who was silent for many seconds while he gathered his thoughts. When he spoke it was in a quiet, matter-of-fact tone. "The situation today was handled as well as it could have been. No one lost face, the priest Zanton had his sacrifice, and the Saxon prisoners were not the victims, the alliance is still intact. But I agree with Orius; the Anglo-Saxon army is very confident of success, which could be used against them. The battle, when it comes, should be of our choosing, and the place of battle should be selected with great care. It has to be decisive; we have to inflict severe casualties on the enemy, we also have to have the will and fortitude to pursue them after we have routed their army, and destroy them wherever we find them. We have to drive them back to the far northern kingdoms at least, and if possible back to their own lands across the seas. But despite all the strength of our bodies and our prayers to our gods for the willpower to succeed, realistically, I do not think we have the resources to drive them from our shores altogether. The land we reclaim should be given back to its original Celtic owners with whom we should form a strong alliance under King Erion and the Celtic Round Council.

"We should also recruit and maintain a permanent, well-trained army, and continue to train all our young men so that they will be ready if and when they may be needed to assist the regular forces. This will take a great deal of organisation and heavy taxation, but it will be well worth it to maintain our freedom and way of life, and not be driven back into the mountains and wilderness as we were when the Romans were here."

Myridyn was greatly impressed with Aurthora's vision; it was obvious that Orius had been a great influence on the young man's thinking during his years of training, he had taught him to assess situations calmly and with a logical and practical attitude. Katrina too, had been impressed with his speech, and felt so proud on his behalf. He was, after all, usually rather shy, and went to great lengths to try and avoid attention; it was obvious he was very passionate about this issue. She found she had not been able to take her eyes from this man, with whom she had already fallen deeply in love; he was so different from her brother, who was loud and boastful and enjoyed being the centre of attention.

After the meal, Disaylann cleared the table and heated water to clean the wooden and pewter platters, while Orius and Emilia strolled in the small garden and Ethellro conversed with his sister. This was the moment Myridyn chose to beckon Aurthora to join him in the privacy of his dispensary, where the gathered herbs were hanging to dry and various containers of potions and pastes lined the shelves. By the light of the oil lantern that Myridyn was carrying, Aurthora could also make out the shape of the great buzzard on its wooden perch in the corner of the room.

Myridyn bade Aurthora to make himself comfortable on a low stool while he went over to feed the bird scraps of meat left over from their evening meal, at the same time making strange noises that seemed to calm the ruffled bird, unsettled at the presence of a stranger.

Once the bird was more at ease he sat down on a stool facing Aurthora. "Aurthora, my young friend," he began, "I have given much thought to what you told me you witnessed when you came upon the King in the woods, I believe that what you saw and what your senses told you about the threat to the King are quite true. However! We do not have any definite proof as yet against Petrov Joma who, you realise, is also a distant relation of the Great King. What's more he has served the Great Council well, even though he has been ruthless in carrying out its instructions he and his followers have been over zealous in their actions. Nonetheless, he does, I'm afraid, have his supporters on the Celtic Council. As you know we have been having problems with raiding parties of Anglo-Saxons attacking our supply wagons. Our spies inform us that their army is getting low on food so they are scouring the country they have occupied, taking whatever food they can find from the farms and villages, driving the occupants away and killing anyone who resists them.

"The King has taken my advice and dispatched Petrov Joma with his followers to patrol our borders and to try and safeguard our convoys. He has also agreed to my request that I appoint a permanent guard for himself and the Council and to patrol the town day and night. You have proven yourself a worthy subject and loyal to the Council and the King's cause. You are a fine leader, and your men trust and admire you, therefore Aurthora Ambrosius, the Great King has appointed you and your company of Celts the permanent guard for himself, the High Town, the Royal Household, and the Round Council. Until the time this Anglo-Saxon army is crushed and driven from our lands.

"You will take up your post tomorrow evening and relieve Timus Calgacus and his men who are the current guard. Tomorrow you will collect all your men, check their armaments and work out a rota for their duties. You and your men will be guarding the Great King and the Round Council night and day. All of you and your horses will be quartered at the town's barracks you will stay permanently inside the walls of the town unless you are required to leave as an escort to the King or members of the Celtic Round Council."

Aurthora did not know what to say, Myridyn's words had left him speechless, his mind was buzzing. This man in front of him was not only an able physician, he was also a clever and highly-respected advisor to the Round Council, and also a close friend of King Erion.

"And what of my friend and tutor Orius Tomase?" he inquired when he had recovered from the shock of such a prestigious appointment.

"He will be allowed to serve you as before," came the reply.

"Yes, but you must realise that I have never kept any secrets from Orius; he has many contacts and has always been my advisor. Will you release me from my oath of silence so that he, too, can be made aware of this situation?"

Myridyn reflected on Aurthora's request for a few moments, then replied, "Yes, Aurthora, Orius can be informed of the general situation, but in the course of your new duties you will overhear many important discussions, and any idle gossip could cost many Celtic lives. You must use your own discretion about what you disclose to Orius, although you may listen to Orius's advice on various matters you discuss, you must be the one who makes the final decision on any action you take."

Aurthora smiled at the old physician, and replied simply, "I agree!" Then grasping the physician's outstretched hand, he shook it warmly in both of his.

Aurthora rushed to inform Katrina of his new appointment. Being stationed within the town meant they would be able to be together for longer periods. Then he informed Orius and Ethellro, who were both delighted with his news. It was now necessary to organise his men and inform them of their new position. He told the household he would not be back before the curfew imposed within the town's walls, so he would spend the night with his detachment of Celts in their camp outside the town.

As the great oak door closed behind him, he stopped on the short path that led to the gate and the narrow street. He needed to gather his thoughts. Things were moving very fast. A rattling sound in the garden stopped his daydreaming, and turning, he saw Disaylann. The youth had his back to Aurthora and was rattling a box, presumably containing some corn. He was trying to tempt a pigeon perched on the roof of an adjoining house to enter the cote. He felt compassion for this young man who lived in a world of permanent silence; the only person with whom he could converse was Myridyn through their series of signs. He left through the garden gate and along the narrow street, noting the dark storm clouds gathering in the evening sky. *It looks as if this good spell of weather is about to break,* he thought as he made his way along the cobbled streets towards the centre of the town.

Chapter Twelve

When Aurthora left the physician's house there were still several hours before the curfew imposed on the town was due. Then the gates at the three entrances would be closed and guarded, and groups of armed warriors from the Coritani tribe under the supervision of Timus Calgacus would patrol the narrow streets and guard the houses allocated to the King and the Round Council.

No one would be allowed to enter or leave the town without special permission. As this was to be the responsibility of Aurthora and his men from the following day, he decided to familiarise himself further with the layout of the streets in the town, the position of the barracks and the stables, and in particular, the house occupied by the King.

At this hour there was a general hustle and bustle in the streets as the townspeople went about their usual business and tradesmen from out of town were busily closing down their stalls in preparation to leave before the night's curfew. People were making final purchases before they too would be hurrying off to their homes. The King's residence had been well chosen, surrounded as it was by a high wall and with the only means of entrance a sturdy gate guarded by two of Timus Calgacus's tribesmen. He presumed there would also be guards patrolling the inner perimeter of the wall.

The town barracks consisted of a long building without openings in its outer wall, only a series of narrow slits on the inner walls that faced a central parade ground. A high wall also filled the space on either side between the barracks and the stables, and a similar wall stood between the barracks and a large stone building that had formerly been the Roman army's hospital and was still being used for that purpose by the Celtic army. There were some other stone buildings used as storerooms, and one building that housed the baths and washing area, also joined by a high stone wall. Along the top of all these walls ran a protected walkway. The only entrance into the building was through a large, arched stone entrance sealed by two heavy oak doors. Over the years the great King had built and modified the defensive walls to form another fort within the walled town itself. No one was on guard duty at the barracks and no one seemed to be on guard duty at the stables, there were just a few young lads carrying hay and water to feed the many horses in their charge.

As he walked through the stables he could not help but be impressed by the number and condition of these large horses. *A charge by these great animals with well-armed armoured Celts in the saddle using their new long spears would be an awe-inspiring sight for our friends and allies, and a terrifying sight for our enemies*, he thought. *A force like this must not be wasted, but used at an opportune moment in the coming battle when surprise may play a decisive role in helping to rout the Anglo-Saxon army.*

He felt his excitement mount, even though the coming battle against the Anglo-Saxons would delay the announcement of his betrothal to Katrina, and the battle's outcome could possibly change his future forever. He knew the Celtic army: despite rumours that it was well outnumbered by the enemy, it was organised and been well trained, it had the best available armour and weapons that could be provided by the skilled Celtic smiths, the Anglo-Saxons would be unprepared for many of its features. But it also had its weaknesses. Aurthora was aware of these and knew that Myridyn was too. It was of the utmost importance that the Anglo-Saxon leaders did not also discover them.

He left Buxonana by the eastern entrance along with a mixed crowd who were all hurrying to vacate the town before the gates were closed. The motley group included a band of jugglers and acrobats who had been entertaining the crowds, several beggars, and one or two doubtful-looking characters bringing up the rear, who obviously lived by their wits and on what they could beg or steal. On seeing them he automatically checked to see if his small leather pouch containing his few coins was still fastened securely to his belt.

There were also a few men from the encampment who visited the town to purchase extra supplies or foodstuffs as a change from the basic meals provided by the army cooks, or perhaps to visit the houses where prostitutes plied their trade, offering some satisfaction to those who were far from their own towns, villages and families.

He waved down a large, two-wheeled cart containing several large wooden barrels. "Are you going in the direction of the encampment?" he called to the driver. The man nodded grumpily, moving over slightly on the narrow seat to make room for him, but without attempting to stop the slow-moving oxen that were pulling the cart. Aurthora nimbly joined the man on the narrow seat as the cart swayed from side to side in rhythm with the movement of the two great beasts. "What do your barrels contain, friend?" he asked the driver, trying to strike up a conversation.

"Water," the man grunted, "just water! Several of us carters are under employ to collect the water from further upstream and not to take it from the easiest place, which would be the ford in the middle of the encampment.

We do this all day, every day. We take the full barrels to the cooks' shelters in the centre of the camp and collect the empty barrels for refilling. It's our duty to make sure that there is water available at all times for the cooks and the men."

"A most responsible task, my friend," replied Aurthora. "Yes! But it would be made easier if we were allowed to take the water from the ford," repeated the driver.

"Who instructed you to collect the water from further upstream and not from the centre of the encampment?" asked a curious Aurthora.

"It was that interfering foreign physician," replied the driver.

He had made the same complaint over the last few days to many of the men to whom he had given a lift back to the encampment. Many had been there for some dubious entertainment that could be obtained in the narrow streets if they had the coins to pay and were not usually as sober as his present passenger. He was glad to have someone who was prepared to listen to his complaints. "You know the one I mean?" he continued, "the one that's always up the King's arse!" he said, chuckling at his own witticism. Aurthora merely smiled to himself.

Outside the encampment they passed a flogging being supervised by Cimbonda Gilberto of the Cornovii tribe, who was in charge of order in the encampment. Two men had been caught fighting, but fortunately for them no steel had been drawn and no blood spilled, otherwise they would both have risked execution. That was the law.

The men had been strapped, facing one another to the wheels of a large wagon. They were each receiving ten lashes, which would be doubled if they were caught fighting again. *It's not the pain that's the punishment, those men can stand that easily, it's the humiliation of being stripped and beaten that they'll find hard to swallow*, thought Aurthora. With the carter and himself as onlookers, the cart trundled slowly past as the punishment was meted out.

"Do you get well paid for your labours my friend?" continued Aurthora.

"My rate is the same as when I carried goods for the merchants, but this is more regular. It'll rain before morning, though, and that will make my job much harder," complained the driver.

It was quite dark when Aurthora disembarked from the slow-moving cart and joined his men at their encampment. A light rain had begun to fall, but he saw that his small shelter was still standing, so at least he would not have to spend a wet night under the stars.

His men had already cooked and eaten their evening meal when he arrived and were sitting around their campfires discussing the day's events and their implications. "Men!" He called out loudly to gain their attention, and waited while they gathered round. "Tomorrow we take over from Timus Calgacus and his warriors. We have been appointed as permanent guard to the Great King and the Celtic Round Council."

There were murmurs from the listening men as the implications of Aurthora's statement sank home. Not only was it a very honourable and prestigious position, but also one that would mean dry accommodation in the town's barracks – ideal, given that it was obvious the weather was changing for the worse.

"In the morning we break camp at sunrise and take all our belongings up to Buxonana to assume our new duties. The hours will be long and there will be little time for entertainment, but your accommodation will be drier than where you are at the moment. Aurthora turned and walked towards his shelter with the cheers of his men behind him and shouts of "Well done Aurthora! Well done!"

The spell of fine weather had allowed the columns of men and materials to make their journey from different parts of the country to the meeting point at Buxonana without any great hardship, but during the night the weather changed for the worse. The light rain was followed by heavy showers driven on by gusts of strong winds.

The temporary shelters erected by the majority of the warriors in the vast encampment were unsuitable for such severe conditions and many of the men could only sit or stand at the entrances of their leaking abodes, wrapped in their heavy, water-soaked blankets and surrounded by their sodden belongings. The previously hard dry ground around them quickly turned into a sticky, muddy quagmire.

The small stream that had run through the camp the previous day was now a fast-flowing torrent fed by the heavy rainfall higher up in the hills. It had burst its banks flooding the area where the cooking tents were situated. The camp cooks had been forced to evacuate to higher ground, it was impossible to keep any fires alight, so there was no hot food available for the occupants of the low lying valley, which added to their misery.

Aurthora and his men broke camp quickly at dawn and began to make their way over the muddy site in the direction of the road to the walled town of Buxonana. Orius had arrived before dawn loading the pack pony with his and Aurthora's belongings.

On their way they passed the water cart near the cooks' tent. It was stuck in the heavy mud and the two great oxen were straining to move it, verbally encouraged by the old driver from his seat on the cart. Half a dozen men were assisting him, three per wheel, up to their knees in the clinging mud, slowly inching the cart towards firmer ground. As Aurthora passed by he waved to the driver of the water cart, the old man in turn acknowledging him. Orius followed Aurthora leading the smaller pack pony, with the column of heavily-armed warriors behind him, struggling in the deep mud. As they went by the old driver asked the nearest of the men straining to turn the wheel of the water cart, "Who is that man at the front of the column of men? He was on my cart last night." The man stopped, glad of a chance to regain his breath from his efforts, and looked at the retreating figures of Aurthora and Orius.

"That man at the front, my friend, is Aurthora Ambrosius, the scourge of the Anglo-Saxons," the man replied, gasping the words due to his exertions with the cart. "And those following are his men. Rumour has it they have just been appointed permanent guards to the King and the Round Council. They've left this dung heap of a swamp at just the right time, they'll all be billeted in the barracks in Buxonana where it will be warm and dry, the lucky swines!" With that the man put his shoulder to the cartwheel and slowly the cart moved again towards higher, firmer ground. The old driver sat staring in the direction of the fast disappearing group of men, his mouth hanging open.

He had been unaware that he had sat beside a living legend. *Still you have to think positively*, he told himself. *I made my complaint, which was good. And to someone in authority, which was also good. I'll be very surprised if some immediate action isn't taken to deal with my complaint and remedy the situation. Indeed, they might even present me with a reward for my thoughtful suggestion,* he concluded with a great deal of satisfaction.

Once Aurthora and his men reached the paved road they began to make better time. It was still raining quite heavily and the grey colour of the clouds overhead indicated that the bad weather was there to stay at least for the rest of the day. He made a note to inform Myridyn that conditions in the camp were deteriorating by the hour as more and more of the wagons and carts became bogged down in the mire, and as men, animals and wheeled vehicles churned the water-saturated soil into a knee-deep sea of mud. Not that the old physician could do anything to help the sufferings of these men, there were simply too many of them.

At the stone gateway to Buxonana he was met by Timus Calgacus and two of his men. "Welcome Aurthora!" said Timus, "you bring fine weather with you!"

"It's good to see you again, Timus," replied Aurthora. "Whatever bad weather we're having, I hope the Anglo-Saxons are getting it ten times worse." Both men laughed. "My men will guide your column to the barracks," said Timus. "In the meantime, if you agree, I will show you the properties that the Great Council occupy also King Erion's residence, and of course the other two gateways into the town."

"Yes, indeed," replied Aurthora, "it will give my men chance to familiarise themselves with their surroundings, then I and Orius will allocate them their positions and form a rota for their duties."

"Will Orius be your second-in-command?" queried Timus, surprised.

"Yes! I trust him with my life, I will vouch for him with my life."

"I do not judge you Aurthora. But others may. You must watch yourself," warned Timus.

"I thank you for your advice, my friend, and I can assure you we will take great care."

After touring the town and seeing the positions where Timus had placed his men, Aurthora was glad to make his way to inspect the old Roman barracks.

Timus and his guards had vacated the large stone building and Aurthora's men had already taken their place by the time he arrived. There were permanent wooden bunks in neat rows with a storage locker to each bunk, and toilets that had a permanent flow of water to wash away the waste. Alongside the latter was a small bathhouse where water could be heated and directed into a large communal bath. Around the sides of the bathing area were stone beds where the Roman soldiers had lain while they were massaged. Aurthora's men were amazed, never before had they seen such luxury made available to the common soldier.

Aurthora and Orius would each be occupying a small room, used in the past by officers of the Roman army. "I'm glad for the opportunity to change into some dry clothes," he said to Orius as they walked down the passage to their quarters.

"Yes, we are most fortunate, those men camping on the plain outside the town wall have no such luxuries," replied the old legionnaire as the heavy rain continued to pour down from darkened skies, rushing like a waterfall from the roof tiles of their new accommodation.

Under Orius's guidance and supervision, Aurthora and his men settled down into the rota and routine of guarding the three gates into the town, the King's residence, and properties occupied by the members of the Celtic Round Council, as well as being available for escort duties when required. The rain continued for a further two days, and although it was heavy around

Buxonana, further up in the hills it was heavier still, so that the stream that had broken its banks was by now a raging torrent, and the army encampment ever more flooded. The warriors had been forced to move into the surrounding woods and higher ground above the valley, where they had made shelters as best they could using whatever materials they had been able to find or salvage from the original camp. The conditions were so bad that supplies of food for the men and fodder for the animals stopped as wagons and men became bogged down in the terrible mud, and even the stone paved Roman roads had become impassable to man and beast.

It was a very busy time for Aurthora. This type of soldiering was completely new to him and the men under his command. The duties attached to the position stretched the small number of soldiers at his disposal to the limit. Both he and Orius shared a rota of nine hours on duty and nine hours off. They had decided on this rota for all the men since it meant the guard changed at a different hour each day and night. They also made a point of regularly changing the checkpoints in the town where the soldiers were positioned, so that no one travelling after the curfew would know when or where they might be challenged.

They both continuously patrolled the town, checking on the men in their different positions, so had little time to converse except to discuss the change of rotas or the allocation of men for various escort duties. Aurthora called at the physician's house whenever time allowed in order to see Katrina, who by then had made a complete recovery from her injured shoulder, but his visits were short and infrequent.

Because all the lodgings in the town had been taken weeks before, Myridyn had suggested that Katrina stay on in his property since there was ample room for her and Emilia. This offer had been gratefully accepted, the alternative would have been to camp out in the woods indefinitely in atrocious conditions.

It was during one of the short meetings between Aurthora and Orius as they exchanged guard duty, that Aurthora had the opportunity to tell him of the episode in the forest when he had felt the Great King's life was in danger, and how Myridyn had at first sworn him to secrecy, but that now he had been relieved of that promise.

"Who were these men and where are they now, Aurthora?" asked Orius after his companion had finished his tale.

"Myridyn managed to have them deployed guarding our borders so they are not a direct threat to us at the moment," replied Aurthora. "Their leader is a cousin to the Great King, his name is Petrov Joma." Aurthora stopped in mid-sentence when he saw the look and the colour drain from Orius's face.

"I know this man!" exclaimed Orius, as the memories from many years before came flooding back, accompanied by the feeling of guilt he always felt at the way he had betrayed his comrades. "He was to have taken me prisoner when I escaped from the legion. If he had, I would not be here today. Your father has my eternal gratitude for saving me from that evil, torturing butcher Petrov Joma!" Orius spat out the man's name. "He has a reputation for taking no prisoners alive, and if by some chance they are taken alive, they are horribly tortured until they die. He has surrounded himself with all the kingdom's bullies and savage killers you would never wish to meet; he blames the rest of mankind for his disfigurement."

"I have heard these rumours too," replied Aurthora, "but he has some support in the Great Council, and he and his men have a reputation as ferocious fighters."

"That may be, Aurthora, but never turn your back on a man like that, unless you have a trusted friend protecting it." With that warning Orius prepared to leave on his tour of duty.

"Orius, wait!" called Aurthora as Orius went through the open door, "The other man was an ex-legionnaire like yourself. You may know him, his name is Victor Aberuso."

The name seemed to echo around the corridor as Orius pulled the door shut behind him and leant against it, his head swimming. "Victor Aberuso," he muttered to himself, "the bastard that slaughtered my younger brother. He's still alive!" His hand moved to grasp the handle of his pugio, the short dagger that he always kept in his belt, his knuckles showing white against the skin, so tight was his grip.

It was several moments before he moved from the door and made his way down the passage. He did his rounds that night with his mind in turmoil, but by morning he had calmed a little and made a promise to himself. *"I will avenge your death, my brother. And as for you, Victor Aberuso, your days are numbered. On my brother's life and to all the gods I make this pledge!"* He swore this out loud; the two Celtic guards at the town gate who overheard him did not understand, for the pledge was made in Latin, his mother tongue.

It was during this time that an incident took place that raised Aurthora's reputation amongst the gathered tribes still further. At their established daily meeting, Aurthora and Orius had finished discussing the rotas for the men, the minor breaches of discipline that had occurred, the improvements that could be made for the better security of the town and several other minor details – all of which required attention and would keep Aurthora busy well into his rest period – when Orius spoke again: "Oh! There is one other item that requires a decision by you, Aurthora. I've been approached by a man named Selecia Cunobelin. This man is brother to Arranz Cunobelin, the leader of the Dumnonii tribe, who, as you know, have been staunch supporters of King Erion and his policies for many years. He asked if you will grant a favour to one of the King's most ardent followers: he asked if you will give permission for a wedding ceremony to take place within the walls of Buxonana. I know these ceremonies and celebrations are usually carried out on the plain outside the town, but that area is now heavily waterlogged.

"This man," continued Orius with a smile on his face, "is most eager to see his daughter betrothed. She is a rather buxom woman and older than most brides, and I have yet to see a knife as sharp as her tongue, but the large dowry on offer has tempted some man to ask for her hand. As you can understand Selecia is most anxious for the wedding to take place as soon as possible."

Aurthora thought for a few moments. He had seen and, what was worse, heard this woman, she did indeed have a vicious tongue, as many of the young cleaning girls who had been in her employ could vouch. It was true the meadow where these events usually took place was under several inches of water and it would be many days before it had dried out sufficiently to allow such gatherings. The celebrations would mean posting extra guards, but if the ceremony were held in the morning, hopefully most of the guests would have left by the curfew. Orius probably stood to make a few coins out of the arrangement, which was why he was putting forward the proposal.

He turned to Orius, "Tell this man Selecia that my answer is yes on condition that the wedding is held in the morning, and that the guests who are not resident within the town vacate it by curfew, unless they have made prior arrangements for accommodation. And Orius, make arrangements for extra guards to be on duty in that area of the town during and after the ceremony."

Having received his instructions, Orius left Aurthora's quarters and went in search of Selecia to pass on the good news, and hopefully, to be suitably rewarded for his services.

It was a Druid ceremony and was held the following day. Aurthora had been on duty all night and was sleeping in his quarters, but had he known that the High Priest Zanton was to be in charge of the proceedings he might well have changed his duty rota. It was late morning when a loud banging on the door of his room woke him from a dream where he was in the hands of his beloved Katrina. "What is all this noise? What's happening?" shouted Aurthora as he quickly pulled on his breeches.

"Orius has sent me, Sire," called a voice from the other side of the door. "Your presence is needed urgently, there is a serious disturbance at the wedding ceremony."

A serious disturbance? thought Aurthora, as he quickly pulled on his loose woollen shirt and leather boots, drawing his gladius from its sheath as he opened the door. If there were to be fighting, the short sword would be an advantage in close combat.

"What is the nature of this disturbance?" he asked the young, wide-eyed Celt who was standing panting in the open doorway.

"It is the groom at the wedding, Sire, he is trying to fight everyone. He is wielding the Druids' great ceremonial two-handed sword. He threatens to behead anyone who approaches him," gasped the young man.

Aurthora leant down and picked up his rectangular shield, thought better of it, and placed it back on its rack: if he needed a shield there would be enough of them there for him to borrow one. "Keep up with me, Darius," Aurthora shouted to the young man as he jogged in the direction of the large stone building that had been allocated as the venue for the wedding ceremony. Darius was surprised that a man of such high rank as Aurthora should know his name. But Aurthora, on being appointed and placed in charge of one hundred soldiers, had with the help of Orius made a point of memorizing the names of all the men under him who had not journeyed with him from his father's estate, including a brief account of their history.

He knew that Darius was from the southern colonies of the island and was not a member of any of the tribes. His mother was Celtic and his father was a retired Roman soldier who had stayed when the legions departed. Darius had volunteered to join the northern tribes rather than to be enlisted into the loose-knit southern amalgamation that supported King Erion. The young soldier in his heavy combat armour was struggling to keep up with Aurthora as they came in sight of the large stone hall.

There were groups of wedding guests milling about outside the entrance. *They've probably vacated the building for fear of being injured,* surmised Aurthora, as he went in through the main door that led to a small room packed with his armed men. "Make way there, make way!" he shouted as he passed through a corridor of his men to enter the main hall.

Chapter Twelve

Confronting him in the middle of the room and standing on a large wooden table was a thickset, middle-aged man, holding above his head a great two-handed, double-edged Celtic battle sword. Below him, but out of reach of the great blade, were Orius and several guards, all in full battle dress. Standing on his own in the far corner of the room Aurthora noticed the High Priest Zanton watching the scene. Several of the guests were scattered around the room in small groups, well out of harm's way, while an older man was pleading with the groom to relinquish his weapon, but with enough sense to keep well out of striking distance of the long blade.

That must be the bride's father, Selecia, assumed Aurthora.

There was a wide staircase that led to another floor with a balcony, from where several people were watching the unfolding events in safety. Aurthora thought he recognised Myridyn amongst these figures but he couldn't be certain. He took in all this with one glance around the room. The man standing on the table was the only one who was any threat or creating any kind of danger.

Grabbing a shield from the nearest guard, he walked quickly up to the man on the table. The blow launched from the two-handed sword and directed to decapitate Aurthora was deflected by the shield that he raised above his head. He then smashed the handle of his gladius into the side of the man's knee. Even the groom's befuddled brain felt the pain as his knee bone cracked under the blow and collapsed under him, throwing him heavily, head first onto the solid table, and from there onto the floor. In the process he instinctively let go of the sword to grasp his damaged knee, the weapon clattering down onto the stone paving.

Aurthora bent to pick up the heavy sword, ignoring the man who was writhing in agony in the centre of the hall, and slowly walked to the far corner of the room to stand in front of Zanton.

A hushed silence fell as he raised the sword, held it poised for several seconds, and then proffered it to Zanton's shaking hands. "This belongs to you, Priest," he said in a loud, clear voice so that everyone in the hall could hear.

The accusation, though not spoken in as many words, was clear to everyone present: *I hold you responsible for this incident* was the message. Turning quickly Aurthora called to the guards who had remained rooted to the spot during all that had taken place, and pointing to the man still rocking and moaning in pain on the stone floor, said, "Take that man prisoner. Fasten him in chains until his punishment has been decided." The guards responded instantly, snapping out of their daze by the sharpness and authority in their commander's voice.

"And Orius," Aurthora continued, "see that the rest of the wedding guests are escorted out of the town, and send the men back to their duties." Then without a backward glance, he strode out of the hall and through the throng of guests and onlookers who had congregated at the entrance, jostling with one another to try and see what was happening. They quickly parted to form a corridor as one of the guards shouted, "Make way there for Aurthora Ambrosius, Commander of the town guard and protector of the Great King and the Celtic Round Council!"

Aurthora was already in the street outside the hall making his way back to the town's barracks when he suddenly stopped, changed his mind, and went back to the rear of the hall. He sent one of the guards with a message to Myridyn, asking to speak to him. This was arranged and they met at a quiet spot close to the hall.

"Myridyn! Greetings! When will the Celtic Council meet to pass sentence on this man, Longinus Caratacusi?" he asked.

Myridyn looked at Aurthora, a half smile playing on his lips as he replied, "The Council have already passed laws to cover this period of engagement against the Anglo-Saxons; every man is aware of these laws and the punishment for breaking them. When you accepted the position of Commander of the Town Guard, you also accepted that it would be your duty to enforce these laws, and carry out the appropriate sentence." Myridyn's answer left Aurthora icy cold; he had never contemplated that he would have to order the beheading of a fellow Celt. He watched as the old physician turned and made his way back into the building.

He looked at his hands; they were shaking, his knees felt as if they would collapse under his weight, and he could feel a cold sweat on his forehead. A thin trickle of blood was running down his face from his forehead, where a splinter of metal from the shield had cut his head just below the hairline. The onlookers would have seen the blood: things were not looking good at all for the groom. To have drawn steel was a serious offence, but to have drawn the blood of another Celt meant there was little hope under the existing law for this newly-married man.

The sound of hurrying iron-studded sandals behind him caused him to quickly turn, his gladius at the ready. It was Darius, the young soldier who had banged on his door earlier. He stopped, panting in front of Aurthora. "Orius has sent me to escort you to your quarters, Sire," the young man gasped, "and to stay on guard outside your door until I am relieved."

Aurthora smiled, *Orius is still looking after me just like a mother hen*, he thought as he turned and strode on, the young man dropping in step beside him as they negotiated the narrow streets of the busy town on their way to the barracks.

Aurthora went back to his bunk but could not sleep. The afternoon's events were too fresh in his mind. Zanton was involved somehow. The groom, now in chains, had drawn steel and also blood. The law was quite specific: the only sentence possible was death by beheading.

Since he was in charge of security within the town's walls, he was the one who would have to pass sentence and see that it was carried out. No one else could interfere. It would be an ignominious end for the groom; quite possibly he had not even consummated the marriage. *Yet perhaps spending a lifetime with that woman with such a loud, sharp tongue would be a much harsher sentence than a quick beheading*, he thought during his restless and fitful attempts to sleep.

Aurthora pondered his problem all through his following tour of duty. Once again Zanton was attempting to create disunity amongst the gathered army: arresting a man on his wedding day, a man who was now a member of a prominent Celtic family, then beheading him the following day, would not go down well with the families of either bride or groom, nor the members of their tribes and supporters. But if the sentence were not carried out it would indicate to all the gathered clans and warriors that favouritism had been shown to a high-ranking family, and this would discredit him along with the Great King and the Celtic Round Council in the eyes of the common soldier.

The time and place designated for the passing of sentence was the following morning at sunrise, outside the town's West Gate. Orius had mustered the full complement of the Town Guard, also called upon the services of Timus Calgacus, and the young Cimonda Gilberto, to bring all the troops they could spare, sensing that there could be severe unrest amongst the anticipated large gathering of warriors.

Two of the town's gates were closed and guarded; only the West Gate, which the prisoner would be led through, was open. Early that morning Aurthora passed through this gate closely followed by Orius and Darius. During the night a simple wooden platform had been erected at the side of the road outside the gate. The three-man-deep, heavily armed contingent, under the supervision of Timus Calgacus and Cimonda Gilberto, were struggling to keep the large, jostling, hostile crowd clear of this raised timber structure.

Standing on the battlements of the town, overlooking the proceedings, but out of sight of the ever-increasing mass of men, was Great King Erion in the company of the Celtic Round Council's senior advisors, Boro Sigurd, together with Albion Egilos, Neila Gilberto, and several other tribal leaders and high officials, including Selecia, the bride's father, with his brother, Arranz Cunobelin, the leader of the Dumnonii tribe. Standing alone in the background was Myridyn the Physician.

Below them in his armour strode Aurthora in front of two armed Celtic guards. As he leapt lightly onto the raised wooden platform, Orius moved to one corner of the structure and bade Darius to take up a position opposite him at the other side. Aurthora raised his hands for silence, and the large crowd, by now near the five thousand mark, slowly quietened.

The crowd was not in the best of moods: because of the severe storms most of its members had not had a hot meal for several days, and all of them were wearing damp or sodden clothes.

Aurthora did not speak until even the low murmuring had stopped and the silence became a deathly hush. "My friends!" he shouted, "you that are Celts and speak the Celtic language and are here to fight for your continued freedom and your way of life, also you of Roman origin who are amongst us and support Great King Erion, we are all here to see Celtic justice and its punishment." There was a low murmur from the crowd at his last sentence.

Aurthora waited until the voices had subsided, then continued. "We all know the law, it is quite straightforward: if a man is found fighting with another, the punishment is a flogging; if, within the boundaries of this town and its surrounding encampment, a man draws steel against another and blood is drawn, the penalty is death by beheading." There was another angry response from sections of the crowd at Aurthora's last sentence.

Aurthora turned and signalled towards the town gate where the prisoner, with his damaged leg in wooden splints and heavily strapped, obviously the work of Myridyn the Physician, appeared escorted by two guards who were practically carrying the injured man along.

Surrounding them were men in full battle attire, with polished chain mail and burnished leather, their rectangular shields forming an impregnable wall of steel. All in step and keeping perfect formation, they approached the wooden platform. The sight of the prisoner brought another bout of shouting from sections at the front of the crowd who had a better view, which was quickly picked up by the rear of the crowd as the message was passed on and they realised what was taking place.

The guards at the front of the mass of people were struggling to restrain them as those behind pushed forward. Aurthora raised his hands for quiet again, but this time it took a lot longer before the crowd had settled down, and still the occasional shout from the crowd could be heard as he prepared to pass sentence.

Orius, meanwhile, could sense the crowd was changing from a noisy gathering into an unruly mob; he had been in this situation on several occasions in the past when the Roman army had imposed severe sentences on those whom they called robbers, thieves, brigands and terrorists, whereas the occupied population saw them as freedom fighters.

There were several agitators amongst the front row of the crowd, Orius decided that if things turned nasty they would be the first to taste his steel. "I will announce my sentence for this prisoner," shouted Aurthora, above the noise of the crowd which slowly quietened and eventually stopped. "The law states no man shall draw steel against another in this encampment on pain of death." There was another great roar from the groom's supporters and members of his tribe. "But this man Longinus Caratacusi…" continued Aurthora, indicating the groom, who had been lifted onto the platform by the guards and was standing beside Aurthora with all his weight on one leg, and looking very sorry for himself; "… this man," repeated Aurthora, "was not fighting any other man, but was fighting the demons in his own head, the placing of these demons was not of his doing, and therefore I do not hold him responsible for his actions." Aurthora stopped so that what he had said could be passed back through the crowd; he then continued.

"My decision is…" Here Aurthora stopped until there was not a sound to be heard amongst the crowd as they all strained their ears for his next words. "… that he continue with his chosen partner, hopefully they will have many years of happy married life." Aurthora turned to the prisoner beside him, took a small dagger from his belt and sliced through the ropes that bound the man's wrists, then turning to the guard he shouted, "release the prisoner into the custody of his new wife!"

There was a deathly silence as the great mass of onlookers absorbed the implications of Aurthora's speech, and then a loud murmur as word of the sentence was passed round the vast crowd. It was common knowledge that Selecia had been trying for years to offload his nagging daughter with her high-pitched screams and short temper. What was more, the groom would be bedridden with his damaged knee and would not be able to distance himself from his new wife. Most of the crowd felt that the groom had in fact drawn the short straw, and his damaged knee was punishment enough for his escapade, after all, as Aurthora had said, his actions were not of his doing. There were several shouts of complaint from within the crowd by those who had come hoping to see a beheading, but the vast majority were happy with the decision and the logic behind it.

This was especially true of the groom's friends, the bride's family and the Dumnonii tribe, many of whom were present in the vast assembly. One joker in the crowd shouted in a clear voice, "The sentence is too severe! The man should be beheaded to save him from a life of torment." This brought a great deal of laughter from those around him, which helped to relieve the tension of the large gathering of men.

As Aurthora left the platform he was followed by Orius and Darius, the guards dropped in behind them as they marched through the gates of the town to a growing chant from the crowd of "Aurthora! Aurthora! Aurthora!"

The group of men on the town wall who had seen and heard what had gone on below them were very quiet. It was Boro Sigurd the senior official who spoke first, but to no one in particular. "We have just witnessed the work of a natural statesman. He has shown the wisdom of King Solomon, a king that these new Christians have in their scriptures. This young Aurthora Ambrosius could be a great leader of men and a salvation for the Celtic people."

As the group left the battlements on the town wall Myridyn, ever observant, noticed a strange expression on King Erion's face as the crowd continued to chant, "Aurthora! Aurthora!" In the past the chanting had always been for Great King Erion, Saviour of the Celtic Nation.

Aurthora left Orius to work out the changed rotas for the guards. Feeling mentally drained and physically exhausted, he returned to his quarters in the barracks. With Darius outside his door, he slumped on his bunk and was soon in a deep sleep, his mind at rest now that such a pressing problem had been resolved without bloodshed.

On waking later he felt much more mentally alert, after sluicing himself down with cold water in the nearby washhouse, he also felt physically refreshed. He noticed that Darius had been relieved and another, slightly older youth was now positioned outside his door.

It was while he was finishing off the leg of roast chicken and freshly baked bread with goat's cheese that had been left in his room (obviously the work of Emilia) that Orius called to make his usual daily report. "All went well, Aurthora," he said in his usual matter of fact tone. "The crowd dispersed amicably enough; they were all happy with the decision. You handled the situation in a most masterly fashion."

Praise from the lips of Orius is praise indeed, thought Aurthora to himself.

"I must congratulate you, too, Orius," said Aurthora, "the guard looked exceptionally smart, efficient and well disciplined. And they were excellently drilled! Those men are a credit to you."

"I thank you for your compliment, Aurthora. I only hope that when the time comes they can fight as well as they look. I have taught them all I know, the rest will be up to them," he replied seriously.

"I am sure they will not let us down. They are young, eager and have great confidence in their own ability; they know that their future and that of the Celtic nation is in their hands," commented Aurthora.

Shortly after, with their business concluded, Orius got up to leave. "Tell me Orius…" began Aurthora, "…Darius's father. Did you know him from your time spent in the legion?"

"Yes," replied Orius, as he stopped at the doorway. "He was in charge of the cohort of soldiers I was posted to when I first came to these islands of Britannica. Later he retired and married a Celtic woman. The boy Darius is the product of that union."

His question answered, Aurthora continued, "Orius, will you make enquiries in the town to see if there is anyone who can operate these baths? If so, employ them, and we will see if the men and ourselves can have the luxury of bathing in hot water." Orius smiled and nodded, then closed the door behind him.

A short while after Orius had left, Aurthora was preparing for his tour of duty when he had an unexpected visitor in the form of Myridyn the Physician. He offered Myridyn the stool while he perched himself on the edge of his bunk.

"I was with the Great King and some members the Celtic Round Council this morning," stated Myridyn. "We were on the town fortifications overlooking the West Gate. We were all most impressed with the way you handled a very delicate situation."

"I thank you for your compliment, Myridyn, it seemed to be the right decision to take," he replied, embarrassed at the compliment from the King's adviser.

"I treated Longinus Caratacusi, the groom. His injuries are painful but not serious: the knee bone is cracked but not broken and he will make a full recovery in time. Unfortunately, he'll be bedridden for a while and won't be able to escape his wife's terrible tongue," said Myridyn, smiling ruefully, and Aurthora could not help but smile with him.

"But now on to a more serious note," said Myridyn leaning forward on the small stool. "While I was treating Longinus Caratacusi he told me that one of Zanton's priests had offered him a potion to be taken in his cider. It was supposed to increase his virility on his wedding night. He has no recollection of anything that took place after taking it and certainly not the incident with the ceremonial sword."

"It was as I suspected," replied Aurthora. "Zanton was up to his old tricks again, trying to create disunity within the gathered tribes. But what can he hope to gain from this dangerous meddling?" he asked the old physician.

"Like the Celts, the Angles and Saxons have their own ancient gods," replied Myridyn. "Zanton may feel he would maintain his power if a Saxon or Angle king ruled the Kingdom of Elmet. They might not be as tolerant with the Christians as King Erion, at present it is the Christians who are the greatest threat to the Druids. An Anglo-Saxon alliance could potentially drive the Christians and all their followers out of the kingdom."

Aurthora was stunned by Myridyn's blunt speaking. "But if what you say is true, Zanton is committing acts of treason!" he exclaimed in a shocked voice.

"You and I know that, my friend," said Myridyn wearily, "but to prove it is another matter. Zanton has many followers and many powerful friends and allies. He is a clever and wily old fox, and to compromise him will be very difficult, nigh impossible, even. Incontrovertible evidence would be required in order to convince the King and the Celtic Round Council that the Druid High Priest Zanton is a traitor. And, I'm afraid, time is not on our side."

"And what of Petrov Joma and his pet wolf Victor Aberuso? What is their role in this conspiracy? They always seem to be around when Zanton is trying to cause disruption," added Aurthora.

Myridyn paused for a few moments, as if choosing his words carefully before replying. "I have not revealed these thoughts to any other living soul, Aurthora, but you are a true Celt and a loyal supporter of Great King Erion. His dream is to have a united Celtic federation to rule this island, to have representation on the Great Council from all sections of the country and the community, not only the privileged few such as the Royal Household, tribal chiefs, members of prominent noble families, large estate owners and the wealthy merchants. All these people enjoy the luxuries and benefits that are obtained through trading with other distant countries and civilisations. The Great King has a dream in which all the Celtic peoples in this kingdom, from all walks of life, will eventually benefit and share in all of these goods."

Aurthora felt very humbled and also very privileged that this wise old man should share his inner thoughts and secrets with him, and also the dreams of his King. After all, he was only a simple Commander of the Guard.

"But to answer your question, Aurthora," continued Myridyn. "If any fatality should befall the Great King, his distant cousin Petrov Joma, with the assistance of Zanton and the supporters they have in the Round Council, would lay claim to the throne and the Kingdom of Elmet; in the short term there would be no one strong enough to oppose them. Then, for a short-sighted gain, they would make a treaty with the Anglo-Saxon alliance. Never again would the Celts be as powerful or as organised as they are now, and never again would they be in such a strong position to defend their borders and way of life. If Zanton and his disciple Petrov Joma succeed, in the fullness of time the Celtic tribes will simply be swallowed up by the Anglo-Saxons."

Aurthora grew cold as the full impact of Myridyn's words sank in and he visualized a country run by the psychopathic Petrov Joma and his followers. He could think of only one thing he needed to know from Myridyn at that moment, his mind was already full with what the old physician had already disclosed. "Where are Petrov Joma and his men now, Myridyn?" he asked.

"They are camping several days' ride from here in a deserted village close to the western border until this storm with its heavy rain ceases and the tracks become accessible again. Then they are under instructions to continue to patrol the border," replied Myridyn.

Aurthora was amazed that Myridyn seemed to know everything that was happening within the town, the surrounding camp and the country as a whole.

"All that I have confided in you I tell you so that you will be more vigilant, Aurthora," continued Myridyn. "I and my assistant Disaylann will be away for a few days collecting herbs for my potions for I will require many during and after this coming battle. Katrina and Emilia will continue to stay at my house since there are no lodgings available anywhere in the town."

Myridyn had noticed that both Aurthora and Orius paid regular visits to the house when they were on duty in that area, and the old man knew that both were deeply in love with their respective women. His and Disaylann's absence would give both men some privacy with their loved ones. After all, only the Gods knew if either of them would survive the coming battle against the Anglo-Saxon army.

Myridyn rose to leave, thus indicating that the conversation had finished. Aurthora noticed that the physician looked weary of late, it seemed the old man was more stooped than usual. He was now using a staff to assist him, which he had not needed before.

He closed the door to his quarters after Myridyn departed. He had much to think about, and needed to consider how much of what he had been told he would divulge to Orius.

Still, it was good news that Myridyn would be away for several days; he and Orius would have the house to themselves when they next visited Katrina and Emilia.

Myridyn took several steps down the passage from Aurthora's quarters then stopped. *Oh well, it's of no consequence,* he thought to himself, *I can leave the soap Orius requested for the hot baths with Katrina or Emilia. No doubt in my absence either Orius or Aurthora – more likely both – will be visiting my house very shortly.*

As Aurthora had suggested, Orius had made enquiries within the town for someone who could operate the furnaces for the saunas and maintain the baths within the barracks. He had been directed to a small, wood-frame cottage just outside the town walls, quite near to West Gate and only a few minutes brisk walk from their quarters. As he approached the building he could see that the thatched roof was in a terrible state of repair, and that the wicker fence around the small garden had fallen down in places.

Chapter Thirteen

The old man who eventually answered the door to Orius's knocking was obviously slightly deaf, but truly delighted when Orius managed to make him understand that he was needed to operate the saunas again, and to clean and maintain the large, communal, hot spring baths.

As both men made their way through the town towards the building where the baths and washhouse were situated, the old man, Oengus by name, told Orius that he used to be the caretaker for the barracks when the Roman legion had occupied the town more than twenty years before. Orius remembered the legion bathhouses well, they were mostly of the same construction, with stone or wooden walls and floors, and great slabs of stone where the men who so desired, and as long as they had the money to pay for the service, could be massaged with scented oils after they had soaked in the hot mineral waters. Even though Orius had lived amongst the Celts for twenty years he still missed these hot baths and the small rooms alongside, where water was poured onto red-hot stones, cleansing the body with the vapours that rose as a result. He recalled how refreshed and revitalised one felt afterwards, and all of this had been available to every soldier in the Roman Army, no matter what rank or position they held.

The old caretaker Oengus had negotiated a good fee for his services, and if these soldiers were like the previous ones, he could make extra by providing the scented oils and women to massage the men, and, of course, further professional services if the men had the means to pay.

"Yes," said the old caretaker, as he gleefully informed his wife, "our fortunes have certainly changed. Yesterday I was scratching out a living helping anyone and everyone in the town market, at the beck and call of every trader or merchant, whereas today I am in permanent employment – with the possibility of earning a little extra besides. No! much better than that, *I* will become an employer. I will engage an assistant; I will employ my nephew, Gwion. He's young, strong, and not too bright. He can do all the hard work and lifting, but he's not sharp enough to learn about the furnaces. That way I keep my position, my authority and all the extras for as long as the barracks are occupied."

Feeling quite pleased with himself, he had a spring in his step he had not had for many a year as he went off to find his young nephew and tell his family how hard he had to negotiate in order to obtain such a good position for their son. And if he hurried he would arrive just before they started their main meal of the day, as the bearer of such good news he would no doubt be invited to join them as a privileged guest. Afterwards, he would find the merchants who used to employ him and negotiate with them for regular deliveries of the black stone that burnt, plus wood to fire the bath's furnaces. But he would strike such a hard bargain, he would make them cringe – yes! He would nail them to the floor! He liked that expression, it had a nice ring to it, that would be his revenge for all the years they had employed and cheated him, paying him a mere pittance in the process.

Aurthora finished his tour of duty shortly after dawn had broken and was making his way along the narrow streets near Myridyn's house, his mind full of their previous evening's conversation. *What would I do if I were Petrov Joma and wanted to assassinate the King?* speculated Aurthora. *First I would remove or weaken the security around the King, possibly by killing the commander of the security guards and creating some form of diversion. Then, during the ensuing confusion, I would make my assassination attempt on the King's life.* He was so deep in his own thoughts that he was startled when he was stopped by a shout of "Halt! Identify yourself!" two of his men emerged from the shadows. "It is I, Aurthora Ambrosius!" he quickly responded.

"Sorry sir!" replied the soldier who had issued the challenge, obviously embarrassed at not having recognised Aurthora in the half-light. The two guards quickly passed him and proceeded on their rounds. He was pleased. For the most part the men under his command had adapted well to guarding the town and its occupants, he hoped Orius was making progress with the hot baths as a reward to them for their dedication to what some might consider a very boring assignment.

His next few steps brought him to the gate of Myridyn's property, but when he saw the tall gate slightly ajar his heartbeat quickened. All the occupants of the house, as well as Orius and himself, had agreed to always close the gate securely behind them when they entered or left the property. He was undecided about what to do, and whether or not to call back the patrol. If there was a prowler in the garden, whoever it was would be forewarned and ready, but if there was no one he would look silly in front of his men. Quietly he drew his gladius, the short sword that would be ideal in a confined space, and slowly opened the gate.

Keeping to the shadows he entered the garden, where he stopped, sword at the ready, while his eyes adjusted to the dim light of the walled area. At first he could see nothing, but as his eyes adjusted he made out the dark shape of a crouching human form. He moved his head slowly from side to side, his eyes scouring the rest of the small garden. There appeared to be only one prowler.

Suddenly he slammed the heavy gate shut with a bang, making the dark form jump like a startled rabbit before it tried to move more deeply into the dark corner where it was attempting to hide. Aurthora, too, moved into the shadows, and in doing so must have trampled in the herb garden for he could smell the scents of rosemary, sage and mint rising from the crushed plants underfoot. Using his most authoritative tone he called out in the direction of the dark shadow: "Who are you and what is your business here?" There was no reply, only the thumping of his heart – which to him sounded like a beating drum – and the cooing of several pigeons from the cote, disturbed by his loud voice.

He tried again, this time louder. "Show yourself or risk feeling the sharpness of my pilum!" Even though he was not carrying the short throwing spear, he knew the figure in the shadows would not know this. There was an instant response and a scuffling sound from the shadowy figure in the corner. Aurthora braced himself for the expected charge, his short Roman sword pointing in the direction from which he anticipated the attack would come. By now the sweat was dripping from his forehead and he could feel the hairs on the back of his neck standing upright.

A frail figure emerged out of the shadows and into the half-light. Aurthora could see the man was shaking with fright. "It... It... is I, Lucius..." he stammered, still shaking. "I am a student of Myridyn the Physician, he asked me to feed and water the pigeons while he was away. I... I... was frightened by the guard patrol," continued the young man, "so I hid near the pigeon loft."

Aurthora relaxed, he recognised the young man's voice from their conversation on the journey to Buxonana. "You realise you're breaking the law to be out and about before the curfew is lifted?" he said gruffly to the trembling young figure standing in front of him. "If you'd been arrested, it would have meant days spent in the prison compound as punishment. I suggest you wait here until the curfew is lifted before you go wandering around the streets of the town. And the next time you come here, come in daylight. And keep this gate closed in future!"

Feeling he had rebuked the young trainee physician sufficiently, he turned towards the large oak front door of the ex-merchant's house.

"I have left the parcel of scented soap in the kitchen as requested, Sir," whispered Lucius as Aurthora turned the large iron key given to him by Katrina in the lock of the great door and slipped quietly into the house. While he made his way slowly down the dark passage, he thought to himself, *the fright must have unhinged young Lucius's brain. What do I know about scented soap?* At the end of the passage he stopped and listened: all was silent.

The slight disturbance in the garden had not woken anyone in the house. He gently opened the unlocked door, and quietly entered the bedroom Katrina occupied.

Several days later Aurthora and several of his men who were off-duty were relaxing at the barracks in the warm afternoon sun, idly watching several ox-drawn wagons of black stone being unloaded, and piles of chopped logs being stacked near the furnaces. As always, he was amazed by the weight these teams of oxen could pull. The work was being supervised by an old man who was shouting instructions to the wagon drivers. These in turn were then loudly repeated word for word by a much younger man standing at his side.

It was while this work was in progress that the court official, Boro Sigurd, appeared, accompanied by one of Aurthora's men who was acting as his escort. On seeing Aurthora he waved and directed his horse in his direction. Stopping several paces from Aurthora, he dismounted and gave the reins to his escort. "Greetings, Aurthora! I hope I find you and your men well," he said with a pleasant smile.

"Yes, Sire," replied Aurthora. "Now that the heavy rain has subsided, both my men and I are dry and well."

The court official placed his hand on Aurthora's shoulder, and as he spoke directed him away from the group of men. "There is a small service that requires your type of skills, Aurthora. The Great King and the inner circle of the Celtic Round Council would be extremely grateful to you if you and some of your men would be prepared to carry out a mission."

Aurthora was intrigued. He was finding the day-in, day-out, repetitive nature of guard duty rather boring. "I'm sure I would be interested if you told me what this mission was," he said to the still smiling official.

Boro Sigurd stopped and looked around. They were now far enough away from the group of men not to be overheard. "It is quite simple," he said, still smiling. "We wish you to escort several wagons filled with barrels of ale and loaves of bread and allow them to be captured by the Anglo-Saxons."

At Aurthora's look of amazement, Boro Sigurd's smile broadened.

"But you already have Petrov Joma and his men patrolling the borders to stop this kind of thing happening," he said.

"Yes, that is true," replied Boro Sigurd, "Petrov Joma is indeed patrolling the borders on the western side of the kingdom; however, you will be escorting these wagons to the eastern border, in other words, where the Anglo-Saxons are congregating in great numbers, and from where we think they will launch their army against us. The information I give you now is for your ears only: the ale in the barrels has been treated by Myridyn with a slow-acting poison, and the bread has been baked with fungus-infected wheat. The men you select to ride with you can be told this, but only when you have left Buxonana."

"You will put up some resistance before you retreat – just enough to make it look convincing. This is a dangerous mission, but if successful it will inflict many casualties on the Anglo-Saxon forces even before they go into battle."

Aurthora considered what the court official had told him. He knew, and Boro Sigurd also knew, that he would be unable to resist such a mission, it appealed too much to his spirit of adventure.

"Will I be allowed to choose my own men for this venture?" he asked, already making a mental list in his mind.

"Certainly!" replied Boro Sigurd instantly. "Then when do we leave?" said Aurthora eagerly.

He decided he would not take Orius. He knew his old tutor would be terribly disappointed, but he needed the experienced legionnaire here in the town to take over the duties of guard commander in his absence. He would take Roderick Tristan the master bowman and several of his men, also his friend Ethellro, who had just returned with a great herd of his large horses. He, too, would jump at the chance. Katrina, however, would not like the idea of both of them going on this mission, he pondered for many hours before asking Ethellro if he would join them, for he knew there could only be one answer. He would also take several men from his own town whom he knew he could rely on. Later, when he informed Orius of the mission, on the latter's insistence Aurthora decided to take Darius. All the men who did not possess one of the large horses were provided with one for this mission since they would then be able to easily outrun the small mounts used by the Anglo-Saxons.

Buxonana was a good two days' ride from the eastern border of the kingdom. The group of men quietly left the walled town the following morning as the first rays of light were beginning to show on the horizon. Arrangements had been made for them to join their wagons two hours' ride from the border, and for the first mile they followed Aurthora, walking their horses in order to make the least possible noise. He checked that the small cage carrying the pigeon was securely fastened to his saddle, then mounted his horse. At this signal, the rest of the men mounted their own animals and all set off at a steady pace towards the rising sun.

None of the men had been told the exact nature of the mission, it was only when they were well clear of the town and the encamped Celtic army that Aurthora stopped his horse allowing the men to gather around him. He then informed the curious group of the plan and what they hoped to achieve.

The group of horsemen maintained a good pace over the now dry ground. They were all quiet, deep in their own thoughts, but each one was determined to make a good account of himself when the time came. Later during the journey Ethellro called to the group, "Look!" and pointed upwards. Flying in large circles high in the clear sky was a large buzzard. "It's a good omen from the gods for this engagement with our enemy; we will strike with the speed of this great bird of prey." Aurthora smiled at the cheer that Ethellro's statement raised from the men.

Aurthora and his band camped that night in a small valley surrounded by thick woodland that would shield them from any prying eyes. A small stream provided water for the animals, but they did not light any fires or attempt to do any cooking. Aurthora had emphasised that stealth, secrecy and surprise were of the utmost importance if their mission was to have any chance of success.

After riding most of the night with only several hours of rest, by the following morning the mounted group of men made their way to the designated spot where the loaded wagons were waiting for them under the escort of men from the local Brigante tribe. With the arrival of Aurthora and his horsemen, and after the usual greetings, the Brigante escort departed, taking with them the wagon drivers who were replaced by Aurthora's men. Then the slow-moving wagons and the group of mounted men set off in the direction of the small Celtic outpost that was the supply wagons' purported destination.

This outpost was situated close to where reports had been received of groups of mounted Anglo-Saxons foraging in the surrounding countryside. Aurthora could feel the tension rise as they drew ever closer to the small, defended outpost; nevertheless, when the attack came it took Aurthora and his men by surprise. He expected Anglo-Saxon horsemen to be the first to make an appearance, but it was armed men on foot that sprang as if out of nowhere at both sides of the wagons and their escort.

The Anglo-Saxons had dug shallow trenches alongside the track, then lay in them while their companions covered them with loose soil and grass.

When the wagons pulled level, they jumped to their feet and attempted to attack the nearest mounted Celt. The sudden appearance of these screaming men spraying soil and grass everywhere frightened the large horses, which shied away from the advancing men, lashing out with their hooves in the process.

This panic reaction by the horses probably saved the lives of their riders, allowing them time to draw their swords and defend themselves. The first Saxon to reach one of the mounted Celts had his jaw broken and his chest caved in by the rear hooves of the startled horse.

Standing on the wagons, Roderick Tristan and his fellow long bowmen quickly picked off several of the Anglo-Saxon warriors, and the Celtic horsemen quickly dealt with several more. Aurthora's attacker took a blow to the neck from his sword, and fell to the ground to be trampled underfoot by Aurthora's horse. Having disposed of his opponent he had the chance to look around him: Ethellro had eliminated his attacker with the great Celtic battleaxe that had belonged to his father. Darius, sitting with one of the cart drivers, had reacted quickest of all. The attacking Angle had barely stood upright when the pilum Darius threw penetrated his flimsy shield and body armour and entered his heart, killing him instantly so that he fell backwards into the shallow hole he had just vacated.

Another young member of Aurthora's group was Cynfelin Facilus. His father had been in the Roman Thracian cavalry and, on his retirement, had moved to a small farm that was now within the kingdom of Elmet. He was a member of the large, mixed, Roman Celtic community from the south of the island. His father had obviously passed on his riding skills to his son, for Cynfelin was the first to regain control of his horse and rode down an Anglo-Saxon who was attempting to climb onto the rear of one of the wagons.

Seeing they had lost their advantage of surprise, the rest of the attackers scattered, running in the direction of a large group of mounted men who were bearing down on Aurthora and his small party. Shouting for the drivers to leave their wagons and mount their own horses, he indicated for his men to beat a hasty retreat, leaving the wagons as they had planned.

Aurthora was pleased with the results: all his men were mounted and riding clear, leaving great clouds of dust in the process. None of his soldiers were seriously injured, and the young men whom Orius had recommended had indeed proven themselves in their first encounter against the enemy. What was more, they had deposited their lethal cargo to the Anglo-Saxons in a truly convincing manner.

He was spinning his horse round and preparing to follow his fast-disappearing men when the horse stumbled over the inert body of one of the Saxons, going down on its knees, and in the process throwing him over its head and landing him heavily on the ground. He was badly dazed and winded by the fall his sword had landed yards away from him. By the time his head had cleared his horse had recovered; its rear end was fast disappearing in the dust cloud as it chased after its companions.

He had landed on the far side of one of the wagons, out of sight of the fast-approaching enemy horsemen, who would not have seen what happened, especially with all the dust that had been churned up during the skirmish. He realised that any attempt to flee on foot would be pointless, he would be run down within twenty paces.

Neither was fighting an alternative: he was by far outnumbered and would certainly be quickly overwhelmed and cut down. He did not even consider the alternative of surrendering. As he desperately looked about him he thought there was maybe one slim chance – if he was lucky and his gods were smiling on him that day. He quickly crawled under the nearest wagon, and placing his legs over the great wooden front axle and his shoulders over the rear one, he pulled the rest of his body up close to the underside of the rough, wooden plank floor. In this way he was hidden from view by the wagon's solid wooden wheels, except in the event of a thorough, close inspection of the underside of the wagon.

More dust was created by the arrival of the group of mounted Anglo-Saxon horsemen, who rode past the wagons as they chased after the group of mounted Celts. They were followed by foot soldiers who stopped, leaning on the sides of the wagon gasping for breath. After checking on their fallen comrades they loaded the dead onto the first wagon. Only one man was left alive – the one young Cynfelin had run down with his horse, but fortunately for Aurthora he was semi-conscious and not seen him crawl under the wagon.

There were whoops of joy from the soldiers as they opened one of the casks and discovered what it contained. The other mounted Saxons returned, having given up the chase against the much better mounted Celts, they quickly joined the foot soldiers in enjoying the contents of the tapped cask of ale.

As time passed, Aurthora became concerned about his hiding place. The soldiers had been drinking for some time to the occasional shout of *wassail!* as one of them would again dip his empty drinking horn into the large cask of ale. The dust had long since settled; it would only take one of them to look under the wagon and his hiding place would be instantly exposed. His men would have realised by now that something was seriously amiss, he feared that the headstrong young Celts would make a futile attempt to rescue him, even though they would be greatly outnumbered.

As the strong ale began to have an effect on the soldiers, they became quite boisterous, laughing and joking together. When one late arrival who had been acting as rearguard accidentally dropped his drinking horn, another kicked it under the wagon to great bouts of laughter from his companions. The horn landed just below the place where Aurthora lay straddled between the axles. He realised that as soon as the man attempted to retrieve it he would be discovered. It would take him several moments to release himself from his position, by which time the wagon would be surrounded and he would be caught like an animal in a cage.

As the man bent down to crawl under the wagon, he was pushed from behind by the boot of one of his companions, which led to another burst of drunken laughter. The man landed flat on his face just beneath Aurthora, raising a cloud of dust in the process, which fortunately for Aurthora partially blinded the man as he groped around for his drinking horn.

From his position above the man, he noticed that he had three middle fingers missing. The sight of the man's hand brought back memories of his last encounter with the Saxons many years ago.

(*He had been on the last pirate boat, the one nearest the shore. When the returning raiders had swum out in an attempt to reclaim their ships, he had fended off several of the crew with a pole, but one who seemed more determined than the others had managed to partially pull himself on board the drifting boat. Aurthora had swung his sword at the hand of this Saxon, the man had screamed and fallen back into the sea, leaving three of his fingers behind twitching on the wooden deck.*)

The now furious Saxon was scrambling on his hands and knees from under the wagon, banging his head on the wooden framework as he attempted to rise, which brought more laughter from the rest of the soldiers.

He eventually staggered to his feet, holding his bruised head with one hand and drawing his dagger with the other, angrily demanding that whoever had pushed him under the wagon should make himself known and be prepared to defend himself. It was then the leader of the group decided things were getting out of hand, shouting orders, and dispersed the men from around the wagon to the loud protests of the fingerless man who complained because he had been late arriving he had not had chance to savour much of the ale, which brought more bouts of laughter from the remaining Saxons. Some of them mounted the stationary wagons, and with the crack of whips and a lot of shouting they set the patient, slow-moving oxen in motion, heading in the direction, Aurthora assumed, of the main

Anglo-Saxon army encampment. The Saxon soldier with the three fingers missing rubbed the dust from his eyes, revived his drinking horn as the wagon slowly moved away, then ran to join several of his merry comrades who were sitting on the back of the wagon, their legs dangling over the rear.

The group of mounted Celts had easily outrun the pursuing Anglo-Saxon soldiers on their smaller horses, the latter quickly giving up the chase to go back to their comrades at the wagons, concerned that the foot soldiers would have the first choice of its contents and there would be little left for them. The Celts regrouped, and it was only then that they realised Aurthora's horse was with them but Aurthora himself was missing. Ethellro and the younger Celts were in favour of going straight back to fight the Anglo-Saxons and rescue their leader if he'd been captured.

It was Roderick who persuaded them not to try such a foolhardy attempt, convincing them that if Aurthora was being held by the Anglo-Saxons, as soon as the band of Celts appeared he would almost certainly be put to the sword. Instead they decided they would stay well hidden in the nearby woods while he, Roderick, would creep back to the group of noisy Anglo-Saxons to see what was happening.

He observed the soldiers and the wagons from several positions but could see no sign of his commander. If he'd been killed, they would certainly leave his body behind. Roderick waited until the wagons and the group of soldiers departed, then left the cover of the thick brush and began his search. When the rest of the Celts arrived on the scene he was still combing the surrounding area for any sign of Aurthora.

"They loaded their dead onto one wagon. Only one of the group that attacked us was left alive – an injured Saxon they put on the other wagon," Roderick told the men as they gathered around him, "Aurthora's not here, let's search further afield."

Despite discovering Aurthora's sword, found under loose soil, they remained baffled: there was still no trace of their leader and nowhere he could have hidden if he had been injured.

"We can only presume that Aurthora is with the wagons," said Roderick to the small group standing in a semicircle around him. "We will follow at a distance and keep out of sight, but we will be prepared to attack if and when we think it necessary." After a short discussion, the small group reluctantly accepted this as the most logical action to take.

While Roderick released the pigeon from its small wicker cage, the rest of the Celts mounted their horses, and taking Aurthora's riderless animal with them, they proceeded to follow the tracks left by the heavy wagons.

Aurthora's slow journey under the wagon was extremely painful; every jolt sent pains across his shoulders and thighs where his body rested across the wagon's axles. The dust created by the wagon wheels covered him in a fine powder, blocking his nostrils and forcing him to gasp for air through his mouth, which left him with a terrible thirst and an almost irresistible urge to sneeze. If he had he would almost certainly be heard, discovered, and killed.

The jolting of the wagon also caused the ale to spill from the wooden cask the Saxons had tapped, and it dripped through the rough wooden wagon floor all around and over him. The temptation to moisten his lips with this was beyond belief and became an unbearable torture for the duration of what seemed a never-ending journey. But he knew that although the slow-acting poison Myridyn had added to the ale would not take effect for a day or so, it would eventually prove fatal.

He heard the name of Eboracum mentioned several times by the men on the wagon, and presumed that this was their destination. It was an important, ex-Roman fortified town close to the border of Great King Erion's Kingdom of Elmet, now occupied by the Anglo-Saxon army.

Matters improved somewhat for Aurthora when the wagons came off the dirt track and joined a paved road; at least there was not as much dust created by the wagon wheels and the hooves of the oxen. The light was now beginning to fade and he was contemplating whether, when it became dark enough, he could disengage himself from the wagon axles and lower himself onto the ground, rolling to the side of the road between the wagon wheels, and out of the way of the mounted soldiers following behind. The group had set off quite cheerfully, laughing and joking, but the amount of ale they had consumed was taking its effect, and some of them were already dozing in their saddles. If he was quick, there was a good chance he would not be noticed.

He had already swung his legs clear of the rear axle and allowed them to drag on the cobbled road when the wagons stopped and orders were shouted to the group from the front of the wagons. It seemed they had reached the outskirts of the Anglo-Saxon camp and were being challenged by the perimeter guards. There was a brief exchange of words, which he was unable to understand, but it was clear that the group were known to the guards since the wagons slowly moved forward again, and he was forced to swung his legs back into their previous, painful position.

The road that the wagons were now travelling along was much higher than the land on either side, and he could see the hundreds of campfires of the encamped Anglo-Saxon army. The rumours in the Celtic camp were obviously true: this army certainly appeared to outnumber many times over the troops of the Celtic Alliance.

Chapter Fourteen

It was fortunate for Aurthora that it was now almost dark, since any sharp-eyed individual looking up at the wagons from the encampment would have seen him straddled under the wagon and immediately raised the alarm.

The mounted escort and the men on the wagons dropped away one by one as they passed their own section in the vast encampment, until there were only the drivers on the top of the wagons and himself below.

They eventually came to a stop in a large compound where the drivers unhitched the placid oxen and led them into a stockade, leaving them fodder and water. Leaving the animals contentedly feeding, they went off to their own particular part of the camp, presumably to get their evening meal.

All was very quiet. Aurthora strained his ears for any unusual sound, but all he could hear was the steady munching of the oxen. He was in the centre of the enemy camp, badly bruised, stiff and very sore, but at least he was still alive, and with luck he had the rest of the night to plan and, hopefully, make his escape.

The small band of Celts had followed the two wagons at a distance. On two occasions they had to ride quickly into the undergrowth and hide as groups of mounted Saxons rode up behind them, then passed on their way to their main encampment. From their hiding place they observed the perimeter guards stop the wagons and it was obvious that they themselves could proceed no further.

It was now dark so they decided they would make camp in a small wood they had passed further back along the trail. The pigeon that Roderick had released would have informed Myridyn and the inner circle of the Council that the plan had succeeded, but they would not be aware that Aurthora was missing.

Roderick and Ethellro decided they would stay in their present position that night and take turns watching the camp entrance. There had been no movement of men or wagons along the road since the two they had been following had entered the camp at dusk. At first light they would have to fall back and find a safer position than the small wood where they were presently hidden. There would be too great a risk of being discovered in the daylight hours. Once a safe place had been found they would send one of the young Celts on the fastest horse to inform Myridyn, who in turn would inform the Great King and Celtic Round Council of their present situation. Roderick and Ethellro had decided they would stay in the area as long as was necessary, or until they received orders to return.

As Aurthora slowly and painfully eased himself from under the wagon, he found that when he tried to stand his legs simply buckled under him. It took several minutes of stretching and massaging his calf muscles before he could walk, and even then only with jerky movements, as if his legs were not his own. He realised how fortunate he had been not to have attempted an escape earlier in the day; it would have been a foolhardy, suicidal attempt in his present condition, and would have inevitably ended in failure. Looking around he found he was in an area enclosed by a low, interwoven, waist-high willow fence. There were several more wagons besides the two he had arrived with, and several more pairs of oxen besides those that had pulled the two wagons. All were in the same small, fenced paddock.

All around him were the hundreds of campfires belonging to the vast army of men that had gathered at this point, he could see their shadowy figures as they moved about the camp by the light of the fires. He felt on the floor of the wagon for the sacks that had been used to dampen and cool the wooden casks of ale in order to prevent it from going sour in the strong summer sun.

He decided it would be too dangerous to walk all the way down the raised paved road the wagons had followed into the camp, even though it would be by far the quickest route. He would be too obvious, he would also be cast in silhouette by the many campfires alongside the road. But most important of all he could not risk being challenged by any patrolling guards. After a great deal of thought he made up his mind to use this road only until he entered the main area of the enemy camp; he would then take the risk of moving between the many fires and groups of men, making his way all the time towards the outskirts, and the guarded perimeter.

Wrapping one of the sacks around his shoulders, he went over to one of the wooden water buckets but it was empty; the second bucket had been knocked over by the oxen. In the third he found sufficient water to ease his burning throat and to partially quench his terrible thirst. The ox lying near the bucket chewing its cud watched him with large, dark, disinterested eyes. "My needs are greater than yours, my friend," he whispered to the great beast as he gulped the remains of the water from the bucket, patting the ox's rump.

He placed a bunch of sticks he found nearby over his shoulder and quietly left the safety of the small compound, ambling slowly down the paved road.

He soon reached the main area of the camp and left the road as planned. He had only travelled about twenty paces and was passing between two groups of men sitting around their fires, when a snarling, wolf-like animal lunged at him from out of the shadows, forcing him to throw himself backwards.

The great hunting hound stopped short of his prone body, held back by a thick metal chain fastened to the collar around its neck that had snapped taught. The dog was slavering at the mouth, showing great pointed teeth, and straining to reach Aurthora, who pushed himself away with his heels and elbows. The actions and noise of the great beast had set the rest of the pack baying and howling and straining at their leashes. A voice from one of the nearby campfires shouted, "Maro!" receiving no answer, shouted again much louder in Latin, "Maro! See what's wrong with those hounds." Maro replied from the other nearby campfire, "Yes, Maddoc! I will attend to it at once." Grumbling, he left the game of dice he was playing with a group of men, and strolled over to where the hounds were tethered.

Aurthora stood upright and replaced the old sack around his shoulders, hunching them up as much as possible and, stooping from the waist, began to retrieve his scattered sticks as Maro approached. "You stupid old fool!" he shouted at Aurthora. "Do you want to be eaten alive? Keep away from these dogs!" giving Aurthora a hefty kick that sent him sprawling.

Aurthora scrambled slowly to his feet, gathered his sticks and scurried off into the darkness. Maro went back to the hound. "Settle down Hadrian", he said to the great dog, scratching its huge black head beneath its ears. You're as aggressive as your father was before you! It's only an old man collecting wood for his fire." He returned to his game of dice.

Keeping to the darkest areas of shadow, expecting to be challenged at every step, Aurthora slowly made his way back in the direction of the camp entrance, passing groups of men heading towards the compound where the wagons he had arrived on had been left. Word about the latest acquisition – free ale for all and sundry – had quickly spread amongst the encamped army.

Slowly but steadily he progressed from one dark patch of shadow to the next, planning his route as he went along. His leg muscles had now fully recovered and he was walking normally, feeling more and more confident of not being challenged since there were many figures moving around the camp.

He was about two-thirds of the way across the large meadow, passing between two groups of men standing around their fires, when a noisy party of about twenty men began to emerge from a large tent ten or so paces away. For several seconds he had a clear view into the interior of the tent, which was lit by many oil lamps and candles. Then, as the last of the men left, the opening was closed behind them from the inside. The men were laughing and joking as they came towards him. It was clear to Aurthora that the occupant of the tent must be of some importance since it was the only tent that Aurthora had passed with armed guards posted outside its entrance. It was also obvious to him that the group of men were about to intersect his path.

To his right was a small group gathered around a fire that had an iron cauldron swinging just above the flames. Judging from the smell that drifted to where he was standing the cauldron contained some form of stew that several of the men were ladling onto their wooden platters. He changed direction, and with a sense of purpose walked up to the fire, placed his bundle of sticks to one side of the burning embers, took a wooden platter from several at the fireside, and ladled himself a helping of the cauldron's contents.

He nearly dropped his plate and the ladle into the fire when a man a few paces away from him turned and spoke to his nearby companion in the Celtic tongue. Aurthora stiffened in astonishment. Quickly regaining his composure, he turned, walked several paces away, and sat down out of the light of the burning logs. His actions did not appear to have attracted any attention at all. As soon as the large group of men had passed by he would continue to make his way through the camp. The strain was telling on him, for although it was not a warm night, his clothes were sticking to him; he was sweating so much it was dripping from his forehead and into his eyes. He wiped his brow with the sack and cautiously studied the men who were nearest the fire.

Their attire was similar to his own, the odd fragment of conversation he could hear was definitely in the Celtic tongue. His heart missed a beat and his body tensed as the large group of men from the tent turned and passed within a pace of where he was sitting.

They too stopped at the nearby fire and began helping themselves from the steaming cauldron before settling down to eat their food, several of them sitting close to him. Frightened in case they tried to open a conversation with him, he curled up on the ground, pulling the sack around him, and feigned sleep.

His mind was racing. How many of these Celtic traitors were there in the enemy camp? There must be a considerable force for them to be welcomed at the tent of someone of such importance. What Celtic tribe did they come from? Were they betraying their comrades for monetary gain, or were there more sinister, long term motives behind their actions? He listened intently to the conversation of the several men seated near him, and the more he heard, the more he could feel his anger rising.

The conversation was related to recent events and the reward they would share for the parts they had played. Apparently, this group had been patrolling the border and came across several Celtic families, their wagons loaded with their hastily gathered possessions and driving their small herds of goats and sheep before them. They were the occupants of a small hamlet and were fleeing the Anglo-Saxon forces that had occupied their land.

These men were bragging about how they had swept down on the unprotected families, cut down the menfolk, raped the women, bringing their captives back to the Anglo-Saxon encampment. They had sold the sheep, goats, wagons and their contents to the highest bidder, and sent the women and children off to be sold as slaves.

There was also mention in their conversation of the leader of this Anglo-Saxon army, the Saxon King Ælle, and his three sons, Raedwald, Aethelbert, and Aethelfrith. *If these members of the Saxon royal family are here,* thought Aurthora, then this is where the invaders will most probably launch their attack across the border against the Celtic Alliance and the Kingdom of Elmet. He watched through half-closed eyes as a man left the group near the fire and walked over to the three men nearest him. As he stood in front of them with his back to Aurthora, their conversation stopped. He began to speak to them in crude Celtic with a distinct Latin accent.

"You there! Your leader Petrov Joma, your future king of the Celts, is dividing the takings from the recent patrol. Go and get your share before it's all gone." The men jumped to their feet with a whoop of joy. "Thank you, Victor Aberuso!" shouted the last one as he followed his companions to the nearby fire where everyone seemed to be congregating.

As more wood was thrown onto the fire, no longer was Aurthora's figure partially hidden in the shadows, but well lit by the leaping flames. With his foot, Victor Aberuso roughly nudged the curled up body. "Wake up, Celt, if you want your share of the spoils," giving Aurthora another shove with his foot.

Aurthora tightened his grip on the handle of his short dagger strapped to his calf, and waited a moment before replying. "Yes, I thank you, in a moment- in a momen…" giving a muffled yawn from under the sack. He was praying that Victor Aberuso did not recognise his voice, or make him stand, for even if he did not recognise him with his hair matted and his face and clothes covered in a thick layer of dust, in the light of the now large fire one of the nearby group of Celts surely would. If this happened it would be pointless fleeing. He decided he would catch Victor Aberuso by surprise with his dagger, then charge the group around the fire, hoping to reach Petrov Joma and strike a fatal blow before being inevitably cut down himself. He could sense Victor Aberuso standing over him, waiting for some reaction.

Aurthora had tensed his body ready to spring when a shout came from one of the group around the fire. "Victor! Victor Aberuso! Come and join us. Petrov Joma is coming."

This took Victor Aberuso's attention away from the motionless form at his feet, and with a "You lazy Celt!" he moved away to join the chanting group of men around the fire, cursing as he went about how there were no longer any good fighting men left, he had met them all in the arena – these so-called hard fighting warriors, the Scoti from the island to the west of Britannia, the Picti from the far north, as well as Anglo-Saxon pirates – all had eventually succumbed to his sword.

Victor Aberuso's thoughts wandered to his last fight. Only one man had ever matched his skill, but since he had known this beforehand, he had taken precautions. It had been expensive, but well worthwhile to have this man's last meal before the contest drugged. Victor Aberuso proved he was not just any gladiator – he had an animal cunning and was always aware of the quality, or lack of it, in others. He knew that this Mattos was an exceptional fighter and might well have beaten him. Aberuso lived for the sound of the crowd cheering his name as they now cheered their leader Petrov Joma. The next time Victor Aberuso looked in the direction of the dozing Celt wrapped in a ragged sack, the figure had gone.

As soon as Victor Aberuso moved away from him towards the fire Aurthora had silently risen and slipped away into the shadows, quickly blending in with the other figures moving about the camp. He now had the vital information that Myridyn the Physician required in order to expose and challenge the instigators of the plot to remove King Erion and attempt to replace him with his scheming cousin Petrov Joma.

Aurthora stopped behind one of the few remaining trees on the encampment, going through the pretence of relieving himself against its large trunk, for the benefit of any casual onlooker. All the brush and smaller trees in the immediate area had been taken for the fires, but several large beech and elm trees with too wide a girth to be cut down had been left. Looking back, he could see by the light of the large fire that had now been built and was sending great clouds of sparks into the night sky, the band of more than a hundred renegade Celts carrying their leader Petrov Joma shoulder high around the burning bonfire. Even from where he stood he could hear their chanting drifting over the camp: "Petrov Joma! Petrov Joma!"

Taking his time to pass through the camp, he gathered together another bundle of short branches and twigs, and hoisted them onto his shoulder. Still keeping to the shadows and taking care to avoid any contact with other people, he was fortunate and went unchallenged. If anyone thought his garb was strange, they probably assumed he was one of the Celts with Petrov Joma, or another one of the many foreign mercenaries in the employ of King Ælle.

Eventually he reached the outer fringe of tents and shelters just as everyone was settling down for the night, except for occasional faint shouts of *wassail* coming from the direction of the beer wagon. From his position he could see that sentries were patrolling the perimeter of the camp. Beyond the sentries' route lay a good stretch of open ground where the brush and trees had been cut and carted away for firewood. Then the brushwood began again. It was quite possible a further ring of sentries might be stationed at this point.

He realised the problem he faced was that even if he avoided the sentries on the inner circle, as he crossed the open ground any sentry on the outer circle looking towards the camp would certainly see him, challenge him, and raise the alarm. For several hours he stayed well back from the inner perimeter but observed no movement on the far edge where the brush and scrub still grew. He timed the gap between the patrols, and calculated he would have just time enough to reach the far undergrowth before the patrolling guards on the inner circle met.

Hoping and praying that there were no guards on the far perimeter he waited while the two guards crossed and stopped to say a few words to each other, both looking longingly in the direction of the sounds of merrymaking that came drifting across the valley from the ox compound. They moved off once more on their patrol. Aurthora thought to himself that the two guards did not realise how lucky they were. *In several days' time they'll be cremating their comrades who are now enjoying themselves.* Taking several deep breaths, he waited.

As soon as the guards had moved out of earshot he rose and, crouching low, began to cross the exposed ground as quickly and quietly as he could. As he neared the far edge of the cleared ground he could make out the outline of the brush and scrub.

Since all was deathly quiet except for the distant noise of revelry, his own breathing and the sound he was making as he brushed through the long grass seemed deafening to him. A short distance ahead a dog fox cried out to its mate, but there was no outcry from behind him, which meant the guards had not yet reached their crossover point. All was going well.

He was about forty paces from the safety of the brush, when he saw the faint figure of a man outlined against the light of the moon. Without slowing, he grabbed his dagger from its sheath on his calf. The guard had heard Aurthora's movements through the long grass and turned. With a distance of fifteen paces between them, the man raised his spear in Aurthora's direction.

Now he'll shout for help and I'm done for, he thought as he tried to force his tired limbs to move faster. The shout of alarm died in the guard's throat. Instead, he fell full length in front of the advancing Aurthora, a slight gurgling sound issuing from his mouth, the shaft of a yard-long arrow projecting from his back.

Roderick Tristan the master bowman had been on watch. He had been observing the camp and the perimeter guard when he was quietly joined by Ethellro, who came to relieve him. Both had seen the dark shadow of a figure leave the camp between the patrolling guards. They attracted the attention of the guard on the outer perimeter by imitating the call of a dog fox, giving Aurthora just enough time to cover most of the open ground nearly reaching the scrub and safety. Roderick only had time to shoot one arrow from a distance of over fifty paces, in semi-darkness. "I compliment you on your skill, Roderick," gasped Aurthora as all three men grasped hands and Ethellro hugged him.

"You do not realise how fortunate you are, Aurthora," said Roderick. "If the guard had not stopped my arrow, you were directly in line behind him. But come, we must leave this place at once, there are other guards patrolling this section."

"Let's bring this Saxon with us," said Aurthora, still gasping for breath from his run, "it will give us extra time if they do not find his body. If we hide him well, they may think he deserted."

Ethellro easily lifted the dead guard onto his shoulder, and all three quietly made their way to where the rest of the group was still in hiding. Aurthora did not want the Saxons to know they had been spied upon, or Petrov Joma to suspect he had been seen in the enemy camp. For now he could not tell his companions all that had occurred, he held vital information and he needed to consult with Myridyn as soon as possible.

The rest of the group were overjoyed at Aurthora's safe return. Roderick had to reprimand them for making too much noise since sound carried a great distance on a still night. They listened intently to Aurthora as he told them his tale – deliberately omitting the episode concerning Petrov Joma and his followers. He was deeply moved by the loyalty his small band had shown in risking their lives by following the wagons then remaining in the vicinity.

The younger Celts wanted to attack the camp while the enemy slept, kill as many as possible as they rose bleary-eyed, while Roderick and his bowmen covered their retreat. Ethellro, too, had been much in favour of this escapade. It also appealed to Aurthora, if the Saxon king's tents had been nearer the perimeter, he might well have considered it worthwhile to remove some – if not all – of the Saxon royal family.

But it was more important for him to return with his information and report back all he had seen and heard to the King and the Celtic Round Council. "I understand how you feel," he said in response to the rest of the group's wish to do a swift hit-and-run on the enemy, "but during my time in their camp I discovered vital information that could be far more beneficial to our cause, especially if the Anglo-Saxon army is unaware we have been here. So I suggest we bury or hide the body of this Saxon and make our way back to our own part of the country as soon as possible. Dawn is not far away, I suggest we leave at the earliest and cover as much ground as possible before daylight.

The men reluctantly agreed to his wishes. He could have ordered them to do as he wished, but by discussion he would get their full support, and they would feel they had played a part in the decision. They buried the body of the guard with soil and stones then covered it with brushwood. It was unlikely that he would be discovered unless in the near future a thorough search was launched.

They left the small wood just as dawn was breaking, careful to leave no trace of their presence. At first they walked their horses in order to make the least possible noise until they were well clear of the enemy encampment and any marauding bands of Anglo-Saxons. They mounted their animals, and with a rider well in front and one well behind for security, they set off on the long ride to the Celtic camp and Great King Erion's headquarters.

By the time the group eventually reached Buxonana, Aurthora was so weary that Ethellro was riding alongside his friend, his brawny arm around him, supporting him in his saddle.

On their arrival the rest of the group went for some well-earned rest in their dormitories at the town's barracks. Before they parted company Aurthora reminded them all that they were still under oath to say nothing of the previous days' events, or of the mission they carried out, even though they might be sorely tempted to do so.

Aurthora and Ethellro continued to Myridyn's house, Ethellro leaving for the barracks soon after, embarrassed at his sister's great show of emotion at Aurthora's safe return, throwing her arms around him, crying, and kissing him passionately.

Myridyn was not at home, and neither was Disaylann, nor did Katrina know when they would return. Aurthora was so weary he simply wrapped himself in a blanket, left instructions with Katrina to wake him the moment Myridyn returned, then lay down on a couch, falling into a heavy sleep within seconds.

Katrina woke him after he'd been asleep for a good eight hours insisting that he must eat something from the platter of food she'd prepared before he left the house. He did so in haste, still deep in thought, he left the physician's property. He was still chewing on a leg of chicken as he made his way to the barracks; he was hoping to find Orius and receive his report and any gossip or information the old soldier had acquired in his absence. But Orius was away attending to his many duties, which had increased in Aurthora's absence. So instead, Aurthora inspected the barracks. Passing through them he came to the washhouses where he found the old stone baths full of steaming water with towels laid out at the side. He was staring in amazement at the clear hot water in the deep communal bath when he was approached by a wizened old man who was closely followed by a tall, rather vacant-looking youth.

"What are you doing here?" shouted the man. "These baths are for the personal use of the Town Guard based in these barracks, under the direct instructions of Aurthora Ambrosius, Commander of the Town Guard and Protector of Great King Erion. They are *not* for vagrants, so be off before I call the guards." Aurthora had never seen the old man or youth before and could only assume that this was the old caretaker that Orius had mentioned.

"My friend," he replied, looking down on the old man, "you have done a splendid job in restoring these baths and it will give me great pleasure to put them to the test." He stripped off his torn, sweat-stained and dust-ridden clothes and walked down the steps into the waist-high hot water of the large bath. He had never felt anything more pleasurable or relaxing as his tired, aching limbs sank into the hot water.

Chapter Fifteen

The old caretaker realised by the man's actions that he must be somebody in authority, even though he looked like one of the many beggars who frequented the town, so he and his nephew slipped quietly away to continue their chores. Leaving Aurthora soaking in the hot bath for quite a while, using the scented soap and sponges to wash away the grime and dirt of the last few days. When he came up the steps from the bath, the youth appeared with a loose gown made of soft woven wool, which Aurthora wrapped around his body while the youth indicated that he was to follow him to a side chamber.

On entering, the heat hit him like the opening of a baker's oven. There were slabs of stone on which to recline while the youth poured water onto other stones, creating great clouds of hot white vapour.

He then took the robe and Aurthora lay naked on the stone slabs, sweating profusely but totally relaxed.

Every so often the youth would enter and poor more water onto the stones, creating more steam. Aurthora's thoughts drifted to the fortunate soldiers of the old Roman armies who all benefited and enjoyed the pleasure of these facilities in their barracks, when they returned from a long and arduous campaign or tour of duty. He dozed in the hot, humid atmosphere until he was awakened by the young man shaking his shoulder and beckoning him once more to follow.

The boy seated Aurthora on a stone bench then proceeded to dowse him in several buckets of cold water. Aurthora was startled and could not help letting out a cry at the unexpected shock. The youth smiled at his reaction, then proceeded to dry him with one of the thick woollen towels. Next, he was directed to lie on one of the stone slabs. He reluctantly obliged and the youth began to rub his body down with warm, sweet smelling oil. Aurthora was quite tense at first, but the youth was obviously a gifted masseur and his deft fingers relaxed the tired muscles in his body and he eventually slipped into a relaxed doze. Dreaming he was sitting by a river on a warm summer's evening, watching the trout jumping for insects, his beloved Katrina by his side, as the sun set over the distant tree tops. What a wonderfully peaceful scene!

This pleasant dream was disturbed by the sudden noisy appearance of Orius, in his iron-studded sandals. He went to rise but Orius came towards him, bidding him to remain lying on the stone couch. They grasped each other's wrists in a warm salute and Orius told the youth to carry on massaging Aurthora's lean body, while he sat on a stone seat opposite.

Orius knew the mission had been accomplished by the return of the pigeon, but was not aware of any details. "I am glad to see your safe return, Aurthora," he said.

Unable to keep the sense of relief from showing in his voice, Aurthora replied with a smile for his old friend and tutor. "It is good to be back Orius. But you have obviously been busy while I've been away hunting" – this last word chosen for the benefit of the young masseur, who may have been a little slow, but was certainly not deaf.

"All this luxury that you and the Town Guard have been enjoying in my absence!" he joked.

"This is what a legionnaire in the Roman army came to take for granted; there is nothing finer to lift a man's mental and physical sense of wellbeing after several hard and dusty days' marching, or a little foray to put down a rebel disturbance, than a long soak in a tub of hot water," Orius replied smiling.

Aurthora dismissed the boy, and began to tell Orius in detail about the success of the group's mission, but without mentioning the Saxons or Angles, so that if the youth was listening, it would have sounded like a hunting adventure being discussed between two friends.

Orius listened intently. He understood when Aurthora mentioned campfires as far as the eye could see, but sat bolt upright when he said he'd seen two 'old friends': one with a scarred face, the other his Roman 'lap dog', together in the camp of many fires.

Orius knew exactly what Aurthora meant: Petrov Joma and Victor Aberuso, along with their followers, were traitors. The thought that immediately flashed through Orius's mind was that now he did not need an excuse to kill Victor Aberuso on sight. His second thought, which he spoke aloud to Aurthora was: "If these men think the way they do, how many supporters do they have in our camp?" Aurthora simply opened his hands, and with an emphatic shrug said, "I don't know."

"I will increase the guard around the King's dwelling at once," said Orius, and got up to leave. "Orius!" shouted Aurthora after the retreating figure. Orius stopped in the doorway and turned. "My group of companions should be awake by now. Find them and send them here to soak in these hot baths, they deserve this small pleasure for their loyalty." The old legionnaire raised his hand in acknowledgment and continued along the passage across the parade ground towards the soldiers' dormitories.

Orius had a lot on his mind. He had grown very close to Emilia, Katrina's handmaiden. Over the years he'd been with many women: during his time in the legion women had been brought to the barracks to satisfy the men's desire. It was an accepted practice the officers had always turned a blind eye. After all, they did the same. He also visited the brothels that could be found in any occupied town, but he'd never felt about a woman the way he did about Emilia. They both had so much in common. It was the first time Orius had discussed his future with anyone, all his needs had previously been taken care of as a member of Prassat Ambrosius's household. But now he found he was discussing Emilia's future together with his own: how after the coming battle he would retire from his present position and they would open a *mansio*. Not the ordinary type of lodging house but one of quality where excellent food would be served.

They would only cater for the more wealthy clients: merchants, government officials, members of the King's Court and the country's ruling families. He told Emilia about the hot baths, how he had come to an arrangement with the caretaker. He would arrange things so that the soldiers used the hot baths and tubs in the morning, leaving the bathhouse and sauna free in the afternoon for private clients. Word would soon pass around the nobility, traders and merchants, and when they came to visit the baths, he and Emilia would be there to provide the accommodation for these wealthy clients.

But first things first! He had to get Aurthora's travelling companions out of their bunks into the baths and away, before his private clients arrived later that afternoon, as he'd arranged with the caretaker.

The caretaker's nephew was a rather dim-witted young man: if he was told to stoke the fires he either built them too high or let them sink too low. He also made a poor job of cleaning the tubs and the sluices, they all had to be done a second time. But when it came to massaging, he was a natural. Orius had never known anyone like him for relaxing tight, bunched muscles and relieving tension in the spine. The boy had long deft fingers that probed and worked the tension in the body to the extremities of the limbs, and from there, away. Orius knew from past experience that a good masseur was essential for a successful and profitable sauna and baths, and in Gwion they had an excellent one. It seemed he was quite happy to work for his keep and a few coins given to him by his uncle, which he could take to his family.

Orius roused the men as instructed and, promising them an experience they would never forget, herded them like a mother hen towards the bathhouse and sauna. By the time he arrived with the bleary-eyed group, Aurthora had already left. With the help of the caretaker and Gwion, Orius quickly had the soldiers stripped and soaking in the hot baths; soon they were whooping with joy as they splashed about in the waist-deep hot water. As promised, they had never experienced anything like it before.

Aurthora smiled as he left the barracks; he could hear the shouts of joy and laughter coming from the direction of the bathhouse. He still had not seen Myridyn, the importance of what he had seen and heard while he was in the enemy camp needed to be discussed with the old physician before he reported to the Round Council. But Myridyn was not at home and left no message with either Katrina or Emilia. Neither was Disaylann anywhere to be found.

He told Katrina he would complete his tour of guard duty and call back at the dwelling later that evening, by which time Myridyn would hopefully have returned. The hot baths, sauna and massage with warm scented oils had removed the soreness and stiffness from the battering he received from being under the wagon so he now felt totally fresh and relaxed. Even Katrina noticed and remarked on how sweet he smelt. As he went on his rounds checking the guards at their posts, they all made the same comment: nothing unusual to report.

True to his word, Orius increased the patrols and the guards around and inside the town walls. It was dark when Aurthora finished his tour of duty and handed over to Mallus Calvus, another Roman ex-legionnaire and a friend of Orius. This man had been in charge of the Thracian cavalry attached to the Roman legion, and taken the opportunity to desert after the pack of hounds had left the camp to track Orius and his two companions. Orius had vouched for this man when Aurthora promoted him, and he had no reason to doubt his friend's word.

It was with a jaunty step that he made his way back to Myridyn's house. Not a soul was about since the curfew was still in force, the narrow cobbled streets were quite dark. As he approached the house he saw there was still a lantern burning in Katrina's room. *Perhaps she's expecting me?* he thought happily to himself, *but what's this? That fool of a student Lucius has left the gate unclosed yet again!* he noted with irritation as he pushed the gate wide. "Lucius!" he shouted at the dark shadow near the pigeon cote.

He was about to reprimand the young man when a sixth sense warned him of danger: the movements he saw were not those of a timid youth. He sensed rather than saw the blade in the hand of the man lunging towards him, blessing the gods for the attention he had received that day – for without the hot baths, the sauna, and the skills of Gwion the young masseur, he would not have been supple enough to sidestep the dagger that was aimed at his stomach.

The blade cut through his tunic and sliced along the thick leather breastplate that covered his chest and midriff. The impetus of the man's thrust took him past Aurthora, who crashed the hard palm of his hand against the man's ear and head as he passed. He heard the man wince in pain as he stumbled slightly, but he recovered quickly turned to face Aurthora again, who in the meantime had drawn his own dagger from its sheath on his calf. There was nowhere for the man to go, Aurthora stood between him and the gate the garden walls were too high and could only be climbed with difficulty. He could feel the adrenalin pumping through his veins, this man was an assassin? This was a struggle for life or death, no quarter could be asked or given.

The man made another desperate lunge with his dagger. Again Aurthora sidestepped, slashing at the man's throat but only succeeding in cutting his face from chin to temple, forcing him to reel back heavily against the oak door. The assailant realised he was coming off second best in this engagement: the wound was now pumping out blood which he could feel soaking into his woollen shirt, while his head was still ringing from the blow to his ear, which also seemed to have affected his vision.

As the man leant heavily against the doorframe desperately pondering what his next move would be, the door suddenly opened slightly, and there was Katrina carrying an oil lantern, the light of which fell for a brief second on the pale face of the man. Realising that the open door not only offered the man an avenue of escape, but also opened the possibility of injury to Katrina and the other residents of the house. Aurthora moved away from the gate towards Katrina and the open door. Seizing his opportunity to depart from this uneven fight, the man made a dash for the opening, scurrying as fast as he could into the street and away into the darkness, followed by Katrina's terrified scream.

Katrina had been expecting Aurthora, and opened the door on hearing the sounds outside. Instead she found a stranger leaning against the doorframe, a long dagger in his hand, with his face covered in blood. Her scream as the stranger dashed through the open gate preceded her fainting.

The next thing she remembered was being comforted by the man she loved. "Don't worry, Katrina," whispered Aurthora as he pulled her closer to him, "you're safe now, the assassin has gone." Katrina let herself relax in his arms. She could still smell the scented oils from his visit to the baths earlier that day. He in turn breathed in the fragrance of the sweet-scented soap Katrina used as he nuzzled his face in her hair. Holding each other close, time seemed to be of no importance, it merely slipped away as they enjoyed each other's tight embrace.

It was Aurthora who eventually broke the spell. "Katrina! Has Myridyn returned?" he asked as he looked into her eyes at her beautiful face, which he could never imagine growing tired of gazing at. Her reply, however, brought him back down to earth: the old man was still missing. It was unusual for him to be away for so long, especially as the time to fight the Anglo-Saxons was drawing ever closer. The man he disturbed in the garden might just have been an opportunistic thief. Far more worrying, and the most likely, he could well have been a hired assassin.

He decided that for Katrina and Emilia's safety he would stay the night. In the morning he would instruct Orius to place two permanent guards at the house. If the man was an assassin then someone had informed the enemy of Myridyn's great value as an advisor to the Great King and the Celtic Round Council, if that was the case Myridyn's life was compromised.

The following morning he was up at dawn. Although he found it difficult to leave Katrina's bed there were too many unanswered questions occupying his thoughts. He began by searching the garden to see if his assailant had left any clues to his identity, but there was nothing besides a bed of flattened herbs to mark the previous night's encounter.

It was while he was there that Myridyn's young apprentice arrived to feed and water the pigeons. "Lucius! Do you know the whereabouts of your master?" he asked.

"No, Sire. He told me he would be away for a while collecting herbs and I was to attend to the pigeons in his absence."

Aurthora left the garden and hurried to the barracks to find Orius. He needed to inform him about the previous night's incident, and have him post guards at the physician's house.

When he arrived Orius was on the parade ground shouting commands to members of the town guards who were not on patrol. He stopped and watched as Orius put them through their drill, all the soldiers carrying the rectangular metal shield that was not dissimilar in design from that of the Roman Army. Armed with the short gladius, each man in the front row placed his shield alongside that of the next man to create a wall of steel.

This was a set piece of Roman infantry defence. The second row carried their shields above their heads, thus protecting themselves and the men in front of them from airborne missiles. In their right hand they carried a pilum, a short throwing spear, which allowed them to reach over their comrade's left shoulder and use the spear in a stabbing motion. This was a Greek method of fighting; Myridyn had suggested to King Erion both these proven methods be combined and practised; his suggestion had been accepted.

On Erion's orders the Celtic warriors had been using this method in their training since the King first formed the Federation. In this way any advancing enemy infantry was first met with a shower of the short throwing spears from the front row. These heavy spears had a long steel shaft that easily passed through the enemy's shield, if it did not penetrate the infantry light body armour, it still dragged the man's shield down, making it awkward to wield and of little use to him. The second wave of spears came from the second row of soldiers, and a third wave again from the first row. The Roman infantry had perfected this method and it was ideal against opponents attacking in mass.

He watched the troops as they practised their training; only time would tell whether or not the untested young Celtic soldiers would have the discipline of the ex-Roman legionnaires who were training them. The soldiers were sweating profusely when Orius eventually called a halt, Aurthora went over to join him. He quickly explained what had happened the previous night, and voiced his concern for the old physician's welfare. Orius immediately ordered two of the soldiers from the parade ground to go to Myridyn's house and stay there until they were relieved.

He also called over Darius, and brushing aside Aurthora's objections, ordered the young Celt to reassume his duties as personal bodyguard. "Believe me," he said, facing his ex-pupil, "if your Great King and Myridyn the Physician are targets for an assassin, I can assure you that you are also on that list." Aurthora was moved by the concern for his welfare that showed on his old tutor's face, and ceased making any further objections.

Both were still talking battle tactics and the best methods to deploy the heavily armed troops, when one of the soldiers sent to guard Myridyn's house returned to say that the old physician had arrived and was requesting Aurthora's presence as soon as it was convenient.

Aurthora immediately took his leave of Orius and, accompanied by Darius and the guard, returned to the physician's house. As he entered he left the two guards and Darius outside, sampling fresh scones dotted with chips of hazelnut and ginger, and covered with a thin layer of recently made goat's cheese, which Emilia had brought out for the men.

Myridyn was alone in his workshop the old man greeted him warmly. "It is good to see you returned safely, "he said, grasping both of his friend's shoulders with his thin outstretched arms. Aurthora was surprised at the strength in the physician's grip considering his condition: he was still using a staff to assist him and he shuffled his feet when he walked. "The pigeon returned, so I knew the mission had been successful, but I also knew there had been problems, which caused me great concern," continued the old man. He indicated with his staff for Aurthora to sit down on a low stool while he sat down on a well-padded chair, supporting his elbows on the high armrests. Myridyn allowed Aurthora to tell his story without interruption, including the part about the intruder in the garden. It was only then that he fired several questions at the young man seated before him.

"Did you actually see Petrov Joma?"

"Yes!" replied Aurthora.

"Did you personally see the Saxon King or any of his three sons?"

"No!"

"Can you estimate how many of Petrov Joma's followers there were in the camp?"

"I'd say about one hundred."

"They left early the following morning," continued Myridyn.

"Ah! What a pity they did not stay to enjoy the presents we left them!" said Aurthora, wondering how Myridyn was able to know so much.

"Yes! More's the pity," agreed Myridyn. "I will discuss with King Erion what you saw in the enemy camp, which only confirms our suspicions. I do not think he will inform the Round Council at this stage, we do not want any of the conspirators going to ground at present. However, it would be good for the morale of our troops if a successful attack was launched on the enemy's camp – just a hit and run – don't you think?" suggested the old physician with a twinkle in his eye.

"And who would you choose to lead such an attack?" inquired Aurthora, already certain of the answer.

"Well, it would have to be someone who knows the position of the camp and the lie of the land in order for the attack to inflict the maximum amount of damage in the shortest possible time. Preferably someone who has already been in the enemy camp, wouldn't you say?" Both men laughed simultaneously.

"I will organise it straight away," said Aurthora, grasping the old man's hand in a warm handshake before leaving the room. Later, he spent some time with Katrina and, before he left accompanied by Darius, he told her that sadly it would not be possible for them to see each other for several days.

He knew he needed to move quickly and organise his men if the group were to set off during the quiet hours of darkness. He had decided that the raiding party would travel by night, and rest hidden during the following day. They would then travel the remaining distance to the enemy camp the following night. He planned to be in position to attack the enemy camp at dawn. He found Orius talking to Oengus, the old caretaker of the baths.

Orius dismissed the old man as he saw Aurthora approaching.

"We have a mission to plan, Orius," said Aurthora in a low voice as he drew close, quickly passing on the details he'd discussed with Myridyn. They decided that Aurthora would take three-quarters of his men, selecting those who were the best horsemen, including Ethellro. In addition, Roderick Tristan and twenty-five of his bowmen would mean about one hundred men in all would be involved in the raid. To cover the shortfall in men to police the town and carry out the duties of the depleted town guard, Aurthora made contact with Timus Calgacus and Cimonda Gilberto and arranged for them and their men to make themselves available. He realised there could be problems regarding who would be in charge as the young Celts would not take kindly to being under the authority of Orius. But during his discussion with his old tutor Aurthora had emphasised the need not to ruffle the young chieftains' feathers, to request, rather than order or demand. This would be very hard to swallow for the old legionnaire, but promised Aurthora he would do his utmost to comply with his wishes. Aurthora also asked the two young Celtic chieftains to be tolerant of the old soldier and his manner as it would only be for several days.

None of the men selected by Aurthora were to be told the details of the mission until they were well clear of the camp. All would be riding the large horses and travelling light, leaving their heavy armour behind. He calculated that in the event of any pursuit, the Anglo-Saxon mounts would find it difficult to catch the Celtic raiding party's much larger and far superior animals.

So as not to arouse suspicion, the well-armed band left the town in small groups well after dusk, rendezvousing at a prearranged point several leagues from the Celtic army encampment. Tension spread among the men as Aurthora told them of his plan and what was expected of them. All the men who had taken part in the previous expedition were once again part of this group, Aurthora deployed them evenly among the rest of the men since they were already familiar with the route. They placed a scout at about six hundred paces in front of the main group and one at the same distance behind them to guard the rear. He did not anticipate any problems since the Anglo-Saxons disliked travelling at night in what was for them a strange part of the country.

Led by Aurthora, the mounted group travelled a large part of the distance on the old, paved Roman road, making excellent time, then moved across country following a lightly defined track that was well lit by the full moon. Travelling in single file, the men were under orders not to talk to one another, as sound travelled great distances at night. The horses' hooves made little noise on the hard-packed soil, and as dawn approached they moved into the thickest of the nearby woods to wait. No fires were lit, the men rested and groomed their horses during the day. As night once again fell, they continued the rest of their journey.

At a few miles' distance from the outskirts of the enemy camp, they dismounted, fastened the leather covers they had brought for their horses' hooves, and began to walk alongside their mounts, one hand on their muzzles the other guiding their animals as they silently made their way to the small wood they had used as cover during the episode several nights before.

Roderick Tristan, acting as a front scout, came to report to Aurthora that most of the wood had been cut down, possibly for cooking fires in the nearby camp. The system of sentries in force was the same, and no one had disturbed the shallow grave of the buried Saxon guard in what remained of the wood.

Tristan then slipped away with several of his bowmen to deal with the guards, a short time later one of the bowmen returned to tell Aurthora that the sentries had been silently dealt with, it was now clear for the horsemen to advance. Still walking his horse he led the rest of his men as quietly as possible to the edge of the now unguarded Anglo-Saxon encampment. Dawn was just breaking as he looked down onto the vast array of shelters and small tents.

The low-lying areas of the camp were covered in a layer of mist, thickened by the still smouldering embers of a number of large fires. "*So*", thought Aurthora, "*that's why the wood was cut down; it was to provide fuel for these funeral pyres. The poisoned ale and bread have obviously taken their toll.*"

He mounted his horse and signalled to his men to do the same. Each horseman had three of the short throwing spears, plus a sword that was longer, thinner and lighter than the usual issue; this lethal weapon was held in a sheath fastened to their saddle. The men were under strict instructions that there was to be no shouting of tribal battle cries as they advanced.

Chapter Sixteen

The line of mounted troops moved forward at a trot. Aurthora, Ethellro, Darius, Longinus Facilus, the young Roman Celt who had excelled in the previous encounter, and several other hand-picked men of the party moved ahead at a faster pace than the main body of mounted Celts: their target was deeper within the Anglo-Saxon camp.

Aurthora and his small party were several hundred paces from their target when the screams from behind them told him that the main body of mounted warriors had entered the encampment. The Celts were slowly walking their horses up to the shelters and small tents and throwing their short iron spears through the fabric or the bracken and heather covers, piercing the sleeping soldiers where they slept. The screaming was unabated when Aurthora and his small band emerged from the mist twenty or so paces from the two large tents that accommodated the Saxon King Ælle and his three sons.

The two guards at the tent entrance had heard the screams of their comrades, but could not see what was happening because of the low mist. Suddenly from out of this grey cloud appeared Aurthora and his band. The two guards collapsed, clutching the short iron spears that had easily penetrated their body armour, as they fell to the ground a partly dressed figure came out of the tent, alerted by their screams from the valley below.

On seeing the group of strange horsemen bearing down on him he turned to re-enter the tent. Before Aurthora, who was nearest, could reach him, an arrow flashed past his shoulder following the path of the retreating man.

As Aurthora leapt off his horse and threw the reins to Ethellro, he noticed young Cynfelin Facilus was already fitting another arrow to his short bow, while the rest of the mounted men were throwing their short spears into the nearby large tent. Three short steps and he burst through the opening of the tent, expecting to be confronted by an armed Saxon or Angle, but there was no one, only the body of the partly dressed Saxon spread-eagled on the ground with an arrow projecting from between his shoulder blades.

He quickly scanned around the tent but did not immediately see what he was looking for – which was what he had glimpsed through the open tent flap several nights before, lit by oil lamps and candles. A pile of animal skins lay over what looked like a stool or a chair, and on pulling them aside Aurthora let out a shout of glee as he exposed two chests.

By this point the screams of the wounded and dying had woken the whole camp, and several of the mounted Celts were now using their swords to ride down and slash the Anglo-Saxons as bleary-eyed they rushed from their tents and shelters. Ethellro had passed the reins of both horses to Darius and rushed into the tent moments after his commander. "We will have to go now, Aurthora", he gasped, "they are beginning to regroup and organise themselves".

"I see you have tested your father's battleaxe, Ethellro", said Aurthora, indicating Ethellro's bloodstained axe.

"Yes! The Saxon skulls are not very thick", laughed Ethellro, and watched puzzled as Aurthora tore down four large drapes from the side of the tent and spread them on the floor.

Both men turned as there came a ripping, slashing sound from behind Ethellro, and the side of the tent was cut from the outside with the blade of a two-handed battle sword. Bursting through the gap came a large Saxon, the owner of this awesome weapon.

Aurthora shouted a warning to Ethellro, but he was already spinning around, his great axe forming a wide arc as he directed the double-edged blade in the direction of the Saxon's chest. But the Saxon was obviously no novice, he deflected the axe away with the blade of his double-handed sword and moved threateningly into the centre of the tent facing Ethellro.

Aurthora seized his chance and grabbing the corner of the drape that was lying on the floor, he yanked it sharply with all his strength, causing the tall Saxon who had one foot on the drape to stumble and spin around as, at the same time, Ethellro's second swing of the axe caught him and sent him crashing to the floor of the tent with a broken and mangled back.

Aurthora then grabbed one of the large chests, emptying the contents in roughly equal piles on the four drapes. There was a gasp from Ethellro as the gold and silver coins cascaded onto the centre of the drapes. "We will see how long their mercenaries stay with their Anglo-Saxon masters without being paid," shouted Aurthora as he pulled the four corners of the drape together and fastened it tight with its cord. He quickly did the same with the other three. He then fastened them together in pairs so they would lie over his horse's saddle.

While Ethellro took the four drapes filled with coins to the horsemen outside, Aurthora untied a stout rope from around his waist, which he then fastened around the remaining chest. Taking the loose end, he went outside and mounted his horse, fastening the rope around the horn of his battle saddle.

The rest of the Celts, who had made their way through the camp, slashing and cutting the enemy as they stumbled from their shelters, now joined Aurthora at the two large tents. Facing them were groups of armed Anglo-Saxons merging together and increasing by the second as they realised where their enemy had congregated. It would only be a matter of minutes before they felt they had sufficient numbers to charge the isolated group of mounted men. Indeed, a ring of Anglo-Saxon armed warriors was now forming around Aurthora and the rest of his group. In addition, the Anglo-Saxons had formed a line of men five deep at the point where the Celts had entered the enemy camp. As Aurthora moved his mount forward, taking up the slack of the rope fastened to the chest, two Saxon archers ran from between the two large tents.

Cynfelin Facilus turned completely round in his saddle while his horse was cantering forward, stopping one of the Saxon archers with a shaft in the chest fired from his short bow. His father had been in the greatly feared Roman Thracian cavalry and passed on his skills to his son.

The second Saxon bowman drew back his bow, aiming for the group of tightly packed moving horsemen. As he did so the rope snapped taut, and the iron bound chest that Aurthora's horse was pulling hit the archer, knocking the man sideways, sending his arrow over the heads of the mounted Celts and into the line of Anglo-Saxon warriors.

The Celts were now gathering speed, shouting their war cries as they drove their large battle horses forward. It was now daylight and Aurthora could see some of his warriors had painted their faces and arms with blue woad in the old Celtic tradition when going into battle. They headed their mounts straight towards the densely packed lines of Anglo-Saxons, with hundreds more enemy warriors giving chase from behind, the situation was looking decidedly grim for Aurthora and his small band.

While the enemy faced the charging Celts on their powerful horses, Roderick and his twenty-five bowmen were unnoticed as they left the cover of the tall grass in which they had been lying and moved nearer to the edge of the encampment. Taking their yard-long arrows from their sheaths, they stuck them in the ground in front of them. On a signal from Roderick the bowmen began to fire their arrows as fast as they could into the unprotected rear of the packed Anglo-Saxon warriors, quickly forming a corridor of dead and injured soldiers for the galloping Celtic horsemen to pass through.

At that moment the large chest that Aurthora was pulling burst open from the force of being dragged and bounced over the hard stony ground, spilling its contents of gold and silver coins in every direction. Most of the Anglo-Saxon soldiers who were chasing the mounted Celts stopped in their headlong rush and instead began to scramble in the grass and dirt for this unexpected windfall of treasure.

On seeing that the booty he was dragging behind him was lost, Aurthora released the rope and followed the rest of the Celts galloping through the gap created by Roderick and his archers, trampling over the dead and dying soldiers on the ground in the process, some of whom had two or even three arrows projecting from their mangled bodies. Several of the Anglo-Saxon warriors still bravely tried to stop the horsemen, but they were simply ridden down or knocked sideways by the Celts' heavy horses.

Ethellro, riding beside Aurthora, swung his great axe as a Saxon soldier tried to slash at him with his sword. The axe hit the man's shield cutting straight through the wood and metal and slicing off the man's hand. The axe remained stuck in the shield for a few seconds more, dragging the man along before it came free and dropped the man to the ground where he was trampled under the following horses' hooves. A lone Saxon drove his spear at Aurthora's midriff, there was a clang of metal as the spear point entered the sack of gold and silver over Aurthora's horse's neck, then the sudden jolt lifted the Anglo-Saxon off the ground and Aurthora slashed at him with his sword as he passed him by.

The bulk of the Anglo-Saxons on either side of the safe corridor were too busy trying to protect themselves from the deadly fusillade of arrows directed by Roderick and his bowmen from their elevated position at the edge of the encampment to try and interfere with the passage of the large body of mounted men.

The Celts rode up the slight embankment out of the enemy camp while their bowmen continued to send their deadly volleys of well-placed arrows as a deterrent to any would-be pursuers. Aurthora and Ethellro were the last to reach the top of the embankment, at which Roderick and his bowmen left their positions and ran after their fellow Celts to where their own horses were tethered in the small wood.

Aurthora stopped his horse and looked back at the carnage and disarray his group had left behind them in such a short space of time; his men had reacted well throughout the skirmish and he felt immensely proud of them. The Anglo-Saxons had managed to raise some mounted men in the hope of chasing the group, but they were being hampered by the soldiers searching the grass and soil for the silver and gold coins that had been scattered by the bursting treasure chest.

Indeed many of the Saxon horsemen that had grouped together began to dismount and join in the treasure hunt. The gap created by the Celtic archers in the Anglo-Saxon ranks had been closed, and they were now slowly moving forward in the direction of Aurthora, gaining confidence with their ever-increasing numbers.

Behind them Aurthora could see that several groups of the enemy were taking out their frustration on the inert bodies of those of his men who had the misfortune of being unhorsed during the gallop. Hundreds of armed Anglo-Saxons were now running from the rest of the camp to where the action had taken place in support of their comrades.

"We must leave in haste now, Aurthora," shouted Ethellro, ducking to avoid a hastily fired arrow from the advancing enemy.

"You are right my friend," he replied. "This day they have learnt a painful lesson – that it does not pay to send assassins into our camp." Feeling a great sense of achievement and purpose, Aurthora took one more glance at the chaos below him then both men turned, lying flat over the necks of their mounts, galloped after the fast disappearing group of their companions. The pigeon Roderick had just released circled above them several times; then, having found its bearings, it swiftly flew off in the same direction they were heading.

After an hour's hard riding it was obvious that the Anglo-Saxons had not mounted a concentrated pursuit, so posting mounted guards in both directions, Aurthora called a halt at a small stream to count the casualties and attend to the wounded.

It was during this ride that Ethellro casually mentioned to Aurthora that as head of the family since his father's death, he had been approached by Timus Calgacus, who asked permission to court his sister Katrina. Ethellro had politely informed the young Celt that his sister had a mind of her own and would not be influenced by her brother, that she was already seeing Aurthora Ambrosius and seemed quite happy to be doing so. Nonetheless, he would inform her of the proposal.

Aurthora smiled to himself as Ethellro told him the story, for even though it was the Celtic custom to first approach the head of the household, in the case of such a strong-willed young woman as Katrina, it would have been better to ask her first as he himself had done. And given the strength of the feelings he and Katrina shared for one another, he did not consider Timus Calgacus, pleasant though he was, to be a rival for her affections.

Before they left the town of Buxonana, Myridyn the Physician had given each horseman a package which contained a small container of blue fluid to be poured over wounds received in battle. There was also a small jar of honey to be placed on strips of the silver birch bark, and strands of fibre from the stinging nettle with which to bind the bark over the wounds. The men set about treating their own and each other's wounds. Most were minor and superficial, mainly cuts to the thighs and lower part of the body, and some to the chest and shoulders of their horses. They had lost five comrades in the enemy encampment, and two of the young Celts received deep wounds from which Aurthora and his men could not stem the bleeding.

"I am concerned about the condition of Cassivelaunus and Bernicia Deiva," said Aurthora to Ethellro as both stood stripped to the waist in the stream, splashing the cold water over their face and bodies.

"Yes, they have both lost a lot of blood," replied Ethellro, "Bernicia's face is as white as the driven snow, and Cassivelaunus's body as cold as winter. The jogging of the horse is keeping the wounds open, they are bleeding to death."

Aurthora pondered over Ethellro's statement. His friend was right, for the badly wounded soldiers to continue on their horses was certain death, whereas if they remained where they were a wagon could be sent for them. However, there was then the danger they might be discovered by the marauding enemy patrols, that also would mean certain death.

He was also concerned that when Petrov Joma learned of the attack on the Anglo-Saxon camp it might force his hand against Great King Erion. He wanted to be there with his men at the town to counter any such move, so time was not in their favour. He splashed water over his face with his cupped hands and turned his face to the heavens allowing the cool stream of water to run from his face over his body. He opened his eyes and looked above him into the clear blue sky.

There floating high above in great circles was a buzzard. *That bird is a good omen for me*, thought Aurthora as he donned his jerkin. His thoughts were interrupted by the hasty arrival of the mounted guard who had been sent on ahead. He pulled up his panting horse with a jerk in front of Ethellro and Aurthora, and pointing behind him he told them quickly, "There is a wagon coming down the track with about twelve mounted horsemen as escort." Aurthora's men had been sitting or standing around in small, relaxed groups, but at this news they immediately became tense and alert, looking to Aurthora for their orders.

"Roderick! Take half your archers and hide in the scrub at the side of the track. Tell your men to select their targets but only to release their arrows on my signal. Ethellro, take twelve of my guards and join the archers, be prepared to rush the escort on my command.

The rest of you men take your horses back down the track. Stop anyone from passing you. As the men rushed to carry out his orders Aurthora moved into the shade of a stunted mountain oak, and the large group of Celts moved back down the track, away from the approaching wagon. The two badly injured solders were gently carried into the shelter of a small clump of bushes by several of their comrades, before they joined the archers in hiding.

Chapter Seventeen

Orius completed his rounds checking the positions of the guards in the town. His last call before handing over to Timus Calgacus was to the house of Myridyn the Physician. The guard in the narrow side street was outside the front of the property; the second guard opened the garden gate from the inside when Orius knocked. Both these men were members of Aurthora's company of soldiers left in the town. Orius had every faith in their loyalty; he knew they would give their life without question if required.

He lifted and dropped the large iron doorknocker, its deep boom resounding throughout the house. The door was opened by Lucius, Myridyn's young student. Orius entered and made his way to the kitchen where he knew he would find Emilia. As he passed the entrance to a reception room, the sound of laughter caused him to glance in as he passed. Timus Calgacus was standing opposite Katrina with a goblet in his hand, whatever Timus Calgacus said had caused a peal of laughter from Katrina. Orius carried on to the kitchen, thinking on the way: *You are treading on thin ice Timus; laughing and joking alone in a room with a betrothed woman.*

He found Emilia in the kitchen, her hands covered in flour. She came towards him and kissed him, then indicated with her eyes towards the reception room. Orius merely shrugged his shoulders. "What are you preparing Emilia?" he inquired.

"I'm making dough for bread, and preparing peas and beans for the evening meal," she replied. "It will only be a simple soup but you're welcome to join us."

Orius weighed up what he had to do later that day; he knew that the caretaker had several important clients due for the baths, sauna and massage, and he would need to keep the baths clear of any of the guards who were off duty. Fortunately, many of the men who had permission and access to the baths were away with Aurthora. As Orius was debating whether or not to take up Emilia's offer he heard Timus Calgacus' voice in the hallway, taking leave of Katrina. Then Disaylann came into the kitchen and indicated that Orius's presence was required and he followed Disaylann to the old physician's workshop.

"Ah Orius! How good to see you," exclaimed Myridyn, grasping Orius's hand and leading him to a stool. Orius made himself comfortable while Myridyn sat down heavily in a high-backed chair facing him.

"We have received a message from Aurthora and his party, their mission has been successful." Myridyn lifted his hand to stifle the shout of glee that Orius was about to utter. "However, the message indicated that they had sustained several casualties," continued Myridyn. "The message was in code, which does not allow for naming names."

Orius looked at Myridyn, expecting the old man to continue. Myridyn read Orius's thoughts; he knew they were the same as his own. "I do not know if Aurthora is one of the casualties," finished Myridyn.

"When do you expect them to return?" inquired Orius, doing his best to hide the emotion in his voice. "If the injured have only minor wounds and they can still travel, I expect them back at dawn tomorrow; if the injuries are severe and their progress is hampered, then during the following day, or even the following night. But," continued Myridyn, "they will send their fastest rider to inform us of the situation in advance. All being well, he should arrive sometime after midday."

Orius was now on his feet pacing the small room. "Should we not send riders to escort them, in the event of the Anglo-Saxons pursuing them?" He exclaimed, stopping in front of the physician. "I would have thought that if they wanted assistance they would have requested it in their message," replied Myridyn. "But what I have done is to send one of my best students with a small mounted escort to meet them when they reach the paved road. He will attend to their injuries, which will give them some degree of comfort until they reach Buxonana, and then, if necessary, they can be placed in the hospital."

"Yes! You are right," answered Orius feeling more relieved.

Myridyn slowly rose from his chair with the aid of his staff. "I would like you to take the message to the Great King informing him that you have received word that the raid was a success. I believe he's visiting the town barracks accompanied by some of the Celtic Round Council, but at the moment this message is for his ears alone," said Myridyn as he showed Orius to the door of his workshop.

Orius looked at the old man. He seemed to have aged tremendously since they had first met. "I will leave at once," he said, and left the room, saying a quick goodbye to Emilia who had now been joined by Katrina. For the moment he decided not to divulge any of the information about the raid to the two women, he would wait until he had more information about Aurthora's wellbeing.

On entering the parade ground Orius was challenged at the gateway by two guards whom he recognised as members of the Coritani tribe, as he made his way to the bathhouse, there were several more guards from the Coritani tribe stationed outside the entrance to the hot baths. Orius approached them and they stayed where they were blocking the entrance to the building. "I am Orius Tomase, Commander of the Town Guard in the absence of Aurthora Ambrosius," he said to the nearest man, looking him in the eyes. Orius did not recognise any of the guards and they obviously did not recognise him. "If you will wait here for a moment, I will send for someone who can vouch for your position," replied the guard whom Orius had addressed; he turned and went into the baths disappearing into the misty vapours. Orius paced up and down in front of the entrance, frustrated, but also relieved that the soldiers were performing their duty well.

It was several minutes before Timus Calgacus appeared at the entrance, naked except for a thick woollen towel wrapped around his waist, and with water dripping from the rest of his body. *Our paths have crossed again*, thought Orius, who was struck by the amount of hair on the muscular frame of the young Celt. It was thickly matted on his chest and midriff, over his shoulders and back, on his forearms, and covered what could be seen of his legs below the towel.

"Salve, Orius!" Timus said in greeting, then turning to the guard assured him, "Yes I can vouch for this man, you may let him enter. He is, as he says, the acting Commander of the Town Guard." Orius walked past the two guards and joined Timus. Both men went into the building, enveloped by the clouds of warm vapour rising from the hot water of the large communal baths.

"I am sorry you were stopped at the entrance, Orius," said Timus, "but my men did not recognise you and they were simply following my orders."

"You need not apologise, Timus," replied Orius, "I was, in fact, quite impressed." And indeed this was true. For even though Orius had been wearing his full Commander of the Guard attire, the guards had not been over-awed and had behaved correctly.

It was known that many ex-Roman legionnaires were acting as mercenaries in the pay of the Anglo-Saxon army. It had been emphasised to the guards to be particularly vigilant, especially after the discovery of the would-be assassin in Myridyn's garden.

"Have you come to bathe in the waters, Orius?" asked Timus.

"No," replied Orius, "much as I would like to. I am here on official business. I have an urgent message for King Erion, and I would be obliged if you would direct me to his presence."

"You will find the King in that chamber," said Timus, indicating the massage room.

"I thank you Timus," said Orius; he waited while the young Celt made his way back to the hot baths before he entered the small chamber.

Great King Erion lay on his stomach on a towel placed over a large stone slab, his face looking towards the entrance to the room, his eyes watching Orius as he entered. Orius noticed a sheathed sword was leaning against the stone slab within the king's reach. Busy massaging warm oil into the King's shoulders was Gwion, the old caretaker's nephew, who glanced up as Orius entered, recognised him, and continued his nimble manipulation of the King's shoulder muscles.

"The message I bring from Myridyn, Great King, is that they were successful, but there were several casualties." The caretaker's young nephew would not know what the message was about, to the King the few words meant a great deal.

He raised himself up on his elbows, and replied, "The day of reckoning for our enemy is getting ever nearer. As a nation we will never be as well prepared as we are now. You obviously do not know who the casualties are otherwise you would have named them, I too share your thoughts my friend. Most of the members of the Celtic Round Council are either in the hot baths or the sauna. I will announce the good news to them later and it will be all over town and the surrounding encampment by nightfall. Our forces will have a victory to celebrate."

By now Orius's eyes had adjusted to the dimness of the the chamber; as the King was talking to him, his eyes settled on a birthmark on the King's left shoulder. He had seen the same mark many times over the last twenty years: Aurthora Ambrosius, whom he had taught as a boy, watched over and seen grow into a young man, had an identical mark on his very same shoulder.

"If further information is forthcoming on this subject I will inform you at once," said Orius, still transfixed by the mark on the Celtic King's shoulder. He left the chamber and made his way out of the building and onto the barrack square, the bright sunlight blinding him for a moment. He did not even notice the warmth of the summer sun on his face, for his mind was in turmoil at the conclusion it eventually reached.

Chapter Eighteen

Aurthora stood in the shade of the stunted mountain oak, his brown leather jerkin and breeches blending in well with the dappled sunlight that filtered through the branches. The sound of the creaking wheels of the wagon could be heard long before it came slowly into view around the bend. It had been an overstatement to call it a wagon: it was actually a two-wheeled cart pulled by a mule, which was guided by a soldier sitting on the side of the cart. It was loaded with several pieces of rustic furniture, several crates of noisy fowl, several sacks of what was possibly wheat or barley, two sacks of what were either turnips or swedes, and one crate contained several loudly squealing piglets.

Being pulled along at the rear of the cart were two youths, their wrists fastened together with a short length of rope between them and the slowly moving cart. Riding behind them on their small horses were twelve mounted warriors laughing and joking amongst themselves, little realising the imminent danger they were riding towards. It was only as they came nearer that Aurthora realised they were speaking the Celtic language and were not Anglo-Saxon soldiers but Celts, obviously some of the followers of the renegade Petrov Joma.

The cart was only ten paces from Aurthora when he left the cover of the oak tree, and in four paces he was standing in the centre of the track blocking the path of the cart. The mule came to a sudden stop as this strange figure appeared as if from nowhere in front of him. The jolt as the cart halted suddenly woke the dozing driver, who looked up startled at the sight of this lone figure in front of his mule.

Two of the mounted renegade Celts rode from the rear of the cart to see what the delay was, but reined their horses up sharply, level with the mule, as they too saw Aurthora. Trying desperately to control the anger he felt rising within him he shouted in a clear voice that carried to the mounted men at the rear of the cart. "You Celts who have betrayed your culture and sold your brothers into slavery, who have killed and maimed your own people for the gold and silver coins of an enemy, you will now see justice done. Prepare to meet your maker." With his last words he lifted his hand in a signal and at the same time raced towards the horsemen and the cart driver.

Only two of the ten horsemen at the rear of the cart managed to draw their swords before they were struck by several arrows apiece, tumbling them from their mounts and onto the hard ground where their twitching bodies landed with a dull thud; the other two tried to turn their horses to flee, but were blocked by the loose mounts of their fallen comrades. Within seconds they were dragged from their horses by the Celts led by Ethellro, who had rushed from their cover and, before the renegades had the opportunity to use their weapons, they were quickly overpowered and put to the sword.

One of the horsemen in front of Aurthora raised his axe as Aurthora raced forward, but a well-directed arrow from Roderick penetrated the man's body under his raised armpit and entered his heart. The mounted Celt dropped his battleaxe, a glazed look appeared in his eyes and he fell backwards as his horse reared away from the advancing Aurthora. A second enemy Celt drove his heels into his animal's flank, spurring it forward, brushing past Aurthora and galloping off down the track in the direction where Aurthora's main body of men were waiting.

Aurthora watched as the horseman turned round and waved his sword in defiance, thinking he had escaped the ambush. "Little do you know my renegade friend," he said to himself under his breath, "your escape will be short-lived." Then he turned to face the driver of the cart.

The man held a spear the length of his body and was using it to jab in Aurthora's direction, keeping him from getting close, and preventing him from using his sword. The rest of the Celts, having disposed of the remaining renegades, had formed a circle around their commander and the driver, uncertain whether or not to intervene.

Cynfelin Facilus drew his bow and shouted to Aurthora, "let me finish him, Sire, he is but the scum of this earth," but Aurthora waved down the bow of the young Roman Briton, he wanted his opponent alive to bear witness against the actions of Petrov Joma when he delivered him to the Great King and Celtic Round Council in the High Town of Buxonana.

The two men moved slowly in the circle of onlookers. Aurthora could smell the sweat of the driver, who constantly kept the point of the spear directed at his stomach, jabbing it occasionally in his direction all the time looking nervously at the grim-faced men that surrounded him, yet still managing to keep Aurthora at a safe distance. If Aurthora jabbed with his sword, the driver retaliated with a lunge with his spear, but this time Aurthora was ready.

With a quick change of footwork he pushed the spear to one side, spun around towards the driver, rolling down the spear with his back and bringing the hilt of his sword in a broad arc to crash it against the side of the driver's skull. The side panels of the light metal helmet the driver was wearing were no protection against the force of the blow directed by Aurthora. The driver collapsed against the wheel of the cart, his spear dropping from his hands. A cheer went up from the circled group of Celts; at the same time the main force of Aurthora's men came down the track with the lifeless body of the mounted renegade strapped across his horse, which looked like a pony in comparison to the size of their mounts.

"Release the two young men," instructed Aurthora indicating the two youths who were still fastened to the cart, and had watched the proceedings in amazement, "and fasten this renegade in their place," indicating the driver who was beginning to regain consciousness.

By now all the Celts had surrounded Aurthora as he proceeded to question the two young men.

"You have nothing to fear now my young friends," he said to them as they looked uncertainly at the heavily armed men surrounding them. Summoning his courage, one of the youths slowly began to speak: "My father and mother and my brother were all leaving our small farm to travel to the sanctuary of Buxonana where we heard the Great King was forming an army to fight the invaders. These men came towards us as friends, or so we thought. They were Celts like ourselves, they spoke our language, they said they had been sent to escort us. My father put down his sword and we put away our bows; that is when they set upon us.

"They cut down our father without mercy, and when our mother went to his aid they cut her down also. They beat us to the ground then fastened us to the cart and dragged us along until we struggled to our feet. We have been travelling for a day and a night, dragged behind our own mule and cart filled with our family belongings. They talked of the high price they would receive for us when we were sold as slaves. I think that is why they spared our lives." There were angry exclamations from the group of Celts surrounding Aurthora, as the young man finished his story.

"Take the dead renegades and fasten them on their horses, we will take them back with us," ordered Aurthora through gritted teeth. "Keep this one alive and he will bear witness to their savage deeds," he said, pointing to the driver fastened to the cart.

"Make room on the cart for our two injured comrades and let us continue on our way to Buxonana." The men hurried to carry out Aurthora's orders, turning the cart around and finding comfortable positions for the two badly injured young Celtic soldiers amongst the sacks of cereal. They were all eager to continue their journey and deliver their injured friends and comrades back to Buxonana and the encampment as quickly as possible, also to spread word of their successful escapade. Aurthora left Ethellro in charge with a score of mounted men to escort the cart and the bodies of the renegades back to the encampment, while he and the rest of his mounted warriors and archers set off for Buxonana as fast as their horses could take them.

When Aurthora and the group reached the paved Roman road some hours later, Lucius, Myridyn's assistant, was waiting for them with the wagon and escort as the physician had instructed. Aurthora saluted the leader of the escort, whom he recognised as Cimbonda Gilberto, the youngest son of the leader of the Cornovii tribe.

"Greetings Aurthora," called out Cimbonda, "I see you have been on a mission, I hope it was successful."

Aurthora laughed and leant over to grasp his friend's outstretched hand before replying, "You will hear soon enough Cimbonda, but it is indeed good to see you. There is a cart with two of our wounded following behind us, they require the professional services of Lucius," he said, indicating the young student physician sitting alongside the wagon driver. "I would be obliged if you could travel to meet them."

Cimbonda and his men moved to either side of the road allowing Aurthora and his large party of mounted warriors and archers to pass. He watched as the group of mounted soldiers passed him by. Judging from their condition, they had obviously been in some form of conflict. Many had strips of birch bark strapped to their limbs, covering wounds where dried blood had formed around the edges. Also many of their horses had bloody cuts to the chest and shoulders. All the men and horses were tired, dusty and dishevelled, yet the riders were laughing and smiling amongst themselves. Cimbonda concluded that they must have had a successful mission, whatever it may have been. It was also clear that Aurthora Ambrosius had the full loyalty and support of his soldiers, who were proud to fight alongside him. He was fast becoming a legendary figure and a hero of the Celtic nation.

After the last of the dusty horsemen had passed, Cimbonda led his small group and the wagon along the track from which Aurthora had just appeared, heading to meet and escort the cart carrying the badly wounded Celts and the renegade prisoners back to the town of Buxonana.

It began to rain; after several hours of the unrelenting downpour Aurthora and his men had become quite subdued. They and their mounts were very tired, by the time they eventually came in sight of the town of Buxonana, the sun was setting over the distant hills. They kept to the paved Roman road that passed directly through the Celtic army's encampment on its way up to the gates of the town and their warm, dry welcoming quarters in the town barracks.

As the long line of weary men and horses began to pass through the encampment, first one observer then another began to cheer them. This was quickly taken up by other Celts as they came out of their shelters and from around the many campfires scattered across the plain to see what the noise and commotion was about.

They formed a corridor of bodies on either side of the road. The chant of *Aurthora! Aurthora!* rose to become such a roar that it frightened some of the horses and made it difficult for their riders to keep them under control. Myridyn was in his workshop when he heard the chanting, faint at first, then louder and louder until there was not a street or house in the town where the sound did not penetrate.

Katrina and Emilia were clearing the table in the kitchen when they first heard the faint sound, like distant thunder coming progressively closer. They stared at one another wide-eyed as they gradually distinguished the word "*Aurthora! Aurthora! Aurthora!*" Without a word they moved as one, threw shawls over their shoulders and made for the front entrance of the house. They had only got as far as the garden when a breathless Orius met them: "I bring you great news! He is back! He is back!" he shouted, an enormous grin on his face.

The threesome raced towards the town gate, joined by scores of the town's citizens in various stages of dress, some even in their night clothes, but all curious and wanting to see what all the noise and cheering was about, the curfew being completely ignored in the confusion. *Has the enemy left? Has there been a battle? Have we won? What is all the cheering about?* were snatches of conversation the trio heard as Orius led them through the jostling crowd, shouting, "Make way! Make way there! Make way for the Town Guard," slowly forcing a passage through the gathering mass of people all heading in the direction of the town gate and the sound of the loud chanting.

Earlier that evening, the Celtic Round Council had assembled in the Great Hall in the centre of the town to discuss how the federation's dwindling finances could be best distributed. They had rejected one motion that the Round Council should just seize what they required to supply the army and pay their dues after the battle. Great King Erion was seated at the head of the long table listening in turn to the chiefs of the various tribes and senior officials putting forward the list of complaints that had been made to them – mostly because of late payments – and their ideas for a solution.

"The merchants who are pressing for payment, refusing to deliver further supplies to the army! If we do not have food to feed these soldiers, they will leave and return to their towns and villages. There are already many grumblings from the men about the short rations that have been imposed and the conditions in which they are forced to live on the waterlogged plain outside the town. Paying the merchants must be seen as the major priority," insisted Boro Sigurd, but he was shouted down by several of the other members of the Council who had other ideas.

"The most important issue is to maintain the continual supply of weapons produced by the smiths and armourers. They need a regular supply of iron ore from the mines in order to carry on meeting the demand for arms. What use is it to have men here ready to fight if they have no weapons to fight with?" protested Bernicia Calgacus, leader of the Coritani tribe, above the shouts of the others.

"We are running short of feed for the horses, without this we will have no cavalry," spoke out Culvanawd, the official responsible for the welfare of all the livestock the army needed.

Great King Erion listened to the heated discussions and demands of the chiefs and officials knowing that he desperately needed more time to finalise his plans before doing battle with the Anglo-Saxon army. To attack now would be to jeopardise all the years of careful planning, but it looked as if the decision would be forced upon him. The situation was grave: the coffers of the Crown treasury were empty, there was barely a copper coin left to pay anyone.

Slowly, above the noise of the arguing Council, a faint chanting could be heard coming from the plain outside the town. Those members nearest to the windows were the first to hear and stopped their heated discussions with their neighbours. Slowly all the Council members became silent as the faint chant grew louder by the moment. But when they heard a blast of the great boar's head battle horn, the Council members looked at one another in alarm. The great horn was a signal to arms: were they under attack? Had the Anglo-Saxon army made a surprise move? Was the enemy on the outskirts of the town?

Great King Erion looked around his group of Councillors, advisors and tribal chiefs, all wearing startled and confused expressions at the thought of their army caught unprepared on the plain below. All, that is, except two: Selecia Cunobelin and his brother Arranz, leader of the Dumnonii tribe. These two men were standing slightly apart from the rest of the group in quiet conversation between themselves, apparently unperturbed, as if they knew there was no attack taking place.

They looked uncomfortable when, glancing up, they saw the King Erion looking in their direction. Great King Erion and his advisor Myridyn had always suspected there was a traitor or traitors in the Great Round Council; these two had long been at the top of the list, now his intuition told him he had discovered the culprits. The King smiled at the two men then returned his gaze to the main body of the Council.

The chanting of several thousand men shouting the same name was all the clearer the closer it came: *Aurthora! Aurthora! Aurthora!* King Erion had informed the Council briefly at the beginning of the meeting that a raid had been carried out on the enemy and the results were awaited, but they had not been made aware of the exact details.

The Council members followed the King as he hurried out of the hall and onto the battlements of the town wall, from which they had a view of the plain before them and of the stone paved road that passed through the Celtic army's encampment. On either side of the road thousands of Celts were standing five and six deep, some lighting the scene with brush and pitch torches.

Travelling along the road was a line of mounted men, it was to these that the cheering and chanting was directed. No one among the group of Celtic chiefs and officials spoke for quite some time as they gazed on the amazing sight before them.

"I think the raid on the enemy must have been very successful," Culvanawd said, breaking the silence and stating the obvious.

"More successful than we could ever have hoped by the sound of the reception they are receiving," commented Boro Sigurd enthusiastically.

"The Celtic nation in its hour of need has brought forth a man who can lift the hopes and expectations of everyone who comes into contact with, or serves him."

All the Councillors turned to see who had made such a definitive statement. It was Myridyn the Physician, who had quietly joined the group on the battlements. Now, having obtained their attention, he continued, "He has the capabilities the support and the following of the people, as you can see from the spectacle below. He is also a staunch supporter of you, the Celtic Council, and our Great King Erion, he believes in the principles on which the Celtic Round Council was founded."

Murmurs of agreement came from the Councillors.

King Erion turned and watched as the last of the horsemen entered the gates to the town and the vast throng of many thousands of voices continued their chant of Aurthora's name in time to the continuous blowing of the great Celtic battle horn.

Chapter Nineteen

Never in his wildest dreams had Aurthora ever imagined that he and his men would receive such a reception on returning to Buxonana. The rider sent on ahead had not only reported the success of their mission to Myridyn, but he'd obviously passed on the word to others in the camp as well, information this had spread like wildfire throughout the encamped army.

As Aurthora entered the town gate he spied amongst the gathered throng the figure of Orius with Katrina and Emilia by his side. The crowd parted as he directed his horse towards them, leaning forward, he scooped up Katrina with his free hand, placing her in front of him on the neck of his horse. As she turned towards him he kissed her full on the lips and she threw her arms around his neck, continuing the embrace for several long moments to the wild cheers from the nearby townspeople.

When Katrina eventually released him he signalled to Orius that he would see him later at the barracks, slowly turning his mount, he guided it towards the tail end of his soldiers, moving slowly through the packed mass of still cheering bodies in the direction of the town barracks and their quarters.

Orius had watched closely as Aurthora came through the town gate, his soldier's eye also observed that Darius, riding at the side of his captain, was not waving to the crowd like the rest of the mounted column, but was continually scrutinizing the throng on either side of his commander. *I have chosen well*, he thought to himself as he stood watching as the rest of the column slowly made its way through the wide gateway and into the town.

When Aurthora reached the parade ground it was full of men and horses. All the stable hands and the off-duty soldiers were helping the tired men who had ridden with him, attending to their weary horses, cleaning their various wounds dressing them with poultices and lotions. Slowly the parade ground cleared as the horses were rubbed down and taken to the nearby stables to be fed and watered. In the meantime Katrina had gone back to the old physician's house with Emilia to prepare a meal she had agreed to bring to his quarters later.

Aurthora joined his men in the washrooms where they stood naked, washing the grime and dirt of battle and two days in the saddle from their bodies. It was here that he greeted Orius warmly when he entered, as they hugged, Orius's eyes were once again drawn to the birthmark that Aurthora bore on his shoulder.

Aurthora told Orius the details of the raid and how they had surprised, killed or maimed at least three to four hundred of the enemy, losing, as far as he knew, only six Celtic warriors. He also entrusted Orius with the safekeeping of the four bundled drapes bulging with gold and silver coins, showing him the rip in one where the Saxon's spear had been embedded. "There is also a wagon and a cart on its way with two of our wounded, a prisoner, and two youths who are witnesses against Petrov Joma and his followers. Guard them well, Orius," said Aurthora, "their lives may well be in danger, even here in Buxonana."

It was while he was finalising his plans with Orius that Katrina appeared with some cooked pork sausages with onions – still warm – a little cheese, some freshly baked bread and a small flagon of wine. She also carried a message from Myridyn that the Great King and Celtic Round Council requested Aurthora's presence in the meeting hall at mid-morning the following day.

With a woollen towel wrapped around his waist and another one over his shoulders, he left his travel-stained clothes in a corner of the washhouse for collection in the morning, and bidding a fond farewell to Orius, who would wait for the arrival of Ethellro with the wagon and cart, he slipped his arm around Katrina's waist and the young couple slowly crossed the empty parade ground to his private quarters in the barracks.

Orius watched them go. He felt proud to have been involved in the upbringing of this exceptional young man who had the gift of bringing the best out in anyone who was prepared to serve with him or accept his authority. Orius felt he had been more of a father to Aurthora than Prassat Ambrosius, who spent so much time away on the Great King's business. He certainly loved Aurthora as he would if he had been his own son.

Attracting the attention of two stragglers who were leaving the washhouse, he had them carry the heavy sacks of coins to the guardhouse at the entrance to the barracks.

His friend Mallus Calvus was on duty at the stone building. "Greetings Mallus," said Orius, as he and the two heavily laden Celtic guards approached across the parade ground.

"Greetings to you, Orius," replied Mallus, looking curiously at the heavy cloth sacks that the soldiers were struggling to carry.

"I need to put these in a secure place and under constant guard until tomorrow," said Orius indicated the drapes.

"They will be safe with me Orius, I will be here on duty until noon." Mallus knew what the bags contained, he'd heard of the raid on the enemy encampment, and during his career in the Roman Army he had seen similar sacks of booty many times.

Mallus guided the laden soldiers to a small chamber with a narrow, arrow slit window and a low, heavily studded iron door. An iron bar dropped down into place on the outside, which in the past had made it a secure prison for detaining any unfortunate Roman legionnaire guilty of some minor infringement of the army's laws, or unlucky enough to fall foul of the sergeant of the guard.

The sweating soldiers left their heavy burdens in the chamber, their task completed, Orius dismissed them and they returned to join several of their comrades who were still on duty in the guardroom. Orius sat for a long while on a seat cut into the stone wall of the chamber, staring at the improvised sacks containing what Aurthora had taken from the Anglo-Saxon camp.

After a short while he leaned forward and put his hand into the slit of the thick cloth where the Saxon spear had penetrated and pulled out a fistful of coins. He looked at the gold and silver in the palm of his hand. *Even this small handful would keep Emilia and myself in luxury for a good while,* he thought to himself as he gazed down at the dull coloured metal. *After this coming battle, if the Celts are successful and things settle down again, it would be enough to purchase the mansio of our choice. It would make us independent and at the beck and call of no one."*

The temptation for him to slip the coins into his jerkin was overwhelming. "No one would be the wiser," he thought, and years ago he would not have hesitated. But now he could not bring himself to do so. Aurthora had entrusted him with the sacks: he could not bring himself to betray that trust. *This is exactly the type of loyalty,* he thought, *that this man brings out in his soldiers and their officers.* Feeling guilty that he had even considered taking the coins, he replaced them, left the chamber, closing the door behind him and dropping the iron bar into its slots.

He went to the short corridor between the main guardroom and the chamber, taking a candle and its container, lit the candle with his flint. He waited a short while, then poured the melted wax onto the iron bar as it sat in its slots. Next, he took a ring from his finger, and using the flame from the candle, warmed the crest on the face of the ring before placing it on the wax across the bar. The door was now sealed with his crest. Anyone attempting to enter the cell would have to break his seal. Satisfied, Orius returned to the main room of the guardhouse where two off-duty soldiers from Aurthora's command were in the company of two guards from Cimbonda Gilberto's men of the Cornovii tribe, who replaced Aurthora's men when they left for the raid.

Lecturing to them was the old Roman soldier Mallus Calvus. Orius smiled to himself, he knew what the lecture would be about for he had heard it many times before. Mallus Calvus was a devout convert to the Christian religion taking every opportunity to proselytise the 'pagans', as he called those who did not adhere to 'the one true religion'. Orius listened for a while to his old friend, but just as he was about to take his leave Mallus broached a subject Orius had never heard him mention before.

"…And across the water from the green island of the Scoti came a disciple of the true religion, with him he brought a sacred relic, which was used by the true God's only son at the last meal he took with his followers, hours before being brutally dragged from their midst and crucified like a common criminal by the disbelievers of the one and only true faith." Mallus stopped to pour himself a mug of water, allowing one of the soldiers to raise a question.

"What was the sacred relic that the Scoti friar brought to our island, Sergeant?" Mallus looked at the upturned faces all waiting eagerly for his answer, while he slowly sipped his water."

"The sacred and priceless object was a small drinking goblet. It was forcibly taken from the disciple, he was left for dead by his attackers, but unknown to them he lived long enough to inform his fellow friars who his attackers were."

Mallus stopped here, waiting for one of his audience to broach the question. No one spoke. The tension was overwhelming. Finally one of the soldiers burst out, "Who were his attackers, Sergeant?" Mallus waited several more agonising moments before he answered. "His attackers were the Druid priests, those of the old Celtic religion."

"Never! You tell a tale made up of lies!" shouted one of the off-duty guards. Orius watched as the man stormed out of the room, still bearing traces of the blue woad on his face from his expedition with Aurthora. Orius bade farewell to the rest of the group, who were now uncomfortably silent, then he, too, left the guardhouse. As he walked across the parade ground his thoughts returned once more to the cache of coins and the small goblet he had buried while deserting more than twenty years before. *There had been a rumour circulating then amongst the legionnaires about the goblet.*

Could it be true? Marcus the engineer had believed it, he had gambled all his winnings to possess the goblet. The dog handlers, too, had pursued him much further than was prudent, and had all been captured or killed for their pains! And even Mallus his old friend believed the story. Orius could not clear his head of these thoughts. *Perhaps he was the one who knew where this famed and priceless goblet was hidden, and even if it proved worthless, there were many silver and gold coins in the leather pouch. If they were still there and he retrieved them, they would provide a good start for Emilia and his new future.*

He paid a brief visit to Emilia at the physician's house and checked that the guard was still on duty before leaving to take up a position at the town gate, where he made himself comfortable to await the arrival of Ethellro and the transport. Yet all the time his thoughts kept returning to the leather pouch he had buried at the stone pillar near the crossroads by the river, those many, many years before. Over that period he had been in the same area on many occasions when Aurthora's fathers duties dictated, but he'd never felt the need or the necessity to retrieve the pouch.

Chapter Twenty

Aurthora was not awakened from his deep sleep by Katrina the following morning as she quietly slipped from his bed at dawn. Before leaving the barracks she made her way to the washrooms to collect his soiled clothes. She then joined the rest of the town's womenfolk who were doing their washing at one of the hot springs that surfaced nearby. Bringing the scrubbed clothes back to the barracks, she spread them out in the sun to dry, much to the amusement of several of the soldiers who were lounging about in the early morning sun waiting to go on duty.

Orius arrived and joined her as she made her way back to Aurthora's quarters. "You look tired, Orius," she said to the elderly legionnaire as they walked across the deserted parade ground.

"Yes, it has been a busy and noisy night," replied Orius, continuing eagerly, "but your brother is well; he arrived back in town just before dawn and is stopping at the physician's house."

Katrina's relief could be heard in her voice, "Then I will go to him as soon as I have seen Aurthora."

They found Aurthora awake, still wrapped in the towels, and finishing off the remains of the sausage and cheese from the previous night's meal. Orius waited outside the door until Katrina took her leave, then entered. "Ethellro arrived back safely without any mishap. The Celtic renegade is safely locked away and is being questioned."

Aurthora did not ask for details since he knew Orius had associates who specialised in extracting the truth from stubborn prisoners.

"And what of the two youths?" he inquired.

"The two boys have been billeted in the barracks with the men who returned with you, they will be safe there until you require them." Aurthora pondered for a few moments, his back to Orius, looking through the narrow opening in his cramped quarters, gazing out on the still deserted parade ground. "I have been called to a meeting to report to the Great King and the Round Council, Orius," he said. "In the meantime this is what I would like you to do…"

As Aurthora explained his idea to his old tutor, his tired face began to smile as the plan was unfolded to him. "Go now, and act upon these instructions. In the meantime I will meet with Myridyn and tell him of our intentions."

Orius left to carry out his orders while Aurthora dressed in the clean clothes that Katrina had taken from his chest and spread out for him.

The Great King and the full Celtic Round Council were seated when he entered the Great Hall. He felt nervous in the presence of so many dignitaries, advisors and leaders of the Celtic nation. But he had formed his plan and intended to follow it.

First he told the assembly the details of the raid against the enemy: of how well his men had performed, the great number of casualties they inflicted on the Anglo-Saxon army, and the relatively few casualities they had suffered in return. There were many murmurs of approval as he continued with his report, but shouts of disbelief broke out when he reached the episode of the renegade Celts.

"I would not make these accusations lightly against my fellow countrymen," he said, raising his voice above the discontented murmurings of the Council. "I would only make them if I had proof to confirm my claims."

He turned and signalled to Orius who was standing by the entrance to the Hall. Orius opened one side of the great door and beckoned two guards who led in the captured renegade Celt in chains, supporting him on either side as he was having great difficulty in standing or moving on his own. Behind him came the two very nervous youths.

"These young men will tell you their own story in their own words," he said, moving aside as if to give the two youths more room, but in reality because he wanted to be in a position to observe the expressions on the faces of all the Council members as the story was told.

There were cries of anger and shouts for revenge from the gathered Council as the boys told of their frightening experience, the younger one sobbing as the older boy told of the slaughter of their parents.

Aurthora, watching from the sidelines, noted that all the Council members appeared genuinely angry, apart from two who looked exceptionally uncomfortable and were throwing the occasional covert glance in the direction of the renagade prisoner, being held near the door by the two guards. Aurthora was not alone in his observations: both Myridyn and King Erion were both aware of the discomfort that Selecia and his brother Arranz Cunobelin, leader of the Dumnonii tribe, were suffering. As the young men finished their story Aurthora moved again to the centre of the room. It was there he waited quietly until the members of the Council had finished their exclamations and demands that the perpetrators of these crimes against their own kind should be brought to justice.

"Your demand for justice has already been carried out, my Lords," stated Aurthora. "If you will follow me I will show you these renegade Celtic mercenaries who have turned on their own people in exchange for payment from the invaders."

Aurthora turned and left the room. Slowly the Council rose, led by the Great King, Myridyn and the full Council followed, with Orius and two guards bringing up the rear. Aurthora led them onto the battlements where, looking down on to the courtyard below, they saw fastened to upright stakes driven into the ground the bodies of the twelve Celtic traitors.

There were hundreds of soldiers from the encampment viewing the bodies, and many more were thronged at the gate waiting to enter and witness the spectacle. Surrounding the hall in lines two deep and back-to-back were Aurthora's men of the town guard in full battledress, one line facing the hall, the other facing the courtyard.

He allowed the Council to absorb the scene below them before he spoke. "You wanted justice my Lords? Below is justice for the deceased family of the two young men whose story you have just heard, and the many other Celtic families those men have slain."

There was a subdued silence amongst the group on the battlements as they continued to watch the scene below. It was at this point that King Erion took Aurthora by the shoulder and walked him several paces out of earshot of the rest of the group. Speaking quietly he said to him, "Aurthora, I think your next move may be a direct accusation against several members of the Round Council, but I beg you to hold. I can assure you on my oath that you will be satisfied with the final outcome." Erion then moved away from Aurthora and joined the rest of the Council, who were now all in deep conversation amongst themselves except for two of the members, who were holding a heated discussion together a slight distance away from the main group.

"My Lords!" King Erion called out, waiting until he had their attention, "I think we should give Aurthora Ambrosius a vote of thanks on behalf of us all. His achievements in the last few days have been magnificent, we owe him everlasting gratitude on behalf of the Celtic nation." Aurthora was embarrassed by the praise and the ensuing back slapping and shouts of agreement from the Council who were queuing to shake his hand and congratulate him on his actions.

King Erion made his way back into the Great Hall in a sober mood.

There were still many problems that needed to be resolved, even though Aurthora's action had been a sun-filled moment in an otherwise cloudy sky.

After the rest of the Council followed their king and entered the Great Hall, Aurthora remained alone on the battlements, looking down on the scene below as hundreds of the Celts from the encampment moved slowly past the bodies of their traitorous countrymen, some cursing the bodies, others spitting in their direction. As he turned to make his way back into the Great Hall, Orius approached him looking very agitated. "Aurthora, both of the young injured Celtic warriors that rode with you, Cassivelaunus and Bernicia Deiva, have died. I thought the plan was to denounce the traitors in the Round Council? We have the proof. The renegade Celt we captured alive eventually denounced them."

Aurthora raised his hand to calm his friend. "Do not fret Orius. I can assure you the matter is not over yet. Have the guards bring in the sacks when I have finished speaking to the Round Council. Oh, and you can dismiss the extra guard from around the Great Hall, I do not think they will be needed now."

Aurthora left a puzzled Orius to carry out his instructions while he re-entered the Great Hall. The Round Council were once again seated around the table talking amongst themselves, but they fell silent when Aurthora appeared. He walked slowly towards the table and stopped at the side of King Erion. Turned and faced the rest of the Council. "My lords, if I may be permitted, I will continue my report on our raid into the enemy camp. We lost seven Celtic warriors during the battle and two more young soldiers have died recently because of their wounds. But we inflicted around four hundred fatalities and casualties on the invaders. We also reduced their capacity to pay their mercenaries by bringing their treasure back with us." Aurthora raised his arm and at the signal, Orius opened the doors to the Hall allowing four of the guards to enter with the bundles.

These they set down in the centre of the large table removing the cords from the neck of the fastened drapes. The gold and silver coins with a scattering of semi-precious stones spilled out, covering the table and glittering in the sunlight that entered the Hall from the arrow slit openings in the walls.

The King and the Celtic Round Council looked in amazement at the great pile in front of them: it was more gold and silver than they had ever seen before in their lives.

"This is a king's ransom," continued Aurthora, "in fact it is several kings' ransoms from the kingdoms that the Anglo-Saxons have invaded and conquered. Now it is back in its rightful place, for the use of the Celtic people. He then bowed in the King's direction, turned, and with Orius following close behind him, left the Great Hall leaving the King and the Celtic Round Council speechless.

Orius instructed the guards to remain, for when the king requested them to take the booty to his treasury. Then the two men set off together for Meridyn the Physician's house where they knew Katrina and Emilia would be waiting. There were several points he wanted to discuss with his old tutor concerning the raid he had carried out on the enemy camp, he needed his opinion on a few new ideas he had in mind.

Orius and Emilia sent Aurthora and Katrina out of the kitchen and into the garden while they prepared the evening meal. Emilia had purchased a large piece of pork and was busy wrapping it in rosemary, thyme and mint, with an outer layer of large dock leaves. The meat was placed amongst the warm ashes of the open fire and covered with hot stones. They then prepared beans, sliced turnips and peas and set them in an iron container next to the fire. While Orius gutted and cleaned a large pike that the old caretaker had given him, Emilia made a thick sauce of parsley and dill.

Orius stuffed the large fish with herbs, wrapped it in large dock leaves and placed it in the ashes at the edge of the fire. They had decided that the fish would be served first. Then taking some stone ground flour, he added water, some goat's milk and a little salt, prepared a thick dough, which he also placed on the hot plates near the fire. Fresh celery, almonds, and dates were also set out on the table. Emilia sliced a cabbage which she mixed with several sliced onions, she and Orius laughing together as the tears streamed from their eyes from the freshly cut onions. The cabbage and onions, splashed with olive oil, would be placed on the hot iron plates near the fire and turned until they became a golden brown. This was one of the many simple recipes that Orius had learnt on his foreign travels, and it would be served hot with the pork and other cooked vegetables. They decided they would finish with the freshly baked bread, fresh goat's cheese and blackcurrant jelly.

"The delicious aromas coming from this kitchen are overpowering," said Aurthora as he and Katrina stood arm-in-arm at the kitchen's entrance.

They were all about to sit down to their meal when Myridyn arrived escorted by his young assistant Disaylann and Ethellro. Disaylann retired to his own quarters while the four made room at the table for Myridyn and Ethellro.

Before he sat down the old physician went to his workshop and returned with a clay flagon. "This is wine from the pale grapes grown in the far south of this island," he explained, smiling as he placed it on the table. "And a better wine cannot be found in the known world."

There was little conversation during the meal, everyone seemed to be concentrating contentedly on the food, it was only at the end that Myridyn expressed their mutual appreciation. "Orius and Emilia! Once again I must compliment you on a meal that my taste buds tell me I have never enjoyed the equal of before. Your talents are wasted. You, Orius, should not be a guard, and you, Emilia, should not be a maidservant. I know you will both be a great loss to Aurthora and Katrina, but when this conflict is over you must open a *mansio*! People will travel great distances to eat such wonderfully prepared fare, and I will be one of your most regular customers!"

It was Emilia who replied. Orius, unused to such praise, was too embarrassed. "You are too kind Myridyn. Not only are you are great physician, but you can also read people's minds!" The group laughed at the witty reply, while Katrina and Emilia cleared the table and moved into the kitchen area, Aurthora broached the subject of the recent raid on the enemy camp.

"I think it is important that the heavy horses and their riders be better protected. Our mounts received many injuries to their chests and shoulders, and the riders' calves and shins were also exposed to sword and spear.

"I've noted," joined in Orius, "that you employed a different strategy with the heavy horse compared with the lighter horses of the past, in which the light cavalry used to skirt the enemy troops using their bows to inflict casualties. This new heavy cavalry charge is directed straight at the enemy formations, causing chaos and disorder amongst their troops as they smash through their lines."

"Yes, that is so," joined in Aurthora. "There is more direct contact with the troops by the cavalry than before, and the use of the new leather straps Ethellro designed, which are fastened to the saddle and support the rider's weight, means they have more control of the horse. This is especially so when they use the long spear in a charge."

"I have been thinking about this too," joined in Ethellro. "I have discussed the problem with the smiths and they say they can make a breastplate for the horse, which can be fastened to either side of the saddle and supported from around the horse's neck. It can be of metal or of hard leather; both can be shaped to the horse's chest. The same can be done for the rider to protect his shins and thighs." There was an exclamation of agreement from the other three men. Ethellro continued, "The smiths are already working on the sketch I submitted to them; several of each will be ready by tomorrow, for us to test, then more will quickly follow."

"Well done, Ethellro!" exclaimed Aurthora, "time is so precious to us that any delay could prove disastrous."

Further conversation was halted by the loud banging of the doorknocker.

Orius was nearest opening the door to the guard who was on duty outside the house. He returned to the room where the four men were sitting, all looking expectantly towards him as he entered.

"There is a messenger from your town, Aurthora," said Orius quietly. "Your father's sickness has worsened. He is alive but cannot be wakened. His last wish before he fell into this deep sleep was for him to be brought to you, so that you would not have to leave your command during this crucial time, he his already on his way here."

Aurthora understood. Were his father to die here, he would be able to make arrangements for his funeral and see his father had suitable provisions for his journey to the other side, according to the Celtic custom.

"The journey will be slow for your father and his attendants; according to the messenger all being well they hope to arrive in two days' time."

Katrina entered the room at the sound of the knocking hearing the news. She went over to Aurthora laying her head on his shoulder. She did not need to speak to share his grief. The news deflated the bright atmosphere of the gathering, and the three men prepared to take their leave of Myridyn and the women. As they were leaving Myridyn called Aurthora back and briefly informed him that the Great King and the Celtic Round Council wished to see him again at mid-morning the following day. Then Aurthora left quickly catching up with his friends as they strode towards the barracks.

The dark, narrow streets were empty. Curfew had been in place since sunset. They were challenged by two guards on patrol but had no difficulty identifying themselves. Just as they were passing the guards at the entrance to the barracks the alarm was sounded from the section of town they had just passed through, one where several members of the Great Round Council were known to be in residence.

Aurthora and Ethellro raced towards the sound of the hunting horn, carried by all the guards on duty to call for assistance. Orius waited until the guard was roused at the guardhouse before following. The alarm had been raised by the same two guards Aurthora and his companions had met shortly before. A servant had rushed from the house occupied by Selecia and Arranz Curobelin shouting that his masters had been murdered in their beds. When Aurthora and Ethellro arrived on the scene, breathless after their sprint, they found the two guards searching the rooms of the property.

Lying unconscious at the entrance to the property was the Celtic guard on duty, who represented part of the increased security that had been enforced to provide greater protection for all the members of the Round Council since the assassin's appearance in Myridyn's garden.

A quick inspection of the house revealed that the intruder or intruders had long since left. The bodies of the leader of the Dumnonii tribe and his brother were both dead, stabbed through the heart while they slept. Orius and the soldiers from the guardhouse arrived as Aurthora and Ethellro were attending the guard who was slowly regaining consciousness. "He remembers nothing and the assassins have fled," said Aurthora to Orius, "He received a blow on the back of the head and is fortunate they did not take his life as well."

"I will double the guard on the residences of the rest of the Council," said Orius and shouted orders to the soldiers with him, who quickly dispersed to carry out his instructions.

"Should I send someone to inform Myridyn and the King?" inquired Orius in a low voice to Aurthora.

"I have a feeling they will already be aware of what has happened tonight, Orius?" replied Aurthora in the same whispered tone. "I think we can wait until the morning before we inform them officially."

"I have spoken to the two guards who were patrolling this area," said Orius, "and only Nicolas of Mesopotamia was in the street after the curfew, he was returning after his duties as personal bodyguard to Albion Egilos of the Celtic Council. "MM!" sounded Aurthora through pursed lips at this information.

After double checking on all the guards, it was late when the three men eventually made their way wearily to their own bunks in the barracks. Within a short while two of them were fast asleep, while the third, Aurthora, could not help but go over in his mind what the Great King had said to him in private earlier that day.

He was as requested at the Great Hall early the following day. The King and Celtic Council were still in session when he arrived, he was asked to wait. He left Darius in the courtyard when he entered the building, while he was waiting he had time to reflect on his recent bad news. His father was being brought to the High Town to die. He was a highly respected leader amongst the Celtic community he had been a fearless and brave warrior. Aurthora had a tremendous amount of feeling and respect for his father, but had never been very close to him. Prassat Ambrosius had always been away, either fighting or on some business or other for Great King Erion. He often wished his father could have found as much time to spend with him as he had spent with Orius, his tutor. He felt guilty that he felt more spontaneous affection for Orius than he did for his own father. His thoughts also turned to Katrina. He hoped she loved him as much as he loved her – but he was sure she did, she showed so much affection towards him. No, he decided, he

197

must follow his heart in this matter. He smiled at the approach that Timus Calgacus had made towards Katrina through her brother Ethellro. He liked Timus and it showed the young Celt had excellent taste. Timus would not bother Katrina again now that he knew she favoured him.

His daydreaming was interrupted when the door to the chamber opened and he was beckoned inside. As he passed through the door he noted that all the members of the Celtic Round Council were present – except, of course, for two vacant seats among the group of leaders who represented the Celtic Alliance. Aurthora felt uncomfortable and embarrassed as all eyes in the room seemed to focus on him. At the end of the table sat King Erion, leader of the Celtic Alliance. Aurthora decided to concentrate his attention on him.

"Aurthora Ambrosius!" exclaimed the king. "Since this campaign against the Anglo-Saxon invaders began you have shown exceptional skill and personal courage in confronting our foe. Your father before you was a brave and fearless Celtic warrior, a personal and trusted friend and companion of mine. You have shown by your previous actions that you are of the same stamp and quality as your father, you stand for all that is true and good in our Celtic way of life. It is the wish of all here present that you be offered the seat that has been vacant since your father's illness. You have shown a considerable knowledge of warfare and tactics far beyond your youthful years. It is the unanimous wish of the Great Round Council that in addition to being asked to join the Celtic Round Council, you also be offered a voice on the Inner War Council, on whose decisions the future of this nation depends."

Aurthora was left speechless: the prestigious proposal for him to become a member of the Celtic Round Council at his age was already a tremendous honour in itself, but to be also invited to become a member of the Inner War Council was unheard of for one so young as he. He stood for several moments, completely overwhelmed as the King's words registered and he was sure he had heard them correctly.

King Erion was smiling, indicating a vacant seat, he slowly walked around the table and placed himself behind the chair, an indication that he had accepted the offer that the Great Council had made. "I accept your most generous offer," he said, looking at the men around the great table. "My only wish is that I can fill this seat as well as the previous occupant, my father Prassat Ambrosius.

There were shouts of "Well done, Aurthora! Well done!" from the Council Members as they clapped, and those near to him also slapped him on the back and grasped his hand. The noise slowly subsided, and King Erion brought the meeting back to order.

"My Lords, we must now turn to a most serious matter. Last night, as you have probably already heard, two of our loyal Council members were brutally assassinated as they slept. We can only assume that this act was committed by the Anglo-Saxons or people in their pay. Unfortunately, the culprits were not found, even though an immediate and extensive search was made of the town and surrounding area.

"As Celtic law dictates, the elders of the Dumnonii tribe have already met and appointed a successor to lead their people. The brothers Arranz and Selecia Cunobelin had no male offspring; Selecia has one daughter who recently married Longinus Caratacusi. This is the man the elders of the tribe have appointed leader of the Dumnonii clan."

There was a murmur of discussion amongst the gathered chiefs; it did not sit well with many of them that Longinus Caracatusi, who only days before had been marked down to lose his head, had suddenly been elevated to the position of leader of the clan he had just joined, and thus would have the lawful right and duty to represent the tribe as a member of the Celtic Round Council.

"Later today Selecia and Arranz Cunobelin will be buried, at the same time the elders of the clan will inform the mourners at the funeral of their new leader and introduce him to the rest of the tribe. But first I will introduce you, the Celtic Round Council, to the new leader of the Dumnonii tribe."

King Erion indicated that the guards should open the doors to the chamber, into the hall limped Longinus Caratacusi.

There was not the rapturous welcome from the Council that Aurthora had received, merely a polite clapping of hands. Many felt that Longinus was taking his place on the Council as a hasty expedient at a difficult moment, unlike the rest of the Council, who had fought many battles and felt that they had earned their position. His only claim to fame was to have made a spectacle of himself at his own wedding feast.

Once again, low murmurings of discontent were heard from many of the Council Members, which Longinus could not help but overhear as he limped around the table towards one of the two newly vacant seats, his eyes fixed firmly on the floor. Aurthora felt a pang of sympathy and sorrow for the man. Longinus stopped beside him, still several places short of the vacant seat, and surprised Aurthora by holding out his hand in a gesture of friendship. Aurthora stood to grasp the man's outstretched hand and, drawing him close, whispered in his ear, "Walk tall, Longinus Caratacusi! Walk tall!

You are now the leader of a powerful tribe, the Dumnonii."Then he stepped back, as he looked Longinus in the eyes, he saw them light and knew his few quietly whispered words seemed to have had the desired effect. Longinus Caratacusi turned and with a straight back and head held high took the last few steps to his seat at the table.

Much of what was discussed at the Round Council meeting Aurthora found to be doubtless important, but routine, boring and of little interest. Reasons were given for delays in the delivery of various commodities; they discussed the deteriorating condition of the roads and tracks in and out of town due to all the extra traffic; they dealt with merchants' promises that were not kept and problems in the mines producing iron ore... the list was endless. Aurthora's mind wandered to the seat his father had occupied for many, many years, the one where he now sat. *I wonder whether he was also bored by this kind of talk? If he was, why didn't he come home to spend more time with me, his only son?*

The meeting was called to a close by the distant trumpeting of the boar's head horn, a mournful sound that carried across the town and surrounding encampment. It was blown to inform everyone that the funeral of members of a notable family was about to take place. The Council members slowly made their way out of the Great Hall and down to the courtyard, where they were met by an escort of mounted guards led by Orius. Aurthora could not help but admire how smart and professional the men looked in their burnished chain mail armour, with their highly polished leather straps and coverings, seated astride their large, well-groomed mounts. It was while he was waiting to mount his horse that Myridyn approached him.

"The Great King and I will pay our respects to the family of Arranz and his brother and then we will depart. We would like you to join us, we have something of particular importance we think you should see." Myridyn moved towards his mule, held by his assistant Disaylann. The column then set off on its slow journey. Orius led the escort at the front, then came the Great King on his large grey, followed by the Council on a collection of horses, some riding the large breed and some astride the sturdy local ponies and small horses. At the rear rode Myridyn on his mule, led by Disaylann, and Aurthora with Darius riding at his side.

King Erion expressed his condolences to the wives and immediate family of the two brothers, pointedly ignoring the presence of the High Priest Zanton who was presiding over the service. According to Celtic custom their bodies were then placed on a cairn of stones together with their favourite possessions and several weapons. Food and drink was also provided for the journey their spirits were about to undertake. The ceremony would last for the rest of the day, and much food and drink would be consumed that night to celebrate their past life.

Over the next few days their bodies and possessions would be covered by well-placed stones; these in turn would be covered by soil into which plants from the surrounding area would be embedded. Within a very short time the cairn would look like a small, overgrown mound: no one would notice it, and hopefully their remains would go undisturbed for many years to come.

It was during the placing of the bodies on the platform of stones that Myridyn and the Great King slipped away, shortly followed by Aurthora, Darius, and Orius with the two guards appointed as the Great King's personal escort. They rode in silence taking the track that circled the town until they came to a path that led off onto the moor and wet marshland. This was the path the small party followed.

Chapter Twenty One

Aurthora calculated they had been travelling approximately one hour when the track petered out, before them appeared an old man whose attire indicated he was a shepherd. He wore a coat made from sheepskin that hung below his thighs and was fastened at the waist with a leather belt, a fur hat, possibly hare or rabbit skin, and leather boots that came up to his thighs. In his right hand he carried a staff the height of a tall man, and in his left he held two stilts. Behind him was a vast stretch of dark water with the odd clump of marsh grass projecting here and there. Aurthora had seen both men and women performing with these contraptions in the many fairs and festivals he had attended in his youth, and marvelled at their sense of balance. Myridyn moved to the front of the group and spoke to the man whom it seemed was going to be their guide for the rest of the journey. The language Myridyn used Aurthora knew to be Celtic, yet he was only able to decipher a few words. He looked around him. It was now well past midday and a mist was beginning to settle over the marsh; visibility was diminishing by the moment.

Myridyn moved to each of the mounted travellers, he was obviously giving instructions. He reached Aurthora at the rear of the group. "Aurthora, it is important that you follow the person in front of you. On no account must you take a different route or stray from the track, to do so will cost you your life and that of your companions."

Leaving him with this stark warning, Myridyn turned, making his way back to the front of the group, mounted his mule and signalled to the guide to proceed. The guide slipped into his stilts and proceeded to make his way through the dark peaty water. The horses followed very uncertain at first, tentatively feeling their way, but gaining confidence as they found solid footing even though at times the dark water came up to their bellies. They travelled slowly for well over an hour, changing direction on numerous occasions. The marsh mist had closed in, blocking out the sun and leaving a dark grey light, just enough for each man to see the shadowy form of the figure in front as the party continued to move through the clinging wet vapours that covered the peaty waters.

Gradually, the terrain began to change. They were now travelling through tall reeds, well above the height of a mounted man, and the level of water was much lower, just above the horses' hooves. They had left the mist behind them and the sun was shining once more, the marsh was giving way to dry ground and grassland. They passed a herd of white cattle, their wide horns sweeping the long grass on either side of them as they grazed in the lush meadow. They continued along a well-worn path entering a small hamlet of single-roomed dwellings, thatched with rushes. There were also several temporary shelters where men could be seen working on long benches. As they approached, Aurthora recognised Lucius, Myridyn's young student; the young man was carrying a metal jar towards the centre of a cleared area where there were many patches of burnt grass. He set the jar down on the ground and walked towards Myridyn who had dismounted from his mule. "Greetings, Sir!" said the young man as he approached and made a short clumsy, bow in the direction of King Erion.

"I think we have perfected the formula, Master," he said to Myridyn. "You have arrived just in time to see us test the result." Myridyn nodded to the young student and turned to face the rest of his party who were still mounted.

"I beg you to dismount gentlemen, and have the guards remove your horses to the far end of the clearing and behind the thatched huts. Aurthora and Orius dismounted and gave the reins of their mounts to Darius. The King also did as was requested and the two guards took his horse then followed in the direction of Darius and Disaylann, the latter leading Myridyn's mule. When Myridyn was satisfied the animals were out of sight he signalled to Lucius, who, taking a flint and piece of steel went to the centre of the clearing and bending over the jar proceeded to strike the flint, causing the sparks to ignite a short piece of rope coming from the sealed opening of the jar.

When Lucius was satisfied this was well alight and smouldering he scampered back to the group placing his hands over his ears. King Erion did the same, Myridyn turned and indicated that Aurthora and Orius should also cover their ears with their hands.

Aurthora noticed that all the workmen under the shelters had stopped what they were doing, and were standing watching with their hands pressed tightly over their ears. All eyes seemed to be on the metal jar in the middle of the clearing, with the fine plume of dark smoke indicating that the short length of rope was still smouldering.

It seemed to Aurthora that the rope smouldered endlessly, until his keen eyes noticed the smouldering had stopped when it reached the neck of the jar. He was about to remove his hands from his ears when there was a blinding flash of light like lightning, a crack like thunder, and a great cloud of dust enveloped them, with pieces of the metal from the jar falling several paces short of where they had all instinctively taken up a crouching position. There was a whinnying and the sound of galloping hooves as one of the horses bolted, quickly pursued by one of the mounted guards on a very frisky and frightened horse. Aurthora looked at Orius and then at Myridyn.

The old physician was smiling and clapping Lucius, his young student, on the back. King Erion stood slightly apart from the group, but he too seemed to be wearing a very satisfied expression. Myridyn signalled to the men under the shelters, and they began to drag into the centre of the clearing a contraption of some kind with only its wheels showing; the rest was partially hidden by a cover made of sewn animal skins. In charge and directing operations was a one-armed man whom Aurthora recognised as Aidas Corrilus, Orius's old friend.

Aurthora turned to Orius who nodded. He, too, had recognised his cantankerous old friend with whom he had spent so much time – when they were both in the Roman army.

Aidas instructed the men to remove the covering, exposing a machine that resembled a cross between a scorpio catapult and a ballista crossbow. It was set on four wheels, with a series of ratchets to increase the tension of the throwing arm.

"So that's why Aidas was moved so quickly," said Orius from behind Aurthora. "He was brought here to develop this machine". Aidas gave instructions to the two of the men on the ratchet, and the tension on the hybrid crossbow was increased, forcing the arms back.

Two more of the men carried a basket containing four, metal sealed jars, similar to the one that had exploded earlier, and each with the short length of rope hanging from it.

The horses of King Erion, Aurthora and Orius were brought from behind the buildings by Darius and the two guards, and all three men mounted and rode five hundred paces down the clearing to where a hundred or so upright logs of wood were fitted into the ground several paces apart, all about the size and height of a man. Turning to Aurthora and Orius, King Erion said simply, "Aurthora! Note the timbers." He then turned his horse riding away upwind to the far edge of the clearing with Aurthora, Darius, Orius and the guards following close behind. When the three men had dismounted, Darius and the guards led the horses, as before, back to the rear of the far low buildings. Then King Erion raised his arm and Myridyn waved back in return.

There was the sharp sound of a thwack as the tension on the crossbow was released and a small, dark object sailed through the air. When it was just above the upright lengths of timber, it exploded as before with a blinding flash and a crash like thunder. Another thwack sounded from the direction of the large cross bow-catapult as another projectile was sent on its way, quickly followed by three more flashes and loud explosions.

Aurthora could not get over the sound of the explosion and the flash that left him disoriented and unable to think clearly, or the terrible acrid smell of burning, one he had never encountered before. Myridyn waved to indicate that he had finished; it took several moments for the smoke to clear, then Aurthora and Orius followed King Erion as he walked to where the logs had been sunk into the ground.

As they made their way to this point Aurthora bent and picked up several of the small pieces he had seen land nearby after the explosions. They were pieces of razor-sharp flint, slightly larger than an arrowhead. When they reached the man-sized logs of wood he was amazed at the damage inflicted on the timber. Great lumps had been gouged out of the upright posts, sharp splinters of flint were deeply embedded in the baulks of tough timber, and many that had taken the full force of the blast had been blown out of the ground completely.

"So this is the Greek fire you told me about?" Aurthora said to Myridyn as he joined them on his mule.

"Yes, Aurthora. This is what we have been trying to develop for many years, we have come closer and closer to doing so. Now, as you have observed, we have at last achieved perfection."

Aurthora gazed at the mangled and splintered wood around him; he could imagine what devastation this new weapon of war would cause against the packed ranks of the Anglo-Saxon army. "And how many of these machines have you working, Myridyn?" he queried.

"With the knowledge and technology of Aidas Corrilus, we have made fifteen machines, and by nightfall we will have ten projectiles for each machine. They will be taken to the Town of Buxonana at first light tomorrow under the escort of Neila Gilberto and his sons Camara and Cimonda with their warriors of the Cornovii tribe. The Great King and I will also return tomorrow with Neila Gilberto and the Cornovii warriors as an escort."

Aurthora and Orius decided they would return immediately as both had duties to perform, even though it was late in the day and would be dark when they eventually reached Buxonana. Before he left Orius rode over to his old friend Aidas Corrilus to say a few words, then Aurthora, Orius and Darius took their leave. Following their guide they proceeded back along the faint path through the meadow towards the edge of the marsh.

During the ride back he asked Orius what he thought of the weapon they had just seen demonstrated.

Orius pondered for some considerable time, Aurthora was about to ask his old tutor the question again, thinking he had not heard him the first time, when Orius began to reply. "I think it would be a lethal weapon used against packed foot soldiers, as was demonstrated. But its range is short and the conditions today were ideal. The enemy needs to be coming forward in packed formation toward it for it to be effective. And it has to be in the right position at the right time. It would be of little advantage if the projectiles fell too far behind or too far in front of their target. These machines would be rendered useless by a persistent cavalry attack.

"But on the other hand, having never been used before, the element of surprise and the shock sustained by the attacking troops would be devastating to them, it would lower their morale and give ours a tremendous boost. On their own I do not think the new machines can win the battle, but they could help turn it in our favour – especially if we took immediate advantage of the confusion caused to the attacking troops by these new machines and this Greek fire."

"You have read my thoughts perfectly, Orius," replied Aurthora. "We have to pick the battlefield with extreme care, we have to dictate all the moves in order for the outcome to be in our favour." They continued riding in silence, all three deep in thought over the spectacle they had seen that day. Aurthora was already planning how the machines could be used to their best advantage against the invaders.

It was already dark when the three horsemen left the marsh saying their farewells to the guide on his wooden stilts. He carefully placed the coin Aurthora had slipped to him into his small leather pouch, then quickly turned and made his way back into the wetlands, the light from his lantern fastened to his staff soon swallowed up by the encroaching mist.

It was late when the trio eventually reached the High Town. The curfew was already in force when they presented themselves to the guards at the town gate before continuing on to the barracks, their horses' hooves sending up a ghostly echo as they clipped along the stone paving of the narrow, empty streets. There was only a lone guard patrolling the stables; they removed the saddle and harness and rubbed down their sweating horses themselves, then settled them in their stalls with hay and water. It had been a long, tiring day; the three men said their goodnights and made their way to their individual quarters. It seemed to Aurthora that he fell asleep as soon as his head touched his straw-filled pillow, and as if only moments passed before he was awakened by a loud banging on the wooden door of his quarters, and a voice that he recognised as Mallus Calvus the ex-Roman army friend of Orius in charge of the town guard that night, shouting on the other side of the door.

"Aurthora! Sire! Awake! I bear important news! There is a threat to the encampment, we must sound the alarm." He was awake and out of his bunk in an instant. He slid back the bolt on the door of his quarters and flung it open. Mallus Calvus was standing there dressed in full battle order; he had obviously been running as his face was blood red and he was panting for breath. As the soldiers had done when he was in the Roman army, when on duty he always wore full battle dress, and insisted the soldiers under his command did the same. Now before him stood a well-built, almost naked young man with nothing but a gladius in his right hand.

On seeing Mallus Calvus Aurthora lowered the short stabbing sword. "I thought I recognised your voice Mallus, what is this problem that causes you such haste? Tell me your news," he asked the panting man in front of him.

"One of our scouts has just arrived from a sighting near the Anglo-Saxon camp," gasped Mallus. "A large force of mounted men left the enemy camp the night before last and were followed by our scout. The scout nearly killed his horse to bring the news as soon as possible, when he realised they were heading towards our encampment. They could be here by dawn, which is but several hours away."

Aurthora realised at once what was happening. This attack would be a retaliatory raid for the one he had mounted on their camp several days before. "How have the Anglo-Saxons organised so many mounted men, Mallus?" he asked, more to himself than to the old Roman soldier standing in front of him.

"From the description given to me by the scout I would say they were Flavians," volunteered Mallus. "They were employed by the Roman army as light cavalry and are deadly accurate with the bow while on horseback. They were used for scouting, to harass troops, and for hit and run attacks against enemy columns and supplies. They worship a god they call Mithras; they are very anti-Christian."

"You surprise me with your knowledge of these people, Mallus," replied Aurthora.

"We had a section of them posted with our legion when I was in the Roman army. I thought they had all returned to Gaul with the legions. But if the Anglo-Saxons are paying them enough, they may well have returned to these islands as mercenaries.

"Well!" said Aurthora grimly, "We will see what this Flavian cavalry is made of when it faces Celtic steel!"

He continued giving instructions to Mallus as he pulled on his breeches and shirt. "Raise the alarm in the barracks only. Do not sound a general alarm in the town. There are fifty horses in the stables, they need to be saddled immediately and fitted with their new protectors. Their riders need to be in full battle armour and provided with the long spear. Send a rider to Ethellro in his camp. Tell him to mount as many men as he can and be at the South Gate within the hour. Tell him to use the road at the back of the town. Oh! And tell him to arm his mounted men with the long spear. Also rouse Roderick Tristan and his master bowmen who are billeted near the South Gate. Tell them to join the Guard at that point."

He shouted the last message down the corridor as Mallus hurried off to carry out his orders, passing Orius who was coming in the opposite direction on his way to Aurthora's quarters. Aurthora was fastening his breastplate and looked up when Orius, also in full battle dress, entered his chamber.

"Ah! Orius my friend, the enemy has sent a detachment of light cavalry to try and catch us unawares. I have not raised a general alarm for I want to catch them in a trap. If they suspect we are prepared for them they will just disperse into groups and create havoc around the countryside behind our defences, and if that happens it will take us days and many men to hunt them down."

Orius nodded. "I see the logic behind your plan. How much time do we have?" he asked as he fastened the buckles on the rear of Aurthora's breastplate.

"Mallus has informed me we may have less than two hours."

Orius grimaced on hearing this. "And what are your orders for me, Aurthora?" he inquired, hiding the panic that he felt rising in his stomach. *To organise a defence within such short time without raising a general alarm was practically impossible,* he thought to himself. *They could be caught with no defences at all.*

"I want you to send a rider to Neila Gilberto and his warriors. They are camping on the marsh road to the east of the High Town. They are waiting to escort the Great King and the machines when they arrive out of the marsh this morning. Neila is to keep his men hidden and allow the enemy cavalry to pass unhindered. He is then to block the pass with his warriors and that will close the door on the trap. When you have done that, Orius, I want you to raise the guards that are off-duty and all the soldiers within the town. Leave the minimum of men to protect the town gates. Take Roderick Tristan, who will meet you at the South Gate, and as many of his bowmen as can be raised in such a short time, proceed at the fastest pace possible along the paved road from the South Gate. Spread your men out along the road. I require a double line, like a testudo: the first line will face the enemy with their shields forming a wall of steel while the second line will use their shields as overhead protection for both lines against arrows. When you are in position Orius, order the men to lie down on the road, until we are ready to spring the trap. As you know the road there is a man's height above the surrounding meadow, your men will be too conspicuous if they are standing upright."

Orius nodded, his feeling of panic receding as Aurthora quickly outlined his plan. "And you, Aurthora? What will you be doing?" Both men were now hurrying down the corridor as Orius asked his question.

"I will take all the heavy horses and mounted men that are available. I will ride through the Celtic encampment on that side of the road and warn them of the raid. I will send them as quickly as possible to you. You will position them behind you, at the top of the embankment at the far side of the road. If the enemy cavalry charge you and manage to break through your lines, these men will be our second line of defence. If they are strong enough to break through them also, the main Celtic encampment below them will be at their mercy. But before that happens I will charge their cavalry with my men. We will see if all the hours of practice with the long spear have been worthwhile. I will ride through their cavalry and join up with Ethellro and his mounted men at the town's South Gate; we will then turn and ride through the enemy again. Inform Roderick Tristan and his master bowmen of the plan. I do not want to end my days because of a carelessly fired Celtic arrow."

By the time Aurthora had given his instructions to Orius they had reached the stables where the stable lads were frantically fastening the saddles and the new apron breastplates to the last of the horses. Aurthora climbed onto his horse, grabbed the long spear that was handed to him, checked that the long sword was in its sheath at the side of his saddle hooked the narrow, rectangular shield on to the saddle horn. He then turned, seeing all his men were mounted, dug his heels into his horse and galloped out of the parade ground followed by fifty of his well-armed fellow Celts.

Mallus Calvus had already sent several men mounted on the local ponies to rouse the men in the encampment on the side of the road that would be attacked first by the enemy cavalry.

The men that had been awakened were tumbling out of their shelters and small tents, still half asleep. Most at that side of the road were from the Dumnonii tribe who had buried their leader and his brother the previous day. The wake had carried on well into the early hours of the morning a large majority of the men stumbling in the direction of the raised Roman road were still suffering from the excessive amount of free mead and ale they had consumed.

He noticed in the early morning light the limping figure of Longinus Caratacusi valiantly striving to hurry his half-dressed fellow tribesmen towards the raised embankment, where, if things were going to plan, Orius would be placing his men. "As quickly as possible, Longinus," shouted Aurthora in the direction of the limping man. Longinus lifted his free hand in acknowledgement, and with the other hit a slow straggler with the flat of his sword. Seeing that he could do no more here, Aurthora gathered his men and rode a short distance to where the road curved in a long bend. Here, he would be hidden and out of sight of the enemy cavalry.

Orius meanwhile had raised the alarm in the barracks before he had proceeded to Aurthora's quarters, so that by the time Aurthora rode out of the barracks with his fifty mounted cavalry, the off-duty guard were already assembled on the parade ground fitting the buckles on their protective armour; the guards on duty in the town had been rallied and were rushing through the entrance of the barracks to join their comrades.

Orius led the men at a fast trot out of the barracks and through the town towards the South Gate. When he reached the gate he called a halt to give his men an opportunity to regain their breath and also to give Roderick and his archers time to join him. Orius could see from the south entrance the town where streams of men camping on the east side of the paved road were dragging themselves up the embankment and staggering over the road to collapse on the other side. *If the first line fails, these drink-sodden Celts will be a liability to themselves rather than a second line of defence,* Orius grumbled to himself as a half-clothed Celtic soldier with no sword or shield staggered across the road and stumbled into the stone pillars of the town gates where he collapsed in a drunken heap, heaving and retching the contents of the previous night's drink over himself and part of the gate supports. In the half-light of the approaching dawn Orius could just make out the outline of Aurthora and his cavalry riding slowly through the encampment towards the bend in the paved road. He could wait no longer. Shouting orders to his men he moved forward, placing two men at every two paces, which allowed a gap for the Celts leaving that part of the encampment to filter through. He was halfway to the bend in the road when looking back he could see his old friend Mallus Calvus with Roderick Tristan, placing their archers with his men.

As the archers joined the soldiers each group of three lay down on the paved road. *There is still no sign of the enemy cavalry*, thought Orius, *we might just make it in time.* It was now quite light, and it was possible to see to the end of the encampment, even though there was a mist to the height of a man's waist lying over the meadow.

Orius had just positioned the last two of his men at the end of the column when Roderick joined him. "Mallus has remained at the centre of the line of men, I will go back and join him," he shouted to Orius as he placed an archer between the two end soldiers. Orius signalled he had heard, then looking behind him he recognised Longinus Caratacusi limping along, struggling to organise a line of armed warriors on the rear of the raised road, shouting to wake and raise the men camped on that side of the highway.

Suddenly, above the noise of men slipping, cursing, and struggling to scramble up the embankment to the road, came the distinctive sound of a large body of mounted men, their horses' hooves pounding the ground accompanied by the rattle of harness and buckles. In sight at the edge of the encampment came the enemy's mercenary cavalry of Eastern troops: the Flavians.

The sound penetrated even the alcohol-soaked brains of the Celts as they struggled towards the road, the added screams of tail-end stragglers being cut down at the far end of the encampment by the Flavian archers adding impetus and panic to their efforts, forcing their unresponsive legs and befuddled brains to carry them across the meadow to the beginning of the embankment. The Flavian cavalry had stopped at the edge of the Celtic camp, their mounted archers picking off the Celtic stragglers as they left their tents and bivouacs and stood upright, the top half of their bodies showing above the low-lying mist.

What Ashur Nabin the Flavian cavalry leader saw when he reached the edge of the camp was several hundred or more half-dressed men rushing towards and scrambling up and over a low embankment. The smell of panic was in the air, his archers were picking off the dazed men that were nearest to them as they appeared out of the mist. He would seize his opportunity: he would charge the panic-stricken soldiers in front of him, his cavalry would drive them onto one another and roll them up like a carpet against the road embankment and there his men would slaughter them like chickens, he would ride back to the Saxon camp and collect the large bonus offered by the Saxon king. Excellent payment for a successful morning's work.

Riding to the front of his mounted followers he drew his long curved sword, waving it above his head in an action that was quickly followed by the rest of his cavalry, he drove his heels into his horse's thighs and set off at a fast gallop towards the Celtic troops who were five hundred paces away, milling together at the bottom of the embankment. He wanted to be the first to ride amongst them, to hear their screams as he slashed and cut his way through their terrified masses.

He had covered about a hundred paces, his cavalry now in full charge, hearing his men shouting and yelling behind him. He was laughing wildly as, with his heels, he spurred his horse on to greater exertions. The men at the bottom of the embankment had turned and were facing him now. They were trying to form some sort of line, but even at that distance he could see they were poorly armed, many were not even carrying shields. Others were standing on top of the embankment, these did seem to have shields – indeed, there seemed to be a continuous line of shields…

Alarm bells began to ring in Ashur Nabin's brain.

He tried to slow his horse but it would not respond. He turned and waved for his men to stop, but those that saw him simply waved back, driving their horses faster. Ashur Nabin was not killed by the flurry of arrows that fell amongst his charging men, but indirectly by the arrow that struck his horse's heart, causing the animal to collapse and throw him over its head. It was the horses behind him that trampled him to death in their panic as they too were being killed or crippled by the fusillade of arrows.

Chapter Twenty Two

Each of Roderick's marksmen archers had three arrows in the air before the first hit its target. The front riders and horsemen of the enemy cavalry collapsed under the onslaught of flights, those following behind could not avoid riding onto the kicking bodies of injured horses and screaming men. The rest milled around uncertainly. A quarter of their number were already either maimed or dead, and their leader was nowhere to be seen. They had a small respite: the deadly flight of arrows seemed to have stopped, they would have time to reorganise themselves. Cyrus Judah, the second-in-command, began shouting instructions, pointing desperately to their flank. As the Flavian horsemen struggled to turn to face this new threat, Aurthora and his heavy cavalry smashed into their jumble of horses and men; the Celts first used their long lances, but as these were broken against the bodies and horses of the enemy forces, they then drew their long light swords from the sheaths on the saddle to cut their way through the ranks of the disorganised Flavian cavalry.

Aurthora from his position on the bend of the paved road had seen the Flavian cavalry leader take the bait; he had also seen him try to turn his men when he realised it was a trap, then be trampled by them and their horses. The Flavian horseman nearest to Aurthora was unhooking his bow from around his shoulders when Aurthora's long spear struck him in the chest, lifting him bodily off his horse and dumping him on the flattened and churned-up grass of the meadow. A second Flavian slashed at Aurthora with his curved sword, but he took the blow on his shield, and then rode the man and his horse down, cutting the man across the head and neck with his own sword as the man tried to rise from his fallen animal. Spurring his mount forward he slashed at another Flavian rider before he was clear of the melee and driving his horse towards the South Gate of the town, followed by the majority of his men.

From his raised position on the road, Roderick Tristan had watched the Flavian cavalry as it charged in his direction. He had shouted to his men, "Rise and loose your arrows!" They in turn had shouted the order down both sides of the double line of soldiers. He saw the flight of arrows from his bowmen inflict devastating casualties on the men and horses of the front ranks of the approaching enemy cavalry and shouted to them, "Cease firing!" as he saw Aurthora leading the Celtic cavalry charge into the enemy's flank. The order was repeated down the line of archers, when he repeated the order, "Loose arrows!"

By the time Aurthora and his men had ridden through and clear of the mercenary horsemen, there were a number of mounted Flavian archers returning fire with their short bow, but it was inconsistent and not of any great volume and most of their arrows were falling short of their intended target. Tristan, watching from his position, saw Aurthora wheel his horse around as he reached the closed South Gate of the town. There were several rider-less Celtic horses following the main group of mounted men as they followed their commander as they wheeled their horses into position behind him. Suddenly the South Gate of the town swung open the troops guarding that entrance came running out carrying the tall spears, one in each hand, which they passed to Aurthora and the horsemen around him.

Clever thinking by Orius or Mallus Calvus! thought Aurthora as he grabbed one of the long spears from a soldier. At the same time, cantering along the paved road at the side of the town wall, he saw a group of horsemen with their long lances held high in the air. Leading them on a great black horse was a large man with a mass of red hair blowing in the wind.

Aurthora gave a sigh of relief, and dropping his spear from the vertical to horizontal kicked his heels into the flanks of his trembling, sweating mount spurring it in the direction of the remaining group of enemy cavalry, closely followed by his companions and joined by the yelling group of horsemen led by Ethellro Egilos.

From his position at the end of the line of soldiers and archers Orius had seen the enemy cavalry stopped in their tracks by the archers, then the charge led by Aurthora smash into their flank. As the archer next to Orius sent another of his deadly accurate missiles into the group of Flavian horsemen, Cyrus Judah realised they had been tricked into a trap and that his leader Ashur Nabin was dead. He saw the Celtic cavalry stop and wheel around at the Town Gate, he saw them being handed the long spear that inflicted such casualties on his men, he also saw the other large group of horsemen led by a red-haired Celt arrive; he also saw his comrades still falling from their horses from the continuing, devastating flights of arrows.

Cyrus Judah, his leader before him, and the entire Flavian cavalry were no amateurs at war, nor were they cowards. His men would die for him if he so wished, but the time was not now. He had been fighting mounted battles for over twenty years, he could assess situations at a glance and this one was not in their favour. He could charge the fast approaching mounted Celts with their long spears and heavier horses, but they had the advantage. He could alternatively charge the foot soldiers at the bottom of the embankment, whom in theory he knew he could slaughter, but not while they were protected by the archers from the road above with their deadly bows and long arrows. No, he and his remaining men would retreat the way they had come. They would live to fight these Celts another day when the pendulum swung in their favour.

Cyrus Judah turned his horse, shouting instructions to the remnants of what had been once a large cavalry force, spurred his horse into a gallop away from the mounted Celts and out of range of the bowmen on the raised road.

Aurthora at the front of his mounted Celtic warriors saw the remains of the Flavian cavalry turn away in the face of his charge. He knew from speaking to Mallus Calvus, Orius's old friend and ex-commander of the Roman cavalry, that this was when the Flavian horsemen were at their most dangerous. They had perfected the technique of running away from their pursuers, turning in their saddles, and firing their bows at the chasing foe, keeping just sufficient distance to inflict heavy casualties on their enemy without allowing them to catch them. He knew his breed of horses had the stamina to eventually outrun the Flavians' lighter mounts, so he shouted, "Keep your distance!" to the men on either side of him, waving them back. "Do not increase your speed!"

The order was repeated down the line of horsemen, yet a group of six young riders at the end of the line either did not hear the order or chose to ignore it. Their blood was up and they had the thirst for battle in their hearts. They had already smashed through the Flavian ranks once and knew they had the speed in their mounts to catch the enemy in front of them and they intended to do so.

These six quickly pulled ahead of the group led by Aurthora and were rapidly gaining on the Flavian cavalry in front of them. Aurthora watched as the small band drew nearer and nearer to the retreating Flavians. He had to admit they did look a spectacular sight, their horses at full gallop, their riders in their chain link armour, their family crests painted on their narrow shields, long spears pointed towards the enemy with the steel tips glinting in the morning sun.

Cyrus Judah was pleased at the way his men had so far responded to his shouted commands. They were now clear of the Celtic archers and their deadly longbows, they were also clear of the pursuing Celtic cavalry. He smiled to himself: this was a situation they were familiar with, one they could use to their advantage with devastating results. The Celts were gaining. Soon they would be well within the range of his men's short bow. There seemed to be a group of Celtic riders racing ahead of the main force; it did not matter, he would deal with them first.

As Cyrus Judah shouted his instructions, the Flavians turned and fired their arrows in unison. One moment the group of six magnificent Celts were gaining on the retreating Flavians, the next they had disappeared in a cloud of dust as both men and horses stumbled and collapsed under a hail of flying arrows. As Aurthora and his men rode past they could see three of the horses lying motionless along with their riders. Two of the horses had regained their feet but were obviously seriously injured and one was still on the ground struggling to stand, its rider trapped screaming under its body. Two of the riders were on their feet, staggering around, badly dazed and wounded.

It was now near midday. Aurthora kept up a regular canter; a steady pace for him and his men's mounts. For the smaller Flavian horses in front of him, however, it would be impossible to maintain that speed for long. They were coming to where the ground was rising on either side, forcing the Flavian cavalry to bunch closer together. As they drove their horses towards the gap they could see in the hills in front of them: and the pass out of the plain.

Aurthora found he had time to look around him, which Ethellro, riding close to him, noticed. "Why do you keep looking at the sky, Aurthora?" he shouted. "The enemy are in front." "I am looking for my lucky omen, Ethellro," Aurthora replied.

"And what may that be, Aurthora?" returned Ethellro.

"The buzzard!" Aurthora shouted back.

"Well look no further, it is there in front of us over the Flavian cavalry!" came back the shout.

Cyrus Judah saw that his men's horses were beginning to pant heavily and that their riders were having to force them to maintain their speed in order to keep their distance from the Celts giving chase. But it mattered little. Shortly they would be through the pass and into the rougher, higher ground beyond, which was much more suited to the lighter, more nimble-footed horses ridden by his men. Once there he would deploy his men into smaller groups, which would force the Celtic cavalry to divide, then he would pick them off at his leisure.

Aurthora watched the Flavian horsemen draw closer to enter the neck of the pass. *Cramped together like that they will not be able to use their bows to their best advantage*, he thought. *Now is the time for us to increase our pace.* "Faster!

Faster!" he shouted to the men on either side of him and spurred on his own horse with his heels. The ground through the pass was much rougher than on the plain the bunched Flavian cavalry were concentrating on riding and guiding their tiring mounts rather than firing arrows at the chasing Celts, who were now rapidly closing the gap between them.

Orius from his elevated position had seen the Flavian cavalry turn and run for the pass from which they had come, little knowing that this escape route was at that very moment being sealed. He had cringed as he watched the small group of Celtic horsemen ride ahead of the main group and suffer the consequences of their youthful folly, and he had watched as Aurthora led the Celtic cavalry in pursuit of the remains of the Flavian horsemen until they were out of sight. Now he set about organising individual Celtic horsemen as they responded to the call-to-arms that was now being sounded from the battlements of the High Town, sending three score of them to assist and report on the situation that was taking place at the pass. He looked around the plain where the cavalry action had taken place and as he took stock of the large number of injured and dead horses he thought cynically, *the Army will dine well tonight on all this fresh meat.*

He would send Mallus Calvus to confiscate some; he would also have some of the best cuts delivered to Emilia at the physician's house and to the old caretaker of the baths – he would send him several pieces. The old man had been doing very well of late. The Town Guard being otherwise occupied, there was more time for private clients in the baths and sauna, so his and Emilia's savings for their *mansio* were increasing by the day.

Neila Gilberto had risen early that morning, his back aching from the hard earth floor of his small shelter. How he missed his own soft bed! This camping out business was for the young men of his clan and not for senior members like himself. In future he would leave these escapades to his sons. But he was curious to see these new machines about which he had heard many rumours, when his tribe had been asked to provide an escort for the Great King and the vehicles from the settlement in the marsh as far as the High Town, his curiosity had got the better of him. He was the first one to rise from the small encampment of bivouac shelters laid out at the side of the track that led into the marsh.

He had just checked that the horses were still tethered to their grazing lines and was relieving himself at the side of one of the few trees in the area, when his attention was drawn to a lone horseman galloping towards the camp.

Neila Gilberto came out of the shadow of the tree shouting "Cimbonda!

Cimbonda! Rise from your bed, a rider is heading for our camp, he is in great haste." As Neila came out of the shadows the horseman seeing him, changed his direction and came racing towards him. As he advanced, Neila could see he was riding one of the large-framed horses, from his attire that he was one of the soldiers designated to patrol and maintain security in the High Town, which was under the command of the newly appointed member of the Celtic Round Council, Aurthora Ambrosius. The rider pulled up his steaming mount in front of Neila Gilberto just as his son Cimbonda came bounding out of his small shelter, sword in hand.

"I have a message, Sire, from Aurthora Ambrosius, Commander of the High Town Guard and member of the Great Round Council," gasped the messenger to Neila Gilberto and his son.

"I know of Aurthora Ambrosius, replied Neila. "I knew his father well, a finer, truer Celt you could not wish to meet."

"That is true, Sire, and as you say that of his father, I can say the same of the son." This reply from the messenger greatly impressed Neila Gilberto. He had heard much of the heroics of this young Celt who had been given high authority at such a young age; privately he doubted the wisdom of the Great King. But this Aurthora had obviously earned the respect and the loyalty of his men.

"What is your message for us, rider?" interrupted Cimbonda as he pulled on his jerkin.

"The Anglo-Saxons have sent cavalry to attack the main encampment at the High Town; they travelled through the night and entered the pass earlier. My commander Aurthora Ambrosius and his men are ready for them, he will drive them back towards you and onto your swords at the end of the pass, if you can be ready."

Cimbonda was the first to react to the startling news by calling out to the rest of the men in the small encampment, some of whom had left their shelters at the sound of the galloping horse and raised voices. "Awaken and dress for battle, you men of the Cornovii Tribe. Today you will have the opportunity to test yourselves against the Anglo-Saxon enemy." The Celts sprang into action to prepare themselves and their horses for what would be for most of them their first armed conflict.

For Cyrus Judah and his men of the Flavian cavalry, the end of the pass was in sight. As soon as they cleared its entrance he would order his men to disperse so that they could pick off one by one the pursuing Celtic cavalry on their clumsy heavy horses, just as they had done so many times before with other enemies.

Neila Gilberto, mounted in front of his band of Celtic warriors, could see from his side of the pass across to where his son Cimbonda waited with his men on the other, many of the young, untried Celts shivering with excitement as they anticipated the coming conflict.

Aurthora and his men were closing fast on the smaller horses of the Flavian cavalry – several of the stragglers had already fallen to the Celts' long spears, but Aurthora realised that even at this pace, before his men could bring the enemy to battle they would be clear of the pass and amongst the rocks and scrub beyond, yet there was still no sign of Neila or Cimbonda Gilberto and their men.

At less than fifty paces from the end of the pass, Cyrus Judah was just beginning to think that he and his army had reached relative safety when from seemingly out of nowhere they were suddenly confronted by sword-wielding wild men on large horses that smashed into their tired smaller mounts from both sides.

Aurthora, from his position at the front of his men, saw the Celtic horsemen led by Neila Gilberto and his son Cimbonda attack the flanks and front of the enemy cavalry, bringing their flight to a sudden halt. Aurthora and his horsemen were soon upon the stationary, packed rear ranks of the Flavians, first using their long spears, and then their long swords as they sliced into the disorganised enemy. The pass was blocked by wheeling horses and screaming men.

Cyrus Judah ducked to avoid a crushing blow from a great battleaxe swung by the leader of the group that had attacked his flank; his return backward slash cut through the man's long grey hair and severed his spine where it joined his head. He then swung low in his saddle, his head level with his horse's knees to avoid a thrust from a Celtic spear. He saw a gap in the encircling enemy and spurred his horse in that direction, slashing his sword across the face of the horse that blocked the gap causing it to rear and buck uncontrollably throwing its rider in the process, then he was clear of the fighting, and on a track that led towards a nearby marsh.

When he turned, only five of his companions had managed to fight themselves out of the tightening circle of Celtic horsemen. The rest of his cavalry were fighting for their lives, slowly being overcome by the skilled handling of their opponents' taller and larger horses and the savage ferocity of the Celtic mounted warriors.

Cyrus Judah's thoughts flashed back to the two hundred or so mounted Flavian mercenaries who had set off, in such high spirits and with such high hopes, from the Saxon camp several days before. Within a few hours the most experienced and feared cavalry that had ever been in Roman employ had been reduced to a handful of survivors, sitting astride their blown and weary horses.

Aurthora's name had registered in Judah's brain. The soldiers on the road earlier that morning had been chanting it, *Aurthora! Aurthora!* as the archers amongst them sent fusillades of death into his men. The Celtic cavalry that had charged into his flanks with their extra long spears and caused such carnage amongst his companions had also chanted that name, *Aurthora! Aurthora!* The Celtic cavalry that had just charged into his rear had been shouting it again: *Aurthora! Aurthora!* Even the horsemen that ambushed them at the end of the pass were now screaming the same name, *Aurthora! Aurthora!*

As Cyrus Judah watched the remnants of his once proud cavalry destroyed he saw a tall Celt with hair the colour of fire, riding a great black horse wielding a long-handled battleaxe as if it were a toy, move round to his side of the one-sided battle. *This must be the one they call Aurthora*, he thought to himself.

At least he now had the opportunity to avenge his leader Ashur Nabin, also all his fellow companions-in-arms who had perished that day. "Load your bows!" shouted Cyrus Judah to his remaining fellow Flavians who had surrounded him expecting an order to scatter.

They looked at their new leader in surprise; it was obvious to them the battle was lost and they should be running for their lives while they had the chance. Any delay would be fatal. But they were professionals and never disobeyed an order. They unhitched their bows from around their shoulders and each drew an arrow from its sheath. "Your target is the large Celt on the black horse, the one with hair the colour of fire. Avenge your leader and your comrades my fellow Flavians. He is the one they call Aurthora!"

Chapter Twenty Three

King Erion, along with all the members of the hidden hamlet, had risen early that morning. They had a long, slow journey ahead before they reached Buxonana and the Celtic army. The machines had been hitched to the great white bullocks, while all the accessories that the machines required were loaded into separate, mule-drawn carts. Soon they were on the move, the mechanics and machine operators finding a space on the wagons if they could, or else walking beside the transport as the long column followed the guide with the lantern into the thick, early morning mist that enveloped the whole area.

They had almost reached the outer fringes of the marsh coming to the end of the tall rushes that grew out of the murky water, when the unmistakeable sound of a nearby battle reached their ears. King Erion, accompanied by two mounted guards, several of the machine operators on ponies, who were armed with their Celtic swords and battleaxes, and Myridyn on a mule stopped in their tracks; behind them, the line of mule drivers armed with the Celtic longbow did the same. From his position at the edge of the marsh, King Erion was astonished to see a horde of mounted Celtic tribesmen in armed conflict with a strange cavalry.

At a short distance from this melee a small group of the enemy horsemen were unhitching their bows from around their shoulders. Their intention was obvious: they planned to pick off the Celtic horsemen one by one. "Quickly! Archers to the front!" shouted the King. Within moments the mule drivers and Erion's personal guard were in front of him, their arrows strung in their bows. "Your target is the mounted bowmen," shouted King Erion. "Fire at will".

The Flavian archers had already strung their bows and were in the process of sighting their target when the Celtic arrows fell amongst them. These Celtic bowmen were not of the standard of Roderick and his group of specialist marksmen, but nonetheless, at such a short range the volume of arrows were lethal. Several of the enemy were hit and fell from their mounts, severely wounded by the arrows fired from so close. A number of their horses were also struck, causing their riders to abandon their shooting in order to try and control their terrified animals. With a great Celtic battle cry, King Erion drew his sword and spurred his horse forward, followed by his two guards and the four mounted machine operators, armed with their various weapons.

As the Celtic arrows found their targets amongst his remaining men and their horses, Cyrus Judah spun round to face the direction from which this new threat had suddenly emerged. Charging towards him and the remnants of what had once been his fearsome cavalry was a motley group of armed mounted men. Leading them was a tall, grey-haired man on a large grey horse. Even from this distance Cyrus Judah could see by the quality of the clothes the man was wearing that he was obviously a high-ranking official, or a person of noble birth. At this point, Cyrus Judah decided that if he were going to die, then this man would die with him. Shouting to rally his remaining men, "Follow me, fellow Flavians! In the name of Mithras, the one true God!" he spurred his tired animal towards the fast approaching group of horsemen.

The first rider that Cyrus Judah encountered was one of the King's guards. He ducked below the wild swing of the man's sword and lashed out at the man's back as they passed, the force of the blow so powerful it knocked the rider over the neck of his horse, yet it did not penetrate the interwoven chain mail armour the guard was wearing. Swinging his arm around in a half circle Cyrus Judah lunged in the direction of the grey horse, his sword entering beneath the raised sword arm of its rider.

He tried to turn his horse to finish his opponent but was forced to defend himself from attack by the other rider who was also wearing chain mail armour. He was a more experienced soldier and knocked Cyrus Judah's sword thrust away, countering with an upward lunge that slashed through his reins. Given its head, Cyrus Judah's horse bolted down the track towards the stationary carts and wheeled vehicles.

Hanging on to his horse's mane, Cyrus Judah looked back: the tall, red-haired Celt and several others had left the main conflict to join the man on the large grey horse. The majority of their men were completing the disposal of the remnants of the Flavian cavalry, some were even now chasing towards him. None of the archers had fired at him in case any stray arrows hit their own men. Judah's tired horse stumbled as it entered the shallow water, regained its footing as it approached the first cart and then veered away as a man stepped out and swung something in his hand. Cyrus Judah felt the blow on his temple but did not feel any pain. He was aware he was swaying in his saddle but it was the abrupt stopping of his horse that sent him over its head and shoulder to land in the slimy water of the marsh. Hitting the cold water revived him a little, but when he tried to stand he found he was already up to his knees in clinging mud.

Everything was very dim. He could just make out his horse as it backed away from him, he could faintly see his sword sticking upright five or six paces away, but hard as he tried, he could not lift either foot out of the clinging mud. Gradually his vision cleared a little, he could now make out the figure of a man approaching. The man was about ten paces away when he bent and retrieved from the water a long handled pair of iron pincers. He looked at Cyrus Judah, who was now up to his waist in the clinging ooze, then he turned, making his way back to a small two-wheeled cart and threw the long tool into the rear, where it landed with a clang among several other iron implements.

Even though Cyrus Judah's vision was still slightly impaired, he could not help but notice that the man had only one arm. He – Cyrus Judah, who for thirty years had been one of the chief terrors of Rome's enemies, and then of all the enemies of the kings and princes who had employed the Flavian cavalry as mercenaries – had been unhorsed by a one-armed old man with a crude instrument from a blacksmith's forge.

A rider was approaching Cyrus Judah on one of the large, heavy horses. A powerful, well-built young man, one of the typical Celts Cyrus Judah had come into contact with so many times before, so different from his own slightly-built race who he could trace directly back to his Scythian ancestors. The mounted Celt leant over and plucked the upright sword from the soft ground, turned his horse and approached the one-armed man on the two-wheeled cart. "A souvenir for you Aidas. I believe it was you that unseated this leader of the Flavian cavalry."

"That is true, Aurthora, it was the first thing that came to hand, a pair of iron tongs."

Both men laughed at the situation, and the weapon that had been used.

Cyrus Judah overheard but did not understand all of the conversation between the two men as he strained to focus on their dim figures, unaware of the cold, viscous fluid that was engulfing his body. But one thing he had understood: the name of the man they called Aurthora. So this was the man who had destroyed his cavalry. Cyrus Judah had waited twenty years to lead the world's mounted elite; he had achieved his ambition only to lose all of his men in the same day. This large Celt was the one who had led the raid on the Anglo-Saxon encampment and, if the rumours were true, had also stolen the Saxon King's treasure chest. Cyrus Judah could understand some of the language these Celts spoke, he had served in these islands for many years with the Roman legions. "What do you intend to do with him, Aurthora?" asked Aidas, indicating Cyrus Judah who had now sunk to his armpits in the slimy mud.

"This was the man that struck the fatal blow against Neila Gilberto," replied Aurthora, "it is for Cimbonda Gilberto to decide his fate."

"Well, you will not have long to wait, young Gilberto is coming this way now," observed Aidas.

Cimbondo Gilberto pulled up his horse beside Aurthora. "My father died in my arms. It was as he would have wanted: dressed in his armour, his sword in his hand, fighting our enemies."

Aurthora and Aidas both expressed their condolences, then Aurthora said, "There is the man who struck the fatal blow, Cimbonda. His fate is in your hands." The men regarded the Flavian officer, now stuck firmly in the clinging marsh and sinking deeper every moment.

Cimbonda pondered before replying. "My brother is now head of the Gilberto family and leader of the Cornovii tribe, I cannot make a decision about this man. I would like to save him until I can discuss his fate with my brother and the elders of my tribe."

Aidas threw Cimbonda a rope from the back of his cart and the young Celt quickly formed one end into a loop as he had done many times before when catching young horses he was breaking in. By now a crowd of men, some mounted and some on foot, had stretched along the track and were watching the proceedings with interest. Seated on his mount, Cimbonda expertly threw the looped rope around the arms and shoulders of the Flavian cavalry leader, and began to slowly draw the man from the dense, sucking slime.

Suddenly Cyrus Judah began to shout at the gathered group of Celts in a broken version of their Celtic language.

"I am Cyrus Judah, a follower of Mithras, the greatest God. I, and all my companions were his disciples. We will destroy all you Christians who have persecuted us. I, and the followers of my God are not afraid of death. Death is but a stepping stone to everlasting life."

Cyrus Judah then took a short curved knife from his belt and slashed through the hemp rope. He was still proclaiming his faith and hatred of Christianity as the thick, rank-smelling mud slowly covered his head, stopping his tirade, which ended with a gurgling, spitting sound as the green water entered his lungs. All watched in silence as the occasional air bubble rose to the surface, the last evidence of Cyrus Judah's existence.

"So, you will not need to consult your brother, Cimbonda, the decision has been made for you by the culprit himself," said Aidas as he turned on his seat and proceeded to drive his small cart along the track and clear of the marsh, followed by the rest of the wheeled vehicles and their handlers.

Chapter Twenty Four

Aurthora rode back to where he and his men had caught up with the remains of the Flavian cavalry, closely followed by Darius and Cynfelin Facilus, who had never left their leader's side during the day's campaign. Myridyn and his assistant Disaylann were attending to the wounded Celts while the rest of Aurthora's men were either stripping the dead Flavian cavalry of their weapons and anything else of value on the bodies, or collecting their enemies' horses, which were so tired they had not wandered far away. "Do you know the number of our casualties, Myridyn?" he asked the physician. The old man was bending over a young Celt whom Aurthora recognised as a member of the Cornovii Tribe. As Myridyn rose with a sigh, Aurthora could see an arrow projecting from the young man's chest.

"Ah, Aurthora," exclaimed Myridyn, as he came towards him, "your casualties are about one score dead and perhaps the same number of wounded, of whom half should survive with proper treatment, which I will organise once they are brought to Buxonana. But Aurthora, I have to tell you, this is for your ears only. King Erion was also wounded in the conflict.

"Is the wound serious?" exclaimed Aurthora in alarm.

He was deeply shocked and concerned, yet at the same time, on another more logical plane, recognised that it was of the utmost importance that the morale of the Celtic Alliance should not be undermined at this stage in the campaign against the Anglo-Saxons.

"The wound is deep, I have covered it with herbs and bandaged it, but I am unable to see the damage within his body. Only time will answer your question. I will take the Great King on to Buxonana ahead of the rest of you, we will enter the High Town quietly from the East Gate; it would not be good for the army or the townspeople to see their king wounded just before they go into battle. Rumours fly and are apt to be exaggerated in the telling. But," he continued, "I believe your campaign against the Flavians was a magnificent success. With one stroke you have removed one of the most manoeuvrable and powerful forces in the Anglo-Saxon army. You have deprived them of an immeasurable advantage against the Celtic Alliance."

"I was but one man," replied Aurthora, "the damage to the Flavians was inflicted by the warriors that followed me."

"You are too modest, Aurthora," replied the old physician as he mounted the mule brought by one of the cart drivers and set off towards a small, covered wagon to which the Great King's grey horse was tied. Two mounted guards had taken up their positions: one in front of the wagon and one at the rear. Aurthora followed the physician to the wagon. As he drew alongside, the cover was parted from within to reveal the figure of King Erion propped upright on some sacks. Aurthora was shocked at the pale, drawn face confronting him.

"Congratulations are once again in order for your leadership, Aurthora. This recent campaign against our enemies was wholly successful I am told."

"Yes, Sire," he replied, attempting to hide his dismay at seeing the Great King in such a weak and pitiful condition. "Our army is well trained and ready for the coming conflict," he continued.

"Yes, what you say is true, Aurthora, but all could be lost without proper and dedicated leadership. I feel tired now, we will talk again later." King Erion closed the canvas flap and the cart with its escort moved off slowly down the pass where only a short time ago Aurthora and the Celtic Army had chased and destroyed the mighty Flavian cavalry.

It was a very slow column that proceeded towards the town of Buxonana. All the horses and men that had been involved since early morning were weary, but their spirits were high. They had just destroyed one of the finest cavalry forces in the known world. The men removed their heavy chain armour the wounded had been lifted onto the carts and on temporary platforms fitted on the wheeled machines. It was late in the day when the line of vehicles slowly approached the walled town.

Word of their success had already reached the Celtic army encamped outside the town walls, and for a mile both sides of the road outside the town were lined by cheering crowds as the mixed collection of vehicles, followed by the Celtic cavalry leading the Flavians' riderless horses, passed through the corridor of wildly cheering warriors.

The men in the column dispersed as they joined their own groups camped outside the walls of the town. Eventually, only the covered machines and the wagons carrying the wounded and dead Celts with Aurthora and his cavalry passed through the gates of the town.

It was here that he met Katrina, who had been waiting since Myridyn had returned earlier with the injured King. Katrina was tearful with relief and happiness as she and Aurthora embraced, also because she had to tell him

226

that in his absence his father Prassat Ambrosius had arrived, still in a state of permanent sleep, with two of his loyal servants who were nursing him to the best of their ability. "I have made arrangements for your father and his servants to take lodgings in the house previously occupied by the two assassinated brothers, it was the only property available in the town," said Katrina.

Aurthora had no objections at all. He hugged her tightly, he was so glad to be back with her again and exhilarated that his plan had met with success and the dreaded Thracian cavalry had been destroyed.

"I have seen your father, Aurthora, and you must prepare yourself for a shock. He looks very ill, so pale and thin," she continued.

"I will go and see him now," he replied.

"If I may say so, I think it would be much better to do so in the morning. Your father's servants have had a long and tiring journey and will have only just settled your father down for the night. I have also spoken to the caretaker of the baths. You and your men can enjoy the waters: go and bathe and relax and I will come to your quarters later." She hugged and kissed him again before slipping away into the gathering dusk.

Aurthora made his way to the stables where the rest of his men were already bedding down their horses with the help of the stable hands. He told them of the arrangements that had been made for the hot baths; this was greeted with noisy approval and cheers from the tired, battle-stained soldiers.

After soaking in a steaming tub of hot water, he went into the massage chamber where there was a young soldier lying on the bench being attended by Gwion, the caretaker's young nephew. Aurthora took a seat to wait his turn. The young soldier had his head turned away from the door and did not see who had entered. Presuming it was one of his comrades he began to talk: "What do you think of our commander Aurthora! He must be blessed by the gods the way he keeps getting away unscathed after kicking the Anglo-Saxon backsides. There's also a rumour in the camp that he is to be appointed to lead us into battle against the enemy. So what do you think of that, my friend?" he concluded, turning to face Aurthora. Startled at discovering the identity of his audience, the man jumped off the bench as he recognised Aurthora.

"I am sorry Sire, I did not realise you were waiting. Please, I have finished." Standing there naked and extremely embarrassed, the young soldier's face had turned bright red; he quickly grabbed a nearby towel leaving the chamber, averting his eyes from the smiling Aurthora as he passed.

He eased himself onto the bench, and under the sensitive hands and fingers of the young masseur he relaxed into a semi-sleep, feeling as if both his body and mind were floating. The faces of the Great King and his father appeared, both were white and drawn. In his dreamlike state he was riding the King's great grey horse at the head of a horde of mounted Celtic cavalry. When he looked skyward, the buzzard was gliding above him. Then the scene shifted to the episode with the Saxon pirates. Once again he and his companions cut their six ships loose and let them drift out to sea. He saw again the pirates attempting to board them, then in close-up the Saxon who had managed to reach the boat that he was in; how the man had pulled himself up at the side and simultaneously swung his sword at him and how his own sword had come down on the man's hand. He relived the moment the man fell back into the sea screaming, his three bloody fingers twitching on the deck. Now his thoughts took him back to his desperate position under the cart as it rumbled along the raised road and entered the Anglo-Saxon encampment. How lucky he had been that it was dark and no one had observed him from the shelters below.

He recalled his raid on the Anglo-Saxon camp and the boost its success had given to the Celtic army's morale. And now this latest escapade, during which the cream of the Anglo-Saxon mercenary cavalry had been destroyed. Here his thoughts stopped and focused on the long conversation he had with Ethellro earlier as they journeyed back with the carts and weapons to the High Town. It revolved around the damage the Flavian archers had inflicted on the small band of eager young Celtic cavalry, despite them protecting the horses with breastplates, and the men with shields and chain mail. He pondered the heavy losses Roderick and his archers had inflicted on the Flavian light horsemen in front of the High Town, yet again how the ordinary Celtic bowmen in charge of the wheeled machines at the final battle at the end of the pass had routed the remains of the Flavian cavalry. It was this, the damage the archers could wreak, that kept returning to the forefront of his thoughts.

His daydreaming was brought to an abrupt halt by the voice of Orius Tomase calling for him. "Aurthora! Where is Aurthora Ambrosius?" A voice called out to Orius that Aurthora was with the masseur. Aurthora was already standing with a towel around his waist when Orius entered the chamber. "Aurthora! I bring grave news, Myridyn is with your father and your presence is requested most urgently." The concern on Orius's face and in his voice prompted Aurthora to hurry towards the changing room, not noticing that Orius had thrown his own cloak over Aurthora to cover him and the prominent birthmark on his shoulder.

Katrina and Emilia were waiting to meet them at the lodgings. He thanked his father's attendants, whom he had known since childhood, for having brought his father safely to him. They then led him to his father's chamber where he was met at the door by Myridyn the Physician. "Ah, Aurthora, it is good to see you again, I am only sorry for the sad circumstances. Your father, I'm afraid, will not awaken from this sleep; it is the prelude to death. I left instructions earlier today that I was to be informed immediately if there was any change in his condition. A short while ago your father awoke and recognised his servants; nonetheless, I am afraid his time on this earth is very short. You must see him now – immediately."

Aurthora did not reply. He took Myridyn's hand in both of his and held it fast as he felt a dam of emotion break deep within him and the tears well in his eyes. He entered his father's room and closed the door quietly behind him. When he emerged some time later he was solemn and composed. His father had passed away he had been by his side. Myridyn had gone. He had known the inevitable outcome and could do no more for Aurthora's father, whereas the lives of many injured Celts depended on his care.

Aurthora informed his father's servants of his father's death bidding them prepare his body for the funeral of a Celtic chief, which would take place on the morrow. His father, he informed them, had chosen that his spirit join Taranis, the Celtic god of thunder. He then joined Katrina, Orius and Emilia in a large room where a wood fire was burning at one end, throwing eerie shadows in the dark corners. Katrina rose as he entered and encircled him in her arms, no words were needed. They both remained motionless for a long time, taking comfort from each other's bodies.

Eventually Katrina spoke. "Aurthora, would you like Emilia to sing at your father's funeral? She has a truly beautiful voice it will surely be an appropriate gesture for the departure of such a great man." "I have no objections," was the simple reply.

"There may be some from the high priest Zanton," continued Katrina, "he seems to frown on any initiative that takes the attention away from himself and his ceremonies."

"Then I definitely have no objection to Emilia singing at my father's funeral, I do not anticipate there being any objections from the high priest Zanton. He has been very quiet of late. I thank Emilia sincerely for the offer, which I accept most readily," looking towards Emilia, who rose in silence at his glance and came over and touched him on the shoulder, in a moving show of emotion, then returned to her seat next to Orius.

It was while they were sitting around the log fire that Aurthora confided in Orius. Despite his grief on his father's death, he could not remove from his mind the coming conflict against the invaders. He asked him for his military opinion of the Saxons, which after several moments' careful consideration, Orius volunteered.

"My experience of the Anglo-Saxon way of fighting was when they last invaded and tested our resolve to defend these islands. This was during the latter stages of my involvement in the Roman legion. They tend to attack in mass, they are tall well-built warriors, quite fearless. They use their large two-handed swords and great double-edged battleaxes to smash their way through their opponent's defences. Their archers skirt the edges of the battlefield, picking off individual enemy soldiers who have been separated from their comrades, they also attempt to eliminate any leaders or chiefs. As an organised striking force their archers are ineffective, more of an irritant. Thanks to your action today they do not have an effective cavalry, only their own mounted men on small horses. These are not an organised cavalry force, and are mainly employed for scouting and harrying purposes. The secret of defeating the Anglo-Saxon army is to blunt, hold, and then destroy the thrust of their heavy infantry, which is their great strength."

"Thank you Orius, as usual your thoughts are most constructive." Yet again, to the forefront of his mind sprang the role the archers and the heavy horses had played in all the actions he had witnessed against the Anglo-Saxons and their paid mercenaries. Even though he tried to join in the conversation of the group, this thought kept returning to the forefront of his mind.

It was late – well after curfew – when the group departed from his father's lodgings. Orius and Emilia headed towards Myridyn the Physician's house while he and Katrina took the opposite direction towards the barracks and his quarters. They were stopped twice on their short journey by patrols of nervous town guards. He was pleased that the patrols were so vigilant he could understand their nervousness after the assassinations. What was more, every one knew that within the next few days the Celtic army would be leaving the town and vacating the nearby encampment moving to the chosen field of battle, to be tested against the experienced and formidable Anglo-Saxon forces.

The following morning he was up and about at daylight; he had much on his mind and many things to attend to. He and Cimbonda Gilberto decided that his father Prassat Ambrosius, and his old companion-in-arms Neila Gilberto, would be given a joint burial. All the members of the Celtic Round Council and King Erion would be present to honour the support the two old warriors had given to the Celtic cause. Despite the earliness of Aurthora's departure from the barracks that morning young Darius was already there, waiting at the guardroom near the barracks' entrance. He dropped in step alongside Aurthora as he set off along the narrow streets towards the lodgings of his late father.

While Darius waited outside, he entered the house and spent a short while with his father's body and the two faithful old attendants, who had worked through the night to prepare their master for his funeral. His body had been washed and treated with scented oils, then dressed in his battle armour, his weapons placed at his side.

"My father would be proud of the way you have prepared him, Eryl and Borode. You have both been faithful attendants to my father for as long as I can remember. It cannot have been easy for you over the last few weeks, I thank you for all your care and attention from the bottom of my heart." This short speech of gratitude brought tears to the eyes of the two old men.

It was Eryl who gathered himself sufficiently to reply. "I think I speak for both of us when I say that your father was a fair and honest master, it was an honour and our good fortune to have been in his service. Both Borode and I have had joy in seeing you grow to be such a fine young man, you should know that your actions and your achievements made your father immensely proud of you."

Aurthora was lost for words. In reply he embraced the two frail old men in turn. Then all three stood in silence for several minutes beside his father, before he bade his farewell, leaving them to complete their preparations.

He strode out of the house, taking care to keep his face turned away from Darius, who sensitively walked behind him as he hurried along the narrow stone paved streets of the town towards the Great Hall for a meeting of the Round Council. When he arrived at the hall, he found he was one of the first and took his seat at the table.

The next Council member to appear was Longinus Caratacusi, who limped over to Aurthora and immediately offered his condolences for his father's death. As each Council member entered the chamber they came and spoke a few words to him. Many had fought alongside his father in the various battles it had taken to consolidate the Kingdom of Elmet, and eventually form the Celtic Alliance. The last member to arrive was King Erion himself. Aurthora was startled by his sallow complexion, visible despite the coating of rouge that had been dusted across his cheeks. His unsteady walk as he slowly made his way across the room to sit down heavily on his seat brought murmurs of concern from the members around the chamber at the obviously distressed condition of the Great King.

Raising his hand for silence King Erion slowly rose from his seated position and stood upright, leaning heavily with both hands on the edge of the table. "My friends and fellow Celts, I apologise for my condition but it need not alarm you. My physician Myridyn assures me that it is but temporary," indicating towards the entrance where Myridyn was standing. Myridyn bowed his head to the members and said loudly and firmly, "That is so."

"Therefore!" the king continued, "let us complete our business. Tomorrow we leave to fight the Anglo-Saxon army. Today we will all attend the joint funeral, and mourn our fellow Celtic Council members, Neila Gilberto, leader of the Cornovii tribe and one of the staunchest supporters of our cause. Also my dear and close friend Prassat Ambrosius who I will dearly miss. I will now leave you to discuss and make arrangements for moving the army. The place I suggest we meet the enemy I have marked on the map." The Great King indicated the large drawing of the Kingdom of Elmet and the lands surrounding its borders that was hung on the wall of the Great Hall. He then turned, and with the help of Myridyn and his assistant Disaylann, slowly and painfully left through the open doors of the Great Hall.

No sooner had the doors closed behind him than the conversation amongst the Council was of the King's obvious ill health.

Bernica Calgacus of the Coritani tribe was the first to voice an opinion. "I think I speak for all of us here when I say I am concerned about the health of our king. I think his condition is more serious than he will admit the morale of our troops on seeing their leader in this weak and pitiful condition may seriously influence their spirit and their will to fight."

There were loud murmurs of approval from the majority of the members of the Council. "I disagree!" The voice was that of Longinus Caratacusi. He had never spoken in the chamber since his appointment, by the tone of his voice he was obviously very nervous. "The Celtic Nation as a man has gathered here to fight, and fight they will to the best of their ability. If they have to die in an attempt to preserve and protect our lands, then they will do that, no matter who is their leader." There were shouts of "Rubbish!" and "Go back to your bride!" from some of the older members at the table who resented this younger upstart, who had only recently been appointed to the Celtic Council, voicing such a strong opinion. Longinus Caratacusi blushed at the insults and was quick to react.

"If the Council member who has just insulted me, my tribe and my family would care to stand and say these things to my face, we will proceed into the courtyard to settle this matter."

It was obvious that the situation was getting out of hand; the last thing the Celtic Alliance needed was for several of its tribal leaders to end up fighting amongst themselves on the eve of the battle.

Aurthora was about to intervene when Boro Sigurd, the senior court official, spoke to ease the situation. "My lords! We have two funerals to attend later today. I beg you, do not add to this tally. We must surely save ourselves for the real enemy, let them be the ones to taste our steel. Come, let us finish the business for which this meeting was called and allow Aurthora to outline the position of the enemy forces and the place the king has chosen for us to do battle." Aurthora had decided he would not disclose his own battle plan at this time, but wait to hear what other proposals were forthcoming from the council members.

With the situation temporary deflated, the Council gathered around Aurthora, who gave them a brief description of the position of the Celtic forces and the approximate position of the enemy. The council listened quietly until he finished. He was then inundated with shouts for an explanation of the Great King's plan for the Celtic forces. "What are the king's plans for this battle?" "How will our forces be deployed?" "Who will lead our forces?" Aurthora was overwhelmed. He could not answer any of the questions that were being shouted at him from all sides. He looked around desperately for Myridyn, but the physician had left with the king.

He felt frustrated and angry that he had been placed in this position. It was then it suddenly dawned on him that it was highly probable there was no battle plan? All the King's and Council's efforts had been concentrated on gathering and holding the Celtic forces together and organising their training and lines of supplies. With the King's injury no thought had been given to the end result: 'The Battle'. He raised his hands for order. "Friends! Please have patience, the King will in due course inform the council of his plan for the coming battle." It was Boro Sigurd who now intervened, going over to Longinus Caratacusi and shouting above the clamouring. "Come, let us depart now. Let us prepare ourselves to see our old comrades leave on their journey to the next world. Then we will return to study in detail the King's map and make preparations for battle." Then leading Longinus Caratacusi from the hall by the arm, he was slowly followed by the rest of the Celtic Round Council, some still muttering amongst themselves over the lack of information on what role they had to play.

Eventually only Aurthora remained. He had just moved to study the large parchment map when Orius, who had been waiting outside, entered. He had seen the King leave assisted by Disaylann and Myridyn, followed shortly afterwards by all the rest of the Council members except Aurthora, so he had entered the hall to look for him. In the course of his long army career Orius had seen many maps from all parts of the known world. It was part of the Roman Empire's success to know the terrain that they would be travelling through, or where they would fight their next battle. He joined Aurthora and both men stood side-by-side studying the large parchment hanging from the wall.

"You see, Orius, the point the Great King has marked? That is where he proposes to fight the Anglo-Saxon army." Orius studied the map for some time before commenting. "The position has many good points, but as with any plan it has its weaknesses also. The Great King has chosen to fight on a plain, with high ground behind him to help protect the army's rear. This is an advantage for your cavalry. But at the same time it also means the enemy's main force can be easily directed at your centre defences. It will be difficult to withstand a prolonged and sustained attack; your troops could well crumble and your forces would be divided. The Anglo-Saxons would then use a holding force to keep you apart while the bulk of their army attacked and destroyed one half of your army before turning to your second half with the full force of all their troops. At that point your cavalry could only harry the outskirts of their forces.

"You have to form a plan to resist and break down that powerful, initial, surging thrust, yet one that still allows you to retain your formation and be in a position to counter-attack as their attack falters. And remember, you are outnumbered by two – or possibly three – to one if our information is correct. They can afford to make mistakes and still win the battle, but your Celtic army does not have the same luxury."

Standing before the large map he absorbed all that Orius had said but did not comment; he remained fixed in front of the large parchment as if it enchanted him, his head moving from side to side while he muttered to himself as if he were trying to solve a giant puzzle. Orius meanwhile went and sat on one of the chairs that surrounded the large table, his thoughts drifting as he looked around this familiar room. He had been in this room on various occasions when he was enlisted in the Roman legion. It brought back distant memories. Nothing had really changed. He was here with the Celtic army helping to plan a campaign against the Anglo-Saxons, just as his officers had done twenty-five years before. In that particular battle the Roman legions had decisively beaten the Anglo-Saxons, and driven them from the island of Britannia, but now they were back, with a much larger and stronger force than before.

Chapter Twenty Five

A large group of people had gathered outside the property where Prassus Ambrosius lay, a converted Celtic chariot stood waiting. As was the custom Aurthora as the eldest, and in this case the only son, took the bridle of the horse; calling Katrina to walk beside him, he led the animal and the chariot down the narrow cobbled street. The clip clop of the horse's metal shoes and the metal-rimmed wheels of the chariot on the stone cobbles were the only sound in the still air as the long procession of mourners followed the chariot towards the gate of the High Town of Buxonana. It was here that the chariot led by Camaro, the eldest son of Neila Gilberto, joined them, and the two groups of mourners merged.

The procession was met by the high priest Zanton and his group of Druid priests, some of whom were blowing on the long, boar-headed horns, while others banged cymbals in time to the slow, regular steps of their procession. It had been the wish of these old warriors to be buried according to Druid custom, rather than in the new Christian manner.

Two stone cairns had been built to the height of a man's chest, on which the bodies of the two deceased members of the Celtic Council would be placed. Aurthora's men in full battle dress formed a corridor, one hand resting on their long rectangular shields. As the bodies of the two warriors passed, the men lowered their heads in homage to two brave fellow Celts. Aurthora was surprised at the numbers that had come to witness the final journey of two prominent members of the Round Council: most of the Celtic army that was encamped outside the walls of the High Town seemed to be present. The majority had come to honour the two warriors, others had come to witness the event, but many had come to see the man they called Aurthora, the one that they had heard so much about, the one who had inflicted so many losses on their enemy, the one they now called 'Hammer of the Anglo-Saxons'.

It was during the ceremony performed by the chief Druid, Zanton, that Aurthora had the opportunity to look around him. Not since the days of the Great Queen, Boudicca, had such a large force of Celts been brought together under one banner; all this had been accomplished by Great King Erion, whose family claimed direct lineage to that same noble woman who had fought the invaders of their island so many years before. Aurthora's gaze returned to the King, mounted on his famous grey horse.

Only those standing close to him could see that he was very pale under the rouge, that he was struggling to sit upright in the saddle. Standing on either side of him were Myridyn and Disaylann. He noticed Myridyn's frequent glances at the Great King, he was obviously concerned about his condition. Reading these signs he feared the wound the King had received from the leader of the Flavian cavalry was more serious than had been let known.

When Zanton had completed his ceremony in the Celtic way and the spirits of the two warriors had been released from their bodies to travel their chosen route, Emilia came forward and stood on a low platform that raised her above the heads of the gathered congregation. Behind her were several musicians with their harps and pipes. It was when these men began to play their instruments that the murmuring of low conversation from the vast crowd slowly ceased.

When Emilia began to sing Aurthora was amazed: never before had he heard a voice so beautiful and clear. The small clearing acted like a natural amphitheatre, with the ground rising away all around, so that even the furthest of the gathered men could hear the clear voice as it seemed to float over their heads and drift onwards to the low hills beyond. Emilia sang a well known story of the Celtic people; several men near to Aurthora began to hum in harmony, then several more in the vast gathering started to sing, hesitant at first, but as more joined them so they sang with more confidence. Spontaneously, groups of men amongst the vast gathering also added their voices to the legend of Great Queen Boudicca, the many leaders who had followed her over many generations, their attempts to keep the Celtic nation free, defending their lands and birthright against foreign invaders. They sang of the sacrifices and the defeats that the tribes had suffered, of their heroes and the victories they had celebrated. Emilia finished by honouring the two dead chiefs who had fought all their lives for the cause, and Great King Erion who had brought the tribes together as one, and was himself one of the great Celtic present-day heroes. When Emilia finished her song there was complete silence amongst the large gathering of men, as if they were being mesmerised under a potent spell; for a brief moment they had all been visited by their ancestors and their past Celtic heroes.

"That young women with her one song has just knitted the tribes together as a nation more than all men's fine speeches could ever do." Aurthora did not need to turn, he recognised the voice of Myridyn, who moved to stand near him.

As Emilia stepped from her platform the Great King brought his horse forward in front of the two stone cairns on which the bodies lay. "Both these men," he declared in a firm voice, "have served me and the Celtic cause without reservation. They sacrificed the comforts of warm fires the closeness of family life to campaign with me in order to retain our culture and to be free to follow the chosen path of our people. They have been true comrades-in-arms and will be sorely missed by their families, their tribesmen, by the Celtic nation and by me.

King Erion drew his sword, kissed the hilt and, moving his horse forward, touched in turn the stone cairns on which the bodies lay. He then returned to the centre of the small clearing. He waited until there had been time for his message to be repeated to the many men who were on the fringes of the crowd.

"I have one more important declaration to make," he continued.

Aurthora could see that the guards keeping the vast crowd back were struggling as they were pushed forward by those behind hoping to hear the King's words.

"I am Erion, descendent of the Great Queen Boudicca. I am also the godfather of Aurthora Ambrosius, the son of my recently departed comrade-in-arms who was my dearest and closest friend. Today I proclaim that Aurthora, having lost his own father, shall now take my name, and from this day forth he will be called Aurthora Ambrosius Aurelianus. In front of all of you present here today who are witnesses to this action, I now present my godson with my own sword, passed down to me from my father and his father before him, back to our great Queen. This steel, blessed by all our Celtic gods, which no man's hand can break or splinter, I give to him so that he may fight the Celtic cause as long as there is breath in his body." King Erion then edged his horse forward and presented his sword, hilt first, to an amazed Aurthora.

As he dutifully took the beautiful engraved weapon he looked into the King's eyes and saw that even the simple action of passing the sword was causing the great man severe pain. Sweat was running down his face leaving lines where it had washed away the coloured rouge. His heart went out to this great man, who even though he was suffering intensely from his wound had made the great effort to honour his comrades-in-arms at their funeral.

The King's statement made little impression on Aurthora, who was still grieving for the loss of his father, and deeply concerned about the clearly distressed condition of the leader and figurehead of the Celtic Alliance. But to the members of the Celtic Round Council, to Myridyn who looked on in amazement, also to Orius, it was strikingly significant. The great Celtic King

Erion, before the entire Celtic army and all its leaders, had proclaimed his godson Aurthora as his successor to the Kingdom of Elmet and leader of the Celtic cause.

Orius was the first to recover from the shock of the King's statement, it was he who began to chant, quietly at first, then joined by Darius, young Cynfelin Facilus, then the Town Guard that had formed the Guard of Honour, followed by Boro Sigurd the High Official and leader of the Celtic Round Council. Timus Calgacus joined in the chant, quickly followed by the members of his tribe, Roderick Tristan the master bowman and his men added their voices to the growing volume, Cimbonda Gilberto with all his followers and clan members who were there to honour their dead leader took up the chant.

Soon all those around the small clearing were chanting, in a wave it spread outwards, rising in volume to include the vast gathering of men that formed the bulk of the army. Soon it became a great roar as more and more of the warriors joined in, all repeating the same name. Over and over and over again.

The people in the town paused in their daily business as the sound rebounded first around their houses and then reverberated from the walls of the town itself, the busy market coming to a standstill as the ever-increasing sound drowned out their conversations. The old cart driver collecting water on the outskirts of the town stopped filling his wooden barrels and straightened his back as the sound reached him. It even carried on the wind as far as the hidden hamlet in the marsh, many miles from the High Town, where the people stopped their daily chores to listen to the faint, but very clear sound: Aurthora! AUrthora! AURthora! AURThora! AURTHORA!

Kuyt Persi was the lone survivor of the Flavian cavalry, alive by chance because his horse had gone lame so he had been left behind at the pass until their return. From his elevated position, he had seen the final engagement and the annihilation of his friends and comrades from the shelter of some rocks where he had been hiding. It was only now he felt safe to make his way slowly back towards his Anglo-Saxon masters, leading his lame horse behind him. He wondered what the reaction of the Saxon King Ælle and his sons would be when he informed them he was the sole survivor of the once great Flavian cavalry.

Before they had left the Anglo-Saxon camp on what had turned out to be a disastrous mission, he had heard a rumour that the Saxon King might be planning to spend some of the gold and silver he had taken from the three kingdoms he had overrun and use it to recruit the equally famous Thracian horsemen as a counter to the Celtic cavalry, who were now using this new breed of heavy horse. He had first seen these great beasts in the Anglo-Saxon camp and had been greatly impressed. The renegade scar-faced Celt they called Petrov Joma rode one, as did several of his followers. He hoped the rumour was true, for then he would try to find a position as a mercenary with these Thracian horsemen.

It was while he was pondering these thoughts as he led his lame horse behind him that he too heard what sounded like distant thunder. As he stopped to listen he could make out the name – faint but unmistakeably clear as it rebounded and echoed between the hills on each side of the pass – *AUrthora! AURThora! AURTHORA*! To Kuyt Persi in his present position it sounded as if the name was mocking him.

The vast numbers that made up the Celtic army had returned from the funeral. They all had much to do; they had already been informed that the waiting was over, the following day they would break camp and march to meet their Anglo-Saxon enemy.

Aurthora was alone with Katrina watching the workmen complete the building of the stone cairn that would cover his father's body. He thought the spot he had chosen for his father's burial place was appropriate: it was here that he had led his cavalry into the flank of the Flavian mercenaries. A short distance away was the ever-present figure of Darius, who moved across to intercept a lone rider coming from the direction of the High Town.

He looked on as the rider conversed with Darius for a few moments, then pulled his mount around and returned in the direction he had come. Darius watched the retreating mounted figure for a few moments then turned and walked towards Aurthora and Katrina. "The messenger was from Myridyn," said Darius as he came within earshot, "he would like you to join him, the Great King, and several of the senior members of the Celtic Council in the Great Hall as soon as possible."

Aurthora sighed. With the army moving out the next day he had been hoping to spend the evening with Katrina, they had seen so little of one another of late. "I'll try and leave as soon as it's possible, Katrina," he said as they both walked towards the raised stone road that would lead them to the South Gate of the High Town.

On their arrival they were met by Orius and his comrade Mallus Calvus, both of whom were on duty and were checking the guards at the gate as part of their rounds. "Orius!" he called as he saw his old friend, "Join me! I have a meeting in the Great Hall. I may require your advice. Your comrade Mallus

Calvus can complete your duties and Darius can escort Katrina to Myridyn's house then return to the barracks later."

Orius dutifully saluted Aurthora, spoke to Mallus for a few moments then accompanied Aurthora to the Great Hall while Darius escorted Katrina to Myridyn's house.

When the two men arrived, Orius remained outside the entrance with the King's personal guards and several other members of the Town Guard who had been appointed to protect the other members of the Celtic Council. Inside the Hall a table and five chairs had been placed near the large wall map. King Erion was seated on one of the chairs with Myridyn standing at his shoulder.

The senior official Boro Sigurd was there together with Bernica Calgacus, the leader of the Coritani tribe. Aurthora paid his respects to the King and the other members of the Inner Council nodding in the direction of Myridyn. The King was the first to speak, and his words were directed to Aurthora.

"Aurthora, first of all, whatever you hear or see in this room tonight we must have your word that you will not disclose to any other." Aurthora indicated that he agreed.

"Over twenty years ago when the Roman legions were preparing to leave these shores it came to the notice of Myridyn, our most trusted court advisor, that a piece of valuable equipment was available at a price from the Roman general in charge of the departing legions.

This piece of equipment was called Ryphomachia. It consisted of a planning board and many pieces. It has been used by the religious and military leaders of all the major civilisations since the beginning of time. No one knows where it originated and there are no written instructions for its use since it has always been considered such a vitally secret piece of equipment. Instructions were only passed on by word of mouth to the most trusted highly placed government and religious officials.

"Depending on how the pieces were set on the board, it could be used to predict events in the movement of the planets and stars many years in advance, or severe changes in the weather that might affect a nation's harvest, even the possible future of kingdoms. But it was also used by army generals and navy admirals of all the great empires to assist them in planning their battles and military campaigns. If supplied with the correct information this complicated tool could assist in gaining its users a prize as great as a kingdom or even an Empire."

At this point the king stopped to allow the fascinated Aurthora to absorb what he had said.

It was Myridyn who took up the story. "The price that was paid to the Roman general for this board and the knowledge of how the pieces should be placed, was four sacks of gold and a safe conduct without harassment or attacks against his troops while they withdrew from their Empire's long occupation of these islands. Before he died your father Prassat Ambrosius was a member of this inner group. All of us here have voted that you have earned the right to take your father's seat on this Inner War Council. We have used this board on many occasions, the result is always the same. So far it is only the Roman legions' method of fighting that succeeds against the Anglo-Saxons. This is the reason for all the training our young men have been subjected to over the years. This is why it is so similar to the Roman way of fighting.

"But in order to counter the possible lack of iron discipline in our troops that the Roman legions enforced in theirs, we have included as the second line of defence the method used by the Spartans of the Old Greek Empire of Alexander the Great. You have seen our troops practising using the pilum, fighting over the shoulders of their comrades in front of them, who form a steel wall facing the enemy with their rectangular shields and short swords. It is a most effective form of defence, and if this line is formed by determined well trained troops it is almost unbreakable."

Myridyn stopped as the small group murmured its agreement, then continued. "We thought the mercenary Flavian cavalry might have succeeded, but fortunately you and your men have recently removed that threat. We are here today to finalise our campaign and the positions of our troops and cavalry. We are aware of the strength of the enemy and the strategy they have used in their past battles, against the three kingdoms they have already succeeded in ravaging and conquering since they landed on our shores. When we have made our decisions, we will place the necessary pieces on the board, and see what result is forthcoming."

It was many hours later that he left the Great Hall. A battle plan had been agreed by the Inner War Council, which would be put before the full Celtic Round Council at first light the following day. Aurthora was concerned and very quiet as Orius and he made their way back towards the physician's house. "You seem to have many heavy thoughts, Aurthora," said Orius, unable to stand the silence any longer.

"You are quite right, Orius," he replied. "The King did not contribute much to the battle plan; indeed, he seemed quite distant. I think he is still suffering from the wound he received from the Flavian cavalry officer."

"I agree," said Orius, "I have seen it many times before, the wound is slowly poisoning him."

241

"You are indeed right, Orius, his mind is not as sharp as usual. Some of his suggestions and the decisions that were taken by the War Council worry me; they do not seem logical. I have a feeling of foreboding."

They walked in silence for a while and then Aurthora stopped and turned to face his old friend and tutor. He had made a decision.

"Tonight Orius, I was accepted onto the Celtic Inner War Council and was shown a strange divining board called Rypho…"

"…machia." To Aurthora's surprise, Orius finished the word.

"Then you've heard of this board?" exclaimed Aurthora in amazement.

"Yes," replied Orius. "It was one of the worst kept secrets in the Roman legions. I know of it, and I have seen it put to use in the same room that you were in tonight, but more than twenty years ago."

Aurthora was lost for words for several moments. "But I was sworn to secrecy!" he gasped.

"Every Roman legionnaire heard some rumour about the board, but I was fortunate to see it in action. The results were quite remarkable."

"So it does work!" exclaimed Aurthora.

"It works, but only if the correct information is placed on it," replied Orius.

"The Great King, Myridyn and the other two members feel confident that their plan will succeed," volunteered Aurthora. Orius's reply had done nothing to quell Aurthora's misgivings.

"In my experience of war involving the Romans and the empires before them who used this arcane board, it was an asset – a great asset – as long as all the information is available for the necessary pieces to be placed on the board. However, in my experience of war, and I have been in many battles, nothing ever goes according to plan, I have seen that at such moments what wins the day is if the general sees a serious situation developing, makes the right decision to rectify the problem and most importantly, acts quickly."

They both continued walking, but now Aurthora's mind was in even greater turmoil than when he had left the Great Hall.

First light the following morning brought a hive of activity from all over the High Town of Buxonana and the army encampment. Wagons and carts were stacked with the temporary shelters, lines of mules and pack ponies were being loaded with all the army's possessions, each clan was moving off in turn, led by its tribal chief. Some of the warriors had been living with their families, a policy that had been discouraged but not banned since large numbers of the Celts were refugees from the bordering kingdoms overrun by the Anglo-Saxons. These families were waving off their menfolk as they remained behind in the camp to await the outcome of the forthcoming battle.

Aurthora, meanwhile, had inspected his men who made up the Town Guard. Orius and his old comrade Mallus Calvus had them parade on the barrack ground. Aurthora could not help but be impressed by the appearance of the lines of soldiers with their burnished metal shoulder and shin guards, shiny metal apron strips that protected their hips and thighs, oiled leather breastplates, their metal-lined rectangular Celtic shields. Each man bore two heavy iron throwing spears, plus the pugio and gladius sheathed at their side.

"Our men look immaculate, Orius," said Aurthora to his old tutor, who followed him during the inspection.

"You must thank Mallus for what you see Aurthora, he has drilled these men until they are as good as any legionnaire."

"Yes, we are indeed fortunate to be able to call upon so many men with so much military knowledge, what our men have learned will certainly be put to the test very shortly," said Aurthora as he turned. "Mallus, I thank you for the time and effort you have spent drilling these young men. When we leave the High Town I would like you to take charge of the Town Militia that we will be leaving behind to defend the town in case of attack. There will also be several of the senior members of the Celtic Round Council to assist you, they have been informed of your appointment."

"I thank you, Sire, it is indeed a great honour. I will not let you or the people of Buxonana regret the trust you have placed in me." He was pleased with Mallus and his reply, he had every faith in the old legionnaire.

Aurthora did not attend the full meeting of the Celtic Round Council, making the excuse that he had to prepare his men for the march against the enemy. But his real reason was that he knew the proposal of the Inner War Council would be accepted: there was no alternative.

However, he was not happy with the plans that had been put forward, yet his suggestions had been dismissed out of hand. He felt that what he had proposed had not been given serious consideration because of his age, because they thought his knowledge of battle was restricted to hit-and-run skirmishes. Undoubtedly they were more experienced in making decisions on the larger scale of a great battle, yet he was still perturbed that their plans for the coming conflict were not flexible enough, he felt that if he went to the full meeting he would not be able to conceal his strong misgivings.

The overall battle plan was reasonably good, but he believed it could be improved tremendously, he knew only too well that there would be no second chance. He rode out of town with his mounted group of cavalry on their heavy horses, the ever-present Darius by his side, while the main force of the Town Guard marched behind them, led by Orius riding one of the smaller local horses.

Cimbonda Gilberto's horsemen were patrolling and protecting the flanks of the large column since this was Cornovii country. Their infantry was at the front of the column under the leadership of Cimbonda Gilberto himself, behind them in his covered carriage was Great King Erion, followed by the members of his clan. Behind them were the members of Celtic Round Council, each leading the warriors from their individual tribes. Then came the Scoti Celts from the Island of Diariada who had responded to Great King Erion's call for assistance; alongside them, the groups of northern Celts who had been made homeless by the advancing Anglo-Saxon army. Timus Calgacus and the members of his Coritani tribe formed the rear of the armed column, behind them came the vast army of wheeled vehicles pulled by a collection of various animals – donkeys, mules, ponies, horses, and buffalo – scattered amongst which were individuals carrying great packs. These were the camp followers: traders and merchants who made their living by providing goods and services the army could not.

Aurthora rode in silence, unable to shake off the feeling of foreboding that had enveloped him since the previous day's meeting of the Inner War Council, which was not helped by the fact that even though he constantly scanned the skies, there was no sign of the buzzard, which he had come to regard as a good omen.

To break the monotony, Aurthora, followed by Darius and the young Roman Celt Cynfelin Facilus, rode up to some high ground looking down onto the long, straggling column of men, animals and vehicles. He could make out the Great King's covered wagon with his grey horse tethered behind, walking close by he saw the figure of Disaylann leading Myridyn's mule. There was no sight of Myridyn, *Is he in the Great King's wagon?* Aurthora wondered.

Behind the Great King's wagon was a wheeled vehicle with a brightly coloured, patterned roof. At first Aurthora was unable to make out what the vehicle was; no one would notice the odd roof unless they were well above it. Then it suddenly dawned on him that it was Myridyn's pigeon-cote, taken from beside his house. The old physician was presumably still receiving messages via his pigeons from spies and informers, even as the Celtic army was travelling to take up its battle positions.

Chapter Twenty Six

That night the army camped at the head of the pass: below them lay the plain where the Great King planned to bring the Anglo-Saxons to battle. While his men were erecting their shelters, Aurthora and Orius, with the two young men Darius and Cynfelin Facilus, rode on ahead to inspect the proposed battle site. As they rode through the lines of the Cornovii tribe where Cimbonda Gilberto was inspecting his troops, positioned to protect the Celtic army from a surprise Anglo-Saxon attack, Cimbonda broke off his task and rode towards them. "Welcome Aurthora," he called as he came nearer, stopping his horse in front of the small group and nodding to Orius and the two young Celts. "It is good to see you again," he said as he grasped the wrist of Aurthora's extended arm.

"It is good to see you too, my friend," replied Aurthora.

"I would be careful if you intend going far onto the plain, Aurthora, my men have come into contact with several of the Anglo-Saxon patrols; they are watching us from a distance, they may think you are easy prey if you travel too far from the pass."

"Thank you for your warning, Cimbonda, it is reassuring to know your men are so vigilant that we can sleep safely in our shelters tonight." Cimbonda acknowledged the compliment and rode with the small group to the end of the pass where his men were patrolling. There he left them in order to check on several of the outlying, manned positions that were overlooking the pass.

Aurthora rode on into the plain; he wanted to get a feel of the area. If this was where the battle was to take place and the future of the Celtic nation was to be decided, he needed to know the lie of the land. There were several low hills that he mentally noted: It would be strategically important for his army to hold that high ground. A plan was already forming in his mind. He had already decided that if there were problems he would not abide by the Celtic Council's war plan for the campaign against the Anglo-Saxons. He would ignore them and follow his own intuition and implement his own plan. He had decided he would discuss it with Orius on their return to camp. He was feeling much better in his own mind now that he had eventually come to a decision. They had just turned their horses in order to return the way they had come when a shout from the ever-observant Darius shook him from his reflections: "Enemy horsemen approaching fast!"

A group of about half a score of horsemen were bearing down on them from behind one of the low-lying hills. "Ride!" shouted Aurthora, driving his horse forward, quickly followed by his three companions. He knew that the large breed of horse that he, Darius and Cynfelin were riding could out distance their pursuers, but Orius had never been a good horseman the mount he was riding was for transport only, it was a local, small breed of horse; it was also old and Orius was a heavy man.

He was aware that Orius was dropping further and further behind the three. Within a very short time he was twenty paces to the rear of his comrades, the group of enemy horsemen were closing on him with every stride of their racing mounts. Aurthora was in a quandary: should he turn and fight the enemy cavalry that outnumbered them more than three to one and risk the lives of Darius and Cynfelin in a vain attempt to try and save Orius? And what if he himself were killed or captured? Who would lead the Celtic army then? The King was sick. He could not lead the army in his present condition. The members of the Celtic Council were quite capable of leading their own tribes, which they had done many times in the past. But Aurthora had doubts if any of them could lead the whole Celtic army, there were too many divisions among the various tribes and their leaders.

The issue was brought to a head by Orius's old horse stumbling, possibly through fatigue, the old legionnaire was sent hurtling over the horse's head to land heavily and spread-eagled on the ground. Cynfelin was the first to react: he pulled his horse to a grinding halt, spun it around on its hind legs changing direction in a matter of moments. Then he headed back towards Orius's semi-conscious, horizontal figure.

Cynfelin stopped about twenty paces from Orius quickly dismounting. Within seconds he had strung his long bow by the time Aurthora and Darius joined him he had two arrows in the air, flying in the direction of the fast approaching, closely grouped enemy horsemen.

The enemy cavalry were caught unawares; they presumed they were out of range of any archers, which was true of most nations' bows – but not the Celtic longbow.

By the time they spread out to make themselves less of an easy target they had lost two men. One had taken an arrow in the chest after it had glanced off the skull of his horse, the other had taken an arrow that passed through his calf muscle and into the flank of his horse, sending it mad with pain. Two other horses were seriously wounded, screaming and kicking out, making them uncontrollable for their riders.

Aurthora, now alongside Cynfelin, sent Darius, since he was the lightest, to assist Orius, who was staggering dizzily towards his three comrades, grasping the reins of Cynfelin's horse to stop it bolting in the turmoil that was going on all around. As soon as Darius had pulled Orius up behind him, he spurred his horse back towards his two comrades.

"Well done Darius," Aurthora shouted as Darius rode past him with Orius clinging for dear life to to the rear of the young man's jerkin. Aurthora waited for Cynfelin, the young Roman Celt, to use up all the long arrows from his sheath, then the last of the shorter arrows originally designed for his short cavalry bow. But the respite gained had been sufficient: The two now riding double were well clear and were already galloping towards the safety of the pass. The Anglo-Saxon horsemen were now giving chase to Aurthora and Cynfelin, who in turn were galloping after the fast disappearing Darius and Orius.

The appearance of Cimbonda Gilberto with a large force of his horsemen coming to Aurthora's assistance convinced the mounted Anglo-Saxons that their pursuit was an unwise venture, they turned around quickly heading back the way they had come, pursued by some of the Celtic horsemen.

"We saw your dilemma from our outpost on the hill," shouted Cimbonda. "The Anglo-Saxon riders have been testing our defences and our reactions all morning."

"I thank you and your men for your timely intervention, Cimbonda," called Aurthora in reply.

"Those horsemen were neither Angles nor Saxons," interjected Cynfelin. Everyone turned towards him in surprise.

"Then who were they?" exclaimed Cimbonda.

"They were the same cavalry that my father was in charge of when he was with the legion. They were Thracian horsemen."

Cynfelin's statement left everyone speechless. They had all heard of the prowess of these legendary horsemen and the skill and quickness of manoeuvre they showed in battle. It was Aurthora who eventually broke the silence.

"Are you sure, Cynfelin? You're not mistaken?"

"He is not mistaken." It was Orius who spoke. "I recognised them too. Depending on their numbers, they could cause the Celtic army a serious problem."

It was a very sober and thoughtful group that made its way back towards the pass and the Celtic army's main encampment.

It was during this ride that Cimbonda brought his horse alongside Aurthora's. "Did you know my brother Camero has relinquished his claim to the chieftainship of the Cornovii tribe in favour of me? He wishes to follow the faith of the new Christian religion and spread the word of this God."

"I am surprised," replied Aurthora. "I have not met your brother but I congratulate you on your new position."

As they arrived closer to the pass Cimbonda and his horsemen left them to carry on their patrol around the low hills on the edge of the plain. Fortunately, Orius's horse had followed them, albeit at a much slower pace, and suffered no more than grazed shins for its stumble. So they entered the Celtic encampment as they had left: Aurthora, Darius and Cynfelin on the large mounts and Orius on the small local horse.

"Your archery was exceptional today, Cynfelin," Aurthora complimented the young Roman Celt.

"I thank you Aurthora. My father was commander of the Thracian cavalry, he taught me how to shoot a small bow from a moving horse, but he paid for the best tuition silver could buy for the Celtic longbow. My teacher was Roderick Tristan."

"Then you have done Roderick Tristan and your father proud this day, Cynfelin," said Aurthora as they entered the Celtic army camp.

"Tell me," he continued, "where is your father now?"

"He is here in the Celtic camp. He offered his services to the Great King when the call to arms went out. He is in charge of teaching the young Celts to shoot the small bow from a galloping horse," replied Cynfelin proudly.

They parted company, Darius, Cynfelin and Orius going to their separate shelters while Aurthora went in search of Myridyn to discuss the latest development: the appearance of the Thracian cavalry. He wanted the advice of the old physician, because later that night he intended bringing the subject to the attention of the King and the Celtic War Council.

Aurthora found Myridyn at the mobile pigeon loft. His young assistant Disaylann was feeding the birds whereas Myridyn was engrossed in reading a message printed on the finest of material, similar to the clothes he had loaned to Katrina after her accident.

"Ah! Aurthora," he exclaimed as he looked up and saw the young Celt standing before him.

"I was about to send for you. This latest message I have received could cause us some problems." He handed the pigeon from which he had just removed the message to Disaylann and grasped Aurthora's outstretched hand. Both men walked a short distance away from the cote, Aurthora was the first to speak.

"Tell me Myridyn, does your problem concern the Thracian cavalry that the Anglo-Saxons have employed as mercenaries?"

"You are as well informed as I am, and just as quick!" gasped the surprised Myridyn.

"We encountered a group of them on the plain earlier today. "I was lucky not to lose Orius; he fell from his horse quite heavily. He'll be very stiff and very sore tomorrow – like a wild boar with a sore head!"

He continued to tell Myridyn of the small group's narrow escape at the hands of the Thracian cavalry, after a long discussion over the changed circumstances they decided that Myridyn would see the King and call an urgent meeting of the War Council for later that evening.

As Aurthora came in sight of his and Orius's shelters standing side by side, he could see the old legionnaire bathing his grazed and bruised limbs in cold water.

"Orius!" said Aurthora, "I have spoken to Myridyn, he has sent you this herbal oil to rub on your bruises; within a few days your aches and pains should disappear."

"I thank you for your concern Aurthora," touched that his ex-pupil should find time to think of him when he had the heavy burden of command on his young shoulders.

"Myridyn said that if you warm the oil slightly before you apply it, it will be more effective," added Aurthora as he passed the small container to Orius. "Also, I would like to speak to your old comrade, Cynfelin Facilus's father. I believe he used to be the commander of the Thracian cavalry when they were in the employ of the Roman army. Apparently he is still instructing young Celts here in the camp. His son tells me he volunteered his services when Great King Erion called his supporters to arms."

"That is true," replied Orius, "Faustus Facilus has erected a small shelter close to where the horses are tethered. I will take you to him at once." With difficulty the old legionnaire rose, and slowly and stiffly put on his breeches and jerkin. Aurthora turned and walked a few paces away; he did not volunteer to help for it would have hurt the older man's pride.

They found Faustus rubbing down some local horses that he had been using that afternoon in his training session with the young Celts. "Salute!" called Orius, and embraced his old friend in a warm hug. "May I present you Aurthora Ambrosius Aurelianus, godson to Great King Erion, and successor to the Kingdom of Elmet," grandly giving Aurthora his full title.

"I am honoured to meet you," said Faustus, bowing slightly.

Aurthora placed himself on the low stool indicated by Faustus, then he began, "First I must congratulate you on the skills you have taught your son

Cynfelin. Today he saved all our lives. On the plain at the end of the pass we encountered a group of Thracian cavalry."

At the mention of the name Thracian, Faustus was instantly alert. Aurthora, observing this, continued:

"These horsemen are now in Anglo-Saxon employ. Cynfelin told me you were their commander when you were in the Roman army. I need to know everything you can tell me about this force: their strengths, their weaknesses, and suggestions on how you would go about defeating them if you met them in battle."

He spoke to Faustus for more than an hour, with Orius making the occasional suggestion. Eventually Aurthora seemed satisfied. "Orius," he said, "I will leave you with Faustus, whom I thank most heartily for his information. You two will have much to talk about I'm sure."

The two ex-legionnaires watched as he walked past the tethered horses in the direction of the King's tent. "I feel mentally drained," said Faustus to his old friend Orius.

"Yes, he has that effect at times, but he also has the capacity of bringing out the best in people, he demands – and it is gladly given – the highest degree of loyalty and commitment from his soldiers." Orius thought for several moments, before his next words to his old friend.

"He is the one and only hope the Celtic people have of retaining their way of life and culture, Faustus. If they lose this coming battle against the Anglo-Saxons, I fear they will be overwhelmed by wave after wave of invaders."

Chapter Twenty Seven

When he entered the Great King's tent, Myridyn and the rest of the War Council were already assembled. All of them were standing around the Ryphomachia board except for the Great King, who was seated on a high-backed chair. Aurthora could not help but notice how pale he looked, his eyes were very bright and seemed to have a distant, vacant look.

It was Boro Sigurd the senior court official who turned and spoke to Aurthora as he entered. "Ah! Aurthora, it is good to see you. Myridyn has told us of your exploits with the Thracian mercenary cavalry, and we are all relieved that you came away from that encounter unscathed."

"I thank you all for your concern," replied Aurthora.

It was Myridyn who spoke next and he could not hide the disquiet in his voice. "Aurthora, we have placed on the board the pieces that indicate the threat from the Thracian cavalry it indicates that the outcome of this coming battle is not in our favour."

Aurthora looked at the faces of the rest of the War Council: all bore the same expression of anxiety.

"Does the board show that we will lose?" he asked. It was Bernica Calgacus, leader of the Coritani tribe, who answered.

"No Aurthora, the board leaves no winner or loser, but it indicates there will be many casualties on both sides. I think I speak for all of us here when I say that if this board is correct, and even if we do not lose this coming battle, the advantage will then turn in favour of the Anglo-Saxon invaders and their larger army."

He looked round at the War Council members. They were all looking expectantly at him.

Even though he was only half their age and they had all been in many battles and were all experienced warriors and leaders of men, they were treating him, Aurthora Ambrosius Aurelianus, as an equal. He also realised that they did not have an alternative plan for the coming battle. So, now, here was the opportunity to put forward his plan of campaign, it was essential he convince them that it would succeed, for then he would lead the Celtic Army into battle with their agreement and support.

It was dark when Aurthora left the Great King's tent and made his way towards the small shelter Orius had erected. His eyes smarted from the smoke of the thousands of campfires that were burning as the entire Celtic army, which it had taken King Erion more than Aurthora's lifetime to mould, waited ready to be led into battle.

As was typical when large numbers of Celts found themselves together, they felt an irresistible urge to sing. Perhaps it was because the exploits of their heroes had always been recorded and passed on in song, from generation to generation by the tribes' bards and storytellers. As his gaze scanned the many fires, the sound of groups of men singing in harmony could be heard as it drifted over the vast campsite. As he stopped to listen with the voices floating around him, it seemed that all the history of the Celtic peoples was contained in the rich, mellow tone. Aurthora had a vision of groups of ancient Celts from previous centuries, sitting around their fires singing in exactly the same way as those he was witnessing that very moment. His thoughts wandered back to when he first set off from his small town with his father's group of trained warriors. So many things had happened to him since then, so many things had happened in such a short number of days; he turned towards his shelter with the sound of singing still in his ears, knowing the biggest test was about to take place.

Orius was cooking the carcass of a waterfowl over a small fire when Aurthora joined him. "Greetings Orius!" said Aurthora huskily to his friend.

"What is the matter with your voice Aurthora?" Orius asked, looking up at his ex-pupil.

"I have never spoken for so long at any one time," said Aurthora, "but I have managed to convince the War Council to accept my plan for the coming battle. I have theirs and the Great King's blessing, that means the full support of the Celtic Round Council. Orius, I am now in total command of the entire Celtic army. Tomorrow we must put my plan into practice. Every soldier involved in the coming battle must know exactly what is expected of him. We have two days to perfect our manoeuvres before we take up our permanent positions. Myridyn informed me tonight that the Anglo-Saxons have started to break camp and will reach the plain in front of us in just over two days. This is where we will do battle with the invaders of our country."

Orius looked at the young man in front of him; he was definitely growing in stature and confidence by the day. *The Celtic nation of Britannia has given birth to a son who could be their greatest hero of all time. He is indeed a born leader of men,* he thought.

He recalled the story that the Great King was a descendant of the daughter of the Celtic Queen Boudicca, who, if the story was true, was raped by the Roman general Paulinus. The mark that Orius had seen many times on Aurthora's shoulder was identical to the one he had seen on the shoulder of King Erion. It was clear to Orius that either Aurthora was the son of the King or, alternatively, at some time a bonding between the two families and this mark was carried by the male descendents. However, it could not have been on Prassat Ambrosius's side of the family for Orius was certain he had not borne such a mark.

Orius's thoughts were interrupted by Aurthora, who began to outline to his old tutor his battle plan for the Celtic army. They talked long into the night with Orius putting forward many objections to Aurthora's plan, but each time his ex-student had a ready answer.

Aurthora was convinced his plan would succeed, whereas Orius worried that his young friend was about to take a great gamble, with the future of the Celtic nation as the stakes. Eventually, mentally exhausted, they both retired to their shelters.

The following morning both Aurthora and Orius were up and about before the break of dawn. The late summer weather had been kind to the Celtic army, camping as they were at nights under their makeshift shelters. But the clear blue skies that had been the norm over the past seven or eight days were now beginning to change, and grey clouds were appearing on the horizon.

The King had called for a meeting early that morning of all the clan chiefs and their commanders, along with the members of the Celtic Round Council. The meeting was primarily to outline Aurthora's battle plan and to make sure that all the leaders and officers of the Celtic army knew their positions and what would be expected of them and their men, to deal with any queries they might have. But it was also to demonstrate to the tribal leaders that he was still active and alert, and that the wound to his side would not stop him from leading the Celtic army he had created over long years in battle, against the invaders of his kingdom.

Standing by the side of the seated Great King was a young woman. Aurthora and the other Celtic leaders present were surprised; never before had women been allowed at the Great Council meetings. When the gathering had settled down, the Great King rose from his chair with the assistance of the young woman. Immediately all attention became focused on him. Aurthora noted that his godfather was looking much better than he had during the previous days, which he realised was solely due to Myridyn's superhuman efforts and skill. But even as the Great King had improved, for his part the old physician had become gaunter, older and very tired looking.

Aurthora could not help noticing the striking beauty of the woman at the King's side. "My friends!" Great King Erion began. "First I would like to introduce to this gathering my daughter, Elemar, who on hearing of my slight wound made all haste to be with her father to offer him her support. I call you 'friends' from the bottom of my heart. Many of us have fought together on more than one occasion. We have all lost comrades and relations but they all died believing as we do, they too shared the dream of a united Celtic nation; they made the ultimate sacrifice for that belief and we will not disgrace their memory in the coming conflict.

"They will be watching us from afar, we will have their strength in our sword arm, and these Anglo-Saxon invaders will pay with their lives for having dared to set one foot, uninvited, into our country. In the next few days our shared dream will be put to the test when we meet the invaders on the plain below the pass. My godson Aurthora has presented the War Council with a battle plan that we have unanimously accepted. He will now present you with the details of his plan, we will practise the necessary manoeuvres with our army over the days that remain before battle." The Great King paused, took a deep breath and then continued.

"I have also named my godson Aurthora as my General; he is in complete charge of all our forces. He has the full support of the Celtic War Council I know he will have the support of all of you standing here at this moment. My friends, I now present to you my commander, the General of the Celtic federation, your commander in the coming battle against the Anglo-Saxon army, my godson Aurthora Ambrosius Aurelianus."

The Great king had made his speech to the gathered leaders of the Celtic nation who stood before him. As he now sat down heavily in his chair there was a deathly silence. Aurthora had not heard all the king's speech, he had been mesmerised by the beauty of the King's daughter. It was the sound of his name that startled him and brought him back to reality.

He began to move forward, turned, then stopped, an immense feeling of panic overwhelming him. Everything seemed to swirl in front of his eyes, and he felt as though he had passed out on his feet.

He returned to his senses several seconds later to the sound of flesh being slapped on leather. As his vision cleared he made out the figures of Timus Calgacus, Cimbonda Gilberto and Longinus Caratacusi, the young leaders of their tribes, slapping the flat of their hand against the hard leather breastplate they were all wearing. Others began joining in, it was a tribute to him: without uttering a single word they were sanctioning Aurthora's appointment as commander of the army. Outside the king's large tent where the meeting was being held, the two guards of the king's own tribe who were stationed at the entrance of the tent and could hear the conversation within, were also beating their own leather breastplates, joining them was a watery-eyed Orius with, at his side, Darius, Aurthora's young bodyguard, and the young bowman Cynfelin Facilus.

As Aurthora stood waiting for this unexpected tribute to end he could sense the penetrating gaze of Elemar's eyes on the back of his head. It was some minutes before the drumming ended and Aurthora could proceed to explain his plan to the Celtic chiefs and their lieutenants. He felt the rising resentment amongst some of the older tribal leaders as he gave them their instructions and orders, and indeed they went away muttering among themselves, yet there were no such problems with the younger clan leaders, who listened enthusiastically to his plan and cheered when he had finished outlining the details.

The entire army would be involved in the manoeuvres, but only as separate units and in different sections of the plain. Aurthora did not want any spying eyes to see the full picture of his plan, or the reason behind the units' individual manoeuvres.

Gradually the group dispersed. The leaders still had to inform their subordinates of the battle plan details before the manoeuvres, and to organise the units under their command and make their way to the plain. Soon only the King, his daughter Elemar, Myridyn, and Aurthora remained in the large tent, with Orius and the bodyguards waiting outside.

"Aurthora," began the Great King, "this is my daughter Elemar, who arrived a short while ago. Elemar, this is Aurthora. His father was my great friend and comrade-in-arms and I have adopted him as my godson."

Elemar moved forward. She was tall for a Celtic woman quite slim, with shapely bosom and a graceful, proud walk. Her hair was black but it was her eyes that fascinated Aurthora, they were so dark they were nearly black, and it was as their eyes met that his heart missed a beat. He held her gaze for several seconds and knew that his reaction to this woman was disloyal to his beloved Katrina. He looked away, focusing his gaze instead on Myridyn, whose face wore a worried expression. Quickly excusing himself to attend to all that was required before the manoeuvres, he left the Great King's tent. But as he walked along in the company of Orius and his bodyguards Aurthora could not shake the image of the beautiful, dark-eyed Elemar from his mind.

For two days, from before dawn until after dusk, Aurthora drove the army hard, using his reserves as the opposing Anglo-Saxon forces. These were men from tribes beyond the area of the King's influence who had volunteered their services, plus others who had been displaced by the advancing Anglo-Saxon army making their way as refugees to the area controlled by the Celts. The brunt of the enemy's attack would be taken by the Celtic troops who had been training for many years in the Roman legions' way of fighting, combined with the Greek method of a second line of spearmen.

Aurthora had decided he could not risk demonstrating to the army the weapon that Myridyn had perfected with the one-armed Roman engineer Aidas Corrilus. But what he did do was to inform all the tribal chiefs and their subordinates that all the frontline troops should be prepared for the fire and brimstone that would rain down on the Anglo-Saxon charge, that the Celts should not panic at the sight or sound of this new weapon. He also informed all his commanders and the tribal chiefs that he wanted them in position before first light on the third day; to achieve this they would start to take up their positions as darkness fell the night before. He wanted to reduce as far as possible the risk of any prying eyes seeing the Celtic formations moving into their selected positions. For on that day the Anglo-Saxon army and all their mercenary forces would arrive on the plain prepared to do battle with the greatly outnumbered Celtic force.

The different units' manoeuvres were practised time and time again against the reserves. At first it was chaos as units collided with one another, obstructing each other's movements, while the mock invaders pushed their way through the disorganised units with considerable ease.

The fact that the fine weather had broken did not help, and the troops were subjected to torrential showers that slowly settled into a continuous drizzle. Aurthora could sense that the men were becoming demoralised, but he persisted in practising the manoeuvres. Slowly as the day waned the Celtic units began to move into their allocated positions more fluidly, the mock enemy found they were held back, and were now unable to penetrate the line of Celtic defenders. As dark fell the army left the plain, passing Aidas's machines as they were wheeled into their positions under cover of darkness, his operators struggling to move the heavy devices over the sodden ground. The Celtic army made its way back into the pass, progressing slowly towards the men's temporary shelters. They were cold, hungry, wet and muddy – but also satisfied: they realised they were improving and they still had another day to perfect their manoeuvres.

Chapter Twenty Eight

Aurthora and Orius joined the queue of wet, bedraggled soldiers collecting the hot stew dished out beside the cooks' campfires. Alongside great log fires, rough benches and tables were arranged where the weary soldiers could sit to eat the warming stew while their clothes steamed from the heat generated by the nearby fires. All the spaces on the forms were taken near the fire where Aurthora and Orius stood with their bowls of hot stew. One of the men on the nearest table recognised Aurthora. "Move over there!" he called to the men at the end of the table. "Move over and make room, and feel privileged to sit at the same table with Aurthora Ambrosius Aurelianus, Hammer of the Anglo-Saxons." The men looked up from their meal, and as they recognised Aurthora, they quickly edged closer together, leaving two spaces at the end of the long table.

It was while Aurthora and Orius were eating that Aurthora brought up the subject of the King's daughter. "I have never seen a women of such beauty, Orius," he said to his older companion. "Have you ever seen her? Her looks remind me of the women from the Green Isle of Diariada."

He looked across at Orius, and could see in the flickering light of the log fire that his old friend had the same worried frown at the mention of the King's daughter as the one he had seen on Myridyn's face earlier that morning.

"I would have thought you had a good woman in Katrina?" observed Orius.

"Oh, but I have, and I could not wish for a better partner," came back the quick reply. "I was just commenting as any man would on her exceptional beauty." Orius did not answer for a while, but in his mind he thought that Aurthora had responded to his question rather too quickly. When he did reply he said, "You are right in observing that she favours the Scoti women from the Green Isle, your Great King married a princess from the largest tribe of that land. She was the eldest and favourite daughter of the Scoti king Fergus of Dalriada. He held great tracts of land won in battle from the Picti, the far northern tribes of this island. The Great King's daughter is a result of that union, but unfortunately his queen did not survive the birth of their daughter.

There is a strong bond between the Great King and the Scoti king Fergus. At this very moment King Fergus is fighting a campaign against the northern Picti in order to retain the lands he has claimed there. That is why we have only a token force of the Scoti Celts here, they came in response to an appeal from Great King Erion to his daughter's grandfather, they came to answer the Great King's call to arms."

"You forever amaze me with your knowledge, Orius," said Aurthora. "You constantly have your ear to the ground; you know of happenings in this country even before Myridyn or the Celtic Round Council." Orius smiled, and the two men finished their meal in silence, then rising they bade farewell to the rest of the men at their table before making their way wearily through the camp towards their damp shelters.

As they walked between the bedraggled groups of men sitting closely around the burning fires, they passed the area where Myridyn and his students were treating the soldiers who had been injured in the over-enthusiastic charges made during the day's manoeuvres, helping them were several of the Christian monks and friars of the new religion.

Aurthora stopped to have a few words with the old physician and accepted a mug of water from one of the monks. Aurthora could not help but notice how tall the monk was: he was a good head above him and all the other men. As he looked around at these young men he knew they would shortly have more serious wounds to deal with than the minor cuts and bruises they were now tending. Then once again his thoughts turned to Elemar, the Great King's daughter; he was confused by the attraction he felt towards this woman.

Orius, meanwhile, was deep in his own thoughts about his last meeting with Emilia. She was many years his junior, but that had not affected their relationship. They had discussed their future after this war; they even looked at prospective properties close to the hot baths and sauna. Emilia forecast that trade at the sauna and hot baths would slow down when the army moved out, but the tradesmen and merchants who were supplying the army had taken a liking to the hot baths and the sauna. They had become a social gathering place where business was discussed and deals were struck.

Also there were visitors from further afield who were beginning to make a special journey to use the baths, and all these travellers required accommodation. Orius had given all his silver and gold to Emilia for safekeeping. He recalled how she had cried uncontrollably at the thought that he might not return, and how he had consoled her by telling her he was a survivor; he had been in many battles and tight corners yet had always come out of them alive.

But it was Emilia's last statement that remained imprinted on his mind. It had struck him like a thunderbolt: "Come back to me, Orius, we have such a good future before us, we have so much in common. I am also carrying your child."

After leaving Emilia, Orius had been to see the old caretaker. "Oengus, my friend," he said, as the old man answered the knocking on the door of his small cottage, "I will be with the army for several days; while I am away I want you to pass my share of the profits from the baths and sauna to my partner Emilia." The old caretaker agreed, but Orius knew that if the crafty old scoundrel heard that he had been killed or seriously injured in the coming conflict with the Anglo-Saxons, the payments to Emilia would instantly be reduced or may even cease.

The following day dawned damp and misty, and as the men queued for their pottage and tried to warm themselves around the cooks' fires, the mist turned into a fine wet drizzle that seemed to penetrate their clothes even more than the heavy downpours that struck them at regular intervals. Aurthora accepted a container of water from the man with the water barrel, who was wrapped in such a large cloak against the bad weather that only his hands were exposed. He took only a small sip then handed it back to the man as Orius approached.

The water carrier took the container and watched as the two soldiers walked away, but he did not pour the remains of the water back into the barrel as he had done on previous occasions, cursing he threw it instead amongst the well-trodden grass at his feet. Then began to walk slowly towards the transport wagons, pulling his hood further over his face to hide the vivid scar that stretched from above his eye to below his chin. The water barrel on its little cart was left abandoned in the muddy field.

The morning progressed slowly; the individual units, cold, wet, and miserable, completed their manoeuvres, but without any enthusiasm. However, as the day progressed and the rain stopped, rays of a weak sun broke through the grey clouds and things began to improve so that by the end of the day all the units were completing their manoeuvres efficiently and confidently, even though they were now up to their ankles in sticky, clinging mud. It was during the latter part of the day that Aurthora sensed he was being watched, and looking around he spotted the Great King's grey horse on one of the small hills at the entrance to the pass. He waved and the figure on the horse waved back. "The Great King must be feeling much better to come and watch our manoeuvres on such a miserable day," he said to Orius who was standing beside him.

"That is not the Great King," said Orius. "It is his daughter. She has been there all morning I don't think she has come to watch our men ploughing through the mud."

He ignored the last remark and asked instead, "What is your opinion of our army's manoeuvres, Orius?"

"They have improved beyond belief. If I had not seen it with my own eyes I would not have thought it possible in the time they had available. It is all credit to you."

"No!" replied Aurthora, "the credit is not mine. It is the Great King who should take the credit. Over the last twenty years of training this force it has been he who has imposed the discipline that you now see before you."

"However, your battle plan depends on the Anglo-Saxons keeping their existing formation. If that changes before the morning you could find yourself with some serious problems." Aurthora did not seem to be listening, he was looking towards where the King's grey had been, but now it had gone.

Aurthora followed the Celtic army back to the entrance of the pass knowing that he could not improve on their performance. Also, earlier that day he had seen the great buzzard floating above them. He had come to see it as his good omen and felt happier for its appearance. He also received reports from Myridyn about the manner in which the Anglo-Saxon army was advancing and the position of their forces, which was of the greatest importance in the execution of his battle plan. Using this information, he had informed the clan chiefs and their subordinates of their positions for the following day's battle. The men would now have a hot meal, and when the sun had set they would move forward under cover of darkness to take up their battle positions on the edge of the plain.

The men of the Celtic army moved quietly, there was only the occasional clink of a shield catching some piece of body armour, or a muffled curse as someone stumbled in the semi-darkness. They had trodden the same path several times in the last few days and it was little different in the dark of the night. The moon appeared occasionally from behind clumps of cloud passing across the night sky, and it gave just enough light for the men to get their bearings and keep them heading in the right direction. The cavalry were walking their large horses, their heavy chain link armour lay over their saddles and their heart-shaped shields were fastened to the high pommel of the battle saddles.

They were accompanied by a large group of archers carrying the long spears that were to be used by the horsemen. Both these groups would be positioned close together on the battlefield, on the flank of the main Celtic force. They would be facing the mercenary horsemen of the Anglo-Saxon army: the dreaded Thracian cavalry.

Aurthora's battle plan was quite simple, it aimed to slow down and break up the anticipated initial savage charge by the Anglo-Saxon army, thus stopping them from smashing their way through the opposition as they had done in their previous battles against the northern Celtic kingdoms. Man for man the Celt was as good a fighter as the Angle or Saxon warrior, but the Celtic army was outnumbered three to one by the invaders. In a fight based on numbers, Aurthora knew his army would most probably lose the battle. For this reason he had placed his Celtic troops in their heavy armour in a series of ten defensive squares, each consisting of five hundred trained Celts from the tribes that made up the Celtic Alliance.

The Romans had called this formation the *testudo*: a wall of shields like the shell of a tortoise. Aurthora had placed these contingents twenty paces apart and two men deep. The front line of soldiers linked their rectangular curved shields together to form a square of steel that left an arm free to use their short stabbing sword, the gladius. Each of these soldiers also had several of the short iron throwing spears to hand, behind them, their shields above their heads forming a roof of steel, stood the second line of soldiers with the long pilum in their free hand; together with a spare. These they would hurl over the shoulder of the man in front of them. In the centre of the square were the reserves who would replace any soldier who went down in the first or second line of troops. They, too, held their shields above their heads, completing the steel roof, a perfect defence against arrows or thrown spears.

Aurthora moved his troops back slightly from where he had held the manoeuvres over the previous days. This left a quagmire of sticky, shin-deep mud just in front of his defensive squares. Forty paces back from the squares were the rest of the trained Celts in three rows. The front row stood shoulder to shoulder with their shields interlocked, the second row held their spear and placed their shield over their head so that it protected the man in front of them and themselves from airborne missiles. The third row was more sparsely spaced and its men would act as reserves for the front two rows.

These three thousand heavily armed men stretched across the pass from east to west, from the start of the high ground on one side to the rising ground on the other.

Forty paces to the rear of them as the ground began to rise slightly were a line of a thousand archers; behind the archers were five thousand reserve Celts from the various tribes on the outskirts of the island who volunteered their services to the Great King and Celtic Round Council, or had been forced from their lands by the advancing Anglo-Saxons. To their right, protecting the flank but out of sight of the Anglo-Saxon army, were five hundred of the Celtic heavy cavalry in their chain mail and carrying their long, lance-like spears. Above them on the slightly higher ground also hidden from view were six hundred of the Celtic longbow men, lying in the long grass or behind the gorse, rocks and brush of the hillside. To protect their flank Authora had placed five hundred of the volunteer Celts.

On the far side of the pass there was a similar pattern. Protected by five hundred of the volunteer Celts were the other five hundred Celtic horsemen, but these were mounted on the smaller, lighter local horses and they did not wear the heavy chain mail armour of the heavy cavalry, or carry the extra long spears. Just over the brow of the hill Aidas Corrilus and his operators had set up their converted ballista machines, the operators also had a protective guard of five hundred of the volunteer Celts. It was here, where he had a good view of the battlefield, that Aurthora placed himself with Orius and his own cohort of six hundred trained men in full battle armour. In a prominent position nearby, astride his large grey horse, was Great King Erion, so that when daylight came he could be seen by the entire Celtic army. Surrounding him were all the senior members of the Celtic Round Council and their personal guards, and at his side was the ever-faithful Myridyn.

Under his command Aurthora had about twenty thousand warriors, and coming towards him was a force of over sixty thousand Germanic tribesmen: the Angles, Saxons and Jutes and their mercenary forces, which included the renegade Celts under Petrov Joma and the dreaded Thracian cavalry. Dawn was beginning to show on the tops of the hills at the rear of Authora's position when a shout went up from the leading defensive square from below him.

"Riders approaching on the road!" The road was a continuation of the old paved Roman highway that led from the High Town and continued the full length of the island, right to the far northern kingdoms of the Picti tribes. From his position it was still too dark for Aurthora to see the riders approaching.

"Do you think it is an exploratory cavalry attack to test our defences?" he called to Orius as he continued to gaze blindly into the semi-darkness.

"If it is, it is a deviation from their usual plan of attack," replied Orius. There was a long moment of strained silence; both Aurthora and Orius moved to the edge of the slope and strained into the shadows, yet they could see nothing. Then a shout from the commander of the leading square carried up to the men on the hill. "It is the garrison from the tower at Castleton, they are being escorted by Cimbonda Gilberto and his men."

There was a babble of conversation as the group around Aurthora heard the message. "Send a messenger to Cimbonda Gilberto, I wish to speak to him most urgently," said Aurthora to Orius. Almost immediately a horseman was sent down the slope and galloped off in the direction of the paved road.

The light of dawn could be seen spreading swiftly from the east when Cimbonda Gilberto came galloping up the slope, closely followed by the messenger who had been sent to fetch him. *Bore da* Aurthora!" called out Cimbonda as he pulled up his horse in front of the group.

"Good day to you, too, Cimbonda," replied Aurthora. Then he continued, "Have you seen the enemy forces?"

"I have!" replied the mounted Celt. "They are approaching in formation with mounted riders in front."

"What position has the Thracian cavalry taken?" asked Aurthora.

"As far as I could see and hear – and you must remember it was still dark as they approached – the Thracian cavalry has taken up a position on the right-hand side of the main Anglo-Saxon army as they approach our defences."

This message was a shock to Aurthora. He had placed his forces according to the last report he had received on the positions of the enemy forces. If Cimbonda was correct, it was obvious that the Thracian cavalry had changed flanks during their night's advance.

"I thank you for your message and for escorting the garrison troops to safety, Cimbonda. "Good fighting!" said Aurthora, with a wave, Cimbonda Gilberto turned his large horse and made his way back to join the warriors of his own tribe. Aurthora watched him go. He knew that Cimbonda would lead his tribe courageously until only death could stop him. He then turned to Orius, a worried look on his face.

"We need to move the heavy cavalry and the long bowmen onto the opposite flank, Orius, and place the lighter cavalry in their positions. Also we need to move the two squares on the right flank and change them with those on the left flank." A look of startled amazement appeared on Orius's face as Aurthora's words registered.

"But... but... Aurthora..." Orius stammered, "you cannot change your battle plan at this late stage, the enemy is practically in sight. If they attack halfway through this movement of troops you will be destroyed, and even if they do not attack, it will be light shortly and they will see your troops' positions. That way you will lose the advantage of surprise and they will not fall into your trap as you hope. Your light cavalry is already in that position and they will just have to do the job." There was panic in Orius's voice as he spelt out the dangers to Aurthora. What his ex-student was about to attempt was madness and could jeopardise the whole outcome of the battle.

"The Celtic light cavalry will not have the impact that will be needed to defeat the Thracian horsemen, who will quickly reform causing havoc and chaos on our flank. We have to change the positions of our two cavalry forces in order to destroy their mobility."

Orius looked around him for support but within earshot there was only Darius, Aurthora's young bodyguard, and Cynfelin Facilus, the young Roman Celt bowman. Aurthora was already shouting instructions to his group of Celtic soldiers. "Send men to gather brushwood and gorse, the wind is blowing away from us, fire the brushwood at the bottom of slope on this side of the pass. Move the troops under the cover of the smoke and the morning mist. If we act quickly we can achieve our objective. Tell the bowmen to hold onto the harnesses of the horses of the heavy cavalry, they should not move faster than a trot. I do not want the horses blown or winded, neither do I want the archers to be dragged along and risk being trampled.

Men were running around carrying out Aurthora's shouted instructions, riders were already galloping on their way to the heavy cavalry and the archers who were positioning themselves at the far side of the valley. It was now quite light, and from his elevated position Aurthora could see over the pass and the plain beyond, but he could not see the Celtic army, they were still hidden by the morning mist. His nostrils could smell the pungent smoke of the burning brushwood and gorse as it drifted across the valley and over the low hill.

A rider came galloping up the hill, stopped for a while and looked around. Then, seeing the pennant of the swooping buzzard fluttering in the morning breeze, he turned his horse in that direction, pulling his panting animal to a grinding halt in front of Aurthora. The rider was wearing leather breeches and a sleeveless jerkin of cowhide fastened at the waist with a thick leather belt. His forearms and shoulders were covered in dark tattoos and his face was patterned with the deep blue woad. There was a long sheath fastened to the high pommel of his saddle that bore a large two-handed sword. The rider called out a greeting in the Celtic tongue and Aurthora waved his hand in acknowledgment, at which the rider turned his horse and trotted back the way he had come.

Orius, at the rear of the group of men, turned to Cynfelin who was standing close by. "Cynfelin, who was that rider?"

"He was a rider from the Coritani tribe. Timus Calgacus and some of his warriors are monitoring the progress of the Anglo-Saxons. He called Aurthora a 'Celtic Royal Lion', and told him the enemy is approaching." Orius left Cynfelin and went to the top of the slope.

The morning mist had cleared from the plain and in the distance he could just make out what looked like a dark shadow moving slowly towards them. There was no movement at the foot of the hill but it was difficult to see through the clouds of thick smoke that drifted up the slope from the valley floor and made his eyes water.

He looked again across the plain: the dark shadow was definitely moving closer and was beginning to take shape. A movement at the bottom of the slope caught his eye; he strained his eyes into the billowing smoke and slowly made out the shape of human forms making their way up the slope and positioning themselves behind the boulders and gorse bushes. And from his elevated position he could see the squares on the flank reforming in their new position.

"The archers are here!" he shouted, "tell Aurthora the archers have arrived!"

Orius could not disguise his relief. Aurthora heard the shout of his old tutor, hearing also the relief in the old soldier's voice. "Extinguish the fires," Aurthora shouted; the last thing he wanted was not to be able to see the movement of the enemy or his own troops because thick smoke was blowing across the valley. "Signal to Aidas's men across the valley that the enemy are in sight and to prepare their machines."

Aurthora's order was immediately obeyed and a highly polished piece of metal was used to catch the morning sun's rays and flash a pre-arranged message to the hill at the far end of the pass.

A runner was also sent to Aidas, who was just over the brow of the hill from Aurthora.

The blowing of Celtic war trumpets from the rear and a great deal of loud chanting heralded the arrival of the contingent of Druid priests and their junior understudies, followed by the banging of swords on shields by the Celts who were being held back in reserve near the entrance to the pass. Druid priests in their white robes, followed by their students and the musicians playing their harps and flutes, made their way in a long column through the cheering Celts. The students were handing the Celtic warriors clay tubs of blue woad, which they then used to daub various patterns on their faces and other exposed parts of their bodies.

The column began to climb the low hill, heading in the direction of Aurthora and the small group of men around him. The line of priests made slow progress up the slight slope: the chief priest Zanton was leading them and the old man was struggling even though the incline was a gentle one.

As the group drew level with Aurthora, Zanton pointedly ignored him, and led the horn and harp-playing column past and on towards the Great King and the group of senior members of the Celtic Round Council. Orius was standing beside Aurthora as Zanton, the priests and novices walked by. Aurthora declined one of the tubs of woad offered him by a passing novice who was wearing a headdress of stag's antlers.

"But it has been blessed by the high priest Zanton himself and will protect you in the coming battle!" the surprised novice exclaimed. But since Aurthora still refused the clay tub the novice hurried off to catch up to the tail end of the procession, which was slowing to a stop in front of King Erion.

"That man is searching for favour with your King. He has been quiet and in the shadows for too long," observed Orius as he stood beside Aurthora watching Zanton's staged performance.

The old priest was being helped onto a low wooden platform his servants had carried up the hill; once he had been safely settled on the platform the blowing of the great boar war horns stopped. "My Celtic friends!" shouted Zanton, holding out his hands for quiet. "You people who are the believers in the only true religion and followers of Great King Erion, who has formed this mighty alliance of the Celtic peoples to defend our lands, our culture, our way of life and our Druid religion against these foreign invaders."

"The lying old hypocrite," muttered Orius. "The crafty old fox is associating your king and the great things he has accomplished with his Druid religion." He turned away in disgust and walked to the edge of the slope and looked in the direction of the advancing Anglo-Saxon army.

But Zanton had an audience and he was not going to waste the opportunity to reinforce and proselytize his beliefs, or to elevate his own standing before the gathered Celtic army, their tribal leaders and the Celtic Round Council, so he went on loudly with his oratory.

"The reason you followers of the true way have not seen me, your religious leader, over the last few days is because I have been in consultation with our God of War, Camulos." Here he stopped to let the impact of his words sink in to the listening Celtic chiefs.

"What was the message from the Gods that you bring to us, High Priest?" called out a voice from amongst the musicians.

"I had a vision. In my vision I saw smoke and fire and many injured men. I saw great horse against great horse and long spears broken and splintered, and through the smoke came a rider in Celtic chain mail riding a white stallion that stepped over piles of bodies. I did not recognise the slain men; they were not Celts. I saw many great ships with black sails and long oars, and they had stopped at the end of a silver thread of water. The men who sailed these ships were dressed in the same attire as those that lay dead on the battlefield."

Having finished the telling of his vision Zanton now stood with his head bowed as if in meditation.

There was a low mumble of conversation from the gathered crowd, and it was Boro Sigurd, the senior court official, who called out the question whose answer everyone wanted to know.

"High Priest! What did you conclude from your meeting with the God, Camulos?"

At first there was no movement from the stationary Zanton, and Boro Sigurd was about to ask the question again when Zanton raised his head and spoke in a clear, high-pitched voice.

"My vision showed me those who have followed our true faith will be champions at the end of this battle. The invaders of our country will depart in boats with black sails; they will leave many behind who will never more see their homeland, and those that leave will think most seriously before they dare infringe our territory again."

The crowd broke into low conversation at this statement as they discussed amongst themselves the priest's vision. Led by Zanton, the Druid priests with their musicians moved down the hill to the cheers of the main body of the Celtic army as the religious procession passed their lines. Then a shout came from Orius at the edge of the slope. "The Anglo-Saxon army has stopped advancing; they have halted just out of range of our bowmen."

Chapter Twenty Nine

This news deflected the tribal leaders' attention from Zanton the high priest and sent them scrambling to the edge of the slope to gain a better view of the Anglo-Saxon army. Aurthora heard Orius's shout but he did not rush to the edge of the slope like the rest of the Round Council; he had just noticed Elemar standing near the Great King's horse. He had not noticed her before because she was wearing body armour and had blended in with the rest of the Council's personal bodyguards. On a sudden impulse he took a step towards her and her father. He felt the movement of air as an arrow meant for him flashed passed his cheek and embedded itself in the back of one of the nearby Celtic guards.

The man collapsed, dragging down one of his companions standing in front of him in the process. A second arrow aimed at Aurthora's heart thudded into the raised shield held by the ever-observant Darius. A third arrow passed close by, embedding itself into the flank of Aurthora's horse, sending the wounded animal neighing and kicking in a terrified bolt down the hill. There was a twang as Facilus Cynfelin released a deadly projectile that entered the chest of the enemy bowman, knocking him off his horse and leaving him dead on the ground. Aurthora was running and at the same time shouting orders, "Guards to your rear," he yelled.

He had collected his shield and drawn his short gladius and was running towards the wheeled ballista machines, from where the noise of heavy fighting had suddenly erupted. Running alongside him were Darius and Facilus, and a short distance behind them was Orius with several of Aurthora's town guard on either side. The alarm had been raised Aurthora's cohort of troops, positioned just below the hill, were also rushing to the rear, but a good few hundred paces behind their commander.

As Aurthora came over the brow of the small hill, below him he saw the rearguard of ordinary Celtic soldiers being hard-pressed by a greater number of Anglo-Saxon warriors, supported by a group of about a hundred horsemen, some of them riding the large breed of horse used by the Celtic heavy cavalry. He read the situation immediately, this large group of enemy infantry had moved into position during the night; they had gone unnoticed with all the troop movement in the area.

And while the attention of the Celtic rearguard was diverted watching and listening to the Druid High Priest Zanton and his musicians, the Anglo-Saxon infantry had attacked, supported by the renegade Celtic horsemen. They arrived halfway up the slope before they had been observed and challenged by the Celtic rearguard, which was also guarding Aidas's large ballistaes.

Their intention was clear: they were attempting a pre-emptive strike to remove the tribal leaders and members of the ruling Celtic Council in one fell swoop. All this flashed through Aurthora's brain as he and the small handful of men running at his side were attempting to place themselves between the large group of advancing horsemen and the King and Round Council. He also felt a flutter of panic in the pit of his stomach. He had been outmanoeuvred. He allowed a situation to develop whereby the King and all his senior advisors, himself included, could be slaughtered before the main battle had even begun.

He was aware that his small group were not going to succeed in placing themselves between the advancing renegade horsemen and their intended target, even if by a miracle they managed to cover the distance in their cumbersome armour, which was not designed for sprinting over rough country, there were only eight of them, along with possibly a dozen of the Council's personal guards, against several hundred or more of heavily armed enemy soldiers and horsemen. The horsemen were level, but still fifty paces in front of him and about one hundred paces from the Great King and the group of statesmen, who were frantically trying to form some kind of defences against the fast approaching renegade Celtic cavalry.

Like everyone else in the small group at the top of the hill, Elemar and her father had been watching the high priest Zanton lead his religious procession down the slope and towards the cheering Celtic army's positions. It was only as the loud music became fainter that they had become aware of the noise of the battle between the Anglo-Saxon infantry and its rearguard which was taking place behind them. As they turned they realised that they were the intended target for the advancing group of horsemen, who were galloping unhindered up the hill towards them.

"Guards to the rear! Form a line of shields!" Elemar's shrill shout of command spurred the stationary personal guards into action, and they rushed to the rear of the group as instructed to form a wall of shields. "Father, dismount quickly! You are too prominent a target on your horse," as she helped her father to dismount while Myridyn tried to steady the Great King's horse.

Petrov Joma was leading the group of mounted horsemen as they galloped up the shallow incline of the hill. Some of his men on the smaller, more nimble local horses had made better going and chased on ahead, the bounty of five hundred crowns offered by the Saxon king Ælle for the head of Great King Erion acting as an added spur to their enthusiasm. They moved into position the previous night on the far side of the hill, concealing themselves in the brush and amongst the many scattered boulders in that area. If anybody had chanced to observe the large body of armed men, they would have assumed that they were just another group of the Celtic army moving into position.

Earlier, Petrov Joma with his group of mounted renegade Celts positioned themselves in the woods at the bottom of the hill. The blowing of the Celtic war horns by Zanton's acolytes had been the signal for the Anglo-Saxon infantry to start quietly advancing up the hill. They had taken the Celtic rearguard by surprise, and while they were fully occupied, Petrov Joma led his men unhindered at a gallop up the slope. He could see his intended target at the top of the hill, still sitting on the grey horse surrounded by the leaders of the various tribes. They were trying to form some form of defence and it seemed it was being organised by a woman!

Petrov Joma laughed aloud. His mounted warriors would easily smash through their flimsy wall of shields and knock that upstart of a king off his grey perch. The small group of Celtic warriors running in from his right would never reach him in time to alter the course of events and the much larger force following behind them were also too far away to interfere. *Yes!* Petrov Joma thought, *Everything is going to plan. It's going to be a good day for me. Who knows, by the end of it I may well be crowned king of the Celtic nation? I may have to swear allegiance to the Saxon king Ælle, but I can tolerate that.*

Victor Aberuso was riding alongside Petrov Joma on one of the smaller local horses, but he was not a good horseman and was struggling to keep the pace set by his leader. He, too, saw the small group of armed soldiers attempting to cut off their advance and the much larger group a good distance behind them. From past experiences he knew how they would be struggling. It was extremely energy-sapping to run dressed in the heavy Roman armour; and anyway, they were too far away to be a threat. The leading group of Anglo-Saxon horsemen were now level with the ballista machines, but they would not bother with them now, they would smash them and their operators on their return.

He chuckled to himself as he saw the operators rolling what looked like large stones into the path of the leading horsemen. As if those would stop their charge! He also saw who was directing them. "Aidas Corrilus!" Victor Aberuso spat out the name 'Corrilus'. It was Aidas Corrilus who publicly accused him of cheating when he had disposed of Matos Tomase, in the arena. Still, he had the last laugh by sabotaging one of Corrilus's machines, he recalled the great contentment he felt afterwards when he heard that the loud-mouthed engineer had lost his arm in the ensuing accident.

Orius stopped running. He could not hope to keep up with the much younger and stronger men in the small group. He would wait until the larger force following several hundred paces behind caught up with him; it would give him chance to recover his breath. From his position he saw all that was happening on this, the rear side of the hill. He saw the Anglo-Saxon troops fighting with the Celtic rearguard. The latter, having the advantage of the high ground, were slowly forcing the enemy backwards. He also saw the two groups of horsemen as they charged up the hill. They were ignoring the ballista machines and their operators and heading straight for the group of high-ranking Celts positioned on top of the hill. These had hastily formed a wall of shields, and though heavily outnumbered, were bravely preparing to meet the advancing cavalry. He could also see his friend Aidas standing on top of one of the wagons, frantically waving his one arm and directing his machine operators into some form of action.

Orius ducked instinctively as a series of loud explosions sent dirt, stones and pieces of metal flying through the air to envelop the group of leading renegade Celtic horsemen in a cloud of dust and black smoke. Petrov Joma's horse was bucking and rearing in sheer panic along with all the other horses behind and at either side of him. He was thrown from his mount as were most of his companions, but he managed to hang on to his reins, even though he landed heavily and was dragged for several yards. This action stopped his horse from bolting along with most of the other terrified and wounded animals that had made up the front group of renegade cavalry. Victor Aberuso was also thrown from his rearing animal and landed ungracefully and badly winded on his back, his terrified horse immediately bolting back down the hill followed by several other riderless mounts.

At the sound of the explosions Aurthora and his small group also instinctively ducked and put up their shields to protect themselves, and even at that distance they were peppered with stones and pieces of spent iron. The fighting Anglo-Saxon infantry and Celtic rearguard stopped as one as the flash and sound of the explosions split the air. Only one voice was heard in the deathly silence that followed the explosions, and that was the voice of Aidas, who having been blown from his perch by the explosion, had quickly regained his position standing once more on the wagon from which he directed his machine operators. He was now shouting at the top of his voice in broken Celtic. The Celtic rearguard was quick to respond to Aidas's instructions to destroy the foreigners and recommenced their attack on the confused Anglo-Saxon infantry with renewed fury.

Aurthora recovered quickly from the blast, "Forward!" he shouted, his small band followed him as he rushed into the dust and the smoking bracken, set alight by the explosions. As he rushed forward he heard a loud cheer from the direction of the Celtic rearguard as they savagely fought with the Anglo-Saxon infantry, who were now beginning to break, several score turning and rushing as fast as they could back down the hill.

Victor Aberuso slowly clambered to his feet, gasping for breath from his fall and choking on the thick smoke and dust he had inhaled. He had been in too many conflicts to panic easily. They had lost the advantage, that was obvious, and he now needed a horse. He began to search desperately in the gloom created by the smoke.

Petrov Joma brought his animal under control while the panic-stricken, wounded, riderless horses from the front group rushed past him and on down the hill in a headlong gallop. He saw Victor Aberuso rise to his feet, and further on, another of his men who had been thrown from his horse rose from the ground holding a damaged shoulder. In the same instant there came a sudden swoosh, and an arrow from the direction of the ballista machines entered the bottom of the man's spine so that he collapsed back onto the spot he had just left, screaming and writhing in agony. A man wielding a large, two-handed hammer came out of the smoke from the same direction of the arrow and tried to flatten Victor Aberuso's skull. But even though he was still slightly dazed, Victor Aberuso was still more than a match for the ballista operator. He simply sidestepped the clumsy swing and sank his gladius into the man's midriff. The man made a gurgling sound as Victor Aberuso withdrew his short sword from the man's falling body.

As Aurthora entered the smoke he recognised the same acrid smell he had witnessed at the Greek fire demonstration in the marshland village. He was also aware of the sweat dripping from his forehead, but at least it was not dripping into his eyes for Orius had taught him an old precaution used by the legionnaires. Before going into battle they smeared a thin layer of goose or pork fat on their eyebrows, which directed the sweat away from their eyes and kept their vision clear.

Before him crouched one of the renegade Celts who had been thrown from his horse in the blast. He was on one knee, his other leg had been shattered in the fall and pieces of broken bone were sticking through the flesh of his shin. He was in the painful process of trying to rise. The man saw the outline of what looked like a Roman soldier coming towards him. "Carcharor! Carcharor!" he begged in a panic-stricken voice. But Aurthora felt no compassion as he stopped to slash the man's throat, shouting as he did so, "I take no renegade Celts as prisoners. You chose your path to destruction when you followed Petrov Joma. Your journey ends here, you murdering vermin."

Continuing to move on through the smoke he saw another dim outline of a figure in front of him in the process of pulling his sword from a man's crumpled body. As he approached, the figure turned. Aurthora immediately recognised him as Victor Aberuso! *It's hard to decide who is the more evil, he or Petrov Joma*, thought Aurthora, *but now at least there will be one less!*

As Victor Aberuso swung around he saw the dim outline of a man coming towards him dressed in the heavy armour of the Roman infantry. The man was panting, and Victor Aberuso knew you could not run far in the heavy armour without becoming seriously winded. *This will be another easy kill*, he thought.

"Hello my fine Celtic friend. Yes, you! Dressed as a Roman!" jeered Victor Aberuso. "But it takes more than a suit of Roman armour to make a Roman soldier, as you will now find out to your cost."

As he shouted the last words he swung his sword at the Celt before him, knowing the blow would be blocked by the shield, but at the same time with his left hand he struck with his pugio around the side of the shield at the man's unprotected thigh. He had used this technique many times before in the arena: first you crippled your opponent and then the rest was easy. But this time his dagger thrust did not find its intended target; it was knocked from his hand by the Celt's sword. Victor Aberuso recovered quickly and lunged his sword over and down above the top of the raised shield. This usually caught the opponent in the throat or blinded him, but Aberuso's aim was poor, and the man also averted his head so that the blade simply caught his helmet, dislodging it from his head.

In response the Celt lifted his shield, trapping Victor Aberuso's sword and arm and throwing him backwards, at the same time delivering a thrusting slash with his own short sword at Aberuso's unprotected midriff. Aberuso reeled back, he felt the warm liquid run from the flesh wound in his side, one that would have proved fatal if an inch deeper. Victor Aberuso realised he had been overconfident. This Celt was not going to be an easy victim. The man who stood in front of the ex-gladiator lowered his shield and now, minus his helmet, Victor Aberuso recognised his opponent. There was a large purse of Saxon gold on the head of this man now standing several paces before him. As Darius had followed Aurthora into the thick cloud of dust and smoke, he had encountered a dazed Celtic renegade who blundered into him. The renegade put up a short, fierce struggle before Darius despatched him with a deft thrust from his short pilum.

Leaving the man on his knees dying, he quickly rushed off in the direction he had last seen Aurthora before the smoke had swallowed him up.

Petrov Joma managed to mount his horse, even though the animal was still very skittish and wild-eyed. Joma now saw the encounter between Victor Aberuso and the Celt in Roman armour whose back was facing him, making an easy target. Petrov Joma cursed, he had no weapon to kill him; he had lost it in his fall. He weighed up the situation. Had he been on a smaller local horse he would have had no hesitation in riding off down the hill and away from the skirmish immediately. But he was on the heavier, larger horse which could quite easily carry two men over a short distance – and a man sitting at his rear would also protect his back against Celtic arrows or spears. Once away from the fighting he and Aberuso should have no problem in obtaining one of the many loose riderless horses.

Petrov Joma grinned as he drove his horse into the back of the Celt, knocking him several feet into the air, and watching him land heavily on his stomach several paces away. "Finish him quickly, Aberuso, and let us be away!" he shouted to his companion.

"I need his head!" called back Victor Aberuso as he strode purposely forward. Aurthora had rolled over onto his back and was struggling dazedly to his feet, but a kick from Victor Aberuso sent him crashing back to the ground.

"Finish it! Finish it!" screamed Petrov Joma. From his elevated position he could see a number of figures moving about in the fast receding smoke. Victor Aberuso laughed as he savagely knocked the weakly held sword from Aurthora's hand, and plunged his own sword towards the exposed throat of the helpless man on the ground. The deadly thrust never reached its target. The iron point and shaft of a short Roman pilum knocked his sword to one side, causing it to sink deeply into the ground at the side of Aurthora's head. Victor Aberuso jumped backwards, leaving his sword embedded in the hard ground, but not fast enough to avoid the tip of the spear as it was swung upwards by its young owner, leaving a deep gash in his forearm. Petrov Joma drove his horse forward and held out his arm, "Quickly Aberuso, away from here!"

Victor Aberuso grabbed the outstretched forearm of his leader and using the crumpled form of the dead ballista operator as a footstool, swung himself up behind Petrov Joma, who immediately dug his heels into his horse's thighs so that the still skittish animal bounded off down the hill.

The rest of Aurthora's men had reached Orius who had regained his breath and led them at a steady trot into the smoke of the burning gorse. He had seen the skirmish with Darius and admired how the young Celt had dealt with his opponent. He then followed the young man as he ran into smoke in the direction that Aurthora had taken earlier. He came upon the scene just as Darius knocked Victor Aberuso's sword away from Aurthora's throat. The surprise that overcame him at seeing the ex-Roman gladiator, the very one who had slaughtered his brother in the arena, stopped him in his tracks – but only for a matter of a few seconds. As Petrov Joma's horse with his passenger behind him took the first steps that would lead them both to safety, Orius snatched the pilum from the surprised Darius, and with all the exploding strength that a deep, smouldering hatred could release in a man, flung the heavy iron spear.

The distance was short and the throw was deadly accurate, as the spear penetrated the left side of his rib cage the point and six inches of iron shaft reappeared on the other side. Victor Aberuso knew instinctively he had taken a fatal wound. He also heard the shout in Latin from a voice that sounded vaguely familiar. "Victor Aberuso, my revenge upon you for the slaughter of my brother Matos Tomase!" The message penetrated Victor Aberuso's fading brain. The last image that flashed through his mind as his racing heart pumped his life blood through the gaping hole in his side, was of the contest in the arena, all the crowd chanting, not his name Victor Aberuso, but the name of his adversary lying dead at his feet. MATOS TOMASE! MATOS TOMASE! As his hold on Petrov Joma rapidly weakened, he fell from the galloping horse, the soft iron shaft of the spear inflicting further massive internal injuries as he bounced several times on the hard sloping ground. When he finally rolled to a stop, Victor Aberuso, ex-gladiator and personal bodyguard to Petrov Joma, was dead.

Orius Tomase watched as his hated enemy fell from the galloping horse, and bounced down the hill. He knew the wound would be fatal, and an immense sense of relief filled him, body and soul. *This battle has begun well for me*, he thought as he made his way to where Darius was helping a dazed Aurthora to his feet.

Petrov Joma felt Victor Aberuso's grip slacken from around his waist, and his horse leapt forward as it was relieved of the extra passenger. He risked a backwards glance and when he saw Aberuso's lifeless body on the ground, penetrated by the bent spear shaft, he knew at once that his long serving bodyguard was dead. "You have been a good servant to me, Aberuso, even until the last," he muttered to himself as he concentrated on keeping astride his horse on its mad dash down the boulder strewn hillside, holding his body low over that of his horse in order to make himself less of a target for any Celtic bowman he might encounter.

He cleared the fast disappearing smoke from the burning gorse and could see to his far right the remnants of the Anglo-Saxon soldiers being pursued by the Celtic rearguard. To his left he could see several of his mounted men chasing down some loose horses, so he headed in their direction. *He would gather together as quickly as possible what few mounted men remained and take cover in the woods at the bottom of the hill. The Celtic cavalry would be too occupied to mount a proper search, so for a short time they would be safe and allow him time to assess the situation in more detail. If the Anglo-Saxons looked as if they would win the day he would appear at the final stages for the loot and booty. In the unlikely event that the Celts were successful, he would quietly slip away with the rest of his men, find out where the invaders were regrouping, and show himself then.*

Chapter Thirty

Aurthora held on to Darius's forearm for several moments after he had risen until he regained his balance and his head cleared. "I thank you my young friend; your timely intervention undoubtedly saved my life." This praise from his commander made Darius blush under his helmet, "I was just fulfilling my duty, Sire," replied Darius uncomfortably.

"You did well, Darius," Orius added as he joined them, still panting heavily, "I also saw how you disposed of the renegade earlier."

The conversation was brought to a sudden halt by the pounding of hooves as a large, pale form swerved violently to avoid the small group, then continued its wild canter down the hill. "That looked like the Great King's horse!" exclaimed Orius.

"I think you were correct," confirmed Aurthora. "We must return to our battle formations at once. Orius, take the town guard to their previous positions, I will take Darius with me and see if there are any casualties amongst the Celtic Round Council. And you Cynfelin Facilus," he turned to the young Roman Celt who had just joined them leading one of the renegade Celt's riderless mounts, "see if you can catch the Great King's grey. If it strays onto the battlefield it may be taken as a bad omen by the Celtic army."

Orius gathered together the town guard who were in an elated mood. In the brief encounter they had disposed of the disorientated, horseless, renegade Celts and also managed to trap several of the mounted ones who were in the process of trying to escape. As Aurthora climbed the hill he saw that Aidas was still on top of the cart shouting instructions to his operators. The one-armed engineer waved back in response to Aurthora's salute in his direction. There were several large smoking holes in the hard soil and rock of the hillside where the explosions had occurred, and the burnt scrub and gorse were still smouldering. Many bodies of renegade Celts and their dead horses were scattered around the centre of these explosions. One animal was still alive and struggling to regain its feet, but a glance at its injuries told Aurthora that it was too badly hurt to survive. He indicated it to Darius, who mercifully put the large animal out of its misery.

When he reached the top of the hill he felt a moment of panic as his eyes frantically searched amongst the group of Celtic leaders for the tall figure of the King, but he was nowhere to be seen. He saw the figure of Myridyn treating one of the tribal leader's personal guards, and kneeling beside him holding a bowl of water was Elemar, the King's daughter.

At the sight of her he once again experienced the strange sensation he had felt at their previous meeting; there was something, some attraction this women held for him that he could not quite put his finger on.

"Aurthora!" the voice of the King brought him back to the present. He turned and saw him sitting on a low stool; he had been hidden from view by the many tribal leaders and their guards.

"Sire, you're safe!" he exclaimed with relief.

"Yes, I am quite safe," replied the King. "Several of the mounted renegades managed to reach our lines, but our guards fought well and they could not penetrate our defences. We suffered some minor injuries in the skirmish, but only one was fatal: one of Boro Sigurd's personal guards was struck by a stray arrow, he was a legionnaire, like your man Orius. My horse bolted after the explosion, no doubt it will eventually turn up when it so desires."

The King then took Aurthora by the shoulder and led him to the edge of the small hill, from where they had a complete view of the battlefield laid out before them. As you can see the Anglo-Saxon army is still lined up in front of our forces, just out of range of our long bowmen." Aurthora looked across the valley; it was indeed as the King said.

Facing the enemy were the well-armoured and highly-trained Celtic troops forming squares of interlocking rectangular shields, ready to be raised to form a protective barrier when the enemy began its advance. In the centre of these squares were reserve troops available to replace anyone that fell from the two lines of defences that formed the square. In every square there were also ten master bowmen; their duty was to look for the officers or leaders in the enemy ranks and target them with their deadly accurate longbows. Around each square stood two rows of pointed wooden stakes embedded deep into the ground, their points finishing at the height of a man's stomach or chest.

The ten squares were twenty paces apart, and stretched between the two low hills at the entrance of the pass that led into the kingdom of Elmet. Thirty or so paces away at the rear of the squares was another great line of pointed stakes stretching between the two low hills, but this line of stakes stopped a good hundred paces short of the hill that Aurthora occupied, turned a right angle and continued past the archers and the reserve troops behind them to form a great horseshoe shape out of sight of the Anglo-Saxon army.

Behind these stakes, facing the enemy, were three lines of heavily armoured Celtic soldiers. The warriors in the front line were also protected by a wall of their interlocking shields, each was armed with a short, vicious gladius. The men in line behind them were armed with their short stabbing spears, and the third and final line comprised reserve troops ready to replace any men in the front two lines who fell in battle. These troops numbered three thousand in all. Twenty-five paces to the rear of these lines a thousand Celtic archers were spaced out between the two low hills, under the command of the master bowman Roderick Tristan.

Aurthora could see the bowmen removing their arrows from their leather quivers and placing the points in the ground in front of them. This was to increase the rate of their firepower. Many of the archers were urinating before they placed the steel-tipped arrows in the contaminated soil, a practice recommended by Myridyn, who had informed them that even a slight flesh wound thus infected would later cause an injured man severe problems.

Protecting their right flank was a detachment of five hundred of the Celtic cavalry mounted on the local horses and under the joint leadership of Cimbonda Gilberto, youngest son of the leader of the Cornovii tribe, and Timus Calgacus of the Coritani tribe. Stretching the height of the two small hills were a further three hundred bowmen, and behind them, at the top of the hill, the wheeled ballista machines and their operators, under the command of Aidas Corrilus. Stacked close to these large catapults was their deadly payload.

Protecting them were a further five hundred Celtic tribesmen – not the highly-trained troops of the Great King but warriors sent by neighbouring Celtic kingdoms in support of the Celtic cause. A further thousand of these warlike but untrained troops were being held in reserve behind the great line of long-bowmen.

A short distance below the Celtic Council and the Great King stood Aurthora's town guard and a detachment of soldiers, making in total six hundred heavily armoured, well-trained Celtic warriors under the command of Orius Tomase.

Stilll further below, Aurthora's close friend Ethellro was in command of six hundred reserve troops of the heavy cavalry with their long spears and wearing their chain mail. About twenty thousand warriors now faced an army of over sixty thousand seasoned Anglo-Saxons with their paid mercenary troops and cavalry.

The King turned to Aurthora, "The Council members Aurthora, were asking me why you did not send your reserve cavalry down to destroy the retreating Anglo-Saxon infantry that had just attacked us from the rear."

"With all due respect to the elders, Sire, that section of the enemy had already been defeated; they will play no further part in the coming battle. To send our cavalry to hunt them down in the woodlands and scrub would deprive us of an important and highly flexible part of our fighting force."

The King nodded at Aurthora's reply. "Another point they raised," continued the King, is that the line of pointed stakes does not extend to the edge of the hill on this side of the valley as it does on the other. They consider this to be a weakness in our defences."

"The Council Elders are very observant, and I compliment them on their vigilance," replied Aurthora. Then continued with a wry smile, "I certainly hope the generals of the Anglo-Saxon forces have also seen this weakness and attempt to exploit it."

The King smiled in turn. "I will pass on your answers to their queries. They will certainly be much relieved to learn you have the situation under control."

King Erion left Aurthora looking down onto the valley, and slowly walked towards the group of Celtic leaders who were in deep conversation on top of the far side of the hill. The King was finally and wholly convinced and greatly relieved. He had chosen the right man to lead the Celtic army against the invaders.

He himself had been a visionary and gathered many gifted people around him. He had organised and prepared his subjects and his kingdom for war over a period of twenty years, persuading the surrounding kingdoms to support him. He knew himself to be an excellent orator, one who could raise the spirits of otherwise defeated men. He had also proven himself an able and successful commander in the battles he fought to retain and extend his kingdom. But this young man, Aurthora was both a naturally gifted tactician and a born leader of men.

The King also observed as he watched Aurthora grow from a boy into a young man that he had inherited the good looks of his mother, who had been a beautiful woman, and bore little resemblance to his father, Prassat Ambrosius. The Great King smiled to himself. *Those indiscretions were many years ago, I was a much younger man then. All that is now best forgotten.* He knew Aurthora would make an excellent husband for his only child Elemar; she needed someone of strong character to keep her and the Kingdom of Elmet under control. He had observed them snatching sly glances at one another. Despite Aurthora's betrothal, perhaps there was still a possibility? It had struck him as odd that when he mentioned the fact to his old friend and advisor Myridyn, he had been less than enthusiastic. However, first things first. There was a battle to be fought and won.

Aurthora continued to contemplate the scene. The Druid priests and their contingent of musicians had now reached the far end of the field, and he could still hear the cheering and banging of swords on shields as the religious procession passed the various groups of heavily armed Celts. Very few in the valley below, despite the explosions, were aware of the conflict that had taken place on the far side of the hill, well out of sight of their positions.

Everything that could be done has been done, thought Aurthora. He had kept the Celtic army as tight as possible to limit the amount of manoeuvring required by the heavily armoured front troops, positioned himself to be able to view the battle and make instant decisions himself, without having to depend on unreliable reports from possibly panic-stricken and inexperienced officers. As soon as the opposing Anglo-Saxon commanders were informed that their pre-emptive strike at the rear of the Celtic army had failed they would launch their major offensive against the Celtic lines six hundred paces in front of them.

The Anglo-Saxon forces facing the Celtic lines were growing impatient: they knew they far outnumbered their opponents. They had been in many battles against the armies of the various Celtic kings, ransacking, raping and torching their way through their lands. None had withstood their charge: by simple weight of numbers they had smashed their way through their opponents' defences, giving no quarter and slaughtering any who stood in their way. Once their opponents had been destroyed and no organised resistance remained, they split into bands, mercilessly ravaging and looting the surrounding villages, towns and farms.

From the time of their first successes word had spread throughout their homeland and mainland Gaul that easy pickings were to be had on the Island of Britannica, hordes of mercenaries had flocked from these pulverised and unsettled lands to join the well-paid invading forces of the Saxon king Ælle.

"Look! There is movement at the front of the Anglo-Saxon lines!" It was Darius who spoke from beside Aurthora.

"I can see the movement but I cannot make out the details," came Myridyn's reply; he had accompanied the Great King and now he rejoined Aurthora on the small escarpment near the top of the hill.

"They have your horse, father," said Elemar who had also moved to join the small group at their vantage point. "They also have a person mounted on the animal; his hands are bound behind him and two men on either side have ropes around the horse's neck. They intend the horse and its rider to lead them into battle."

"It will have a deeply disturbing effect on our troops. They will all recognise the Great King's horse," said Myridyn, his concern evident in his voice.

"We must conclude that the rider is Cynfelin Facilus," said Aurthora. His statement was followed by a long silence as each of the group realised they were about to witness the inevitable end of a most likeable young man.

Aurthora looked at the sky: it was quite blue with little puffs of white cloud. The position of the sun behind them indicated it was mid-morning. It would be a fine, late summer's day. High above, as if it were flying amongst the white clouds, he could just make out the faint outline of the great buzzard, its wings spread as it soared on the warm thermals.

"They are moving forward!" The shout from Darius startled him, and looking down into the valley below he saw the great mass of heavily armed men moving forward, slowly at first like some great prehistoric predatory beast. The enemy army began to increase its speed, advancing to the dull roar of war cries and the sound of the handles of their long swords beating on their metal-plated wooden shields.

"Signal Aidas Corrilus to prepare his machines!" shouted Aurthora to one of the four messengers who stood behind the group, holding the reins of their nimble-footed local horses, ready to rush down with any messages to the troops below.

A polished piece of metal was produced and the rays of bright morning sunlight were harnessed to flash a message across the valley. The reply was immediate. Aurthora had his hand raised; when it dropped the catapults would go into action, sending their deadly cargo over the heads of the waiting Celtic lines and into the midst of the vast horde of the charging enemy. But it would also signal the inevitable death of a young friend and companion who had saved his life on more than one occasion.

Aurthora was watching closely as the great tide of seemingly unstoppable armed men, led by a figure on a large grey, came closer and closer to the large pegs with their fluttering markers that had been driven into the valley floor.

Aurthora dropped his arm, the polished metal was uncovered again and a flash of redirected sunlight travelled across the valley. Almost simultaneously came a loud twang that carried around the valley as the tension was released on the catapult arm, and the machines to the rear of them sent their lethal load trailing a fine plume of black smoke in their wake high over the lines of waiting Celtic soldiers.

The explosions were not as spectacular as Aurthora had hoped; they were not as effective as he had seen when they had been thrown manually at the renegade Celtic cavalry. Some were exploding too high in the air to inflict much damage on the Anglo-Saxons below them, others hit the hard ground and broke up before they exploded and simply gave off great clouds of thick evil-smelling black smoke. But about a third of the missiles were devastatingly damaging to the packed ranks of the advancing army. Where they exploded just above or at ground level, they left great swathes of dead and mangled screaming bodies.

Even the Celtic lines who were well out of range of the carnage instinctively backed away from their defensive positions at the sound of the loud explosions the smoke and dust they created. Their officers had the greatest difficulty keeping their men in position. The paid mercenaries who had been in the front lines of the advancing Anglo-Saxon army took the brunt of the effective explosions, and as they turned away in panic at this new form of warfare trying to retreat, they were trampled underfoot by the inexorable multitude of men pressing on from behind them.

Although the explosions had decimated the terrified front lines of the enemy, much of the carnage and destruction it had caused was hidden from the rest by the thick smoke the unexploded and broken missiles were creating. Through this blanket of shifting darkness a large grey horse galloped towards the Celtic lines, and as the horse cleared the smoke and debris a faint cheer went up from the waiting Celtic warriors opposite, which was quickly taken up by the rest of the troops facing the enemy. "The King's horse has no rider," commented Darius mournfully, as several of the defending Celtic soldiers rushed forward and grabbed the reins of the terrified animal.

"The horse may have no rider, but it has pulled a body behind it." This stark statement from Elemar sent the group to the very edge of the small outcrop, straining for a better view, but the swirling smoke in the valley below made it difficult to see what was happening. Aurthora turned to the messengers, "Signal for the ballistae to cease firing and send a rider down to where the king's horse has been taken. Let me know whose body it brought with it."

No sooner had he issued his instructions than signals were flashed across the valley, one of the messengers mounted his horse and galloped down the hill towards the King's horse, which was being led to the rear of the Celtic defences. He then turned to Myridyn who had moved to his side. "The smoke from the unexploding projectiles is covering the advance of the Anglo-Saxon army; to keep using them is to our own disadvantage."

As the smoke began to thin, the group looking down into the valley witnessed the state of confusion occurring in the front ranks of the advancing enemy.

When the explosions had begun to detonate among the front line of mercenary troops they had panicked and tried to retreat, but the troops behind them had been so tightly packed they could not move back, so they had been forced forward by the mass of troops behind them. These troops had heard the explosions and come to a sudden halt, but when the mercenaries in the front ranks had turned and tried to fight their way back through the advancing, packed ranks of the Anglo-Saxon warriors, they had been cut down on the orders of the Saxon King Ælle.

"Order the long-bowmen to shoot at will!" shouted Aurthora, one of the messengers dipped into the flames of a small brazier an arrow whose tip was wrapped in layers of greased lambs-wool, then fired the smoking projectile high into the air so that it landed in front of the Anglo-Saxons.

The flight of the burning arrow was the signal the Celtic bowmen were waiting for and their reaction was immediate. Those on both hills and also those behind the lines of Celtic soldiers began releasing their arrows in the general direction of the milling disorganised army below them. The onslaught was so great that the Anglo-Saxons in the front line slowly forced back those behind them. Their retreat out of range of the deadly fusillade of arrows was so slow that the casualties they sustained in the process were immense. Their round shields sheltered them from some of the blanket of arrows, but many other exposed areas of their bodies had taken a shaft, and some soldiers had as many as three or more arrows embedded in them.

The fusillade of arrows only stopped when the Anglo-Saxon infantry finally backed out of range of the bowmen, to the catcalls and jeers of the Celtic troops. The retreating army left behind a mass of dead and dying bodies, many writhing in agony amongst the smoking pits the explosions had created.

Aurthora looked down along the lines of his troops stretched between the hills: they had received virtually no injuries from the first contact with the opposing forces. He recognised the young lad Ammianus, with whom he had bantered the day they had set forth from his father's home. The boy was filling the thirsty soldiers' leather water bottles from a barrel set on a pair of wooden wheels. Aurthora smiled as he made out the shape of a great two-handed battleaxe fastened across the water barrel.

"They have retreated to lick their wounds. The first blood is yours, Aurthora." He recognised the voice of Elemar and turned immediately. She was standing just behind and to one side of him. Her body armour had been specially made and was a much lighter, finer chain link than the standard issue. The mere closeness of her disturbed him, and set his thoughts racing. What was it about this woman that drew him to her and so affected him in this way?

"The day and the battle are both young," he replied, "they will not give up easily. We have confused them, but only for a short while. They will be back again shortly, and will make a more prolonged and savage attack; they will test our defences to their limits."

He felt his body stiffen as she dabbed a wet cloth below his ear. "You have dried blood on your neck," she said as she re-soaked the cloth in a bowl of water she held in her hand. *So! He* thought, *Aberuso was a mere hair's breadth from killing me.*

The intervention of a messenger leading the King's grey horse curtailed any further conversation between them. The horse had sustained some minor cuts and lacerations had been panicked by the explosions, but avoided serious injury. While the horse was led to where the King was sitting, Aurthora questioned the messenger on Cynfelin Facilus's physical condition.

"He is unconscious and has many cuts and bruises, but miraculously he does not seem to have any internal injuries or broken bones. At present Myridyn's students are treating him." The messenger's report sent a surge of relief through Aurthora's body; there was a fair chance his young friend would recover from his capture by the Anglo-Saxons.

"They are on the move again!" Darius's shout sent them all once again to the small outcrop for a view of the valley.

There was a cheer from the Celtic troops nearest to their hill, which was quickly taken up by the main body of Celtic soldiers in the valley below. Quickly the cheering changed to a chant of King Erion! Great King Erion! Great King Erion!" Aurthora looked to where the chanting was directed, and there, astride his famous grey horse on the highest point of the hill where he could be seen by all the Celtic army, his daughter Elemar beside him and his sword pointing to the heavens, was the leader of the Celtic Alliance: Great King Erion Aurelianus.

"They are moving a lot faster this time," said Darius. "The men behind the front line all have their shields above their heads."

"It is their attempt at forming a testudo," replied Aurthora. "Inform Aidas to launch the catapults, but to use the conventional large stones for the time being, and signal across the valley for the others to do the same." Aurthora's instructions were carried out and the message was quickly flashed across to the far hill.

Within moments the twang and thud of the large ballistas in action on either side of the pass could be heard again across the length of the valley.

The raised shields of the Anglo-Saxon warriors were useless against the great stones that began to rain amongst the advancing army of men, ploughing wide furrows through their ranks. But it was like throwing pebbles

285

at an incoming tide: for as many men that fell, there were still more to take their place and fill the gaps. Even the onslaught of arrows from the bowmen that caused men to drop like the scything of corn could not stem their rapid advance. This only slowed when they were five paces from the embedded wooden stakes that surrounded the Celtic squares. There they were met by the first hail of spears whose toughened tips and long heavy iron shank easily penetrated the thin, metal-covered wooden shields of the Anglo-Saxon warrior and implanted themselves in the human frame behind. But even then they came on, clambering over the piles of their dead and dying comrades.

The next volley of pilum came when they had reached the pointed timber stakes that surrounded the Celts, but it only slowed the advance for several moments before the relentless tide of armed men resurged. Aurthora watched intently the scene unravelling in the valley before him. He knew the Anglo-Saxons could not afford to retreat, they had lost too many men already, and their only hope lay in breaking through the Celtic lines.

As the Anglo-Saxons engaged the Celtic squares, others rushed through the gaps left between the squares and found themselves with another stretch of open ground to cover, providing further targets for the Celtic archers before they could engage the lines of troops in front of them.

"Your strategy is being thoroughly tested Aurthora," said a mild voice at his side. Aurthora turned to answer Myridyn. "Yes. You and your students are going to be very busy after this battle," he replied. "It was never going to be easy, we are outnumbered three, maybe four to one; every mercenary scoundrel and thief from our island and the land of Gaul has enlisted under the banner of this Saxon king Ælle and his sons."

"Well, that is true," Myridyn replied, "but if you are successful, the entire world will know that this island will not submit easily to invaders, and many will think twice before they venture on such an expensive escapade."

"I understand your point Myridyn, my friend," he replied wearily, "but do we have the manpower or the will to train our replacements for what could be a long drawn out conflict?" Their conversation was cut short by a shout from Darius.

"The squares on the left flank are breaking, they are being overrun!" The squares that Darius was referring to were the squares made up of the Romanised Celts, the tribes from the centre of the island that had been colonised and intermarried with the Romans over many, many generations. The more warlike members of the other tribes considered them to be soft and timid. Aurthora had noticed in their training that they did not show the same enthusiasm or the aggression of the wilder mountain people. He had the impression that they only completed their training because to not do so would mean finding themselves working in chains in the Great King's mines or quarries. He had specifically moved them to that position on the end of the line and on that particular flank. If any of the squares were going to break under the onslaught, he had anticipated that theirs would be the first.

"Their cavalry is on the move, it is approaching our left flank. They are hoping to get behind the main force and cause panic and a rout." The shout was again from Darius, whose eyesight was exceptional. "Signal Aidas!" called Aurthora "I want only the catapults on this hill to start using the Greek fire again."

He looked down into the valley below; the long triple line of Celts was now fully engaged by the opposing army, and although completely surrounded by Anglo-Saxon warriors, the rest of the Celtic squares were still holding. Only the two squares on the flank had collapsed, the Celtic archers were still causing immense casualties to the ranks of the Anglo-Saxons. The young lads who were supplying them with fresh shafts looked like ants, scampering from the large supply wagons to the line of bowmen and back again.

The Greek fire started to land once again amongst the advancing Anglo-Saxons. As with the previous bombardment, some of the capsules exploded well above the ground creating a terrible and terrifying sound, but doing little or no damage to the troops below. Those that exploded nearer or just on the ground did immense damage to the advancing infantry leaving great gaps in their packed ranks.

It also had the effect of turning the Anglo-Saxon infantry away from that particular part of the battlefield and diverting them more from the flank and into the centre. Some of the Greek fire capsules hit the hard ground and simply burst into flames, giving off great clouds of acrid black smoke.

This smoke slowly drifted over the area where the two Celtic squares had collapsed, and towards which the mercenary Thracian cavalry were now advancing at a fast canter.

"Inform Orius to be ready to close the door, their cavalry is advancing. And also inform Ethellro Egilos to mount his cavalry and be ready to charge on the signal."

Aurthora's shouted instructions sent one of the messengers galloping off down the hill in the direction of Aurthora's cohort, the six hundred plus men who had made up the Town Guard and were now under the direct command of his old tutor Orius Tomase. A second messenger rode towards the Celtic heavy cavalry, positioned around the bottom of the hill and out of sight of the Anglo-Saxons. From his position at the bottom of the hill Orius had not been able to see much of what had been going on, and even less now the smoke was drifting across his view of the battlefield. The men under his control were stood down and reasonably relaxed. He knew the battle plan, and before the smoke had drifted across this section of the battlefield, he had seen the two squares on the flank collapse.

He had known this would happen and told Aurthora of his misgivings about the quality of these troops when he had first seen them and been involved in their training. His opinion had been further confirmed after watching them more closely in the recent manoeuvres the Celtic army had carried out in the days leading up to the battle.

Chapter Thirty One

Orius had always been apprehensive before going into battle, but this time the feeling had been different. He tried to shake it off by putting it down to getting older, or possibly because in the past he had nothing to look forward to and was very bored. In that sense a good battle broke up the monotony of everyday garrison life. But now he had shares in a profitable business with the hot baths. Soon he and Emilia would have sufficient funds to purchase their *mansio* and take in paying guests. And most important of all, despite his age he was about to become a father.

On reflection he was now glad that he had taken the time to draw a map of where he'd hidden the coins, jewellery, and yes, the goblet that every one at the card table valued so highly and held in such great reverence, all of them wanting to own it.

But all that – his desertion and the ensuing chase – had been over twenty years before. Since the day he had been in the service of Aurthora's father Prassat Ambrosius, his everyday needs had been taken care of he never had the desire or need for material wealth. Now the situation had changed: he had a family to consider the hidden treasure would both afford them many comforts and raise Emilia to an envied position in their society. "A messenger is coming!" The shout from one of the soldiers brought all the men to their feet with the foreknowledge that their participation in the ensuing battle was about to begin.

Kuyt Persi, from on his horse at the rear of the Anglo-Saxon army, had seen the great flood of armed men advancing towards the Celtic lines. He had fought in many battles for the Romans over the years, and since then fought in many conflicts with his old comrades of the Flavian cavalry. But never in his life had he ever seen so many armed men in one place. Surely no army could withstand such a force. He had seen these Anglo-Saxons fight amongst themselves over the most trivial things, especially when they had been drinking their evil-smelling ale. They were vicious fighters who showed no mercy: only death seemed to stop or satisfy them. He watched them advancing, pushing and shoving each other in their eagerness to be in the front lines; they had been laughing and chanting aloud the names of their war gods with the confidence of those who know they are destined to win, and win easily.

The explosions when they came were so unexpected that the Thracian cavalry, of which Kuyt Persi was now a member, were caught unawares as their horses reared and bucked and threw their riders, to scatter in panic away from the flash and bang of the Greek fire. It was several hours before the Thracian cavalry had been able to gather their horses and regain their position at the rear of the advancing Anglo-Saxon army.

Kuyt Persi had managed to keep his seat on his terrified animal, although many around him had not. He and many others had been sent to round up the startled horses that bolted, unseating their riders in the process. It was during this search that he had seen all the wounded Anglo-Saxon warriors being brought to the back of their lines. It was then that he realised that this was not going to be such a one-sided battle as the Anglo-Saxons and their King Ælle had first thought.

When the order to advance came, Kuyt Persi had managed to manoeuvre himself into a position in the centre of the Thracian cavalry. He had seen the results of a charge by the Celtic heavy cavalry before, and felt safer surrounded by as many horses and bodies as possible. From the elevated position on his horse he could see that two of the Celtic squares had been overrun, but he also saw from the number of bodies piled high that the Anglo-Saxons had paid dearly for that achievement. Yet despite having lost many warriors, as the bodies scattered so deeply over the length of the battlefield could confirm, the Anglo-Saxons were now strongly attacking the long line of Celts stretched between the two low hills. He could also see the point the Thracian cavalry were galloping towards: it was a gap where the Celtic squares had been before they collapsed.

The smoke from the projectiles hurled by the great catapults obscured what was beyond that point, but at least those flashes of light and frightening explosions that terrified him and his horse had now stopped, and his mount and those around him settled down into a steady canter. There were so many bodies on the ground in front of them that the leader of the Thracian cavalry, Karnu Arteta, was forced to take a large detour round the edge of the battlefield. Through the drifting smoke Kuyt Persi could see where the Thracian cavalry commander was leading his men. They had followed this manoeuvre so many times in the past, and against so many types of enemy, it was second nature to his battle-hardened mounted warriors.

They would swing in on the flank of the exposed Celtic forces and drive them back upon themselves, and in effect, roll them up like a carpet – which was exactly the expression used by the Thracian cavalry leader when he addressed his men before he led them off at a trot with many shouts and cheers from his supporters. Kuyt Persi began to relax; they had met with no opposition, not even an arrow from the deadly Celtic longbowmen that they all feared, before them was a gap which they could race through unnoticed and attack the Celts from the rear. It had been a serious error on the part of the Celtic commanders to cause so much smoke and allow the Thracian cavalry to advance and attack unobserved.

That mistake will cost you most dear, you Celtic fools! he said to himself aloud through gritted teeth. *I will have my revenge for my fallen friends; your blood will turn this valley into a quagmire before I and my new comrades have finished.*

He drove his horse faster to try and reach the front of the Thracian cavalry charge, cursing himself for having been too cautious at the start. He could feel the excitement sweep through the mounted men around him as the horses' pace was raised to a gallop, he was shouting wildly with the rest as they swept past the area where the Celtic squares had been, past the fighting still taking place at the tail end of the long line of Celtic troops, and through the remains of the fast disappearing smoke. In the distance he heard the unnaturally loud blast of a great horn.

They were swinging around now; soon they would be at the rear of the Celtic defenders. Suddenly there were screams from the front ranks of the cavalry as they tried to stop their horses from the headlong charge.

They had suddenly come upon three lines of sharpened wooden stakes embedded deep in the hard soil, but their attempts to stop were to no avail: the horses following close on the heels of the front line of the charge forced both them and their riders into the stakes. The riders who avoided the pointed timbers in their fall were quickly put to the sword or axe by the waiting Celtic tribesmen, who were positioned five deep on the far side of the sharpened timbers.

Kuyt Persi managed to bring his horse to a skidding halt. Looking around wildly he saw there was no way out, only the way they had come. The riders on either side of him were screaming in anguish, and several horses in front of him went down screaming and kicking in agony as a fusillade of arrows arrived from the Celtic bowmen, positioned on the raised ground at the bottom of the hill, or hidden behind rocks and bracken, or even in the long grass itself.

Now, with their six-foot bows and their yard-long shafts they let fly at the packed, confused milling throng of Thracian cavalry. Every one of the Thracian cavalrymen still mounted on a horse had only one thought: to leave this death trap alive. Spinning their mounts around they headed back to safety the way they had come.

But their escape was not to be that simple. Blocking their way were three lines of heavily armoured Celts. The front line faced them, their interlocked shields forming a line of unbroken steel. The central line behind had placed their rectangular shields above their heads to offer protection from any airborne missiles, the third and last line faced outwards to stop any attempt by the Anglo-Saxon infantry troops to open the trap. The noise of terrified, screaming, injured horses was deafening. Many were on the ground with their riders either trapped underneath them, or if the men were on foot, they were being trampled by the panicking, uncontrollable animals.

Kuyt Persi saw a large group of the cavalry make a desperate charge at the wall of shields, but when at ten paces distance they were met by a hail of the Roman short throwing spears, both horses and riders went down under this onslaught, making it more difficult for the rest of the riders behind to engage the Celtic infantry.

Shouts from the far side of the line of sharpened stakes informed the remaining riders that a gap had been forced, towards which poured the rest of the mounted Thracian cavalry, along with many who had lost their mounts and were now on foot. Kuyt Persi's horse collapsed with an arrow in its neck and one in its flank. The arrow in its neck was the most serious, flooding the straining horse's lungs with blood, causing the animal to suffocate. Kuyt Persi had luckily been thrown clear. To his right, several paces away, two Celtic soldiers were hacking at a fallen and dazed Thracian cavalryman. Kuyt Persi tried to drag a Thracian rider from his horse but the man kicked him in the chest sending him tumbling backwards.

The two Celts having despatched the man on the ground now lunged towards the Thracian rider, who reared his horse so that the Celts retreated from the animal's flying hooves. Kuyt Persi snatched at the opportunity: with four quick strides and a leap, using the still writhing body of his own horse to launch him, he was up behind the rider, his razor sharp dagger thrust upwards through the unfortunate man's ribcage to find his heart. Kuyt Persi had control of the horse and was urging it to follow the rest of the cavalry before the dead man had even hit the ground.

He directed the horse towards the rest of the riders; there was simply nowhere else to go. In the noise of battle, with the shrieks of the wounded riders and the screaming of their injured horses, under the constant bombardment of arrows, it never occurred to Kuyt Persi that they were being directed through this gap that had suddenly appeared between the pointed wooden stakes.

Karnu Artera was glad to be clear of the encirclement of sharpened timbers where he lost a third of his force, now they were back on open ground. That's what cavalry was for – open spaces where their speed and manoeuvrability could be put to the best advantage. But Karnu Artera had been in many conflicts during his thirty years as a cavalryman, he had developed a sixth sense. A sixth sense told him that things were not what they seemed to be. Why had the onslaught of arrows suddenly stopped when they were still in range of the bowmen positioned on the lower slopes of the hill? He could not attack the rear of the Celtic lines since a mass of Celtic mountain warriors were protecting it. He could not attack the slope of the hill for that too had its lines of Celtic warriors, in any case, the closer he came to the bowmen the more deadly and accurate they were bound to become. He also remembered the tale told him by Kuyt Persi, the sole survivor of the Flavian cavalry. The Celtic horsemen with their heavy horses and long spears had smashed into his comrades and decimated their numbers.

Suddenly, it dawned on Karnu Artera! He raised his arm and at the same time pulled his horse to a halt so savagely that it skidded on its haunches, nearly throwing its rider over its head. His actions caused confusion to the riders and their animals following behind him. *We're being led into a trap*! Even as the thought flashed through his brain, the obvious answer was to do the unexpected. If he attacked the line of Celtic warriors on his flanks, even if he broke through their lines, there were more heavily-armoured troops beyond them, and their own cavalry would doubtless appear at any moment. He would also have to deal with that! It might be possible to create gaps in the Celtic lines for the Anglo-Saxons to get a foothold, but his men would most likely be wiped out in the process, and his men's mounts were now growing weary.

There was only one solution: they would have to ride back to where they had come from and smash through the lines of heavily armoured Celtic infantry with their fence of sharpened stakes and their wall of metal shields that blocked the way to freedom and safety.

Signalling for his men to load their bows, they rode around in a sharp semicircle, and quickly building up speed, he arrived at the line of pointed stakes, where they had been let through previously, just as the Celts were attempting to pull the fences together and close the gap. The sudden return of the Thracian cavalry caught the Celtic commanders by surprise, the volley of arrows released from the powerful short bows caused an immense number

293

of casualties to the Celtic warriors who had discarded their heavy shields and armour while they attempted to drag the line of pointed stakes back into position.

The Celtic warriors had no time to organise any resistance as the enemy cavalry bore down on them, firing their bows and cutting and slashing with their curved swords. In no time at all they were through the gap in the fence, and heading at a fast gallop back across the open ground towards the point where the Town Guard had taken up their position, blocking off their escape.

Ethellro Egilos had mounted his Celtic heavy cavalrymen in line five deep when he had received the order from the messenger. At the sound of the great battle horn he had given the order to advance, their speed slowly increased to a fast canter, they were still in good formation as they rounded the base of the hill; he expected the enemy cavalry to be coming towards him at this point, the order to charge was on his lips, but there was no cavalry in sight.

He rode on at a canter and came to the gap in the ring of sharpened stakes to find the Celtic infantry still positioned behind their defences, but looking as if they had been badly mauled. They were treating as best they could their many wounded and injured comrades.

"Which way did they go?" he demanded of one of the soldiers who was trying to staunch the blood from a deep shoulder wound. The man merely looked at him with a dazed expression. Ethellro repeated the question. "Which way did the enemy cavalry go?"

A man standing nearby holding a cloth to a bleeding slash in his face limped towards him, shouting a reply as he did so. Ethellro recognised the voice. It was Longinus Caratacusi; still holding the cloth to his face he pointed with his free hand, "Straight on! They went straight on. They were heading towards the Town Guard." Ethellro saluted and led his men on across the open, churned up ground, following in the same direction the Thracian cavalry had taken.

From his vantage point on the top of the low hill Aurthora could see the battle unfolding before him: another two of the Celtic squares had been overrun by the enemy infantry, the Anglo-Saxons paying a heavy price in dead and wounded men for their prize. The main line was still holding, but he could see places where the odd gap had appeared. Where the Anglo-Saxons had burst through they had been quickly contained by the warriors from the Celtic hill tribes, who had been held in reserve behind the main Celtic line.

He had seen the Thracian cavalry enter the trap, which the smoke had hidden from their view. The Town Guard led by Orius had quickly closed the gap after the last of the Thracian cavalry entered. The archers on the hillside below him had peppered the open ground where the mounted men then found themselves, inflicting ever mounting casualties on the unsuspecting cavalry, who in their panic had taken the easiest route and rushed through the gap left for them in the ring of pointed wooden stakes.

But from then on things had not gone according to Aurthora's plan. He saw the enemy cavalry led by their leader perform a sudden about turn and burst back through the unclosed gap in the pointed stakes, catching Longinus Caratacus and his Dammonis tribe by surprise, bursting through their ranks and inflicting many casualties in the process. They were also well across the open ground before the archers below him realised that they were the enemy cavalry and not Ethellro and his Celts, only a few arrows were sent in their direction.

As soon as Aurthora saw the Thracian cavalry turn their mounts away from the gap and head back the way they had come, he realised the moment had come for him to take a bold and decisive course of action if he hoped to avoid losing this battle. He turned to one of the messengers, "Ride as fast as your horse will carry you across the valley and inform Timus Calgacus and his mounted warriors of the Coritani tribe to attack the Anglo-Saxon flank as soon as he receives this order. Then inform the commander of the infantry guarding the Ballistro machines to take his men and follow behind Timus Calgacus's cavalry into battle."

The nearest horse to Aurthora was the Great King's grey, it had been tethered nearby and provided with a wooden bucket of water and hay to munch, it had obviously recovered from its earlier traumatic experiences. With a shout for Darius to follow him he leapt on the startled horse's back and was heading down the slope towards Orius and the Town Guard before Darius had even mounted his own horse.

After the Thracian cavalry had passed through the gap, Orius and his troops of the Town Guard closed it in exactly the way they had practised over the last few days. The first line of men were facing the direction the Thracian cavalry had gone, with their interlocked shields forming a wall of steel and their short throwing spears at the ready. The second line were also ready with their throwing spears and held their shields above their heads to form a protective cover against airborne missiles. The third line was facing outward as it engaged the few groups of Anglo-Saxon infantry who had followed behind the Thracian cavalry, risking the deadly accuracy of the archers' arrows which were being fired at them from the lower slopes of the hill.

Orius was pleased it had all gone as he and Aurthora had planned.

As Orius was concentrating on maintaining the Celtic line against the few Anglo-Saxons that were attacking his rear, a shout from one of the group leaders turned his attention to the front of the line and the open ground ahead of it. Coming towards them in a mass charge was the full force of the remaining Thracian cavalry. He began to run down the line, shouting instructions for every second man in the third line to turn and face the cavalry, hoping this manoeuvre would not only maintain support for the rear line facing the Anglo-Saxons, but also assist the front line against the oncoming charge of mounted men.

He positioned himself in the centre of the Town Guard where he thought the attacking cavalry would concentrate its attack. As the horsemen came closer, Orius shouted instructions for the Celts to prepare to throw their pelons, but as his men drew back their arms to release their deadly weapons they were bombarded with a volley of arrows from the short sturdy bows of the mounted archers.

Karnu Arteta, leader of the Thracian cavalry, had fought for many years in the pay of the Roman legions, he knew their strategy and their strengths, just as he knew their weaknesses. The best time to release an effective volley of arrows against a testudo of shields, was just as their guard was dropped in order to release their short throwing spears. The accurate volley of arrows found many gaps in the defences of the front line of troops; it greatly restricted the number of spears thrown and the effectiveness of those that were. The cavalry charge did not waver, the riders simply launched their horses in a flying, unopposed leap onto the line of Celtic warriors facing them, concentrating their charge on the centre of the Celtic lines.

Some of the horses in the front line of cavalry with an unrestricted run completely cleared the three lines of Celts, but some of the following horses misjudged their jump and landed in and amongst the defending Celts, or simply crashed into the line. Unable to throw their spears the Celts had no defence against such a bold and reckless charge by the desperate cavalry. The gap that was created was made wider as more and more horses and men poured through. Although the Celtic Town Guard bravely tried to close the gap, they were simply ridden down by the tide of horsemen, who a short while ago had been hopelessly trapped, but who now saw an opportunity to regain their freedom and save their lives.

Aurthora arrived at the tail end of the enemy horsemen's escape, cutting down with his sword the last of the Thracians as they endeavoured to follow their companions onto the open plain. Pulling the large grey to a halt he shouted to the Celts who gathered around him. "Where is Orius? Where is your commander Orius Tomase?" It was a short while before one of the officers came running up. Aurthora recognised him as Gwyddelli, one of the youths who had trained with Aurthora at his father's house. He remembered him as a quick-witted, agile youth.

"Orius is injured Sire, one of the enemy cavalry mounts fell on him during the battle. I fear he has severe internal injuries." Aurthora's heart sank at this news. Orius, who had been his tutor and friend since as long as he could remember, who had seemed indestructible, was now lying injured.

He was off his horse in a flash rushing after the young officer who led him to where Orius lay. They had dragged the horse that had landed on him to one side; it still had Orius's sword embedded deep in its chest. Aurthora looked at the old warrior, he was deathly pale and was obviously finding it difficult to breath. The ex-legionnaire tried to speak as Aurthora knelt beside him, but Aurthora could see the effort was causing him severe pain. He placed his fingers to his lips, and said quietly, "I will speak with you later my friend; I will send for Myridyn the Physician, his herbs and potions will soon have you back on your feet."

He gently squeezed his friend's shoulder, then rose and walked back towards the Great King's horse that Darius was holding. His heart felt heavy and he could feel the tears welling in his eyes, but he knew the importance of controlling his emotions: he could not show any feelings that might be interpreted as weakness. It was then that Ethellro arrived, followed by the contingent of heavy Celtic cavalry.

"Greeting Ethellro," he said to his friend as he pulled up his charger beside him.

"Greetings Aurthora. I fear things are not going well," replied Ethellro.

"You are correct my friend; things have not quite gone to plan, but that situation is about to change. We are going to attack one enemy flank while Timus Calgacus and his light cavalry attack the other. The Town Guard and the rest of the available infantry will follow behind us in two lines. We will squeeze them like an ironsmith's pincers."

"What of the rest of the Thracian cavalry, Aurthora? They are still a formidable force to be reckoned with," queried Ethellro, turning his frisky horse into a full tight circle.

"Fear them not, Ethellro," replied Aurthora. "Their horses are weary and they have many injured; they have gone to lick their wounds, we will not see them again today." Aurthora mounted the King's large grey then called out to Gwyddelli, the young Celtic officer. As the young man came within earshot he shouted his instructions to him. "Gwyddelli, in the absence of Orius, you are now in charge of the Town Guard. Gather all the remaining

Celts in this area into two lines and then follow behind us as we charge the flank of the enemy forces. Show no mercy, take no prisoners, and remember what Orius taught you."

He moved to the front of the heavy cavalry and set off at a trot. As the long column left the confines of the pass he signalled them to spread out in a line three deep, then increased the pace. In no time at all they were in sight of the flank of the packed ranks of Anglo-Saxon infantry as they faced the triple line of Celtic soldiers.

The cavalry was now galloping at the fastest speed the heavy horses could achieve. A shiver of exultation passed through his body as he felt the rush of air blowing past his face, the powerful muscles of the King's horse moving beneath him. On either side of him the men were shouting war chants, the metal tips of their long, vertically-held spears glinting in the sunlight, and the individual family crests fluttering on the small flags fastened at the end. Aurthora dropped his long spear into the horizontal position ready for the charge; this was the signal for every mounted warrior behind to follow suit.

From the top of the hill the Great King and the group of senior tribal elders had also seen what had transpired: the failure to trap the Thracian cavalry and their eventual escape, the collapse of several of the Celtic squares and the gaps that had appeared in the Celtic lines. All of these events had been quickly pointed out to the King by some of the more envious and disgruntled leaders of the various tribes who had disagreed with the decision to make Aurthora commander of their troops. The King was weary, his injury was slow to mend and left him weak and faint after completing the most menial of tasks.

Elemar was most considerate of her father, fetching him water to drink, mopping his sweating forehead, placing a stool for him when she felt he was weakening. She too felt a sense of despair as she watched the battle unfolding below and heard the comments of some of the members of the Celtic Round Council. As the murmurings of disapproval grew louder, it was Boro Sigurd, the court official, who moved to the centre of the group. Holding up his hands, he shouted out to gain their attention.

"My friends! My friends! My fellow members of the Celtic Round Council. You are only commenting on the negative aspects of this battle; you are missing the positive achievements of our army. Look at the dead and maimed Anglo-Saxons below you, they stretch as far as the eye can see. Look at their much vaunted mercenary cavalry, a third of their force lies in the pass below you, the rest have been driven from the battlefield. You talk as if we had already been defeated. Our young men are below us, their line has not broken. They are still fighting. They have not surrendered they will never surrender, they will die where they stand, fighting for the cause they believe in."

The Council members looked at one another in embarrassment, their criticisms silenced at having been so severely rebuked in public by one of their fellow members.

Chapter Thirty Two

"The heavy cavalry are on the move!" The shout from Elemar stopped any further conversation as the group moved as one to the edge of the hill for a better view of the spectacle unfolding below them. It was indeed a wondrous sight as the six hundred heavy cavalry poured from the pass in a long column. They kept to the slightly higher ground, avoiding the lower, more direct but waterlogged route, then spread out in three long lines. There was a gasp from the group as a lone horseman rode to the front of the first line of cavalry. Everyone recognised the large grey horse that was about to lead the charge against the flank of the Anglo-Saxon infantry: it was unmistakeably the king's own, just as it could be seen that the Celtic warrior astride it was unmistakeably Aurthora Ambrosius Aurelianus.

Aurthora waited while the Town Guard and the rest of the Celts jogged through the pass and took up their positions behind the cavalry. In front of them came the more lightly armoured, and therefore more mobile Celts from the Dumnonii hill tribe, led by their young leader Longinus Caratacusi. Aurthora looked to his right and left along the lines of well-armed mounted riders; it was indeed a most magical and also frightening spectacle. *The very sight of these well armoured riders bearing down at great speed would put the fear of their God into any opposing force,* he thought to himself.

It was then that Ethellro with his great booming voice began the chant, followed immediately by Darius and quickly picked up by the rest of the mounted Celtic warriors. It spread in turn to Longinus Caratacusi and his Dumnonii tribesmen who were lined up behind the cavalry, and then to Aurthora's own cohort of the Town Guard and the warriors who had joined them.

The chant was heard by the flank of the hard-pressed lines of Celts, they too began to shout, in patchy small groups at first, but in no time all the men in the line stretching between the low hills of the pass were chanting in unison. The sound swirled around the pass and seemed to rebound and echo off the low hills before sweeping up and over them, with the archers on the lower slopes adding their voices along with that of Aidas Corrilus, who led the chanting of the catapult operators.

Timus Calgacus, Cimbondo Gilberto, and their warriors on their local light horses, positioned at the far side of the pass and waiting for the signal to charge the flank of the Anglo-Saxons, joined in what had now become a booming roar.

The voices of the whole Celtic army were raised in a combined chant that could even be heard in the Saxon king Ælle's quarters. The sound of the chant drifting down the valley sent the old king into a violent rage: the name he could hear was that of the man responsible for the recent deaths, not only of his two sons but also of his brother, as well as the loss of a substantial amount of his treasure. And no doubt the instigator of the loss of half his army.

The sound travelled over the hill where the Great King and Celtic Round Council were watching the proceedings, then down the far side, penetrating to the heart of the woods where Petrov Joma and several of his followers were in hiding in the thickets. "It is the chant of victory," commented one of his followers. "The Celtic army have won the day, we will be hunted down like dogs."

"Leave if you wish, you snivelling dog," snarled Petrov Joma to the speaker. "The Saxon king controls half this island, he will fall back to the lands he has conquered. Since he has lost many troops, he will be glad of our services. We will take the long route around this Celtic army and rejoin the Saxons at a later date."

At the far end of the valley, behind the Saxon king Ælle's quarters, Karnu Arteta, leader of the remains of the Thracian mercenary cavalry, was treating his wounded men and many injured horses. Close by was Kuyt Persi, the last member of the Flavian cavalry. He had emerged unscathed from the battle apart from a few minor bruises sustained in the fall from his first mount. He had just been questioned by Karnu Arteta about how he came to be in possession of the horse belonging to the Thracian cavalry's second-in-command. His explanation that it had been loose on the battlefield had been accepted, as there were no other witnesses to say otherwise. Their conversation was halted by the faint but clear sound of the chant coming from the direction of the distant battlefield. A Saxon on his pony rode straight up to Karnu Arteta, pulling his animal to a clumsy halt in front of the Thracian leader. "King Ælle orders you to attack the Celts and cut the throats of all of those chanting the name of that man."

Karnu Arteta looked at the messenger for a long while before he spoke. "Inform your king," he replied, "that if I had sufficient men and horses who were not injured or maimed, I would gladly carry out his orders, but what horses I have left are badly blown and many of my men are injured; we are not an effective fighting force at the present time. And now I need to continue to look after the well-being of my men and their animals." The Thracian turned and walked away from the man on the pony, who spun his horse around and galloped back the way he had come.

On the low hill, the King had left his stool, and with the support of his daughter was looking down at the young man seated on the large grey in front of the lines of Celtic heavy cavalry. The chant, AURTHORA! AURTHORA! AURTHORA! was deafeningly loud, even at that distance. The King felt a pang of jealousy at the sight. *"It should be me on my horse leading those men into battle,"* he thought to himself as he leaned heavily on his daughter's shoulder. As if reading his thoughts Myridyn, standing close beside him, spoke.

"It was not to be Great King. You were the sculptor, the man below you on your horse was your model, and a better man to lead your forces you could not have found."

The King nodded, as usual Myridyn the Physician, his advisor and old friend, was again correct.

The loud chanting seemed to have unnerved the Anglo-Saxon forces. They had now been battling for several hours yet did not seem to be making a great deal of headway. If a gap was forced in the Celtic line, the Anglo-Saxon forces that tried to burst through were repulsed by the wild Celtic hill tribesmen who were being held in reserve, and the gap was soon closed. They also knew they had lost many men before even making contact with the Celtic lines due to the explosions from the infernal machines. This battle was not turning out to be as easy to win as the previous ones they fought against the Celts. And while they were growing weary, the lines of Celts in front of them were constantly rotating, allowing the men in the Celtic third line of defence a short rest, which meant the Anglo-Saxons were always fighting a fresh opponent. Moreover, the massed charge, which had always been the Anglo-Saxons' greatest asset, had been stopped by the Celtic squares. This meant they had to funnel through the gaps between the squares, thus allowing no room to build up momentum before they were once again up against a wall of Celtic shields and heavily-armoured warriors with their short lethal swords. And behind them, the second line with their deadly stabbing spears. The chanting seemed to have given the defenders a new surge of energy and, for the first time in the battle, the Anglo-Saxons were being forced backwards.

The Anglo-Saxon forces on the outer edges of the flank suddenly became aware of an array of well-armoured men on tall horses forming a long line, their long spears raised high above their helmeted heads, obviously waiting for the signal to charge. The group on the hill looking down from their vantage point saw Aurthora on the king's grey stallion raise his hand as a signal, and at the sound of the Celtic war horn, the lines of cavalry moved forward as one, lowering their spears as they rode in the direction of the exposed flank of the Anglo-Saxon army. First they moved at a trot, but this quickly increased to a canter, and at forty yards from the enemy they broke into a gallop, colliding at full tilt with the breaking ranks of the foreign army.

For the Anglo-Saxon soldiers on the flank of their army it was a most fearsome sight that bore down on them: the great mass of galloping horses, nostrils flared, with their riders crouched over their necks, their dreaded long spears bristling. The vision was too much for many members of the infantry. They had been bombarded by great rocks, fire and exploding canisters, the like of which they had never witnessed before, they had been forced to run the gauntlet of fusillades of arrows, had encountered an organised and well-disciplined line of defenders who had taken a heavy toll of their fellow warriors. Now their front line was being forced back by virtually impenetrable lines of infantry, and they were still being bombarded by the deadly accurate archers, who had already targeted most of their officers and leaders. The advancing cavalry was the last straw for many of these disillusioned men. They simply broke ranks and ran, causing a great deal of confusion and fear amongst the rest of their comrades.

As Aurthora led the Celtic heavy cavalry into the panic-stricken ranks of the enemy soldiers, the first victim of this new development in cavalry warfare, whereby heavily armoured men on strong horses perpetrated a massed attack on packed infantry, was a terror-stricken Anglo-Saxon soldier who had thrown down his weapons and was running back to the rear of the army as fast as his weary legs would carry him. Aurthora's long spear, held tight against his ribcage to help withstand the jar, thrust the weapon into his target, right between the running man's shoulder blades. The momentum lifted the victim clear off the ground for several paces, when he fell, the wooden shaft of the spear shattered.

Another Anglo-Saxon made of sterner material than his companions had stood his ground and was in the process of swinging a heavy battle axe when the splintered end of Aurthora's spear caught him full in the face, knocking him off his feet and leaving him with a broken neck.

The weight and momentum of the great horses were able to knock over the terrified soldiers as if they were chaff in the wind. Aurthora now drew his long sword from its sheath at the side of his horse's saddle, proceeding to attack any of the Anglo-Saxons who were prepared to stand and fight. Many of the enemy infantry who had been bowled over by the charge of the Celtic horses were dazedly attempting to regain their feet, only to be quickly dispatched by the Dumnonii warriors following behind the Celtic cavalry.

Aurthora and Darius fighting side by side had just cut down two of the Anglo-Saxon infantry with their swords when Ethellro pulled his black stallion alongside Aurthora, the glistening stains on the blades of his battle axe showing that he had also been busy. "We need to pursue the enemy fleeing the field, Ethellro," shouted Aurthora above the din of battle.

Ethellro lifted his axe in a salute and with loud shouts directed his mounted men, who had now dispensed with their long spears and were using either long swords or battle axes, towards the enemy infantry, who were fleeing the battlefield in their hundreds. On the other side of the pass the effect of the lighter armoured cavalry on the smaller local horses had not been quite as spectacular as the charge led by Aurthora. Timus Calgacus and Cimbonda Gilberto led their fellow tribesmen with great bravery. With the Celtic hill tribe infantry as support they were now engaging the Anglo-Saxon flank, thus easing the pressure on the front lines of the heavily armoured, but greatly outnumbered Celtic soldiers, who were now inching forward, using their rectangular shields as a barrier and pushing the enemy infantry slowly backwards.

From their advantageous position on top of the low hill, the King and the senior members of the Celtic Council could not refrain from bursting into cheers as they witnessed their heavy cavalry led by Aurthora, mounted on the King's grey horse, ride into the flank of the disorganised and fleeing Anglo-Saxon infantry.

"Notice Sire," said Myridyn to the Great King as they stood looking down on the scene unfolding before them, "the left flank of the enemy was the first to break due to a combination of the Greek fire and the heavy cavalry charge, whereas the other enemy flank is for the moment still intact and organised."

"You are very observant Myridyn." It was not the Great King who spoke but Elemar, his daughter, standing at her father's side. She continued, "The first two you mentioned are indeed a devastating combination."

Aurthora pulled up his lathered and panting horse; he had lost count of the number of fleeing, panic-stricken men he had cut down. The terror had been infectious and the whole flank of the Anglo-Saxon army had collapsed. As soon as the Celtic squares on this side had been relieved of their defensive role, they had reverted to the offensive, trapping the remains of Anglo-Saxon army between themselves and the fresh, advancing Celtic hill tribes. But the noise of fierce battle could still be heard from the far side of the valley as Timus Calgacus and Cimbonda Gilberto with their light cavalry furiously fought the still organised ranks of the Anglo-Saxon infantry.

Gathering as many of the scattered heavy cavalry as he could, Aurthora moved across the plain at a slow trot to give the horses a slight breather before they would, if necessary, make another charge against the rear of the enemy. The destroyed Anglo-Saxon flank they left behind was in complete and utter disarray, with thousands of their troops attempting to flee the slaughter and death the advancing Celts were inflicting upon them. Even the operators of the great wheeled catapults had rushed down the slope to pursue the defeated enemy, as had the archers from the lower slopes of the hill, who only stopped to loose their deadly shafts at fleeing enemy targets.

In the Anglo-Saxon camp King Ælle and his generals watched in disbelief as the remnants of his defeated army rushed past, ignoring the king's orders for them to return to the conflict. A rider rode up pulling two horses behind him. "It is time for you to leave now, Uncle!" the man shouted. "The enemy cavalry are on the outskirts of our camp, if you leave now, you will live to return and take our revenge." The old king looked at the horseman, *this nephew of mine resembles my brother more and more each day*, he thought, as he mounted the horse. Then, with one last look at his once invincible army in its flight from the battlefield, he turned to his youngest and only remaining son, "Quickly Athelbert, mount your horse!" looking at his young son who was staring, apparently mesmerised, by the bloodied and injured men rushing past. The boy was a disappointment to him: whereas his other two sons killed in the Celtic raid had been warriors like Gwandelk, his nephew who had brought the horses, his remaining son was a little simple in the head and needed to be kept an eye on.

Still, his nephew had given sound advice. They could, and would, raise another army. If the reports he had received were true, the Celtic king Erion was a sick man. He would bide his time and consolidate the lands he had already conquered. He had the support of several Celtic warriors, and even tribal leaders, who had been swayed by their ambition and resentment of the power held by their King. Yes, he would bide his time; his spies would keep him well informed of any new developments in the Celtic camp.

Aurthora lined up his cavalry. They numbered only half of those involved in the first charge, the rest were busy chasing and harrying the retreating enemy. Darius was still at one side, and Ethellro had ridden his black stallion to the other. "It is going well for us, Aurthora," said Ethellro, accepting a leather bottle of water from his friend. "It is indeed Ethellro," replied Aurthora, surveying the battlefield in front of him.

The left-hand flank of the enemy was no more; the men that remained were now being engaged by the fresh Celtic hill tribes and the well armoured and disciplined Town Guard under the leadership of Gwyddelli, the young officer who Aurthora had placed in charge. The right flank of the enemy was being attacked by the combined light cavalry of Timus Calgacus and Cimbonda Gilberto and also by the Celtic infantry that had been guarding the catapults situated on the low hill.

The front lines of the rest of the Celtic infantry were pushing forward, forcing the Anglo-Saxons back upon themselves so that they were finding it difficult to swing their two-handed battle axes or use their long swords, whereas the advancing Celtic warriors were stabbing with their spears from behind their metal shields and inflicting great casualties amongst the packed enemy.

"Do we charge now?" asked Darius excitedly as he handed Aurthora an undamaged lance collected from the battlefield.

"Not just yet, we will wait awhile," he replied. Aurthora had noticed that the soldiers at the rear of the Anglo-Saxon army had seen them there, and were glancing over their shoulders at the line of men in their suits of chain mail sitting on their tall horses, wondering when they were going to be charged. He could imagine the word being quickly spread through their rear ranks, and the rising sense of panic this would spark among the weary enemy troops, already battered from all sides, and with very few of their officers left to lead or steady them. They were beginning to feel trapped. Aurthora was aware at this time of his good fortune in having so many capable men under his command.

He had Timus Calgacus and Cimbonda Gilberto leading their cavalry, who, together with the light Celtic infantry alongside, were now making great inroads in the packed ranks of the Anglo-Saxons on the right flank. His friend Ethellro was an inspiration to the men under his command, Aurthora knew they would follow him, if needs must, into the jaws of death itself. He had his trusted guard Darius, whom Orius had so carefully chosen, and Roderick Tristan the legendary master bowman who had initially positioned the Celtic archers to inflict the greatest damage possible on the enemy, then moved around the battlefield repositioning various groups of bowmen in order to give them a better line of fire to hit their foe.

There was Longinus Caratacusi, who excelled in the position that had been thrust upon him as leader of the Dumnonii tribe, the young Gwyddelli whom Aurthora had appointed to be in charge of the Town Guard after the injury to Orius. All these men had proved fearless in battle. *Yes*, he thought, *the Celtic nation is very fortunate indeed.*

Several groups of the Anglo-Saxon warriors were starting to break away in an attempt to travel back along the edge of the battlefield towards their point of departure that morning. As these retreating groups were observed by their fellow warriors, more and more began to join them, until a steady stream of men were rushing as fast as they could away from the fighting. Aurthora stretched in his saddle and looked around at his mounted Celts; the delay had allowed many more of their cavalry to join them, and also provided a brief respite for the horses.

"I think, Darius, that now is the time to make the charge you so desired." He raised his arm, his long spear glinting in the late afternoon sun. The young lad sitting on the pony behind Aurthora blew a long blast on the cow's horn. At this signal the Celtic heavy cavalry began to move forward, quickly picking up speed, the riders roaring and whooping in their excitement as their galloping horses thundered down onto the rear of the retreating enemy infantry.

The desperate Anglo-Saxons facing the charge tried to form a line of defensive shields, but the sheer weight of the galloping animals simply burst through their flimsy wall, with the riders slashing their way through their packed ranks.

Aurthora was at the front of the charge; his first victim fell to his thrusting long spear, which snapped as it entered the man's body. He used his shield to parry a blow from a large battleaxe, then thrust the splintered stump of the spear at a wooden shield that appeared in front of him. The shaft of the spear knocked the shield to one side and hit its owner in the chest, knocking him to the ground. An infantry soldier raised a two-handed sword above his head, but Aurthora launched the broken shaft at the man and then removed its owner's arm with a swinging sweep of his razor-sharp sword. As his horse knocked the man aside, another Saxon appeared in front of him but was trampled down by the large grey. Many of the Anglo-Saxons were now turning and trying to run, but because they were still closely packed there was no escape route. Aurthora was so busy swinging, slashing, stabbing, and thrusting with his sword he had no time to see how the rest of the cavalry were faring, or his two closest companions, Darius and Ethellro.

Hengest was the name of the Saxon whom Aurthora had knocked to the ground with his broken spear. Now the man was on his knees in a crouching position. He and a few others had only just recovered from a great sickness that had taken the lives of many of their companions he was still lacking in strength. He had recognised the Celt on the large grey. It was the same man, albeit a few years older, but definitely the same one who removed three of his fingers when he tried to re-board the Saxon pirate vessel.

Since that incident he'd been the butt of many of his companions' jokes and cruelly dubbed 'the crab', but now he would have his revenge. Hengest could see from his clothes that the man on the large grey was a high-ranking Celt. Hengest watched Aurthora fend off several of the Saxon soldiers, but since Hengest was behind him, Aurthora could not see the man grab the two-handed sword dropped by his injured companion. Hengest moved silently forward, holding the sword in front of him like a spear. He would thrust it in the man's back where the rear section of armour stopped, and when the rider fell mortally wounded from his horse, he would cut off his head. He was one step away from fulfilling his lethal action when he felt a sharp pain in the middle of his back, and the end of a curved sword burst through the front of his chest. He had time to see the sword withdrawn before crashing dead to the blood-soaked earth. Darius, the sword's owner, drove his horse forward to assist his master.

The sound of Timus Calgacus shouting to him made Aurthora realise he had cut through the enemy ranks and joined up with the rest of the Celtic light cavalry forces. Now with the remaining enemy forces split in two the rest of the battle was a rout. Apart from an occasional larger group vainly trying to organise a fighting retreat, the Anglo-Saxons simply turned and ran.

He watched as the bulk of the Celtic army pressed forward on the retreating enemy, the cavalry chasing down small groups as they broke away from the main body running made towards their own lines.

As he sat there on the Great King's horse, watching the enemy flee before the triumphant blue-painted Celtic warriors, he was suddenly filled with a great weariness. His whole body ached with the weight of his heavy armour and he had difficulty lifting his sword arm to place his sword in its sheath beside his saddle. But now it did not matter: the battle had been won.

Chapter Thirty-Three

He could see Ethellro still battling away wherever there was fighting taking place, the ground was covered with the Anglo-Saxons dead. In places where they had come up against the Celtic squares, the bodies were at times four deep, forming piles and taking the shape of the defences. Some were still moving even though they had several arrows projecting from their bodies, and possibly several stab wounds as well. But their agonies would soon be silenced as the horde of camp followers could already be seen descending on the stricken soldiers, looking for easy pickings.

"Darius, let us go and see how your friend Facilus Cynfelin fares," he said to his ever-present bodyguard as he slowly turned the Great King's horse around. "And I will see how Orius Tomase is faring," he said much more quietly, and more to himself than to his companion. On their way back to their own lines they passed many of the monks and friars of the new religion who were assisting Myridyn's young students in treating the wounded. Amongst them Aurthora recognised Camara, the older brother of Cimbonda Gilberto of the Cornovii tribe.

Aurthora was glad to see that Ammianus Camulas the young water carrier had come to no harm in the conflict; he was distributing water to the wounded Celtic soldiers. "Your grandfather will be proud of you this day, Ammianus," he called out as they rode past the youth. The young boy looked up on hearing his name on the lips of such a prominent member of the Celtic Council and he saluted, feeling immensely proud that Aurthora, the General of the Celtic army, had spoken to him, and had even remembered his name.

It was almost dusk when they reached the point where the Thracian cavalry had burst through the trap at the bottom of the hill and where several long, tent-like shelters had now been erected. He passed the reins of the king's horse to Darius while he went in search of Orius.

He passed a long queue of walking wounded waiting quietly to be attended to; in the first tent he entered, lines of badly injured solders had been placed on rush matting down either side of the shelter and were being treated in turn by one of Myridyn's students, assisted by several helpers. At first he was not recognised because of the fading light, but as he came near to an oil lantern hanging from the central tent support, a faint cheer went up from the soldiers lining the sides of the primitive shelter, and they began to chant, "Buddugoliaeth! Buddugoliaeth! Victory! Victory!" As he stood and saluted them, he could see that Orius was not amongst them, so he moved on to the second shelter where he found Myridyn and his deaf and dumb assistant Disaylann. They were both bent over a figure lying on a bed of bracken.

He looked over their shoulders, and by the light of the lamp that Disaylann was holding, Aurthora could see the body of a man covered by a thick woollen blanket, looking up at them, the pain-ridden, ashen coloured face of his old friend and tutor – Orius.

When Orius saw and recognised Aurthora he tried to force a smile, but he only succeeded in a painful grimace. "The battle went well, Orius," said Aurthora with a forced light-heartedness. "We have driven the enemy off with their tail between their legs. They have suffered an immense number of casualties, and have been badly mauled; you cannot see the grass for their dead, I doubt they will stop running until sunrise tomorrow." Even as he spoke he could see his suffering friend was slipping into unconsciousness. Myridyn the old physician slowly stood, then he turned and smiled at him; taking him by the shoulder he led him outside the tent, leaving Disaylann mopping the sweating brow of the injured ex-legionnaire.

As they moved away from the shelter it was Aurthora who spoke first, in a low whisper. "What ails my friend, Myridyn? Is there nothing you can concoct that will help him recover?"

The reply was softly spoken as if to try and soften the impact of his words. "I am afraid your friend has serious internal injuries, incurred when the horse fell across his frame. His ribs are broken and they have damaged his major organs. He is bleeding internally and it is beyond my capabilities to repair the damage."

"But can you do nothing at all?" enquired Aurthora, the sound of desperation entering his voice. "As you have observed your friend is in great agony. I will mix a potion that will help to lessen the severity of the pain, but I do not think your friend will be with us when the sun rises in the morrow."

The old physician's statement left Aurthora rigid and frozen to the spot at the thought of no longer having Orius by his side, having no one there to discuss his ideas with, no one to offer him a word of advice or caution him over some reckless plan he might have. His mind was in turmoil: how would he tell Emilia? She and Orius had made such great plans together to buy a

Mansio close to the baths, He knew of Orius's arrangement with the old caretaker of the baths, but had said nothing. It had not interfered with the efficiency of the Town Guard or their training, and he really wanted his old friend to have a happy and long retirement, which was why he placed him in a safe position behind the main defences, or so he had thought. Orius's gods had called for the old warrior, but at least when he took the final blow he had been wearing his full attire as an officer of his old legion; he would be proud of that fact.

The arrival of Darius made Aurthora realise he still had much to attend to, he was still General in charge of the Celtic forces and had made no plans for after the battle. It was now time to begin issuing orders. Picket lines needed to be organised, the dead and wounded Celts had to be brought in from the battlefield and not left to scavengers and camp followers to rob them where they lay. Patrols of mounted men needed to go and see where the enemy were regrouping and making their camp for the night. He would have to organise his army against a surprise dawn attack, as unlikely as that might be. And despite all these tasks and the little time he had to perform them, he would also have to report to the Great King and the Celtic Round Council, for not to do so would be considered a serious insult to them and their tribes.

"How is your friend Cynfelin Facilus?" Aurthora asked Darius as they moved away from the valley and towards the rise in the ground that indicated the beginnings of the low hill.

"He has taken a severe beating from being dragged over the ground by King's Erion's horse when it panicked, but they say the thick grass helped to soften most of the blows. Even so, he is still unconscious; Myridyn's assistant says the time between now and the rising sun is most important if he is ever to regain his senses and be as he was before."

Aurthora thought for a moment, "Have Facilus taken to the tent occupied by Orius, then go and find either Timus Calgacus or Cimbonda Gilberto, I need the use of their light cavalry. Then see if you can find either Longinus Caratacusi of the Dumnonii tribe, or Gwyddelli, the young officer in charge of the Town Guard. If you do, have them report to me at the King's camp on top of the hill. After that you can stay with your friend; he will need to see a friendly face when he recovers."

Darius began protesting that as his bodyguard he could not leave his post. Aurthora cut him short. "You have served me well, Darius. Both you and Facilus have saved my life on several occasions. Now you must do as I say. If I need your services I will blow on my father's hunting horn." He then reached into the pouch at the side of his saddle withdrawing an elaborately carved, silver-tipped hunting horn. "Be on your way, you have much to do." Realising it was pointless to protest any further, Darius turned his horse and trotted off down the valley to carry out his instructions, Aurthora returned the ram's horn to his saddle pouch and proceeded up the hill towards the Great King's camp.

He stopped on the way to have a word with Roderick Tristan the master bowman, who had just returned with his archers to their small camp after retrieving their arrows from the valley floor before the light failed. "Thank you, Roderick, for your bowmen's accuracy today. Your men's contribution was critical in assuring the failure of the enemy's charge and our ultimate victory. However, they may attempt a dawn attack if they can regroup their forces, so I would appreciate it if you could have your archers in position at first light."

"I can assure you that my archers will be available and in position at dawn, Aurthora," the master bowman replied with a broad smile.

He is obviously pleased with his men's performance, thought Aurthora, *and so he should be. They inflicted tremendous casualties on the enemy with few injuries to themselves, apart from those archers who were lost when the squares collapsed.* He continued up the hill and was met by the sounds and scenes of jubilation. Everyone seemed to be equipped with a goblet, drinking horn or other form of utensil that could hold liquid, they were liberally helping themselves from several casks that had been set upon a low bench. Even the personal guards of the clan and tribal chiefs were participating in the celebrations. As there was no one available to take his horse, he tethered it alongside several other mounts where it would be able to reach the hay and water left there.

As he walked slowly towards the King's tent, he looked around at the merrymaking taking place. Perhaps it was because he was weary, or perhaps it was because he knew that the Anglo-Saxons still had a force left that was larger than the Celtic army, that made him disinclined to celebrate. He knew the Anglo-Saxons would not allow themselves to be caught by surprise again, nor would they be so over-confident the next time the two armies met. Yes, the Celtic army had been victorious in this battle, but they had not won the war.

He stopped outside the King's tent to let two men stagger by, one holding the other upright, obviously much the worse for cider. He was about to enter the tent when he was grabbed from behind and spun around. His hand reached his sword at the same instant he felt a kiss planted firmly on his lips, and caught a glimpse of the laughing eyes of Elemar as she set a goblet of wine in his hand. Then she was gone, leaving only the sweet smell of perfume behind to convince him that what had happened, had indeed been real.

He entered the King's tent in a daze; as soon as he was recognised he was greeted with rousing cheers much backslapping and shaking of hands. He had never seen so many people crammed into one tent before. All the senior members of the Celtic Round Council seemed to be there, by the time he had managed to pass through the jostling crowd and reach the group surrounding the Great King, most of his wine had spilled. King Erion was seated on what looked like a small bench with a built-in backrest. He could not help but observe that he did not look well at all: his face was pallid and he seemed to have shrunk in size since his injury. The appearance of Aurthora brought a warm smile to his face, he rose to his feet to call out: "My Lords, silence! Acknowledge our hero, the general of the Celtic forces and hammer of the Anglo-Saxon invaders, my godson, Aurthora Ambrosius Aurelianus." There was silence for several moments as the Great King's words took effect on the befuddled brains, and then came a wild burst of cheering and shouts of congratulations.

It was clear to Aurthora that night would not be the appropriate time to discuss tactics and future policies. These would have to wait until the morning, but he had at least shown himself to the gathering. Now he had to return to being a responsible leader and general of the Celtic forces, since that was the position he had been entrusted with. He made his way back through the crowd, and once outside took great gulps of the late summer's evening air. It was refreshing, and the light wind that drifted up from the valley below bore a faint scent of honeysuckle.

"You are indeed a hero in the eyes of the Celtic nation, Aurthora." The voice was Elemar's. He had not heard her approach, as he turned to face her she placed her hand on his forearm, reached up and again kissed him on the lips.

"You should not do that," he said, "I am betrothed." She gave a little laugh and pulled him towards her, placing her head on his chest.

"Halt! Make yourselves known!" It was the guard at the edge of the camp challenging several riders who were approaching.

Good, thought Aurthora. *At least someone has his wits about him and is still doing his duty.* There was a rustle and Elemar had vanished.

"It is I Cimbonda Gilberto of the Cornovii tribe and my companion Timus Calgacus of the Coritani tribe. We are here at the bidding of Aurthora Ambrosius Aurelianus, general of the Celtic army."

Aurthora was impressed that his full title had been used, it was obvious by Cimbonda's tone that he was pleased to be called to the presence of the Celtic general.

"Pass friends," replied the guard.

Aurthora moved forward to meet the mounted party of two young tribal leaders with two of their personal guards." Welcome friends!" Aurthora shouted as the riders came into sight. "I would like to thank you, and congratulate you on your actions today: you and your men fought with great courage. We achieved a great victory but I am concerned about the future intentions of the enemy; they still have a substantial number of warriors and enough cavalry to be tempted to reorganise during the night and attack us at first light in the morning, hoping to catch us unawares. I would like you to send out mounted patrols and find where they are congregating and, if possible, what their intentions are. It is most unlikely they will attack, but we cannot afford to be caught unprepared."

The two men acknowledged his orders then the small group turned their horses and set off down the hill. As Aurthora watched them depart he saw them meet three men ascending: young Gwyddelli, commander in charge of the Town Guard, with two of his junior officers. They had removed their heavy armour and were also coming to report. Aurthora overheard their cheerful bantering exchange and smiled, there was an excellent rapport amongst the men. Then, once again, came the worrying thought that this had been a comparatively easy victory, fought in a place the Celts had chosen. The next battle when it came would be much more difficult and the outcome highly uncertain.

He strode out to meet the trio as they came within the light of a flaming brushwood torch placed near the entrance of the tent, and grasped each of them in turn by the wrist in the traditional Celtic handshake. "You and your men fought well today and we have inflicted a severe blow on the enemy, but we have not defeated him completely. He has run for cover to lick his many wounds. I need you to organise a picket line during the night, and inform your men they will come to arms and take up a defensive position at first light."

By the looks on their faces Aurthora could see that they were surprised by his order. Gwyddelli was the first to answer. "Do you think they will return so soon, Sire?"

"I would if I were in their position," he replied quickly. "I would be thirsting for revenge after such a beating. If we had the reserve forces we could have continued our advance, our victory would have been complete. But what is not to be, is not to be."

"Yes, it is right what you say," answered Gwyddelli, "we will attend to it at once." He and his men turned to leave, then Gwyddelli pulled up his horse and turned back. "Longinus Caratacusi sends his apologies for not coming. He is being treated for a leg wound down in the valley."

Aurthora acknowledged this news with a wave of his arm and the three men departed into the darkness. He stood for a while admiring the clear, late summer night sky with its stars and planets, wondering to himself if they would still be there lighting up the night sky when all the recent exploits had long been forgotten. There was a lot of noise behind him from the celebrations taking place in the King's quarters, as he looked through the open entrance he saw the wine, mead and ale were still flowing freely. He decided he would walk back down the hill to the shelter where Orius was being treated and call in to see Longinus Caratacusi on the way. He hoped his injuries were not serious, he needed him to organise his troops before they too started celebrating. He wanted them to bring in all the injured Celts from the battlefield and at least get them under some form of cover for the night. His last view of the Great King's camp before he started down the hill was that of the moths fluttering around the lighted torch at the entrance to the tent, singeing their wings and falling to the ground. He hoped his period in charge of the Celtic forces was not as brief as those fragile winged insects.

Chapter Thirty Four

Septimius did not have a family name. He had disowned his family when his father had signed him into the service of the Roman army in lieu of unpaid taxes. Septimius, his first name, the name of a Roman emperor, it had been given to him because his parents had hoped for great things from their eldest son, but he had turned out to be a wastrel and a drunkard. His time in the Roman legions had not been pleasant: he was crafty and lazy by nature, he always tried to avoid his quota of the company's duties, which meant he had been despised by the other legionnaires; as a consequence, they tried to foist any dirty, unpleasant jobs onto him. He was not a strong man, and therefore had found it difficult to march the great distances achieved with relative ease by the other soldiers, which led to jeering comments. All in all he lived a wretched existence in the army. He had been tempted to desert, but seeing what happened to deserters who were recaptured, the screams of these men as they were burnt alive haunted him and gave him terrible nightmares. As the legion had moved towards the coast for embarkation he had again been tempted to take up the offer of employment the Celtic king had made to any Roman deserter. He also recalled the remains of those deserters being hunted down and caught by the pack of hounds; those men had been much fitter and stronger than he, yet even they had not been able to outrun the vicious dogs. He had been on the outskirts of the crowd in the Roman army camp the night Marcus the ex-engineer had a remarkable run of luck with the dice winning all the coins from Carsius Magon, including the mysterious goblet.

It had been a strange event. Septimius had never forgotten his reaction when the goblet was placed on the table. An uneasy feeling had come over him, along with thoughts of all the dishonest deals and actions he had been involved in up to that present time. He thought that others in the crowd must have been sharing a similar experience for suddenly the noisy drinking tent had gone deathly quiet. Afterwards, when neither the hounds and their handlers nor the auxiliaries returned after going out to hunt for three deserters – one of whom was Marcus – Septimius, taking his opportunity, slipped away the following night. Since then he heard much talk amongst the Romans who stayed behind on the island, that no pouch had ever been found on Marcus the ex-engineer when the hounds had eventually caught up with him.

He eventually surrendered to a group of Celts led by a man with a terrible burn mark on one side of his face, who had in his possession the Roman pack of hunting hounds along with their handlers. It was because of this new prize that Petrov Joma had been in an exceptionally good mood when Septimius stumbled out of the woods and begged for his life. At first Petrov Joma had thought of testing out the hunting dogs on this Roman deserter, but the man looked so pitifully thin and weak he considered he would not make good enough sport. Instead he decided to keep him, fatten him up, and use him for the chase at some later date. For Septimius that day never arrived, he had ended up as a slave to Petrov Joma and his followers. Unfortunately for him, however, they treated him even more harshly than the officers and men in the Roman camp had done; taking many thrashings for being slow and insolent.

Yet familiarity had won out over the many long intervening years. Septimius had gradually worked and schemed his way into the confidence of his new master, finding a position that suited his character: acting as a spy and messenger between the renegade Petrov Joma and several members of the Great King's court who were conspiring for the downfall of the Great King and the Celtic federation. It had been Septimius, following the orders of Petrov Joma, who'd made the attempt to remove Myridyn, the King's advisor. He had been disturbed by Aurthora in the old physician's garden in the High Town. Septimius now carried a vivid scar on his face from that encounter, a much lesser version than his master's. Because of this encounter he had taken a oath to have revenge against the Celtic General, if and when the opportunity arose

Since that night Septimius had kept a very low profile, never venturing out in daylight, only then mixing and travelling with the ragged bunch of camp followers that set up their camp near to the main Celtic army's quarters. Together with the rest of these camp followers he had watched the battle from a vantage point on the side of the hill, ready to run for cover in the thick woodland if the Anglo-Saxons had burst through the Celtic lines.

At the Celtic army's advance, Septimius had become bolder in the hope of easy pickings during the confusion. From a distance he watched Orius being treated by Myridyn the Physician, and then being taken to a shelter separate from the rest of the wounded Celts. From his vantage point under the supply wagon he had seen Aurthora arrive, then leave with his bodyguard and ride towards the Great King's camp at the top of the hill. He had seen the bodyguard return, then gallop off past the tents and shelters where the wounded were treated and then on across the valley.

Just before dusk he observed the two Celtic lords with their guards ride past the shelters and on towards the king's camp. He had also seen Gwyddelli, the captain of the Town Guard walk past the tents with two of his officers, and they too made their way up the hill. There was no permanent guard around the shelters, just the occasional injured soldier being either carried or assisted by his companions and placed in the keeping of the novice physicians, or the monks and friars of the new religion who were assisting them.

It had long been rumoured amongst the ex-legionnaires in the King's employ that Orius was the one who had taken the money pouches from his fellow deserters, but neither coins nor goblet had been found on him when he was captured. Septimius had rightly concluded that he must have hidden the money bags during the chase; if that was the case then perhaps there was a map. And if that map was on his person, there would never be a better opportunity than now, as Orius lay injured, to procure it. If things went well for him, within an hour he could be well on the way to becoming a very wealthy ex-legionnaire. Then it would be his turn to give the orders, and if there was any thrashing to be carried out, he would be the one to wield the whip.

For Septimius the still of night seemed to be an eternity in coming. He could smell the wood smoke from the many campfires that had been lit; it seemed the Celts were camping in their original positions, except for the men from the squares who had joined the troops forming lines across the entrance to the pass. Their campfires could be seen across the pass entrance, from one set of low hills to the others. Mingling with the wood smoke, Septimius could also detect the wonderful aroma of cooking as the Celtic army butchered and cooked the horses that had been killed in the battle, or those that were too badly injured to survive and been put out of their misery. His stomach was tight with hunger; he realised he'd not eaten anything since the previous day. But if all went well and he found the map, he would never go hungry again.

Several torches had been lit and placed near the shelters and tents of the wounded. The moment had come for him to make a move. He crept from his vantage point under the supply wagon and slowly made his way towards the small encampment.

He was carrying a jar half-filled with water which he found in the wagon; there had been nothing else there of any value, just several bundles of arrows. If he was challenged he would say he was bringing water for the wounded. He pulled his hood further over his face so his scar was hidden in its shadow. One good thing about this battle, he thought, smirking to himself as he walked unhurriedly towards the far tent, was that he would be less noticeable now; there must be dozens of men with injuries similar to his own.

He felt relaxed and at ease: he was at his happiest when moving in the darkness of the night, the grotesque shadows thrown by the blazing pitch pine torches thrilled him. The occasional pairs of soldiers still bringing in the wounded Celts, and the novice physicians and Christian monks were all too busy to notice his shadowy figure bearing a water jug as it passed from one dark shadow to the next. A glance through the opening of the shelter, lit by an oil lantern placed on a low table in the centre of the floor, showed that it was empty apart from a figure lying stationary on a bed of freshly-cut bracken.

With a quick glance over his shoulder to check that no one was approaching, he slipped into the shelter. He remained just inside the entrance for a few moments to allow his eyes to adjust to the gloom, listening to the irregular, strained breathing coming from the figure lying on the bracken. He could not quite make out whether it was the ex-legionnaire they called Orius because the body was covered with a large woollen blanket; stacked nearby he spied a metal rectangular shield and two of the short throwing spears, alongside these, a short stabbing sword still in its sheath. Septimius's eyes settled on a small rucksack placed near the shield; it was the type that most of the soldiers carried. It contained their small personal belongings, with anything of value that they did not want to leave behind and risk having pilfered while they were about their duties.

He took another glance outside the tent. Everything seemed to be quiet and calm. Reassured, he moved slowly towards the small rucksack. Still watching the inert figure on the bed, kneeling down he carefully undid the straps. One by one, he removed all the items from the bag. There was a deep wooden bowl, a wooden spoon, a battered metal mug and a finely woven piece of linen of the type he had seen soldiers place over their mouth and nostrils when the conditions were dry and dusty during the march. There was a sponge and a rough piece of tallow soap, a polished piece of shiny metal and a small, sharp, flint razor, all wrapped in a small towel. There was nothing else: no map, no coins. Septimius cursed under his breath as he felt the inside of the bag to see if there was a hidden lining. There was not.

Still on his knees he slowly approached the figure lying on the bed of bracken, gently, an inch at a time, eased the blanket from the man's body. Now that he was close he recognised the face of Orius. *This man is knocking on the door of death,* he thought to himself as he listened to the ex-legionnaire's laboured breathing. Having removed the blanket, his deft fingers quickly unlaced the money pouch from the old soldier's belt and silently transferred the few coins it contained to his own. There was nothing else in the pouch.

He looked at the man; he was still wearing his breastplate and shoulder armour, as well as the overlapping metal strips that formed a protective skirt around his thighs and waist. He could see there was no obvious external sign of injury, so he deduced that Orius must be injured internally, which would be why they had not removed his armour. It would have been too painful a procedure and would probably have increased the damage.

Septimius had seen many men like this before. One of his duties in the legion had been to sweep the quarters where the sick and injured were billeted. When he had been alone in the dormitory he'd taken the opportunity to search these men: looking for the odd coin that may be hidden on their person, ignoring their pleas for water, gave him a great feeling of superiority over those that had previously treated him with disdain. Few men ever recovered from injuries of this type, the few that did were constantly in severe pain. *If he has a map then it must be on his person,* he concluded, *but if I try and remove all that armour he will surely cry out in pain, even if he is drugged.*

Septimius drew his knife; he'd not come this far to be stopped by a sick old man. There was the possibility of a rich and prosperous future in front of him ready for the taking, this would not be the first man he had slain in his sleep. As he studied Orius's throat, searching for a point where he could stab and make it a clean kill, he noticed a leather thong around the neck of his intended victim. Gently pulling the leather he eased a small bronze cylinder clear of the hard leather breastplate. *Now where else would you keep a secret worth a lord's ransom but close to your heart?* he said to himself as he held the metal cylinder with one hand and lifted his knife to cut the leather thong with the other.

The hard palm of a hand hitting him in the nose sent him reeling backwards, sharp pains shot across the back of his head. He must have passed out for several moments for when he recovered the man had struggled off the bed and, with his back to him, was struggling to draw the short stabbing sword from its sheath, using one of the short throwing spears as a support. Ignoring the blood pouring from his broken nose, Septimius was on his feet in an instantand in two strides was behind Orius. He plunged his dagger clear of the breastplate and into the man's side, driving upwards to find the heart.

It had taken all of Orius' sstrength and willpower to strike the blow that had put Septimius on his back, in great agony he'd forced himself upright and staggered to where his weapons were stacked. But he was so weak and in so much pain he did not have the strength to draw his sword from its sheath; when he felt the knife enter his ribs, he knew instantly he had taken the fatal sting of death. His last act as mist enveloped his eyes and all feeling slipped away from his body was to grasp his assassin in a great bear hug, falling on top of him, pinning the small frame of Septimius to the ground with his own heavy body. The last image that flashed through Orius's mind was watching a young boy playing with wooden toy soldiers, and the ex-gladiator Victor Aberuso falling from his horse with the pilum projecting from his back. With a faint smile on his lips, Orius Tomase died.

Falling on his back with the heavy man on top of him in all his battle armour completely knocked the breath out of Septimius. It was only after several minutes that he had the strength to try and escape from underneath the dead weight of the legionnaire. Gradually he worked one leg clear, and placing his knee against the old soldier's neck, he found leverage and pushed with all his might. By wriggling from side to side in the process, he slowly edged himself free.

He was panting quite heavily now, not being used to such hard exertion. No matter how hard he tried he could not roll the dead Orius over onto his back. He tried to force his hand underneath the body to grasp the cylinder but could not locate it. In desperation he looked around the shelter for some inspiration. Spotting the short Roman throwing spear he grasped it, and using it as a lever forced Orius's limp body over onto his back.

He frantically searched the man's neck for the leather cord; not being able to find it, he crawled around the floor feeling with his hands for the leather thong or the metal cylinder. Sweat was pouring from his forehead and dripping into his eyes, his filthy, ripped shirt was soaked. He glanced towards the entrance of the shelter; all was still clear, yet all his senses were screaming for him to leave. He could not stop: he had come too far to turn back now.

Taking the oil lamp from the low table he shone the dim light over the floor, no cylinder, then over the still body of Orius. "By the gods!" he muttered to himself as he noticed that dangling from the clenched fist of the dead man was the end of the leather thong. Bending, he grasped the man's wrist and with one hand he began prizing the fingers open with his other.

Disaylann came out of the long shelter where the Celtic wounded from that section of the battlefield were being attended. He had not stopped since the battle had started, he badly needed a breath of fresh air. Soldiers had been drafted in to carry out the many bodies whose spirit had left to join their ancestors; as fast as a space became available it was filled with another seriously wounded casualty. He picked up a nearby jar half full of water and took several long swallows, then splashed some of the refreshing liquid over his face and head. It was then he saw the moving light from the oil lamp in the shelter a short distance away. Thinking that Myridyn the Physician had returned to give further attention to Orius's injury, he hurried over in case his master needed assistance.

Disaylann entered the shelter and was confronted with the back of a figure crouching over the still body of Orius that was well away from the bed of bracken, with Orius's sword on the floor alongside one of the short spears. 'Pilfering Thief', flashed through his mind. Raising the half filled water jug above his head he took several steps forward and brought it down with all his strength. The figure must have sensed his presence because he began to turn just as the jug came crashing down, and in so doing took the force of the blow on his shoulders and neck and not on his head, the intended target. The jug broke into several large pieces from the force of the blow. Septimius collapsed onto the floor of the shelter, surrounded by the remains of the water jar.

Darius was bringing the still unconscious figure of his friend Cenfelin Facilus on a horsedrawn litter to the shelters as instructed by Aurthora when he saw the distraught figure of the deaf and dumn Disaylann running towards him, gesturing urgently that he should follow him and draw his sword.

Septimius regained consciousness shortly after Disaylann had gone for assistance. He felt a sticky trickle of blood running down his neck from a gash on his throbbing head; a glance outside showed two figures running across the small clearing towards him. Moving quickly to the rear of the shelter he took his sharp knife and slashed the fabric. Grabbing Orius's shield and one of the short throwing spears he stumbled through the opening, then staggered off into the darkness. He did not stop until he reached the line of sharpened wooden stakes; it was there in the darkness that he rested until he regained his senses. There was a line of fires running across the pass where the Celts were bivouacking for the night, also several other fires on the side of the small hill that led up to King Erion's camp.

Septimius decided against joining any of the groups settling down along the pass, instead made his way slowly up the hill.

He did not stop at the first or second group of Celts sitting around their campfire roasting large pieces of horsemeat. Instead he chose the third group. From this position he still had a good view of the two hospital shelters; if a search for him was mounted he would have time to slip quietly away into the darkness. He confidently walked up to the fire and cut a large piece of the sizzling meat off the spit. The glances directed his way only showed him as an injured soldier accepting their hospitality. He settled down just out of the light of the fire and the crowd of Celts around it. To any casual onlooker, he was just another soldier with his shield and spear settling down for the night.

Chapter Thirty Five

Aurthora was glad to be on his own, breathing in the cool night air. He'd removed his heavy chain mail and breastplate, but his shoulders were still sore where the straps had rubbed until his skin was raw, the muscles in his arm ached with the jarring of the lance and the constant use of his sword during the battle. He missed Katrina, and most of all he missed her warm bed, her smooth caresses and the love they shared. He also missed the hot baths and the nimble fingers of Oengus's nephew. The lad had the gift of removing the stiffness and pains of a heavy day's toil. He walked slowly down the hill allowing his thoughts to wander wherever they wished. They settled on the daunting task that lay before him, and the prospect of how he would inform Emilia if Orius died of his injuries, which Myridyn had warned was more than likely.

He stopped at one of the camps halfway down the hill and was greeted warmly by Roderick Tristan and his fellow archers. They had managed to procure the hind leg of one of the dead horses belonging to the Flavian cavalry while they were collecting their arrows in the valley below, and were cooking strips on a spit over their campfire. They had also acquired a barrel of cider and were noisily celebrating their victory.

Aurthora knew that many of the groups of soldiers gathered around the many campfires scattered near the pass would also be drinking an excess of the rough cider purchased from the various tradespeople who followed the army, celebrating the fact that they were still alive. He recalled a statement that Orius had made many days before. You can train soldiers to imitate the Roman army, but you cannot instil the iron discipline of the legions. Roderick waited while what looked like a mercenary, of whom there were many in the employ of the Great King, helped himself to a slice of the horse. Aurthora noticed in the light of the fire that the man was bleeding from a head wound, and was about to shout to him to go and seek attention in the clearing below when Roderick returned with a prime cut of cooked horse flesh passing it over to him.

"I thank you Roderick," said Aurthora gratefully as he took the meat from the knife, passing it quickly from one hand to the other because it was so hot, before fixing it onto his own dagger. When he looked back to the fire, the injured soldier had disappeared into the darkness.

"This was the only good thing the Flavian cavalry left behind," exclaimed Roderick in a loud voice, "some prime horse meat."

"And their injured pride," retorted Aurthora.

This comment brought guffaws of laughter from the group of archers. After some more light-hearted banter he left the group and continued slowly down the hill, still enjoying the remains of the large slice of horsemeat. He had not realised how hungry he was until he began to chew the well-cooked flesh. He had been so engrossed in his own thoughts, and prior to that he'd been completely occupied in planning strategy and issuing orders for the Celtic army.

As he walked down the rest of the hill he could see the campfires stretching across the valley and up the low hill at the far side of the pass. The late summer night was full of the smell of wood smoke and the aroma of cooking meat, and the occasional burst of laughter drifted over from the many groups of men who were now congregating in their separate tribes and clans. He was enjoying the walk down the hill: it was loosening his stiff muscles, and it was a relief to be free of the heavy chain mail. He soon reached the clearing where the shelters for the wounded had been erected, and immediately sensed that things were not as they should be. A crowd had gathered around the second shelter where Orius was being treated, and a guard was posted at the tent entrance.

Pushing his way through the curious onlookers he entered the large tent-like shelter. Darius was there, standing next to Disaylann, behind them was Myridyn, and to the side of them, lying on a rough-cut sledge of poles, was Cynfelin Facilus, the still concussed young Roman Celt. "What has happened?" Aurthora exclaimed. Silence met him for several moments, so he repeated his question, this time louder and with the stamp of authority in his tone. "What has happened here?"

It was Myridyn who eventually answered. "An assassin has struck, Aurthora. His victim was Orius. Your friend has departed this world to join his ancestors."

The words shook Aurthora. He knew his old tutor was seriously injured and had been unlikely to survive the night, but for him to have been assassinated made no rhyme or reason. It would have been obvious to anyone who entered the tent that Orius was seriously wounded.

"Disaylann disturbed the assassin," Darius blurted out. "He entered the shelter and found the murderer crouched over Orius's body, so he smashed the water jug over the man's head and came looking for help. He found me returning with Cynfelin, when we entered the shelter the man had already made his escape by slashing a hole in the rear of the shelter."

"He took Orius's shield and a pilum," added Myridyn. "There is also a trail of fresh blood leading though the slashed rear of the shelter. The culprit has a head wound."

Aurthora's thoughts flashed back to the mercenary soldier in Roderick's camp on the hill. He had a recent head wound and he was also carrying a Roman infantry shield and short throwing spear. *Myridyn's observance may well lead to the capture of the assassin even now*, thought Aurthora. "I think I know where the villain may be skulking. Follow me, Darius!"

With no further explanation, he was off through the tent entrance and running towards Roderick's camp, situated halfway up the hill, with the young Darius following closely behind. Aurthora burst upon Roderick's camp and silence fell on the jovial group of archers as he rushed across the small clearing, sword drawn, closely followed by Darius, to where he had last seen the injured assassin. But the only sign of the assassin's recent presence was leaning against a rock: a Roman infantry shield bearing the crest of Orius's old legion.

"What ails you, Aurthora?" exclaimed Roderick as he joined them with his bow already strung and an arrow fitted ready for flight.

"We have had an assassin in the camp," replied Aurthora, "he has slain my friend Orius."

"I will raise the alarm. We will sweep the hillside, we will hunt this assassin down like the animal he is," gasped Roderick and turned to face his men who were already standing with their bows strung and arrows fitted.

"No Roderick. The man will have slunk into the woods by now. I need your men in position and ready by the first light of dawn. I have no doubt that this murderer's path and my own will cross at some time in the future, I will have my day of reckoning. But I thank you for your offer." With a last look into the darkness, he turned and made his way back down the hill with Darius in step by his side.

When he reached the small clearing the second shelter was beginning to fill with the last of the Celtic wounded from that section of the battlefield. Seeing that the old physician was exceptionally busy, he turned to make his way back up to the King's encampment. But Myridyn had noticed him and came over, wiping his bloody hands on a piece of linen.

"I can see by the look on your face that the murderer eluded your grasp this time, Aurthora," he said, placing his hand on the younger man's shoulder. "You need to rest now. I have a feeling you will have another busy day in front of you tomorrow and you will need to be awake and alert before dawn, even if some of your troops will not be." He indicated a large group of soldiers standing around a fire. They were laughing and joking and starting to sing as the cider they were consuming began to take effect.

"And you Darius," he continued, "stay with your general. Your friend Facilus Cynfelin is in good hands and will be well cared for." Then in a quieter voice he said, "Aurthora, do not concern yourself with your friend's body. I will send to the High Town for your father's servants; they will come and prepare your friend for his final journey." Aurthora did not reply, but the look he gave the old man showed his gratitude.

Aurthora and Darius left the small clearing and the two shelters that were a temporary hospital for the injured; they slowly climbed the hill towards the King's camp and the joyous celebrations they could hear coming from that direction. He felt weak with tiredness and very alone. He was overcome with a ice cold spasm of shivering that racked his whole body, even though he was sweating with the exertion of climbing the hill. It seemed he had no sooner placed his body on the bed of bracken in his small bivouac than he was asleep. He dreamt that he had just left the hot baths in the town of Buxonana and his body felt supple and loose after a massage with the scented oils used by Oengus's nephew. Then he made his way to Katrina's lodgings and slipped into her warm bed. But when he awoke in the morning he found it was not Katrina sleeping beside him but Elemar, the Great King's daughter.

He woke with a gasp and a start: Darius was shaking his shoulder.

"Awaken! Bore da brenhinof Aurthora." The lad was repeating this as he continued to shake him. Aurthora slowly opened his eyes. "Why do you call me 'Royal Aurthora'?" he asked the smiling Darius.

"All the men were singing your praises last night, they were singing Royal Aurthora in their songs. You have become a living legend," explained Darius with awe in his voice. Aurthora had been so tired the previous night he'd slept in his clothes, but now he stripped to the waist and splashed the icy cold water, from the wooden bucket Darius had brought, over his exposed body while his young bodyguard stood by, holding an oil lantern in one hand and a large piece of dry linen cloth in the other.

"I see you are both up and about with the lark." The voice startled them, they peered into the darkness until the slim figure of Elemar came into the faint circle of light shed by the oil lamp. "It is obvious you were not celebrating last night like the rest of your army," she continued.

"The rest of my army is in for a rude awakening as soon as we locate the guardian of the great warhorn," replied Aurthora, and all three laughed.

Taking the dry cloth that Darius handed him, he instructed the young man to go and trace the war horn and its keeper and to bring them to him as soon as possible.

"Are you expecting the Anglo-Saxons to attack us?" inquired Elemar in disbelief.

"I am. I would do the same if I were in their present situation," he replied as he laced on his black suit of chain mail, and struggled to fasten the buckles of his breastplate.

She came behind him and, taking his hands in hers, removed them from the buckles. She then proceeded to fasten the heavy straps that kept his breastplate in position. He could smell her strong perfume remaining quite still while she fastened the leather thongs that held his armour.

"But they took such a beating yesterday," she continued.

"All the more reason for attacking again today. And preferably at first light. They must have heard the celebrations in our camp, they must know we don't have fresh reserves available, otherwise we would have used them to follow up our advantage yesterday to destroy most of their army. This is not meant as a criticism of your father," he stammered. "Without your father's foresight and planning we would have been overrun many years ago. The enemy have but one objective: to destroy us. Whereas we, the Celtic Alliance, are a combination of many tribes and clans all pulling in different directions and beset by petty internal quarrelling and jealousies. I'm afraid, Elemar, that we still have a steep hill to climb." She was very quiet after he had finished, he thought he had said too much and given her a lecture, which had not been his intention. He was about to turn to face her, but she held his shoulders to stop him. He felt her kiss on the back of his neck, and then, like the night before, she was gone.

Darius returned, leading Aurthora's own horse and holding the great Celtic war horn, but without the keeper of the instrument. "I could not waken the man," he replied to Aurthora's puzzled frown.

"Then we will have to blow the horn ourselves," taking the instrument and inspecting it before giving it back to Darius. The two men led their horses to the slight outcrop at the top of the hill that overlooked the valley and the pass below. The first streaks of dawn were beginning to appear on the far horizon, and somewhere below, shrouded in the morning mist, was the Celtic army, who had slept in their clothes around the many campfires after the celebrations that had continued until the cider had run out in the early hours of the morning.

Aurthora indicated to Darius to blow the war horn, but as hard as he tried the young man could not raise a note from it: only a wheezing whistle of air emerged from the trumpet of the instrument. Aurthora took the horn from the red-faced Darius and also tried – and failed – many times. Aurthora stopped for breath in his attempts, now quite concerned. If an attack by the Anglo-Saxons came at this time it would be devastating for the unprepared Celtic army, all the efforts and gains of the previous day would have been for nothing. He was racking his brain as to how he could rouse so many men from their deep slumber in such a short time, when Elemar appeared holding out her hands for the horn. He handed it to her but held out little hope of success. If two grown men could not blow this horn what chance would this slip of a girl have? "It is not always brute strength that is required to succeed, my lord," she said as if reading his thoughts.

She lifted the horn, and placing the mouthpiece to her lips, took several deep breaths. As she did so Aurthora could not help noticing the shapeliness of her slim figure. She puffed out her cheeks and blew the Great Celtic war horn. The noise was loud and piercing, reverberating and echoing between the low hills on either side of the pass.

"Not only will that awaken our Celtic army from their dreams, it would also awaken the dead!" commented Darius as he struggled to hold the horses as they attempted to bolt as the high-pitched notes continued to emerge from the trumpet of the great horn.

"Yes, and it seems with so little effort," added Aurthora.

"It is a matter of technique," replied Elemar as she placed the horn on the ground.

"There is movement amongst the archers below us," exclaimed Darius.

"And I see movement in the valley," added Aurthora. "It seems you have saved the day Elemar."

"If that is true then I will see you later for my reward," she replied, smiling as she turned and made her way towards the King's camp, which was also stirring. He watched her go, and suddenly felt guilty of his thoughts. "*Cast these thoughts from your mind, you fool, you are betrothed to Katrina!* How he wished she was there with him now, then there would be no temptation.

By the time dawn arrived, with the help of Darius and several of the officers, they had managed to raise enough soldiers to form two lines across the pass. Aurthora would have preferred three lines, but many of the Celts were incapable of standing, and indeed many of those in the two lines were being held up by their shields. There had been much cursing and mumbling amongst the men, but at least they were now in position. He'd placed himself with Roderick the master bowman and his archers halfway up the hill; they too were grumbling about the wasted effort. They had been standing there since before dawn and the mist in the valley had all but dispersed. Aurthora could see that many of the soldiers were sitting down. As time slipped by their complaints became louder.

"A rider approaches, and he is travelling fast!" shouted Darius, pointing towards the plain. As the rider came closer it could be seen he had driven his mount hard as it was covered in foam.

"It looks like Cimbonda Gilberto," announced Darius.

He could not trust his men to stay out on the plain when they could hear their comrades celebrating, so he took on the duty himself, Aurthora realised.

Cimbonda pulled up his sweating mount at the line of Celtic soldiers and was directed to Aurthora halfway up the hill. The appearance of Cimbonda had caused a stir amongst the ranks of men, and those sitting down were now all on their feet and back in their battle positions. Cimbonda brought his panting animal to a stop in front of Aurthora.

"The enemy cavalry are fast approaching, I do not know at this point if there are infantry advancing behind them. I have left one of my riders on the plain; he will try and observe their battle plan and then ride to inform us."

"I thank you for this vital information Cimbonda," replied Aurthora. "In the meantime, can you rally some of your horsemen and cover the far flank as before? Ethellro and the men he has managed to get mounted will cover this near flank."

Cimbonda waved in acknowledgment, turned his horse and rode back down the hill and across the pass behind the two lines of now tense Celtic infantry. No sooner had he reached the far side of the pass than a shout came from Darius, "They're coming!" All eyes were trained on the valley below.

Galloping at full stretch and low over their horses' necks with their shields above their heads, the Thracian cavalry was heading straight for the centre of the double line of Celtic infantry. "They have learnt from the battle yesterday," said Aurthora to Roderick who was standing by his side. "They are about to attack our weakest point: they are out of range of the bowmen on the hills and our archers behind our lines have a very limited target. Gather your archers Roderick, and follow me! I need you to support the few archers in the centre as quickly as possible." Shouting to his fellow bowmen Roderick bounded off down the hill after the mounted Aurthora and Darius, closely followed by three score of his companions in a desperate rush to get into position before the charging enemy cavalry came into contact with the weakened lines of Celtic infantry.

Chapter Thirty Six

Karnu Arteta, the leader of the Thracian cavalry, had brooded all night. The sounds of celebration from the Celtic camp seemed to be mocking him. Never before had his men been so humiliated; it was no consolation that the rest of the Anglo-Saxon army had also taken a severe beating. He needed a little victory, just to reassert his authority amongst his men. There had been murmurings amongst his troops on the quality of his leadership and he now lacked the support of his officers since many had been lost in the trap set by the Celtic general they called Aurthora. His cavalry had been specifically targeted by the Celtic archers. All his missing officers had been good, experienced soldiers, had all served with Karnu Arteta for many years. The Saxon King with his backward son and the bulk of his remaining army retreated quietly during the night, leaving his nephew Gwandelk with a strong rear guard; these had spent the night stoking up the many fires to give the impression that the whole Anglo-Saxon army was still encamped there.

Well before dawn Karnu Arteta roused his men. He was in a foul temper, he shouted and cursed those close to him for their delay in fitting their armour and saddles. When they were all armed, mounted and ready for battle, he gathered his remaining warriors around him and addressed them.

"Horsemen and warriors of the Thracian cavalry, as the sun set last night you heard the Celtic army celebrating. They think they have won a great battle and that we too will retreat with our tails between our legs like the rest of the Anglo-Saxon army. But yesterday we left many of our comrades on the battlefield; for our own pride we need to avenge that insult. This morning, while the Celts sleep off their night of drink, we will attack in the name of our fallen friends. They will remember us, not as a beaten force, but one that can inflict a terrible revenge. We are the Thracian cavalry. Ordinary mortals tremble in fear at the sound of our name. And by the end of this morning, these Celts will also tremble at the very mention of the word 'Thracian'."

His speech was received by loud cheers and the waving of swords from the gathered mass of mounted warriors, and chants of Karnu! Karnu! Karnu!

"Follow me, my soldiers! Follow Karnu Arteta and soak your weapons in Celtic blood! Death to the Celts!" With this war cry quickly taken up and repeated by his cavalry Karnu Arteta turned his horse, and followed by his eager warriors, trotted off down the valley towards the Celtic camp, while Gwandelk and the rest of the Anglo-Saxon rear guard looked on with admiration.

The befuddled Celtic soldiers had been slow in getting organised despite the bullying from their officers. When the cry, "Attack by cavalry!" came, they had barely interlocked their rectangular shields before the Thracian cavalry appeared out of the early morning mist, galloping straight towards them like madmen, their horses blowing clouds of vapour into the cool morning air, their hooves throwing up clods of earth as they strained at the reins in their wild charge.

At the Celtic officer's shout of "Prepare pilum!" they drew back their arms, spears raised and ready, waiting for the order to release them. It was at this moment that the Thracian cavalry at full gallop released a volley of arrows from their short bows, all directed at the central Celtic position they were hoping to break down. The deliberate timing of this volley of missiles meant that many of the Celtic soldiers were caught unprotected by their shields. Several officers were also mortally wounded and therefore could not complete the order, "Release pilum!" and in the sections where this was the case confusion reigned. Then the cavalry was upon them, swords flashing as they cut and hacked at the weakened line of defenders.

It was at this, the beginning of the battle, Aurthora and Darius arrived. They were ahead of the Celtic bowmen, who were still several hundred paces behind, panting heavily at their forced run down the hill and across the pass. Aurthora saw at a glance that the situation was critical: many of the Thracian horsemen had broken through the two lines of Celts and were attempting to widen the gap they had created by attacking and forcing the lines back on either side. There were still a number of Celtic soldiers who had been late in reaching their allotted positions on the lines, and who now stood in several small groups wondering what they should do.

It was at these two dozen or so men that Aurthora directed his shout of "Follow me!" driving his horse towards the break in the Celtic lines, followed by Darius and the group of Celts staggering after them, all of whom were still much the worse for the drink they had consumed the night before.

Karnu Arteta was pleased at the way he'd caught the Celts unprepared. He had already cut down two of their number and just slashed another across the face with his sword as the man tried to grab his horse's reins. His horsemen were forcing the gap in the lines wider, and more of his mounted warriors were beginning to fight their way through.

He noticed the two riders come galloping across the plain and saw the group of men following on foot. He also saw the same officer rally the group of soldiers and proceed to rush towards him, obviously in an attempt to plug the gap in the Celtic lines. *Without him, they are leaderless*, he said to himself. *I will remove him.*

Aurthora had charged his horse into the fray, and already cut down one Thracian cavalry soldier with a mighty swing of his sword, when the full force of Karnu Arteta's horse hit his own mount centre on. Although Aurthora's horse was bigger and heavier, the force of Karnu's charge knocked his horse over, throwing him dazed to the ground. Karnu was off his own horse in a second and, raising his sword like a spear, he picked a point at the neck where the chain mail finished and thrust downwards with his sword towards the fallen and still-dazed Celtic general.

The sword stopped inches from its target and fell from the hand of its owner as a yard-long arrow, fired by the master bowman Roderick Tristan, passed through Karnu Arteta's neck and embedded itself in the heavy saddle of the Thracian cavalry leader's horse. Several inches of the arrow also penetrated the horse's flank, which made it bolt in pain in doing so drag the dead cavalry leader, pinned by his neck to the saddle, past the rest of his men. Seeing that they now had no leader, they quickly disengaged from the fight and fled after their leader's unmanned horse in a hasty retreat back down the valley the way they had come, followed by a fusillade of arrows from Roderick's bowmen, pursued in their retreat by the arrival of Ethellro and Cimbonda Gilberto with their mounted troops.

When Aurthora eventually staggered uncertainly to his feet he was met by the cheering Celtic soldiers, who lifted him shoulder high and began marching in a circle to the chant of AURTHORA! AURTHORA! AURTHORA!

Around midday Ethellro and Cimbonda Gilberto returned with their mounted warriors. They had chased the Thracian cavalry across the plain to their encampment, but had been kept at bay by the accuracy of the enemy bowmen, who were capable of turning and firing their bows to the rear while their horses were travelling at full gallop, a skill much admired by the chasing Celtic warriors, who were exceptionally versatile horsemen themselves. On reaching the Anglo-Saxon camp, however, the Celts were confronted by a packed line of foot soldiers behind a defence of sharpened stakes.

Ethellro and Cimbonda wisely decided at this point that as they were unsupported by any infantry, it would be a foolhardy venture to attack this defended position. So after firing a volley of arrows from their short bows at the Anglo-Saxon infantry, they returned, leaving several scouts to report on any movement among the enemy troops.

After the morning's skirmish, the rest of that and the following day Aurthora was kept busy organising the removal and the burial in long pits of the dead Anglo-Saxon and Celtic soldiers. He also made arrangements for the transportation to the High Town of Buxonana of the wounded Celtic soldiers who were not too seriously injured.

In the hot, end-of-summer days that followed, the stench of death began to hang over the battlefield as the corpses of the dead became bloated and began to decompose before they could be collected and buried by the overworked crews of gravediggers. Then the fine weather began to break.

It was while he was attempting to solve the problem of the dead by recruiting more soldiers to dig long trenches, that Darius rode up and informed him that his father's old servants Eryl and Borode had arrived, that Katrina and Emilia were only an hour or so behind them. Aurthora had taken it for granted that Katrina would accompany Emilia and support her during this sad time; he was relieved that it would also mean they would be together again. Elemar had always been present at his meetings with the Great King. He could sense her gaze on him at all times, at every opportunity she would brush alongside him. Try as he might, the more he shared her company, the more his resolve to resist her weakened.

When Katrina and Emilia arrived in the camp, he was there to greet them. It was an emotional meeting: he was so glad to see Katrina, but distraught to see the anguish in Emilia's face: she seemed to have aged tremendously in the few days since he had seen her.

Eryl and Borode had prepared Orius for his funeral dressed as an officer of the Roman legion in his full suit of armour. Most of the Celtic army, together with all the Round Council including the King, had turned out to honour Aurthora's tutor and friend. They stood in the rain that had begun to fall early that morning, forming a human corridor where the carriage and the mourners passed leading on to the flat-topped cairn of stones where Orius was laid and then covered in the Celtic tradition. This, apparently, had been Orius's wish, conveyed to Emilia in their conversation before he had left Buxonana several days before.

The rain continued all that day, and it was still raining on the morrow when Aurthora entered the King's tent for a meeting of the full Celtic Round Council. The Saxon King Ælle had apparently sent an emissary and was suing for peace and a treaty. This news had the effect of splitting the Council like never before.

The Celtic troops were wet, miserable and cold. Their temporary shelters had been sufficient while the weather was fine, but were of little use against the recent prolonged heavy rain. They felt they had won a significant victory against the Anglo-Saxons and had done what had been asked of them. They missed their families, farms and villages. The older members of the Council supported these feelings, while the younger members were of the same mind as Aurthora, who wanted to continue the conflict while they had the advantage. Their aim was to advance towards the Anglo-Saxon settlements, driving all before them until the enemy was pushed into the sea. Each member who so chose was able to put his point of view: voices were raised, accusations made and insults exchanged that would not easily be forgotten. It was a meeting that drove deep wedges into the unity of the Celtic Alliance.

Speaking for those who proposed accepting a peace treaty was Voltigern, a figure who had previously remained in the background, preferring to persuade and influence Council decisions from the sidelines and then have other members argue his point of view. *He must feel he has a lot of support to bring him to the forefront in this debate. He always struck me as being a quiet, but a very ambitious member of the Council, very active behind the scenes,"* thought Aurthora as Voltigern put forward his proposals, trying to paint a rosy picture of the two cultures living peacefully side by side. When a vote was finally taken, the result was a tie. It was the same even after a recount. The final casting vote would be left to Great King Erion.

It was Boro Sigurd who suggested that as this was such an important decision, the King should have further time to reflect on the issues and their implications. It was agreed by all present that noon the following day would be an appropriate time for King Erion to deliver his casting vote. The direction the Celtic nation was going to take would be announced by the very same man who had welded all the different tribes together as one, under his banner.

When Aurthora left the King's tent after the meeting with the Council, he went to the wagon that Eryl and Borode had converted into a mobile, waterproof shelter. The ground underfoot had been churned into a sea of mud by the many horses and the feet of so many soldiers in such a confined area. He squeezed into their shelter with its waterproof cover of closely spun and oiled woollen fabric, where the space was just sufficient to accommodate their raised bunks with a narrow strip in between.

"Eryl and Borode, I would like to thank you for the way you prepared

Orius Tomase for his final journey." Even though Aurthora had known these two men since he was a boy, he had never known their family names, to him they had always been simply Eryl and Borode. The two old friends were pleased that Aurthora, the general in charge of the entire Celtic army, had found the time to come and thank them personally.

"The honour was ours, Aurthora," replied Eryl. Borode continued:

"For all the twenty years that we knew the Roman Orius, from the time he entered your father's service, he has always treated us well. We were privileged and honoured to attend to him for his final journey."

Eryl fumbled in his tunic. "Sire, clutched in Orius's hand, in a tighter grip than I have ever come across, was this small cylinder."

Aurthora took the slender metal container, looked at it for several moments, then placed it in a small leather pouch he carried around his neck. "I must take your leave now," he said. From underneath the cowhide he had wrapped around his shoulders against the rain he produced a jug with a sealed top. He had taken it from the long table in the King's tent when he left after the recent Council meeting. It contained some of the finest white wine produced on the island of Britannia. "This will help to keep the damp out of your bones tonight, my friends," he said, smiling, as he placed the jug between their bunks before leaving their cosy little wheeled bivouac.

Outside, it was still raining heavily, he pulled the soft cowhide more closely around his head; nevertheless, rivulets of water were still finding their way down his neck as he directed his steps towards Myridyn's tent. Since Orius's death he had found himself consulting more often with the old physician, even though he did not always take the old man's advice, he found in him a good sounding board for discussing solutions to the problems that arose amongst the many tribes and clans that made up the Celtic Alliance.

There were still arguments and disagreements amongst the gathered Celtic troops, but since he had banned the merchants from selling wine, ale, mead, and cider to the soldiers on pain of having all their stock and their worldly possessions confiscated, violent and fatal disagreements between the troops had been reduced tremendously; minor disagreements could now be settled by the chieftains and elders of the tribes.

It was while he was in the old physician's tent sipping a beaker of hot mead that he suddenly remembered the metal cylinder Eryl had given him, and took it from his leather pouch. He explained to Myridyn how it had come into his possession while he removed the stopper, withdrawing from the metal tube a silk square on which a fine detailed map was drawn, accompanied by several sentences in Latin. "What do you make of this

Myridyn?" he asked, handing the square of material to the old man.

Myridyn took the cloth to the oil lamp and in its light began to read the Latin script. "In the first few sentences Orius says that the hoard of gold and silver indicated on this map he gained by deceit, and he has regretted his actions against his comrades every day since he first committed them.

"He goes on to write that if the content of this cylinder is opened it is because "I, Orius Tomase, am dead. In which case I would like, in fact I beg Aurthora Ambrosius Aurelianus, if he lives, to use the map enclosed to retrieve the treasures that have lain hidden for over twenty years. Should he find them, I ask him to pass them on to my beloved Emilia and my unborn child."

"Emilia is with child!" interrupted Aurthora in amazement.

"That is what he writes," continued Myriden, looking up from the fine cloth. "I gather from this script that Orius wrote it in the last days of his life?"

"That could well be true. He did seem very unsettled before the battle, which was why I placed him in charge of what I thought was a safe command at the rear of the main battle lines. But it is obvious that his fate had already been determined by a greater force than mine."

Myridyn handed Aurthora the square of silk, "I think this is for your keeping. There is also a riddle that accompanies it written in the Celtic language. I think Orius must have prepared that much earlier than the Latin script, which is, as I said, a recent addition."

"Why did he leave the directions in a riddle? That I don't understand." He enquired of Myridyn. The old man pondered for a few moments before he replied. "I can only assume Orius was obviously concerned that if the map fell into the wrong hands, it would take a clever man to decipher the riddle."

Aurthora took the map, folded it tightly and replaced it in the metal tube, which he then secured in his leather pouch. He would inspect it at a later date. He had more pressing problems on his mind at the moment and he wanted to take this opportunity to discuss them with Myridyn.

He waited until the old physician had settled down on his stool after feeding some scraps of meat to the buzzard, which was settled on its perch in the corner of the tent. *Myridyn never goes anywhere without that great bird of prey,* he thought. *Perhaps the rumours I have heard are indeed true, and he does have the gift of talking to birds and animals."*

"You have no doubt heard about the recent split decision of the Celtic Council, and the casting vote to be given by King Erion at noon tomorrow?"

"I have indeed heard, Aurthora," replied Myridyn. "It will be a hard decision for the Great King: on one hand he has the fire of youth wanting to continue the campaign, on the other, he is trying to hold together a loosely knit federation of arguing tribes, bickering chiefs and elders. They may have trained in the Roman way of warfare, but they are not a permanent professional army, most have farms, families and businesses they have left unattended.

"It will be difficult, in fact nigh impossible, to keep all the Celtic force focused on the aim of annihilating the Anglo-Saxon army. They answered the rallying call of the Great King and Celtic Round Council and feel they have achieved what was expected of them. They have defeated and routed the enemy, and will by now have heard that the Anglo-Saxons are suing for a treaty. If the case was that a treaty be made and then broken, then they might rally again and fight the Anglo-Saxons."

"I hear what you are saying," replied Aurthora. "All this was raised at the Council meeting, but as you well know, we would be very foolish to think that another victory would come as easily as the last one. If we allow our enemies to reorganise themselves and leave them a base in our lands where further families from their homeland can settle, this will give them the capability to increase their fighting force."

"You have read the situation correctly, Aurthora, but could you continue your conflict with a disgruntled army and the possibility that some tribes may withdraw from the federation if you attempt to force them to continue? At the moment the enemy knows you have a consolidated force to oppose them, and the Round Council is in a strong position to dictate the terms of any peace treaty, and include any safeguards they consider are needed."

He knew he was losing the battle of trying to convince Myridyn that his policy of continuing the war was the right one for the Celtic nation; he'd found the same problem when asked to give his opinion at the Council meeting. No matter what the short-term gains of a peace treaty might be, no matter how secure the terms or conditions might appear, he was convinced that the Anglo-Saxons would eventually spread into the lands occupied by the Celts and sooner or later embark on a war of attrition. He left the old physician's tent feeling disillusioned: he had hoped to persuade the king's advisor to see things his way, but he had failed. In any case, half the Council had already made up their minds in favour of a treaty. His pessimistic mood was matched by the miserable weather, with the rain falling harder than ever.

He had spent hardly any time with Katrina due to his responsibilities of administering the Celtic army, and before that there had been Orius's funeral. He knew Katrina would still be consoling Emilia, he wondered if she knew that Emilia was carrying Orius's child. But of course she would, the two women were so close. He was undecided what to do. His small bivouac, like most in the camp, was insufficient to keep out the continuous heavy rain; he might as well have been sleeping in the open field for the shelter it offered him. He decided to check on the injured troops, who were still in the large tents situated at the edge of the pass.

His descent in that direction was quite perilous since cascades of rainwater were pouring down the steep path, turning it into a quagmire of sticky, slippery mud. After several tumbles caused by his feet slipping from under him without warning, he eventually reached the bottom of the hill. It was a very bedraggled, mud-soaked Aurthora who entered the first of the many hospital tents that had been erected. It was here he met Roderick Tristan the master bowman, who had come to enquire on the condition of one of his archers, who had been run down by a loose enemy horse during the conflict. He met him as he was just leaving and inquired how the man was faring. The news was not good: "Camara Gilberto my ex-student informs me there is little hope for the man, he will pass on before nightfall," answered Roderick quietly.

Aurthora's curiosity was aroused. "My condolences over your archer Roderick, but you say that Camara Gilberto was a student of yours before he received the calling of this new religion?" "That is so," replied Roderick, "he was one of my finest students and developed into one of the most skilled archers I have ever taught." Roderick pulled his hood tighter around his head and left the shelter of the tent to return to where the rest of his men were camped. Aurthora watched him go, sliding and slipping in the mud as he climbed the hill.

The injured soldiers had been placed on stretchers woven from thin twigs and branches, which in turn were lying on roughly cut timber frames to keep them clear of the water that lay inches deep on the floor of the shelters. Paddling about in this muddy quagmire was Lucius, Myridyn's young medical student, and assisting him was Camaro Gilberto, who on choosing the path of the new religion had forfeited his claim to the leadership of the Cornovii tribe in favour of his younger brother Cimbonda. They looked up from attending one of their patients when Aurthora entered. "*Dydd da, Aurthora, drygioni tywydd mawr,*" said Lucius in the Celtic tongue, Aurthora acknowledged his greetings.

"It is indeed evil weather Lucius," he replied, noticing that Camaro had pulled the blanket over the head of the patient they had been treating. Lucius moved nearer to the entrance to join Aurthora and out of earshot of the nearest patient.

"Very few of these injured men will survive. They have serious injuries and these conditions do not help," he said in a low voice. Aurthora looked down the lines of wicker bunks arranged along either side of the shelter. In the past, injured men such as these would have been attended to in the open battlefield, he wondered if the conditions they were now in were any worse. He moved on to the second hospital tent, the one where Orius had been assassinated. This, too, was now filled with seriously wounded soldiers, their bunks also built up above the swirling storm water.

At one of the bunks he recognised Darius, who was in conversation with his friend Cynfelin Facilus. Aurthora's heart lifted: Cynfelin had obviously recovered from the concussion he'd suffered several days before. He was about to move from the tent entrance and go over to the men when he saw a mounted rider enter the clearing. It was impossible to recognise the man as he was wrapped in an enormous cloak of animal skins in an attempt to keep out the driving rain, but he immediately recognised the large horse the man was riding. He stepped out into the rain and shouted, "Ethellro! Ethellro Egilos!" The figure on the horse stopped, changed direction and came towards him. "My friend! Where have you been in such vile weather?"

"Aurthora! You are just the person I was looking for," replied Ethellro as he climbed stiffly from his mount.

Chapter Thirty-Seven

He declined Aurthora's invitation to return to the shelter of the hospital tent, and looking around to check no one was in earshot, he began to speak in a low voice. "I took advantage of the darkness and the storm to enter the enemy camp."

Aurthora, unable to contain his astonishment, interrupted him: "But the size of your horse? Surely they must have recognised it was not one of theirs?"

"There were many of the large breed of horse in the camp. The traitor Petrov Joma and his followers have returned to their new master so I went unnoticed," continued Ethellro.

"Can we organise a raiding party and try and destroy that vermin Joma and his followers?" demanded Aurthora excitedly.

"I'm afraid not Aurthora," answered Ethellro, "they all left to catch up with the Saxon king Ælle. He's retreated with his army leaving behind a hundred or so troops to protect their rear. There are also the remains of the Thracian cavalry, all under the leadership of Ælle's nephew, the one they call Gwandelk. But while I was in the camp, one of the novice Druid priests arrived and was directed to Gwandelk's tent. They spoke for a good while and then the priest left with an escort of two of Petrov Joma's men."

"So that son of a swine High Priest Zanton is still up to his evil scheming tricks," Aurthora blurted angrily.

"It would seem so," replied Ethellro.

"You should not have risked your life," he said, placing his hand on the shoulder of his old friend, "but by doing so we now know there are still traitors in our own camp, and to be forewarned is to be forearmed."

"Will you inform the Great King and the Celtic Round Council?" Ethellro inquired.

"King Erion has many problems to solve at the moment and he is still not a well man. We do not know the number of associates Zanton has and what positions they hold. I believe there may be several among those in the Celtic Round Council who support the High Priest and his followers. I think it would be wise for us to keep our counsel and in turn form our own group of men we can trust and who think as we do."

"I agree with what you say, Aurthora. I know of several people I think would swear allegiance to you. I will approach them discreetly and then I think we should hold a secret meeting to discuss our policies and our ultimate aim." Ethellro grasped Aurthora's wrist and then splashed off into the wet and miserable night leading his horse behind him. Aurthora moved back into the entrance of the shelter in order to be out of the driving rain. Darius and Cynfelin were still in deep conversation, the rest of the patients were huddled under their blankets as they lay just above the water on their wicker frame stretchers.

He needed time to think, coming to the conclusion that planning a campaign and leading men into battle was easy in comparison to the scheming and intrigue required as a member of the Great King's court and the Celtic Round Council.

The following morning dawned dark and overcast and it was still raining. Water was running everywhere. The grave diggers had given up their attempts to bury the dead, for as soon as they started to dig a trench it simply filled with water, bringing the bloated corpses to the surface, or else the water-sodden sides of the trench collapsed, making an already difficult task impossible. As noon approached, Aurthora was in the royal tent with all the other members of the Celtic Council, tensely awaiting the Great King's decision. He had positioned himself at the rear and slightly to one side of the group so as to be able to see the reaction of as many of the members of the Round Council as possible.

The King entered the tent, supported by his daughter Elemar. *He does not look a well man*, thought Aurthora. *I've seen dead men with better complexions.* But at the same time he could not help observing how beautiful the Great King's daughter looked in a pair of tight-fitting, calfskin riding breeches and a blouse made of the same semi-transparent material as Orius's map, the one he still carried in the pouch around his neck.

King Erion waited until the low babble of conversation stopped before he spoke. Although he tried to speak with a voice of authority, both the volume and tone were feeble, and Aurthora had to strain to hear what he said.

"My colleagues, my fellow chiefs, my friends. Several days ago we won a great victory over our enemies, the Anglo-Saxons. We were led to this victory by our commander, Aurthora Ambrosius Aurelianus, appointed unanimously by me and the Celtic Round Council." A polite round of applause followed this statement, several in the meeting turned to smile at Aurthora or nod in recognition. The King continued. "The invaders of our lands have retreated back over the borders, away from our kingdom of Elmet." There were murmurs amongst the Council members who had not realised the Anglo-Saxon army had fallen back so far. "They have left many dead and taken with them many injured. Their mercenary Thracian cavalry has been broken like never before: they have been taught a lesson they will never forget." The King paused for effect before continuing. "They have sent an emissary suing for peace. My casting vote is that we of the Celtic Round Council who represent the Celtic nation and all the Celtic peoples and tribes should consider this offer favourably, but we should dictate our terms and conditions without compromise."

There were shouts of "No! Fight on! Follow our destiny! *Rhagair tynged buddugoliaeth*! We can drive them into the sea!"

The Great King waited for the uproar to cease before he continued. Aurthora could see he was leaning heavily on his daughter Elemar, who was bearing her burden bravely, but was straining under the weight of her father. "My friends, one of the conditions of the truce is that the Anglo-Saxons will return the lands of our fellow Celts, the Brigantes, who have fought alongside us in our battle to retain our freedom. This they have agreed. So my casting vote is that we accept the offer of a peace treaty between our two nations."

Shouts broke out on both sides of the Council: from those in favour of continuing the fight, and those prepared to accept a truce. Seeing that the vote had gone against them, several of the members of the Council stormed out of the meeting in disgust. Aurthora recognised all of them: they were mostly the younger element of the Celtic leadership. Cimbonda Gilberto seemed to be their leader, with the still-limping Longinus Caratacusi following up at the rear. There were several moments of hushed silence, then it seemed that every one in the tent began to talk at once. Never before had the Celtic Round Council witnessed such a serious division amongst its members.

The reaction of the few tribal leaders who had stormed out of the meeting had obviously shaken the King: he'd turned even paler and Elemar persuaded him to sit. In doing so he dropped out of Aurthora's sight behind the heads of the crowd standing between them. He felt concern for his godfather; his recovery from the wound received from the Flavian horseman was obviously not being helped by the problems and worries of trying to administer the massed Celtic tribes.

Slowly the meeting dispersed. It had been a no-win situation for the King: to carry on the campaign meant risking the loss of half his army, for some tribes would elect to pack up their belongings and return to their own lands. The remainder would not be sufficient to carry out a full-scale war against the enemy; it was highly unlikely they would be able to withstand another battle against a full-strength Anglo-Saxon force. By taking this decision, King Erion still had an army, even though it was disunited at the present. It would rally to the cause if the peace treaty were broken. The King knew this, and so would the Saxon King Ælle. No doubt his spies would inform him of the disunity within the Council. But once a peace treaty was agreed he could not risk blatantly breaking the agreement, not with such a great victory still ringing in the Celts' ears.

As the leaders eventually left the royal tent, Aurthora saw that the King's chair was empty. Elemar must have helped him to slip out through the rear when the meeting disbanded. He stood outside the entrance to the tent for a while; the heavy rain had stopped and the sun was starting to break through the clouds. He was undecided whether to go and approach Emilia and explain about Orius's map or leave it a few days longer to give her more time to mourn her lost partner. But he did desperately want to be with Katrina; the more he was away from her the more irritable and short-tempered he found he was becoming with those around him.

It was while he was standing there, undecided about what to do, that a soft voice he recognised as Elemar's called his name from inside the King's tent. "Aurthora! I beg a few moments of your time."

Aurthora was in a quandary. Part of him said *go to this woman and see what she wants*, whereas the other half insisted he make some excuse and leave, *otherwise once you are in her presence, you know you will be sorely tempted.*

"Aurthora please!" he could not resist the pleading in her voice and moved to where she stood, just inside the entrance of the tent. He saw she had tears in her eyes. "I thank you Aurthora. I know these are difficult times for you and some decisions in the Council have not gone the way you would have liked, but I am concerned about the health of my father. The strain is telling on him and the wound is taking a long time to heal. I fear that as his chosen successor you may be called upon to take his place much sooner than you may have liked."

The statement shocked him: firstly he had not anticipated this as the reason why Elemar had wanted to speak to him, and secondly he had so many other things on his mind he'd never had time to consider that he would be called upon to take over the kingdom of Elmet so soon. She began to shake with sobs and he automatically reached out and pulled her to him. He could feel her tears on his chest as she relaxed in his arms and looked into his eyes. Where it would have ended he did not know, but a shout of "Aurthora! Aurthora!" from a voice he recognised as that of Darius came from the small clearing outside, and as Elemar stepped back into the depths of the tent, he turned and left.

Darius was astride his horse with Aurthora's in tow. "Aurthora, Sire, I have a message from Katrina. She and Emilia are leaving and going back to the High Town with Myridyn the Physician. He needs to attend to the many injured soldiers who were moved earlier. He is leaving Lucius in charge here along with several other junior students to look to the needs of those unfortunate men who are too weak to be moved and have to remain."

Aurthora knew what Darius meant, even if it was not said in so many words. Lucius was being left to organise the burial of these men, since it was unlikely they would recover from their more serious injuries. He climbed slowly onto the horse that Darius had brought and accepted the two hard boiled eggs that Darius offered him. "From Emilia," answered the youth, to Aurthora's quizzical look, declining one of the eggs his commander offered him, saying he'd already had two himself. Aurthora munched on the eggs as he followed the young man down the hill. He needed to see Myridyn before he left as he had so much to discuss with the old man; he doubted if there would be sufficient time. He also had to see Emilia, who even in her time of mourning was sending him food! He reflected fondly of the many nights the four of them had dined on Orius's and Emilia's magnificent cooking. And it was at that moment that he made a vow: he would honour Orius's request to try and retrieve the valuables for Emilia.

For the moment Orius's map would have to wait. His role as commander of the Celtic forces had been so demanding he had spent hardly any time with Katrina; the following day the Celtic Council was due to meet the Saxon King's emissary. And Aurthora would have to be present at this gathering.

The emissary arrived with an escort of ten Anglo-Saxon warriors; he was announced as Gwandelk, nephew to Ælle, king of all the Anglo-Saxons. King Erion was seated at the front in his finest robe; behind him, forming a semicircle, were the members of the Celtic Round Council, also dressed in their finest garments and cloaks. Aurthora was on the outskirts of the group dressed in the simple worn leather clothes of an ordinary Celt. He wanted the opportunity to unobtrusively observe these Anglo-Saxons at close quarters.

He noted that Gwandelk was a tall, heavily-built man of striking appearance, sporting a great moustache – indeed he and all of his escort were taller and heavier than the average Celt. He moved with the confidence of a man of authority, one certain of his own capabilities. Aurthora sensed that this man would not be content with the lands that had been defined, he was ambitious; if he ever obtained leadership of the Anglo-Saxon forces it would only be a short time before he attempted to extend his kingdom and test the resolve of the Celtic tribes once again.

He also noted that their horses were the local breed, and much smaller and lighter than the heavy Celtic horse. Their saddles were primitive in comparison to the ones that Ethellro and his late father had designed, not having the foot supports Ethellro had introduced that were fitted to the much larger Celtic saddle. Neither did they have the tall front and rear supports that made it possible to sit on a horse wearing the heavy chain mail armour and carry the oblong shield and long lance. He concluded that as a mounted force they were not a threat, their strength was solely in their infantry.

As part of the treaty, the Celtic Council were demanding the return in chains of the Celtic renegade Petrov Joma and his followers. The Saxons said this was not possible as he and his band had slipped out of their camp the previous night and they did not know where he was now. After much discussion between the two parties an agreement was reached: one of the conditions was that Petrov Joma would be refused access to the lands that the Anglo-Saxons occupied, that neither he or any of his followers were to be given assistance or shelter. After much more wrangling and discussion between the two groups, agreement was finally reached and a treaty agreed.

Before the Anglo-Saxon party left, Gwandelk asked if he could be introduced to the Celtic commander Aurthora, but Aurthora, who was still standing on the outskirts of the group, felt any involvement from him in the negotiations and terms of the treaty would only give the impression that he condoned the actions of the Council and agreed to the treaty, which he did not, so he slipped away quietly into the gathering dusk.

After the departure of the Saxon emissary, the Celtic Round Council decided that those with farms and businesses could leave and return to their homes while the rest of the Celtic army would move back to the High Town of Buxonana. Cimbonda Gilberto and his cavalry of the Cornovii tribe, and Timus Calgacus of the Coritani tribe with his cavalry, would escort the Brigantes tribe and all their possessions back onto their land vacated by the retreating Anglo-Saxons.

It was given to Longinus Caratacusi and the Dumnonii tribe to patrol the borders of the Kingdom of Elmet, and under the supervision of Aidas Corrilus the one-armed engineer, they were to build a fortified camp on one of the low hills overlooking the pass in order to protect the entrance into Elmet, the kingdom of Great King Erion.

It was several days after Katrina had returned to the High Town that Aurthora took the same road, accompanied by Darius and Cynfelin Facilus who was recovering well from his injuries of being dragged behind the king's horse. The bulk of the army was also making its slow return journey along the old, stone-paved Roman road – carts, wagons, and horsemen herding the flocks of sheep, goats and the long-horned white cattle that had provided fresh meat for the soldiers. Travelling with these animals were the machines modified by Aidas the master engineer. All were straggling the road in a long snaking column, bringing up the rear rode Ethellro with the heavy cavalry.

It was during this journey that Aurthora had time to reflect on the decisions made by the Celtic Council under the direction of King Erion, and his advisor Myridyn the Physician. The Anglo-Saxon army and all its followers had suffered their first major defeat in battle, and been forced to fall back to the lands that bordered the Pictish tribes of Caledonia, where they would certainly be kept busy defending themselves against these aggressive warriors. The Brigantes tribe declined to become part of the Kingdom of Elmet, and therefore had no seat on the Celtic Round Council, but nonetheless they would act as a buffer between the Anglo-Saxons and King Erion's domain. The younger element of the Council who had disagreed with the Council's decision had been posted away, patrolling the kingdom's borders and searching for the renegade Petrov Joma and his supporters, or been sent on escort duties so that they could not mingle with the rest of the army and therefore stir up any unrest.

Aurthora had to admire the general strategy. Eventually everyone would calm down, and any action that might have been carried out in the heat of the moment which could have led to a permanent disruption or split amongst the Alliance had been avoided. He reflected that being a leader of a kingdom was not just a matter of being successful in battle, it involved the manipulation and balancing of forces that either supported or opposed the leader's strategy.

It was on one of the overnight stops during the journey to the High Town of Buxonana that he was called to the King's tent. As he approached with Darius and Cynfelin in attendance, they were stopped at the entrance by the King's own personal guard. He had never known them to be in such numbers around the royal tent; when he was allowed to enter alone, he was asked to leave his sword with the guards.

Both Darius and Cynfelin objected most strongly that the commander of the all Celtic forces should be treated in this way. Seeing that there was a confrontation developing between the King's guards and Darius and Cynfelin,

Aurthora voluntarily offered his sword to the guard in the knowledge that for his personal protection he still had his dagger hidden in its sheath fastened to his calf. Nevertheless, he was slightly bewildered: Never before in all his meetings with the King or the Celtic Round Council had he been asked to remove his sword and leave it with the Guards.

He entered King Erion's personal quarters stopping in the entrance. The man who had given him his name, now sat on a low stool looking very pale, dazed and slightly bewildered, was the King and leader of the Celtic Alliance. On one side of the King stood Elemar, and on the other, in the place Myridyn the Physician had occupied so many times before, stood Boro Sigurd the senior court official. In a semicircle behind the king were all the senior members of the Celtic Council. Standing slightly apart from these was Voltigern.

Chapter Thirty-Eight

Boro Sigurd was the first to speak as Aurthora entered the inner section of the tent. "Aurthora! It is good to see you again. As you are no doubt aware, our Great King has not been well, but even so some decisions have had to be made during this time.

This statement from Boro Sigurd set Aurthora's mind to work. It was obvious that the King was no longer in charge, the poison from his wound must have reached his brain. He was no longer in control of his own thoughts, and could only act as a figurehead for the Alliance. The running of the kingdom was now in the hands of these, his senior advisors.

Boro Sigurd continued, "Yes Aurthora, you have guessed the truth. Our Great King who has led us to so many victories, who welded the Celtic tribes as one great fighting force, who convinced us to appoint you as supreme commander of these forces, is suffering from a poisoning of his body and brain that even the medicines prescribed by Myridyn have failed to halt." Boro Sigurd stopped and took a sip from a goblet placed on a low table close at hand. Aurthora was startled by these revelations from the highest Council official and wondered where they would lead and why he had been summoned at this particular moment. What was now clear was that if the Celtic army had attempted to prolong the campaign against the Anglo-Saxons and the Great King's state of health had become common knowledge, there would have been grave danger of a breakdown of authority within the Alliance, that would certainly have threatened any hope of a victorious outcome.

The Anglo-Saxons' offer of a peace treaty with terms dictated by the Celts must have seemed like a gift from the gods to the senior members of the Council, whose sole intent was to keep the Alliance together and to show a consolidated front to both the Celtic army, and even more importantly, to the Anglo-Saxon enemy. Aurthora now understood the reasons behind their decisions, but he was also fuming that they had deliberately excluded him from all decision making. He was finding it difficult to keep his temper under control.

Boro Sigurd saw that Aurthora was angry, and was relieved that his supporters had been dispersed on various other duties around the kingdom and were many days' ride away.

"Boro Sigurd," Aurthora began. "I have always had the greatest respect for you and your commitment to the Celtic cause." Here he stopped for a moment: he would have to choose his words very carefully. A saying that his old friend Orius had repeated on many occasions came to his mind: *'speak in haste, regret at leisure'*. He had to control the bitterness and anger he felt welling up inside him. He had to make his point strongly, without any insult to the Council officials, for to do so would confirm what they considered him to be: a juvenile. He would have to play the part of a statesman in order to prove them wrong.

"Fellow members of the Celtic Round Council, I am, as you can imagine, deeply troubled that you chose to exclude me, the commander of the Celtic forces, from participating in forming the policies on which you now embark. The decisions you have made for short-term gain could well be the beginning of the end for the Celtic people." Here he stopped, pleased with his words and the way he had delivered them. His initial reply to the Council officials had been bitter and frank, but not personally insulting. Now he was ready to continue. "After my achievements against the Anglo-Saxon enemy – despite the way I raised the morale of the warriors, the way I formed a successful defence against the enemy's superior forces and forced them to withdraw with the loss of a third of their infantry and practically the total loss of their cavalry, you nevertheless saw fit to bypass me in your decision-making. May I remind you that I am not only a member, like yourselves, of the Celtic Round Council, but also of the inner War Council and have been appointed by the Great King himself in public as his successor. Yet you, the senior Councillors of the Celtic Alliance, chose to ignore all this in arriving at crucial decisions that concern the future of the Celtic peoples."

He saw that his words were having their effect. The council members were looking guilty and distinctly embarrassed. Boro Sigurd had obviously been voted their spokesman; his reply was very apologetic: "We did what we did at the time in the best interests of the Alliance. Rightly or wrongly we made the decision that you were already sufficiently burdened with organising the army against the Anglo-Saxons, and did not need to be troubled by the King's deteriorating condition."

Aurthora realised he had been cleverly outmanoeuvred: all the tribal leaders he could have called upon for support had been sent away on various missions. He had been successfully isolated and it was too late now to alter the decisions the Councillors had made. He spoke again: "Given that you, the senior Councillors, have achieved what you wanted, I will continue my duties as commander of the Celtic army in carrying out the orders and instructions of the full Council. There is still a renegade and his large band of well-armed supporters who need to be hunted down."

He was aware that many of the Councillors present would have been more than happy to see him resign his position in protest: indeed, in the heat of the moment he had at first been inclined to do so. However, that would have been playing into their hands, with King Erion in his present weak condition, both mentally and physically. It was obvious that his resolve to continue the fight against the Anglo-Saxons had disappeared. The power of the army would also have been transferred to them.

As it was, he still had the support of the army and most of the Celtic warriors. Turning quickly he walked out of the royal tent, knowing that none of the chiefs he had just left would like to put to the test, at the present moment, the loyalty of their tribesmen if the gauntlet was thrown down between supporting them, the Celtic Council or himself, the commander of the Celtic army. He was learning fast. He felt he surprised them with his outwardly calm response, and he'd not fallen into their trap by offering his resignation. He'd also told them he would only take orders from the full Council, which would weaken their position. He pushed past the startled guards and walked briskly to where his horse was fastened, followed by his two confused companions Darius and Cynfelin, who had both heard Aurthora's speech to the Council members from their position just outside the tent.

Aurthora kept a low profile for the rest of the journey back to Buxonana. Only half the complement of the Town Guard were accompanying him, men whom he knew were totally loyal. He left the rest of his men with the young officer Gwyddelli, who was under instructions to complete the burial of the many dead Anglo-Saxon infantry still lying on the battlefield. On completion of this gruesome task, Gwyddelli and the rest of the Town Guard were then to report back in the High Town of Buxonana. To be certain that the Council did not try to divert these men to other duties further afield, he sent Darius back to their camp to inform Gwyddelli that he was to ignore any other orders issued to him, and to return to Buxonana with his men as soon as they had finished their work.

He also made a point of contacting his friend Ethellro who was in charge of the Celtic heavy cavalry. He relayed his doubts to him, also his great concern that there was a section of the Council that was not acting in the interests of the Celtic Alliance, but using their position to influence the decisions of the full Council for their own ends. Ethellro listened intently to what Aurthora had to say, just as he had known he would, without any hesitation Ethellro promised his full support and that of the men under his command, whose loyalty he could swear to.

The Celtic army entered the walled town of Buxonana to the cheers of its inhabitants. King Erion, seated on his grey horse, was accompanied by a member of his guard on either side, also one at the reins to lead and control his horse, leading the victorious army through the streets of the High Town. Aurthora had decided he would not appear in the procession, instead he found a position on the battlements from where he could watch events. How much he missed the advice of his old friend and ex-tutor Orius! He'd tried to talk to Myridyn the Physician, but the old man seemed reluctant to discuss anything concerning the Celtic Council or the Great King.

He knew the weight of all these problems were dominating his thoughts and affecting his relationship with Katrina. He found he could no longer relax in her company, his mind was always elsewhere. He saw the actions and decisions taken by the Council as moves to undermine his position as commander of the army; all his time seemed to be taken up with pondering their motives and trying to outwit their schemes. Intrigue and deception were so contrary to his nature that he was mentally exhausted; even the hot baths and capable hands of Gwion the young masseur were unable to relax him.

It was many days later that Cimbonda Gilberto and his horsemen of the Cornovii tribe returned to the High Town after their extensive patrols in search of the elusive Petrov Joma. They had found no trace of him or his band of renegades. The same result was reported by Timus Cagacus and his mounted warriors of the Coritani tribe, also by Longinus Caratacusi of the Dumnonii tribe when they too returned to report to Aurthora. He took the opportunity to approach each one of these young tribal leaders in turn, careful not to be too direct since he did not want to give any members of the Celtic Round Council the opportunity to accuse him of treason. Each one approached indicated similar beliefs to his own and none had any hesitation in swearing their loyalty to and their support of him as the legal successor of King Erion.

Their first meeting was called one night in the old physician's house while Myridyn was away with his young assistant Disaylann, on one of his regular herb collecting trips. Darius and Cynfelin Facilus were placed on duty at each end of the lane to warn the participants at the meeting of any unwanted visitors.

Aurthora looked around the crowded room. Everyone he'd asked to attend had arrived. There was Cimbonda Gilberto, Timus Calgacus, Aurthora's close friend Ethellro Egilos, Longinus Caratacusi, whose limp Aurthora thankfully noticed was becoming less pronounced. There was his old tutor's friend, the Roman Mallus Calvus, whom Aurthora had promoted on the advice of his friend Orius to the position of officer in charge of the High Town militia volunteers; Gwyddelli, the young officer Aurthora had appointed to the Town Guard during the battle at the pass, Aidas Corrilus the one-armed Roman engineer, and lastly Roderick Tristan the master bowman. Aurthora stood on a low stool so as to be seen by all the men in the room.

"My fellow Celts, and Roman Britons: my friends! Tonight we are all gathered at this, our first meeting. We in this room share the same beliefs, we all enjoy the same freedoms that our way of life has given us, and we have embraced the best of the benefits of our previous rulers. Trade routes with many distant lands have opened up to our communities, we have free and unrestricted movement on the roads joining our towns and villages, and within this, the Kingdom of Elmet, our citizens can travel without fear of being attacked by thieves and robbers. All these are great advantages that have vastly improved our way of life.

No man who is willing to work will see his family go hungry, and the same men also have the freedom to choose the gods they wish to worship without fear or prejudice. These things are more important to us than life itself. But all this is under threat by the invasion of our land by the Anglo-Saxons. Our elders of the Celtic Round Council have made peace with these invaders, who for now are confined to the northern part of our island. But even as we speak they are steadily building up their armed forces, bringing their families to join them and fortifying their settlements."

There were mutterings of agreement amongst the gathered men; when these had died down, it was Longinus Caratacusi who asked the question all the men present were concerned about. "What do you propose, Aurthora? We do not wish to be the instigators of a civil war between the Celtic peoples, between those who support the Celtic Round Council and those who support us. If we go to war against the Anglo-Saxons we need a consolidated army to fight them. We need the support of the Celtic Round Council, this, at present, we are unlikely to obtain." Aurthora was ready with his reply.

"For several months many of you have unsuccessfully been seeking the renegade Petrov Joma and his band of followers, but they appear to have disappeared from our lands, as you can vouch. This means that they can only be in one place: under the protection of the Saxon King Ælle. And that being the case, the Anglo-Saxons have already broken a condition of the peace treaty between our two peoples."

There were shouts of agreement amongst the gathering at this statement. Aurthora waited until he once again had their attention, then continued. "I propose that we send an emissary to the Picti and Scotti tribes in the far north of our island; they are already raiding the lands the Anglo-Saxons have settled. If we prepare and organise ourselves to move from this direction against the Anglo-Saxon forces in the spring, and the Scotti and Picti are prepared to move against them in force from their positions, we will trap the invaders of our country in a pincer movement and drive them from our island once and for all."

There was silence for several moments as the impact of his words were absorbed, then the men in the small crowded room broke into cheers, with much backslapping and laughter. The Picti were savage fighters, as the Celts from the part of the island that bordered their lands could testify, they would indeed be a formidable ally in the Celts' fight against the Anglo-Saxon army. When everyone settled down again Aurthora asked all the men swear an oath of secrecy. None of them was to divulge to anyone the names of any of their comrades present in the room, nor discuss their ultimate aim with anyone outside the group. He indicated to the gathered men that it was still too soon to approach the Celtic Council with an ultimation to either join the Celts, Scotti and the Picti tribes against the Anglo-Saxons under the leadership of himself, or to risk a split within the Celtic Council that would fragment the Alliance.

He also told the men to discreetly approach members of their tribes and other tribes who they felt shared the same convictions. Those who would be prepared to join them when the time came in readiness for when they felt they had sufficient support to approach the Celtic Council.

At the close of the meeting, Katrina and Emilia entered with trays of small drinking cups and jugs of strong mead. Longinus Caratacusi proposed a toast to the newly formed Consolidated Celtic Front and its leader, Aurthora Ambrosius Aurelianus. As the meeting closed, the men departed either singly or in pairs so as not to raise any suspicions, until only Ethellro and Aurthora remained. Both Darius and Cynfelin reported that no incident had occurred, everyone involved had been able to slip away quietly. Since no more was required of them until the morning, Aurthora dismissed them and they set off towards their quarters at the town's barracks.

Aurthora and Ethellro remained a while in the small garden at the front of the property discussing the night's events. At one point Ethellro inquired,

"Aurthora, who is the emissary that you plan to send to speak with the Scotti and Picti kings?"

"You, of course," replied Aurthora, and both men laughed.

"But first I have to honour the last request of my old friend Orius; I will be leaving on a journey within the next few days. Once that is completed we can start making our plans in earnest. In the meantime none of our followers are to be isolated; they must always be in close proximity to another of our party and their men.

"Why? Do you believe our comrades are in danger?" exclaimed a startled Ethellro.

"We will leave nothing to chance, the stakes are too high," came back the thoughtful reply.

The two men stood quietly thinking for a few moments as Myridyn's pigeons shuffled about on the perches in their loft. "Those birds are restless tonight," commented Ethellro.

"Yes, all the coming and going has unsettled them."

"Who will be going with you on this quest in honour of your late friend?" asked Ethellro.

"I will be taking no one. I will slip away one night on my own, I hope to be back before anyone has time to realise I've gone. I want to solve this riddle and bring back to Emilia what Orius buried more than a score of years ago. I want to present it to her before she gives birth to his child, which is due shortly. Darius and Cynfelin will still be seen around the town, which will help convince any curious or inquisitive people that I am somewhere within the walls."

"That is true," answered Ethellro. Everyone knew that Aurthora did not go anywhere without either the trusted Darius or Cynfelin close by.

"I beg of you one favour, Aurthora, since you have set your mind to go on this quest alone."

"And what is this favour, Ethellro? You sound quite worried." Aurthora was touched by his friend's concern for his welfare.

"That you leave a copy of the map with Emilia or myself, or with my sister Katrina."

Aurthora thought for a moment. Ethellro's request was a sensible one; after all, he was still commander of the Celtic army, or *Legatus Legionis* as his departed friend Orius would have called him. They would need to be able to contact him in an emergency, although to find him they would also have to decipher Orius's riddles.

"Yes I agree, your request is most sensible," he replied.

"Take great care my friend, the signs show there is severe weather on the way." Both men clasped wrists and parted, Ethellro making his way through the gate and down the lane, Aurthora deep in his own thoughts closing the heavy door behind him, shutting out the sound of the pigeons that were still unsettled in their loft.

As the lamps in the old physician's house were turned off and the light faded through the stretched pigskin that covered the windows, a shadowy figure slipped quietly from the roof of the pigeon loft, stood for a few moments in the garden until the patrolling guard had passed, then silently opened the garden gate, keeping to the shadows made his way silently down the dark empty lane. It was only when he crossed the road towards the town wall that the moonlight caught his face under the dark hood pulled tightly over his head. It showed a vivid red scar from a recently healed wound stretching from his forehead to his chin. The man nimbly scaled the town wall, on reaching the other side, made his way to a distant group of buildings that still had the light of lanterns shining through their windows. These buildings were occupied by the Druid priests and their novices, including their leader, the high priest Zanton.

Authora felt immense relief: at last he had held the meeting that he'd planned since the peace treaty agreed upon by the Celtic Council and the Anglo-Saxons. He had obtained the support of important leaders whom he believed he could trust; what's more, ones who represented the well-trained backbone of the Celtic army. But he also knew that the army could not be efficient or effective without the authority and organisation of the Celtic Round Council. Nevertheless, he was happy: he had started along the path towards a consolidated war against the invaders of his island. This change of mood meant that this was also the first night in many a week that Aurthora found he could relax in his bed and enjoy Katrina's company.

As commander of the army and Captain of the Town Guard, it took Aurthora two full days to make the necessary arrangements before he was ready to slip away on his mission. On the morning of the third day as he broke his fast in the company of Katrina and Emilia, he showed them Orius's map and told them of the silent promise he had made to his lifelong advisor and friend. Emilia begged him not to make the journey on her behalf, but he gently told both women how he felt honour bound to attempt to fulfil Orius's request. Promising to be back before they realised he had gone.

Both women were in tears when he left the physician's house and made his way to the baths in the grounds of the town barracks. He surprised the guards at the gates who were dozing at their posts, but he was in such a good frame of mind that he did not reprimand the two men who jumped to attention when they realised who he was. Darius and Cynfelin were just leaving their quarters when Aurthora passed them on his way to the baths. He had told them of his proposed early start and they quickly dropped in behind him. Oengus the old caretaker was in the process of lighting the fires that heated the stones for the sauna room when Aurthora and his two companions arrived.

"You are early, Sire," the old man exclaimed as they entered the baths.

"Yes, I have a busy day ahead of me. Send for Gwion your nephew, I will require his services shortly."

The old caretaker nodded, it was unusual for anyone to bath so early. His clients usually appreciated a soak and a massage at the end of the day. But customers were customers and having lighted the fires for the sauna stones he hurried off to fetch his nephew. Oengus knew that Aurthora was commander of the Celtic army and been a close friend of the Roman officer Orius. Since the latter's death he had not had to share the profits earned from the baths with anyone; it would suit him to keep on the right side of this highborn Celt.

Chapter Thirty Nine

It was late at night that Aurthora slipped out of the walled town of Buxonana through the quiet East Gate, guarded that night by Darius and Cynfelin. They watched as he disappeared into the darkness and then closed and barred the heavy wooden doors behind him.

Riding his large horse, and with a supply of food fastened to his saddle in watertight leather satchels, he carried in a plain leather sheath at his side the sword presented to him by Great King Erion, while hidden from view at his calf was the dagger his old friend Orius had given him. By dawn he was already a considerable distance from the High Town. So far he'd met no one on his journey, the freshening wind and the faint warmth of the morning sunshine on his face seemed as if it were blowing away the pressures that accompanied his rise in authority.

He arrived at the edge of a moor early that morning after several days travel. He was following a track he could see meandering over the peat and disappearing into the distance. By midday he had reached a large outcrop of rocks where the path divided. From a distance the stones stood out from the moor like a hand with a pointing finger. On the largest of these stones he noticed a bronze plaque with engraved inscriptions in the old language. With difficulty he managed to decipher what it meant. It was a memorial to a faithful hunting hound that had belonged to a chief of that area. The dog had become trapped while trying to follow a wolf into its den, and even after digging, it had been impossible to retrieve the dog from its tomb, so the distraught chieftain had fitted the bronze plate. The story was referred to in the riddle on Orius's map, and much to Aurthora's relief, it came with directions for the path he had to take.

He came within earshot of the bell Orius had mentioned in the next part of the riddle long before he came within sight of the location of the sound. As he drew nearer he saw it was on a stone tower – all that remained of a building destroyed by fire. It had once been a hostelry for travellers using the road over the moor; the bell had been rung to guide the travellers in bad weather. That day the strong wind off the moor was blowing through the shell of the building swinging the bell from side to side, causing it to ring at irregular intervals.

It was much colder at this height, and he was thankful for the thick woollen cloak. Light flurries of snow were developing into a continuous falling mass as dusk approached. There were already several inches underfoot; both man and beast were finding it difficult to keep their footing as they made their way through a steep pinewood. They skirted a group of derelict buildings referred to on the map as 'Roaches'. Aurthora could hear the sound of running water in the distance.

Indeed, as he and his horse cleared the wood they found themselves on the banks of a fast flowing river. Whereas the wood had sheltered them to some degree from the cold wind and kept the snow that was still falling from being driven into their eyes, now that they were out in the open, the weather attacked them with full force. In the distance further along the river he could just make out the light from a number of oil lanterns, and the darker shape of several buildings. "That must be the village marked on the map," he said with relief to his horse as he absentmindedly scratched the animal's ear.

The village lay at the end of the navigable part of the river there was a small port, for the long trading boats that brought their goods in exchange for silver, lead and copper, also the precious blue stones that were mined on the moors at Flash Quarries. The quarries had earned their name generations ago when a severe thunderstorm caused a flash flood which had washed away part of the hillside, exposing a rich vein of lead, tin and silver deposits interlaced with the rare blue stones that were much desired for jewellery by the Celts.

Night was falling, he was having difficulty following the faint woodcutters path since it was covered by a heavy dressing of snow but seemed to lead in the direction of the village. He would need shelter for the night for himself and his horse; both of them were tired and very cold, for even though they were once again out of the driving wind the snow was still falling quite heavily. He remembered Myridyn's parting words. "You must trust no one: you must depend on yourself and your own resources."

No, he could not stay in the village; it was out of the question. There would be too many curious eyes and too many questions. He needed to find somewhere else… and soon. It was now too dark to see the map and he could not risk entering the village and then try to read it by the faint light shining through the cottage windows. He racked his brain to recall the writings on the fine material. What was there beyond the village? Was there anywhere he could possibly find shelter for the night?

As his brain, now numb with cold, struggled to recall the fine details printed on the map and the riddle he had solved as he went along, he mumbled the words aloud to himself. "*Through the village of the blue stone that can cast a spell, over the moor where the flute and fiddle play but cannot be seen, follow the pointing finger with the copper thumb nail, past the ruin where the snipes do stay. Turn to the setting sun at the bell that rings alone, pass through the village in the shade of a sail, through the ring of stone men, and along the path of the old salt trail."*

He remembered that a hostelry had been marked on the old salt trail. If it still existed, perhaps he would find refuge there. To do so, if this was the village mentioned in the riddle, he realised he would have to pass through it. He needed to find the answer to the clue, 'in the shade of a sail,' to know he was still on the right route.

Still leading his horse he came upon a small shelter at the edge of the river. He stepped inside for a moment's respite from the weather, also to plan his next move. Beside the shelter was a small stone bridge spanning the waterway; from his position in the shelter he could just make out through the gloom the track that led on to the village itself. The bridge was a toll bridge, probably installed by the lord of this area he had been lucky to find it unmanned. Most likely the toll keeper had left his position for the night, thinking that that no one in their right mind would be travelling so late and in such atrocious weather conditions.

Leaving the cover of the shelter he set off across the bridge; he was thankful for the thick cushion of snow underfoot that deadened the sound of his horse's hooves. It was a steep climb from the river up and through the village; as he climbed the wind grew stronger. Leading his horse through the main street he avoided the small, windswept areas that exposed the packed shale. On either side were cottages lit up with oil lanterns, but the light did not quite reach the centre of the road, so he was able to lead his horse and remain in the shadows.

The moon had risen, and looking back down to the river between the flurries of snow he could just make out the shapes of a large number of sea-going boats fastened to the quay. *That seems a large number of boats for this time of the year*, he thought, continuing on his quiet course through the village.

Ahead he saw a sign hanging above a doorway indicating the usual village ale and eating house, but he could not make out the name on the snow-covered sign as it swung in the wind. As he climbed he kept looking for some sign or indication that would confirm that this was indeed the village mentioned in the map. Once past the alehouse he turned to look at his tracks in the snow, which were being covered almost immediately by the large falling flakes. This side of the sign now visible was not covered in snow, from a lantern in a nearby window. He could just make out the name 'Barca a Vela'. *'Sailing Barge'. An unusual name for an alehouse miles from the sea*; he passed several more cottages before his numb brain registered the significance

'Barca a Vela', and the line from the riddle '*in the shade of a sail*'. It was the right village! He strode on strongly up the hill away from the oil lamps and buildings.

Because of the noise of the wind he did not hear the door of the inn open, or turn to see the figure of a man walk to the centre of the road to relieve himself, then stoop to inspect the faint tracks in the snow. The man looked up the road in time to see a faint outline disappearing in the swirling snowstorm. The man turned and re-entered the inn, the light from the open door revealing one half of a face that at sometime had been very badly burned.

Aurthora was relieved to be away from the centre of the village, he turned at a junction in the track and passed several low barn-like buildings. He stopped for a while sheltering from the wind, contemplating whether to stay here for the night, but he decided it was too close to the village. The track continued to climb and he could make out the silhouette of trees on either side of him. He only hoped that this was indeed the salt road. As he led his horse higher he could feel the temperature dropping; he now found himself struggling in blizzard conditions and could barely see a pace in front of him. He felt dreadfully cold, isolated, and overcome by tiredness. In fact, he was beginning to stumble in the thick snow, which was rapidly beginning to drift into deep, wind-driven piles.

A dark mass loomed ahead: it was a small wood that offered some temporary relief from the freezing wind and stinging snow. As he entered he stumbled against a man-sized vertical stone. There were more of these stones close by that together formed a small circle, just as described in the riddle. Encouraged, he swung his arms to try and increase the circulation in his frozen limbs. As he cleared the small coppice, the respite he had found in the shelter of the trees was exchanged for the full force of the storm. Very quickly he found he was in deep snow above his knees and every step was becoming a supreme effort. Even his eyelashes were heavy with a layer of ice, and there was no feeling in either his hands or feet. He was leaning heavily on his packed belongings strapped on either side of his horse's saddle, and these plus his weight, were hindering the horse, which was already floundering in the snow.

In desperation he decided he would have to go back to the wood, then down the steep slope to the last building he had passed, and pray he could find shelter there.

Oh my guardian star, he thought, *if ever I needed your help, now is the time.*

He had stopped and was leaning against his horse with his arms around its neck, using the animal as a source of warmth and a shield against the blizzard. He found he was beginning to doze; it was so peaceful when he closed his eyes and he was so weary. A sharp whinny from the horse, together with a straightening of its neck and the pricking up of its ears woke him. "I must not fall sleep, I must not fall sleep," he repeated aloud to himself. He knew well enough that to do so in these conditions would mean he would never wake again.

The horse was moving forward slowly, he let himself be dragged, stumbling, alongside. He clung to the saddle, suddenly, with renewed energy, the horse began to pull him through the ever-thickening snow in the direction of a large dark bulk that was slowly emerging from the swirling blizzard.

All at once they were out of the wind and in the shelter of the courtyard of a large, two-storey building. The light of several lanterns could be seen shining through the windows of the main building; the horse was heading eagerly towards one of two lower buildings that formed wings at either side. Even before the horse had reached the wide entrance, Aurthora could smell the hay and straw and the heavy scent of other horses. He grabbed a handful of straw from the stable floor and began to rub it vigorously between his hands to increase the circulation to his frozen fingers; it was a long time before any feeling returned to his limbs and his hands thawed. As he worked to warm his body, his eyes slowly grew accustomed to the dark; using his flint and dagger with some dry straw he quickly lit a tallow lantern he found near the doorway.

From the dim light of the lantern he was able to see the stable had six stalls, each with a hayrack at the end. Four of the stalls were occupied by sturdy pack ponies, busily chewing the fresh hay that had recently been placed in the racks. His horse had smelt the scent of hay and other animals, and in doing so had probably saved both their lives. The fourth stable was stacked with sacks, which were clearly the ponies' load. A quick examination of the contents confirmed to Aurthora that the ponies were carrying salt. He was on the old salt trail! The circle of large stones he had passed at the centre of the wood had to be the ones mentioned in the riddle, 'through the ring of stone men', and more by luck than good judgement and despite the blizzard he had stumbled on the salt trail and the track that led to the hostelry.

Now that the life had returned to his hands he was able to attend to his weary horse. It had been his saviour and it was only right that he should look after its interests before his own. He rubbed it down with handfuls of straw that was stacked in a corner, filled the hayrack of the spare stall with hay, fitted a bucket of water on a nearby hook and led his horse inside the stall to eat, drink and rest.

Next, he opened a saddlebag and took out a small cage containing the pigeon Myridyn had given him, protected from the freezing temperature by a woollen cloth. The bird seemed lively enough despite its ordeal and he gave it some water in its drinking bowl and fed it some of the seeds Myridyn had also provided. He then buried the rest of his pack beneath a loose sprinkling of straw.

All the time he was reflecting on his position. He could stay in the barn – the animals had been fed and watered, so no one would check on them until the morning, by which time he could be long gone. Alternatively, he could take lodgings in the adjoining hostelry. This, he decided, was the better plan. His clothes were soaked and he was beginning to shiver violently from the cold, hunger and fatigue. He needed the warmth of a fire to dry his clothes and warm his body. And although he still had a supply of food in his pack, he yearned for a hot meal.

Leaving the stable he walked, avoiding the deepest of the drifts, over to the entrance of the two-storey hostel; light still glowed through the stretched pigskins at the window. He drew closer and cautiously peered inside. A large fire burned in a deep inglenook fireplace at one end of the room, and in the centre of the kitchen he could make out the faint outline of a long kitchen table with a bench at either side where the dim shapes of two people sat opposite one another. He assumed they were merchants and that the pack animals in the stable were theirs. A man was tending a stew-pot hanging over the fire. From his attire he appeared to be a monk or friar of the new religion. There seemed to be no one else in the room. He decided that if there was a bed available he would hire it for the night and change into drier clothes. He hoped none of the three men would recognise him. If the snow stopped, he would be on his way in the morning and hopefully would discover Orius's hoard in a matter of hours. The sight of the blazing fire and the thought of the hot stew the monk was tending, which he could smell, helped him to make a fatal decision.

As he entered the smoky, low-ceilinged kitchen, the gust of cold air from the open door caused the flames to dance around the large cooking pot hanging over the fire, the salt merchant who sat facing the door eating his stew looked up in surprise, while his companion turned on his bench to see who could be travelling at that hour in such foul weather. The monk set down the dish of hot stew in front of the second merchant and greeted Aurthora. "Welcome my friend, I am Brother Gildas. Come sit here by the fire and warm yourself, you must be frozen to the marrow. Give me your cloak so that I can hang it up to dry." The monk took several steps forward over the stone flagged floor into the light of one of the several oil lanterns that hung from the beamed ceiling, his hand outstretched.

Aurthora took off his cloak and passed it to the monk, noting that the man was as tall as himself but very thin and frail with rounded shoulders and a prominent stoop. Aurthora judged him to be in his late fifties. The man took the cloak, leaving a trail of water dripping from the garment, brought it to the inglenook. Removing a large shoulder of pork that was being smoked by the open wood fire, he hung the cloak in its place on the large metal hook.

As Aurthora stood in the middle of the room in the light of the oil lantern, he was aware of the two merchants staring – not at him, but at the finely engraved silver hilt of his sword; he had removed the weapon from his horse and it now hung in its scabbard at his waist. A master smith had made the hilt in the form of a buzzard's head with the wings folded back to give the impression of a bird of prey as it dived. When the merchants realised that Aurthora was looking at them, they dropped their gaze to their plates of hot stew and continued eating. Aurthora was concerned: the swooping buzzard was the crest he had taken after the battle, he had the silver hilt fitted to the sword Great King Erion had given him, these well-travelled merchants would have recognised the quality of the hilt, indicating to them that he was someone of high position. He had debated with himself whether or not to leave the sword, which belonged to King Erion and his father before him, in the stable with his horse and other belongings, but decided against it. His sword would be a great asset if he found he had to defend himself when in the hostel.

If the monk had noticed the sword he gave no sign, but busied himself ladling out more of the hot stew. He passed the steaming bowl to Aurthora along with several large thick slices of freshly baked oatmeal bread, then left the room. Almost immediately he returned with a tankard of mead, which he placed beside Aurthora's plate. Taking a white-hot poker from the blazing fire he dipped it into the tankard, filling the room with the smell of roasted honey. "Drink that my friend," he chuckled, "it will drive the winter's chill from your bones." Aurthora recognised the voice and looked up immediately: it was not the monk who had served him the hot stew but Camaro Gilberto, Cimbonda's brother who had foregone the leadership of the Cornovii tribe to follow the new Christian religion.

Camaro put a finger to his lips and signalled Aurthora to follow him, then left the room. Aurthora quickly gulped some mouthfuls of the tasty stew, and noting that the two merchants were engaged in their own conversation, quietly followed in the direction Camaro had taken.

The adjoining room was a pantry where various foodstuffs were stored. A smoked ham hung from a hook in the ceiling and rounds of cheese lay on stone slabs, probably made from the milk of the goats he had heard bleating in the stalls near the stables.

"*Iechyd da*," said Camaro as Aurthora entered the small room.

"And good health to you too, Camaro," he replied.

"I did not wish to speak in front of the merchants, but I am indeed glad to see you," said Camaro, but his words were cut short by the appearance of the other monk, Gildas.

"I thank you for the bread, you are most kind," said Aurthora loudly, and took two slices of bread from a platter on a stone shelf and left the room.

After Aurthora had left the kitchen to follow Camaro, a figure he had not noticed, seated on a form wrapped in a blanket and hidden from view behind the kitchen door, rose and made his way to the table, muttering that his stew needed more salt. As he reached over to take the salt container from the centre of the table, he let a sprinkling of white powder hidden in his hand fall onto Aurthora's dish of stew. The movement was deft, and the two merchants noticed nothing at all as they continued to eat their meal. The man then quietly returned to his wooden bench behind the kitchen door, pulled the blanket over himself and feigned sleep. Aurthora returned with the bread, sat down at the table and continued with his meal.

After several tankards of the warmed mead the salt merchants became more affable and talkative, and the conversation turned to the experiences on their travels around the kingdom.

"These days we always avoid the Whistling Moor," said one. "Of late there's been too many tales of travellers setting out to cross it, but never reaching their destination."

"Terrible tales we have heard," confirmed the other merchant. "That's why we are here tonight. We are going around the moor, even though it takes us several days longer."

"Yes, we have had a lot more travellers stopping of late," said old Brother Gildas as he entered the kitchen with an armful of split logs, which he placed near the fire.

"They say," said the first merchant, "that a pack of wild dogs larger than wolves roam the moor and anyone who travels that road risks his life."

"Strangers or travellers do not seem to be welcomed in the village, either," replied the second merchant. "It used to be the centre of trade around these parts, with it having the moorings for sea-going boats, but not any more." This statement from the merchant seemed odd to Aurthora.

If there was no trade from the village, why were there so many boats at the moorings.

The hard day's journey with the final struggle through the blizzard, the warmth of the room, and two helpings of the hot stew followed by the tankards of mead were beginning to take effect and he felt quite drowsy.

It was only when he rose and turned to go that he saw the huddled form in the corner behind the door. The sight returned him to instant alertness: there had only been the salt merchants' pack animals in the stables. When he'd looked through the kitchen window, the dark figure behind the door had not been visible.

"Do not be alarmed, young sir," said the old monk, standing and stretching his back. "He is just a poor weary traveller like yourself, trapped by the blizzard. He begged for shelter and as Christ's followers we obliged."

"I thank you my friend, your hospitality has driven the cold and damp from my tired body. Now I bid you good night. I will go and join my horse in its stable."

"Hold, Sire," said the monk, "take these garments with you. They are worn but clean and dry and suitable for you to sleep in. Your wet attire will bring you down with an illness."

He thanked the kindly monk taking the dry clothes he handed him, glanced once more at the huddled form in the corner that had not moved at all during the conversation, and left the warm room, closing the kitchen door on the icy wind still blowing outside.

He checked on his horse, which was contentedly chewing the hay placed for it earlier. Changing into the dry clothes, he made himself a bed of straw, pulling more of the straw over himself, and was soon in a deep sleep.

Septimius had been informed of the meeting Aurthora had called at the old physician's house by one of the novice Druid priests. He had not inquired where the High Priest Zanton obtained this information, but he suspected it was from the caretaker of the hot baths. He'd seen the old man entering and leaving the group of buildings occupied by the Druid sect on several occasions. After all, where were men more talkative amongst themselves than after a hot tub and massage with several glasses of wine or tankards of ale that went straight to their heads?

He had not walked down the lane to the old physician's house as he suspected it would be watched, but waited until it was dark then scaled the town wall opposite the meeting place. He'd watched carefully as several men approached the door and knocked. They were all allowed to enter. There had been no permanent guard on the gate or at the door, just the occasional foot soldier from the Town Guard patrolling up and down the narrow street. As several clouds passed and blotted out the faint moonlight he slipped silently across the lane and into the small garden. He knew these surroundings all too well after the incident with Aurthora, and carefully eased himself up onto the roof of the pigeon loft, from where he could observe who emerged.

In the early hours of the following morning he had visited the group of buildings occupied by the Druids. In the past he had always reported his findings or taken his instructions from one of the novice priests, but this time he was ushered into a darkened room whose only light came from several wax candles, leaving the rest of the area in shadow. It took several moments for his eyes to become accustomed to the gloom. He was startled to observe a figure seated in a high chair only several paces from where he was standing. He could not see the face since it was hidden by a deep hood, but the light of the candles were shining on two bright eyes whose stare seemed to penetrate his very brain. He quickly blurted out a report of what he had seen and heard that night; when he'd finished the hooded figure, speaking in a voice that Septimius had to strain his ears to hear, instructed him to inform the novice priest of the number of people at the meeting and the names of any he knew, and then to wait in the building to receive further instructions.

Septimius grew quite concerned. He had done as he had been instructed the novice priest had laboured to write on a sheet of parchment what Septimius had seen and heard. He'd then been led to a small room with a single candle for light, and told to stay there for the time being. The faint light of dawn was beginning to show. Never before had he been in the vicinity of these buildings in daylight; in fact, he only ever went out after dark from the small hovel he rented on the outskirts of the town. He was beginning to sweat and he could feel panic setting in. *Had they forgotten he was here, should he slip away without informing them, he had been here for hours, the candle was nearly burnt out.* To his relief the novice priest re-appeared holding an oil lamp in one hand and a parchment plus a small bag of coins in the other. "You are to take a message to your master Petrov Joma. On this parchment is a map you are to follow." The novice unrolled the parchment and showed Septimius the map. "On no account should you cross this area here," he pointed a clean fingernail to a section on the map. "This area is called the Whistling Moor. Travel around that area; it will take you longer but obey my instructions or you risk losing your limbs. We have transport available and some provisions for your journey. When you find your master report to him what you have told me. He is in this village marked on the map with a cross." Septimius strained his eyes in the poor light from the lantern: the words on the map were in Latin, but the place names were in the Celtic language. The name of the village where he was to make himself known to his master Petrov Joma looked like Swythaily.

Septimius was elated he was to be given transport by the priests. He had misjudged them, they really did hold him in high esteem. The novice priest indicated that he should follow him, which he did, thinking at the same time that as the message was urgent the animal that he was being given could be one of the new breed of great horse. He followed the novice outside into a small walled enclosure. In the light of the approaching dawn Septimius could see, standing on its own in the corner of the courtyard, a small wretched, hollow-backed, very old and bony looking pony. The novice cut short Septimius's protests with a slap across his face. "You are fortunate that my lord Zanton has provided you with any transport at all, do you not realise how difficult it was to obtain this beast? The Celtic army have bought everything available for many leagues around this town."

After following the Druid's instructions and the map for several days, the old pony he was riding had collapsed of fatigue near the hostel, having been driven too hard, the blizzard conditions being the final straw. Septimius had thrashed the poor animal mercilessly until his arm ached but the pony still refused to stand. He had eventually abandoned the animal, arriving at the hostel as the fall of snow began to get much heavier and the drifts much deeper. Ahead of him were a string of pack animals struggling through the snow, with one man leading from the front and another following from the rear of the line. When he also reached the building he was close enough to see the occupants of the hostelry, noting from their attire that they were so-called Christian monks of the new religion. He had seen members of their sect in the High Town of Buxonana, helping the poor and attending to the sick. He had also seen them helping in the hospital shelters after the battle of the pass against the Anglo-Saxons. He decided that if he played the part of a destitute traveller he could well obtain food and shelter for free, and would not have to part with even one of the coins given to him by the Druid priest.

He had eaten two bowls of the stew, drunk a tankard of the hot mead and just settled down on a form at the rear of the room when the kitchen door opened letting in an icy blast from the outside. He instantly recognised the man's voice. Shaking with terror Septimius then heard the man ask if he could have a meal and shelter for the night.

He quietly pulled the blanket over his body and tried to give the impression that he was in a deep sleep. He felt that the man would surely hear the heavy thump of his heart beating uncontrollably like a drum in his chest. Fortunately, he had remained unnoticed. He had taken his opportunity when the high ranking Celt they called Aurthora left the room. Septimius was happy he had at last succeeded, after several previously failed attempts, to poison this man who had been a thorn in the side of his employers. With luck he would be paid by both the high priest Zanton and by Petrov Joma when he informed them of his success.

Chapter Forty

Aurthora was late waking the following morning. He rose stiffly and swung his arms around to loosen his muscles and restart the circulation on his chilled body. His head was throbbing, but he put that down to the tankards of strong warmed mead he had drunk the night before.

Grabbing handfuls of bedding straw he rubbed his horse down vigorously, the animal nuzzling him in appreciation. The blizzard seemed to have blown itself out during the night, leaving piles of deep snow up against the walls of the buildings, with just the tops of the wooden split fencing in the nearby paddock visible above it. During the night he had woken with a start, terrible thoughts passing through his mind before he eventually returned to a fitful sleep. Writing a message in Latin on a narrow strip of cloth similar to that of Orius's map, he took the pigeon from its cage, fastening the strip of material to its leg, and released it into the morning light. The bird flew up onto the roof of the main building and strutted back and forth along the ridge of the thatch, occasionally flapping its wings and looking down at the lone figure in the hostel yard.

He shrugged and crossed to the kitchen of the main building, noticing as he went the deep set of footprints that left the kitchen entrance and headed off across the snow-covered yard towards the faint outline of a track that showed occasionally where the drifting snow had been blown clear.

When he entered the kitchen that morning, the two merchants were sitting in the same places as the previous night, but now Brother Gildas was serving hot pottage from a steaming pot. Looking around the room Aurthora could see no sign of the other traveller, and assumed he was the one that had made the early start that morning.

"Would you like to break the night's fast with us, Sire?" offered the monk, placing a bowl on the table.

"I thank you for your kind offer, sir, I will certainly partake, but perhaps you could also help me by solving this riddle."

He immediately had the attention of the three men, for solving riddles was a pastime practised by many Celtic families in the long dark hours of a winter's night.

He unravelled the silk map and read the last of the directions to the eagerly waiting men. "*Follow in the footsteps of Ludd, enter into the darkness of night, and emerge into the brightness of light. Below you, you will see where the road ends and the waters flow. Behind the long flowing skirt of the stone maiden, your journey ends.*"

The men were clearly racking their brains, but after a long deliberation while he finished his pottage they eventually shook their heads in turn. They obviously could not help him.

Greatly disappointed Aurthora rolled up the fine cloth and placed it back in the cylinder on the string around his neck. To have come so far only to be thwarted at the last hurdle was very frustrating. Thanking them he left the kitchen and started to make his way across the yard back towards the stable and his horse.

"Aurthora!" came the quiet voice of Camaro Gilberto from the corner of the building.

"Camaro! Good morning."

Camero placed his fingers to his lips, and as Aurthora came closer whispered. "My colleague is new to this area and so does not know the country or its history. The man who left early this morning is a certain Septimius. He has been seen many times in the High Town of Buxonana, always late at night, and he seeks out the company of the Druid priests. The path he followed this morning leads back to the village where many foreign strangers are in lodgings. But with regard to solving your riddle, follow this track." Camaro pointed to a faint outline in the snow running in the opposite direction from the one he had taken from the village. "It will lead you to the outcrop of rocks you can see on the skyline. Enter the large crack in the rocks, which was where the disciple of our Christian beliefs, Bishop Ludd, first preached in secret to the converted; it was there he was also assassinated by Druid followers, they also stole from him a most sacred relic of our religion. Below you will see the river, and there at the ford and the crossroads you will find the stone maiden you search for. I think you should make all haste to fulfil your quest, I fear our friend Septimius is again up to his evil work. Go quickly my friend and go with God." Camaro made the Christian sign of a cross and went silently back along the narrow passageway between the buildings and disappeared into an open doorway.

Aurthora stood for a few moments contemplating what he had heard. *How had Camero heard of his quest? And how did he come to be so well informed about the activities of this man Septimius? But what he had said also confirmed his own suspicions with regards to the village, and the large number of boats berthed there.* Puzzled, he went back to the stable. He decided he would leave some of his belongings here, including his clothes from the day before; he had spread them out over a wooden saddle frame the previous night but they were still damp.

Quickly saddling his horse, he rode out from the hostel between the deep snow, following in the direction Camaro had indicated towards the large outcrop of rocks on top of the hill. For most of the journey he zigzagged between the deep drifts but on several occasions he had to dismount and lead his reluctant horse through the deep snow that in places came above the horse's belly.

There was no wind, and in the silence it seemed he was the only human left in this land. But as he cast his eyes skywards he could see the silhouette of a buzzard against the pale sunshine; however, this same sunshine was also reflecting off the snow and into his eyes, and the glare was making them water to such an extent it was becoming difficult for him to see. He came to a small coppice and a wide but shallow stream, which he recalled was marked on his map and was called by its local name 'Shell Brook'. Finding some dry branches he used his flint and his dagger to make sparks and create a small fire. Cooling the embers in the snow he used the charcoal to draw a dark circle around each eye, which effectively stopped the reflection of the bright sunlight from impairing his vision.

It was near midday when he eventually came to the great jumbled mass of rocks that towered above him to the height of eight or nine tall men. Proceeding around the base of the rocks he eventually came to what was a narrow entrance to a deep cleft in the rocks, partially hidden by branches and heather. *If it wasn't for the fact that there are no leaves on the bushes I would have missed the opening completely*, he thought as he pushed through the narrow gap, pulling his reluctant animal behind him. It was not a roofed cave, but the heavy mass of overgrowth created a natural roof at a great height, which only allowed a limited amount of the weak sunlight to penetrate the gloom, but enough for him to see where to place his feet and move towards the faint glow of sunlight at the far end of the large chamber.

Emerging from this exit, he could see the river below, and the occasional outline of a track heading in its direction. It appeared to join the river at what was in fact a crossroads: one track ran alongside the river while the one that he needed to follow to descend the hill crossed the ford and continued on the far side. He cautiously made his way down the steep hill avoiding the deepest drifts, although on many occasions he still had to dismount and lead his horse due to the height of the snow, before eventually reaching what he hoped was the end of his journey.

He sat motionless on his horse for a while surveying the area to check he was not being observed. To the right of the crossroads was a stone pillar. He dismounted and inspected the pillar closely. Writing and symbols in the old language had been carved into its surface; by studying the weathered inscriptions he managed to piece together the story.

Apparently a maiden had accepted the offer of marriage from the man she loved, so overcome with joy she had danced in the meadow amongst the midsummer flowers. A passing Druid priest saw the girl dancing on a holy day and accused her of blasphemy. As a warning to others he used his strong powers to turn the young maiden into a pillar of stone.

"I wonder if that priest was a young Zanton?" Aurthora said aloud to himself. He took the map from its cylinder and read the final riddle: *Behind the long flowing skirt of the stone maiden your journey ends.* Taking his dagger, he began to scrape the soil from the rear of the pillar. He had soon exposed a large flat stone. On its removal he found below a leather pouch, but as he reached for it, the rotten leather disintegrated, showering its contents of gold and silver coins, rings set with precious stones and other pieces of jewellery over the frozen soil. The largest object of all amongst this treasure was a small plain goblet. He picked it up and on closer inspection he could see writing in a foreign tongue engraved on its base. *It seems odd,* he thought, *such a plain goblet amongst a collection of finery like this.*

He placed the contents of the leather bag in a satchel fastened to his saddle, and returned the stone and the soil at the rear of the stone pillar. He then mounted his horse and began to retrace his steps in the snow. He felt a great sense of relief; he had honoured and accomplished the last wish of his old friend and tutor Orius. Emilia and Orius's child would not want for anything, the contents of the leather bag would keep them in fine style for the rest of their days. He felt an immense sensation of wellbeing on this cold but calm and beautifully bright sunny day, so different from the foul weather that had so nearly taken his life the day before. As he retraced his tracks back towards the hostel he was anticipating more of the delicious hot stew he had enjoyed so much the night before, but he told himself he would not partake of any more of the mead, since his head was throbbing more than ever.

It was dark when he eventually reached the hostel. The stables were empty and the merchants gone. He removed the saddle from his horse and rubbed the animal down by the light of an oil lantern. It was only when he was sure his horse had access to oats, water and hay that he crossed the courtyard to the kitchen in the main building.

The fire was burning and the stew was still simmering in the large iron pot positioned over the flames. It would do so for many days with different ingredients being added daily. As he entered, the old monk Gildas came into the kitchen and bade him be seated at the table. Just as he had done the night before, he served him two helpings of the stew before returning to the kitchen. It was Camara Gilberto who returned, bringing with him a tankard of warmed mead, which Aurthora politely refused. Camara placed the unwanted mead on the table and sat down opposite him.

"Was my brother in good health when you last saw him?" he asked.

Aurthora satisfied the monk's concern and then on the spur of the moment brought out the small goblet from the satchel fastened to his belt. He noticed that Camara's hands were trembling as he passed it over the table and the friar took it gently from his grasp.

"Have you ever seen in your studies writings like these on the goblet?" he asked, as Camara held the small drinking vessel up to the light of the oil lamp. He did not expect the friar's reaction, and jumped up startled, sword half drawn as the man in front of him suddenly fell to his knees and began a singsong kind of chant, he had heard these Christians do before. Realising there was no danger, he waited while the kneeling man continued to pray.

Camara stopped his chanting as suddenly as he had begun and placed the goblet gently on the table between them. "I have been most blessed and most privileged to have seen and to have touched the vessel that once touched the lips of one of our Lord's most loyal disciples. You have in your possession, Aurthora, a drinking goblet from which St. Peter drank wine with our Lord at the Last Supper. This small cup is of more value to we Christians than any number of wagons filled with gold or silver. You are indeed privileged to have been allowed to have this priceless relic come into your safekeeping. Our Christ, he must know that you are a man of honour and will protect this sacred goblet with your life. It is said that while this vessel is in your possession, you will have strength and fortitude to lead the peoples of this island against the disciples of evil and the followers of the devil." Aurthora fastened a short piece of twine to the stem of the goblet to form a loop, which he placed over his head so that the small metal cup hung inside his tunic.

He refused Camara's kind offer of a bed in the main building, saying he preferred to sleep in the stable with his horse; his real reason was that he did not want to encounter any strangers who might call at the hostel. His presence in this area was best kept a secret as long as possible, at first light he would begin his journey back to the safety of Buxonana.

He did not sleep well that night, the sky was quite clear and all the stars seemed to be exceptionally bright. Later there was a severe frost, and the penetrating cold, plus his throbbing head kept him awake. It was then that he wished he had taken up the monk's offer of accommodation in the main building. He felt he hadn't slept but merely dozed the night away, waking with a start as visions of men fighting and cavalry charges flashed through his overtired brain. He saw Great King Erion surrounded by the Celtic Council and a grinning Voltigern with a smiling Elemar holding his arm as she stood at her father's side wearing the jewellery he had in the leather pouch under his pillow and drinking wine from the goblet of St. Peter. All these thoughts seemed to compete with one another to keep him awake, but finally he fell into a fitful sleep.

He was up and about before dawn he had rubbed down his horse and fitted the saddle just as the first rays of morning sunlight filtered into the yard. He placed his hand on the animal's muzzle as the unmistakeable sound of horses' harnesses and the faint growl of dogs broke the stillness of the early morning. He felt his body tense and freeze as a large body of men passed quietly by the entrance. He quietly withdrew into the shadows at the rear of the stable.

There were six or so men leading their horses, and like him they were holding the animals' muzzles to avoid noise. The horsemen were accompanied by ten or so foot soldiers and several other men in charge of a pack of great dogs, similar to the ones he had seen in the compound at the Anglo-Saxon camp.

The man who was obviously in charge had his back to Aurthora, but his mount was one of the large breed of horses similar to his own, whereas the rest of the men were leading smaller local horses. No words were spoken. Four of the foot soldiers carried a heavy length of timber the thickness of a man and just as long. They positioned themselves in front of the kitchen door of the main building, and on the signal from their leader, made three lunges with the trunk of wood against the door, smashing it from its hinges and leaving it flat on the stone floor.

Four of the soldiers entered the kitchen returning shortly, pushing in front of them Gildas still in his nightshirt. "Where is he? We know he is here. Where is Aurthora Ambrosius hiding?" As soon as the leader began to shout at the monk Aurthora recognised his voice: it was Petrov Joma.

Quietly mounting his horse and drawing his sword he left the darkness of the stable and rode into the early morning sunlight. It was obvious they were not getting the information they wanted from the old monk, for they had stretched his hand over the block for splitting logs and one of the soldiers was about to swing the two-handed wood axe and cut off his hand. The sudden appearance of Aurthora caught the group by surprise as he rode through them, scattering men and horses, his sword slashing the torturer from neck to chest before the man realised what was happening the large axe he had been holding dropped aimlessly in the snow. One of the foot soldiers bravely ran forward and grabbed his horse's reins; Aurthora thrust his sword into the man's throat. Another tried to unseat him by lifting both the leather strap and his foot in an attempt to throw him from his saddle, but a slash from his sword cut the man's shoulder to the bone and left him on the ground screaming in agony.

He now turned his attention to Petrov Joma. Aurthora's unexpected eruption amongst the men and horses had panicked the animals, and their riders were having difficulty getting them under control. This situation was not helped by the pack of hounds, which were baying furiously and straining at their leashes, dragging their handlers behind them and adding to the confusion.

Aurthora drove his horse forward towards Petrov Joma, who was still trying to mount his own animal, several paces away from him, Aurthora's horse suddenly swerved to the side. One of the hounds had broken free from its handler and was attempting to attack his horse. The horse responded by kicking out with its hind legs, with one hoof catching the great hound at the side of the head, instantly knocking it senseless.

The sudden movement of the horse, however, threw Aurthora from his saddle, landing him in a snowdrift, which fortunately broke his fall. He still had his horse's reins in one hand and his sword in the other. He was back on his feet in a moment but several of Joma's men had quickly formed a semicircle around him, making it impossible for him to safely remount his horse.

"Bring forward the hounds," shouted Petrov Joma who had by now succeeded in mounting his own horse. "We will have some sport at the expense of this general of the Celtic army," he jeered. The men around Aurthora retreated smartly as the pack of howling and snarling dogs were brought forward to see their prey.

Aurthora quickly wrapped his horse's reins around a fence post sticking out of the snow: the last thing he wanted was his only means of escape taking fright and bolting. He then moved slowly away from the horse to where the ground was firmer underfoot, and turned to face the pack of hounds. He was well armed: he had Great King Erion's sword in one hand and the dagger given to him by his friend Orius in the other. If the gods had decreed his time had eventually come he'd decided he would sell his life most dearly.

On the instructions of Petrov Joma, Maddoc the chief dog handler led three of the dogs forward. He was wearing a wide, black and broken-toothed grin at the sporting spectacle he was about to witness, while struggling to hold back the savage hounds as they strained at their leads. He turned to Petrov Joma for the signal to release the dogs.

Petrov Joma moved his horse slightly to be in a better position to view the contest – a move that saved his life. A shaft from a Celtic longbow whistled inches past his chest and buried itself in the skull of one of his nearby mounted followers. Startled and surprised, Petro Joma shouted, "Release the hounds, Maddoc!" at the same time throwing himself down from his exposed position on his large horse.

Aurthora met the lunge of the first hound with his sword through the large animal's rib cage. The second animal leapt at him, its large paws hitting him in his chest and knocking him to the ground. The hound's jaws were inches from his throat when the animal howled in agony as Authora's dagger disembowelled it, spreading the contents of its stomach over the churned snow. Struggling to his feet, he prepared to meet the third dog as it sprang towards him, but it was stopped in mid-flight by a shaft that penetrated its well-muscled shoulder, continued through to its heart and reappeared on the far side. The animal was dead before it crumpled in the snow. Another well-placed arrow hit one of the other dog handlers in the stomach. As he doubled over screaming in agony, his hand released the dogs in his control, which proceeded to savage the soldier with the shoulder wound who was still lying moaning on the snow from what Aurthora had inflicted earlier. During all this confusion he took the opportunity to glance in the direction of the deadly missiles.

Standing on a small cart partially covered by snowdrifts was Camaro Gilberto, still in his friar's habit, but wielding a Celtic longbow. "Take your horse and ride Aurthora," he yelled, "Only you can save the Celtic people and the followers of Jesus Christ. Ride, I beg of you." The howls of the dying hound had unnerved the rest of the dogs, they had also witnessed the slaughter of other members of the pack – who were still twitching in the snow – they were now less enthusiastic about rushing in blindly. But the surprise Camaro had caused was short-lived. Petrov Joma was shouting instructions to his men from behind the safety of his large horse.

"Rush the archer! Spread out and rush the archer!"

For the moment the attention had been diverted away from Aurthora he knew he must take his chance to escape for otherwise Camaro Gilberto's sacrifice would be in vain. Everything suddenly became clear to him. Perov Joma and his followers were based in the village and collaborating with the Anglo-Saxon warriors from the great ships that he had seen fastened to the pier. They were building up a secret force to the rear of the Celtic army and he alone had knowledge of this. The pack of hounds had been used to frighten travellers and keep them away from the village and the surrounding moor.

In a flash he was on his horse and driving through the men as they attempted to surround Camaro Gilberto. He slashed the back of one man with his sword, then raised the bloody weapon in salute to the figure on the cart as he set off at a gallop along the tracks he had left in the snow from the previous day. He knew that if he followed this trail he would avoid getting trapped in the deep drifts of snow, which would make him easy prey for the hounds and the mounted men who were sure to follow him.

The previous morning Septimius had slipped out of the building before first light. Occasional flakes of snow had still been falling in the freezing morning air, but the blizzard of the night before had blown itself out. Even if it had not, he would have preferred to risk reaching the village in a blizzard than face the wrath of the Celtic leader. He had kept to where the snow had been blown clear as much as possible, but in places he had no alternative but to struggle through the deep drifts. It was late afternoon before he eventually reached the village and made himself known, and it was already dark when he was taken to Petrov Joma and was able to tell his story.

The leader of the renegade Celts could not contain his glee shouting out in joy at the thought of claiming the bounty that King Ælle had placed on Aurthora's head, also of taking his revenge for the humiliation Aurthora had caused him. But for the actions of this Celtic general, he, Petrov Joma, would by now have been the leader of the Celtic Alliance and lord of the Kingdom of Elmet.

Exhilarated by the knowledge that he had within his grasp the commander of the Celtic army, alone and with no support or assistance available for many a day's ride, with great haste he ordered the mobilisation of all the men he had available at such short notice. By the light of oil lanterns they set off along the tracks left by his informer, Septimius, who accompanied them back towards the monks' hostel. Septimius was weary; he had struggled through the drifts to the village and with little rest he was now being forced to return with Petrov Joma and his group of armed followers, but he could not refuse. He knew Petrov Joma had a vicious temper which could be roused at a moment's notice, but at least he did have more coins now to add to the few given to him by the novice Druid, and he anticipated some easy pickings at the hostel, for Petrov Joma's men would certainly leave no one alive who would be witness to their actions. He'd purposely dropped behind the main body of men, and was bringing up the rear as they neared the group of buildings.

Chapter Forty One

Petrov Joma had assumed that Aurthora would be in lodgings in the main building since Septimius had not informed him otherwise. Septimius had not had the energy to rush to the front of the group and tell his paymaster that their quarry might be sleeping in the barn with his horse. So by the time he arrived on the scene the men had already broken down the kitchen door, searched the building and pushed the old monk out into the yard. He had seen Aurthora emerge from the barn and fight his way to his eventual escape. He had also seen the aftermath of the brave stand by the monk on the hay cart with his lethal bow. He had kept the foot soldiers at bay until he had no more arrows and was eventually overpowered and brutally put to the sword. It was while this was taking place that Septimius slipped into the barn and brought out one of Aurthora's garments. He gave it to the pack of hounds to smell. Baying eagerly they were let loose, led by a hound that answered to the name of Hadrian which stood out from the rest of the pack due to its unusually pale-coloured body and a large black head.

The dogs immediately took off in the direction Aurthora had taken, pursued by Petrov Joma and the rest of the mounted renegade Celts, with the foot soldiers and dog handlers in the rear. Septimius was pleased with the way he had handled the situation: he had kept well out of sight of the monk on the cart so as not to become a target for his lethal arrows, and he had sent all the renegade Celts and their Roman dog handlers chasing after the Celtic general. This left him all the time he required to ransack the hostel. There were sure to be more coins and others things of value to add to his growing collection, but first he planned to search the barn and the belongings of the Celt they called Aurthora, Hammer of the Anglo-Saxons. He had returned from his quest and therefore might very well have found the collection of gold and silver mentioned in the conversation with Ethellro that he had overheard from his perch on the dovecote at the old physician's house.

Septimius was a professional and it did not take him long to find the satchel hidden under some loose straw at the rear of the barn. His eyes widened as he opened the leather bag to expose so much gold and silver, the likes of which he had never seen in his life. He continued his search to see if anything else of value had been hidden; if it had he would certainly have found it. All he found were clothes spread out to dry and a sleeveless leather jerkin of excellent quality. Though rather large for his frame it fitted him well enough and would keep out the cold wind on his journey back to Buxonana. For this was his next plan. Let Petrov Joma and his pack of two and four-legged dogs chase all over the country to do all the hunting they wanted. He, Septimius, was now a free and wealthy man and he intended to go where he knew his money would buy him the luxuries he had always craved.

His search of the hostel was also rewarding: under a loose floorboard in one of the monks' chambers he found the collection of copper coins left by the many travellers in payment for their shelter and food. In one of the rooms he came across an injured renegade Celt who begged him for assistance, but the man begged in vain. He ignored him and continued to methodically ransack every room. There were also some cold meats in a stone larder, which he also stuffed in the satchel, then, finding nothing else of value, he left the hostel.

He set out on a trail that ran at right angles to the one taken by Petrov Joma and his men, a route that, though very steep and more difficult, would lead him quickly over the hills and onto the moor; from there he would make his way to the High Town of Buxonana. The moor would be safe to cross now that the hounds and their handlers were busy pursuing the Celt, this route would save him several days' travelling, especially as he now had no horse.

Once in the High Town he had sufficient funds to lie low for the rest of his life, and to pay for frequent visits to the gambling and drinking dens situated on the outskirts of the town walls. There in his old haunts he would be safe. He would feign ill health and decline to work for the Druid priest or the renegade Petrov Joma again; they would have to find someone else to carry out their dirty work and be their dogsbody. With a satisfied smile he pulled the collar of the leather jerkin tighter around his neck, then laughed out loud as he considered how well things had turned out for him, whereas that Celtic general was running for his life. He was warm and dry and carrying a fortune in jewels, gold and silver coins.

Aurthora had sped off on his horse. He knew it would be only a matter of time before they overcame Camara, but the young friar had saved his life and bought him precious moments in which to put as much distance as possible between himself and the pack of hounds that he knew would be released on his trail. He took a zigzag route, avoiding the deep snowdrifts following the marks he had left in the snow the previous day. In normal circumstances the horsemen on the local mounts would have difficulty keeping up the pace he set on the large horse, but in the present weather conditions he did not know what might happen. Petrov Joma on the same breed of large horse could possibly keep pace with him, and if that was the case, he could always turn and charge the renegade. He would relish such an opportunity to pit his fighting skills against the traitor. But his biggest worry was the pack of hounds and how they would perform in the thick snow. Would they become bogged down in the deep drifts or would they make good time over the snow he had to skirt, quickly gaining on him and his willing mount?

He stopped his horse on top of a low hill from where he had a good view of the hostel buildings in the valley below. The pack of dogs had left the shadow of the buildings and even from his position he could hear the leading hounds baying as they picked up his scent and began to follow his clear trail left in the patchy snow.

He turned and set off down the far side of the slope to the broad stream at the bottom, the point where he had started the small fire two days before to make the charcoal for his eyes. On the map it was marked as 'Nettle Beds', and indeed, had it been summertime the great expanse of nettles would have caused the hounds something of a problem, whereas today the whole area was covered in a thick layer of snow. It was here that he decided to divert from his chosen path: instead of following the tracks out of the valley he would travel up along the stream, and the hounds would hopefully follow the still well-defined track and faint scent left by him in the snow the day before. This would buy him extra time before they realised they were following an old scent and so would have to retrace their steps.

When Maddoc eventually arrived gasping for breath at the stream, the dogs had already returned from following the old trail. His much younger assistant Maro, who had arrived several minutes earlier, had set the dogs searching to pick up a new scent. Petrov Joma was astride his large horse and a quick glance told Maddoc that his employer was ready to explode.

"If you cannot keep up with your dogs, Maddoc," yelled Petrov Joma, "I will find some one who can."

After several more moments of fruitless searching it was obvious the dogs had lost the scent. "The quarry has taken to the water, Sire," said Maddoc in a servile tone.

"Yes! But which way?" growled Petrov Joma, slapping his thigh in exasperation. "Split the pack! You Maddoc, take half the hounds and half the men and search downstream, I will take the rest of the men with Maro and search upstream. Blow the horn if you pick up the scent and we will do the same."

Petrov Joma set off upstream with several of the dogs on one bank and several on the opposite. Alongside them rode several of the mounted men, accompanied on foot by several heavily panting foot soldiers.

Aurthora had continued to follow the stream, always keeping as close to the centre as possible. The snow had drifted higher than a man on a horse in some places, while in others it had been blown clear. On rounding a bend he came to a small waterfall that he could not climb with his horse. This meant he would now have to leave the relative safety of the stream and risk going across open ground.

He could still see the large outcrop of rocks on the hill in the distance and decided he would try and make his way towards those. It was here that he disturbed a small pony sheltering in a coppice of beech; it trotted slowly off in front of him, following the contours of the hill, avoiding the deep snow drifts. Aurthora smiled to himself, he had no idea where the animal had come from, or how it had arrived at that point but he intended taking full advantage of the situation that had been presented to him. He followed the tracks left by the animal until he came across an area that had been swept clear of snow by the strong winds. It was here that he changed direction, the frozen earth leaving no trace of his horse, this would give him another breathing space if the hounds followed the pony. He was now breaking new ground and would have to pick his route most carefully in order not to get trapped in the deep snow; that would make him easy prey for the pack of hounds and men that he knew would soon be following him again. He realised that even though he had given them the slip for the moment, sooner or later they would again pick up his trail.

At last he came to the break in the rocks marked on the map as Chapel of Ludd. The entrance was still reasonably hidden by the branches and the gorse bushes, unless someone was really looking for it, it would quite easily go unnoticed. There was no snow in front of the entrance, the strong winds had blown it away, but further along the faint trail there was a snowdrift the depth of a man's arm. He walked his horse through this drift then backtracked to the cleft on frozen, wind-swept ground that left no prints of hooves or feet. Taking care not to damage the gorse or bushes at the entrance, he dismounted and led his horse through the narrow cleft and into the chamber, just as he had done the previous day.

From the rear entrance he could see his old tracks stretching down the hill through the snowdrifts until they reached the road and the ford at the river below. However, this time he set off along the windswept side of the hill that took him slightly higher and away from the ford. It was here he heard the baying of the hounds carried on the still cold air as they picked up his scent at the point he had left the Brook of Shells, quickly followed by several blasts of a hunting horn. He was not overly anxious; it would be some time before they realised their mistake and backtracked, and if they found the entrance to the cave, they may well follow his old trail down to the river; that would also give him more time. The day was pressing on and they would not risk hunting him in the dark, and by morning he would be so far away it would be pointless for them to continue the chase. Hopefully, if the carrier pigeon had reached its destination and Myridyn had checked his birds as he usually did at noon, he would eventually meet a strong band of well-armed Celts travelling towards the village of Swythaily. He would joyfully join them and take great pleasure in brutally ravaging and putting to the sword and lance the renegade Celts and Anglo-Saxons encamped in that hamlet.

The pony that had been abandoned by Septimius at the beginning of the blizzard several days previous, had slowly regained a little strength, sufficient for its survival instincts to realise that to stay in this exposed position would be fatal. The frail animal had struggled to its feet and with the icy wind on its hind quarters it had laboriously made its way down from the exposed hill had been fortunate to find the shelter of the small coppice of beech trees. There it had stayed grazing off the short, coarse, poor quality grass it exposed at the base of the trees by digging away the covering of snow with its hooves.

It was from here that it had been startled and forced to bolt by the unexpected presence of the great horse and rider, moving as fast as its tired limbs would carry it back on to the exposed side of the hill.

It had relaxed slightly as after a short while the great horse stopped veering off his track. But the heriditary feeling of fear of The Wolf quickly returned. The pony heard the pack baying and howling as they picked up his scent and joined in the chase.

It was here that he was aware of a nearby familiar figure shouting for him to stop. But the sight of this man only brought back unpleasant memories and forced the weary animal to try and increase the speed of its unsteady stumbling gait.

Aurthora was making good progress along the spine of the range of hills; because of its exposed position it had been swept clear of snow, and it was a route that offered him a view of the road and the ford in the valley below. Once he reached the end of these hills he could descend slightly, and if his sense of direction was correct he would find himself on the edge of the Whispering Moor. Darkness would be closing in by then, and Petrov Joma would be forced to give up the chase, so the rest of his journey back towards the High Town of Buxonana would be relatively safe.

He stopped briefly in the shelter of one of the great rocks to shelter from the bitter cold east wind that blew in icy blasts along the ridge. He was also a little concerned about the dizzy spells which he seemed to be suffering, but he put it down to the dazzle of the sun's reflection off the snow. The silence was broken by another three blasts of a hunting horn, and shortly afterwards there came the sound of a commotion and the frantic baying of hounds on a chase, which drew his attention to the valley where he could make out the small shapes of figures. A man running away from the ford was being chased by the pack of hounds and followed at a greater distance by mounted horsemen. *Some poor innocent traveller going about his business has been caught in the path of those wild hunting dogs,* thought Aurthora. *What a terrible ending to a man's life.* He turned away and carried on along the ridge of the hill, wincing as the screams of the man, caught by the savage hounds, rebounded between the steep sides of the valley.

It was Petrov Joma, from the vantage point of his taller horse, who noticed the cleft in the cliff face as he was watching the hounds circle and search for the scent they had again lost.

The hounds had passed the entrance to the cave and followed Aurthora's short, false trail. But they had back tracked and picked up his scent again. The horsemen following the dogs had broken the scent leading into the cave, which was causing confusion amongst the hounds. Petrov Joma was in a foul mood, cursing the dog handlers and foot soldiers who had been unable to keep pace with the mounted men through the deep snow. Once the bushes at the entrance to the cave had been ripped away, the hounds were once again on the trail through the cave, closely followed by Petrov Joma and the rest of the mounted men. When the hounds burst from the far entrance of the cave, Petrov Joma immediately saw the previous day's trail of prints in the deep snow. Yelling for the rest of the horsemen to follow him, he careered down the hill the dogs following, then quickly overtaking him. The pack had been trained to hunt anything that moved, and their keen eyesight had seen the shambling gait of a pony below them, obviously in distress.

All the dogs, that is, except the leader of the pack, the dog they called Hadrian; he watched as the horsemen struggled to follow the dogs down the hill in the deep snow heading for the river. He, however, had caught the faint fresh whiff of a scent to the left of the cave entrance. His nose confirmed that he was right, and the rest of the pack, led by the man on the large horse, who used his whip all too frequently, was wrong.

Maro emerged from the deep cleft in the rocks into the afternoon sunlight, gasping for breath. He had not seen Maddoc, the head dog handler, since they had parted at the waterfall. When he had found Aurthora's track, blowing the hunting horn he called the rest of the pack to him, but there had been no sight or sound of Maddoc. Maro sat on a low rock while he regained his breath. He was much younger than Maddoc and the rest of the men on foot, but even he was finding it hard to keep up with the hounds.

This was no merchant they were hunting, they were easy enough prey and did not give much of a chase, but this man was a clever fugitive with a good horse and the ability to remove your head if you came too close to him. Which was why Maro had the foresight to take the longbow from the hands of the dead friar at the hostel, and also retrieve several of the arrows from the dead dogs and the injured foot soldier. If the dogs held this Celt at bay he, using the bow, could pick the man off at leisure. That would place him in Petrov Joma's high esteem; he might even promote him to being in charge of the pack, given that it was clear Maddoc could not keep up with the hounds any longer. He might also obtain a share of the bounty that had been offered by the Saxon king, for the Celtic general's head.

Maro could see from his vantage point the group of horsemen in the valley below; he could see no sign of Maddoc or the other handlers. Those below had obviously picked up a trail, whereas Hadrian the pack leader who had stayed behind, kept going in the direction of the ridge of the hill, then coming back to where he was sitting. Clearly he'd picked up another scent. He raised his horn and then changed his mind. He would proceed and make sure before attracting the attention of the group; they would then know that he, Maro the assistant dog handler – soon to become senior dog handler – was on the correct trail.

Septimius was struggling through a deep snowdrift not far from the ford in the river. Once he reached it he knew the going would get easier. He stopped when he heard the long blasts on the hunting horn, but it made little difference to him. If he came across Petrov Joma's hunting party he would say he was making his way to join them in order to hunt down this Celtic general, which would impress Petrov Joma and demonstrate just how loyal a servant he was.

He was surprised when he saw the old pony trotting down the hill in the distance, and coming towards him. He was amazed that the old animal that he had left for dead, had somehow survived the blizzard. The pony ignored his shouts for it to stop, as it passed close by him he could see the terrified look in the animal's wide eyes. He was not unduly worried, he could manage on foot. In fact it gave him quite a thrill and he felt quite superior that his voice could inflict such fear into another animal. He watched the shambling rear end of the animal, its breath giving off clouds of vapour in the freezing still air. The loss of the pony meant nothing to him; with all the gold and silver in his possession he could buy ten grand horses if he wished. He saw the group of hounds the same moment they saw him. There were no handlers or mounted riders in sight. As they ploughed through the snowdrifts towards him, the dogs began to howl the kind of howl that came from a pack that has sighted its quarry and were advancing for the kill.

Septimius felt the pangs of fear pulling at his heart, and began to retrace his steps in the deep snow as quickly as he could. The dogs were confused; they were chasing him. The stupid animals thought he was Aurthora, the Celtic general. Then he realised: it was the leather jerkin! He was wearing the Celtic general's leather jerkin and carrying his satchel containing all the valuables, together with the meat and other possessions he had stolen from the friars' hostel.

He threw away the satchel and was trying to remove the jerkin when the first hound landed on his back, knocking him into the deep snow, its powerful jaws savaging his neck. His screams reverberated around the valley as the rest of the hounds joined in and proceeded to pull the unfortunate man to pieces. By the time the hunting party arrived on the scene he was dead, and it took a long time for them to drive the dogs from the bloody mess that had once been a human being. The only recognisable things were an embroidered leather jerkin and a satchel filled with food and a fortune in valuables and gold and silver coins, which one of the men collected and took to Petrov Joma.

"I recognise the fancy jerkin. It is the same as the one worn by the Celtic general Aurthora; he was wearing it when I and Victor Aberuso attempted to remove Great King Erion from this world and he mysteriously appeared on the scene, but now I will no longer be bothered by him."

"But there is no sign of the Celtic general's horse, Sire," said one of the mounted men cautiously.

"Then spread out and searched for the animal. It probably threw its rider, or bolted – or both – at the sight of the hounds," replied Petrov Joma, but his real attention was taken up by the large number of gold and silver coins and other valuables that weighed so heavily in the leather satchel.

Aurthora was nearing the end of the spine of the high range of hills. He was wearing the thin clothes borrowed from the old monk Gildas, and desperately missed his heavy woollen cloak, especially the padded and embroidered leather jerkin he had been forced to leave behind at the hostel. He was shivering and his head felt as if it were about to explode. He was now coming to the highest point in the range of hills, which formed a small plateau. From this vantage point he could see the whole valley below him He could not see the entrance to the cave because it was hidden by the range of hills, but he could see the track that led down to the river. He realised Orius must have been in this area many times to know it so well, possibly when he was in the employ of his father who would be here attending to the king's business. He had deliberately made the riddle and the map difficult in the event of it being forcibly taken or lost from his possession. He continued and, after several hundred paces, came to a large pool. *Odd that such a sizeable and obviously deep mass of water should be at such a high point without any visible means of supply,* he thought. He had stopped to allow his horse to drink so that he could take a moment's rest and also try to clear his throbbing head.

What he couldn't see, even from this high vantage point, was the pigeon he had released speeding back to its mate in the cosy loft, and neither could he see the deadly peril that was hovering above it. A hawk out hunting had spied the pigeon and moved into a position above. The predator had not eaten for two days because of the poor weather and the pigeon made an easy target. Closing its wings it dived as it had done a thousand times before. It felt the thrill of the wind whistling past its body as it dropped like a stone although still in full control. Only moments before the deadly strike on its unsuspecting target, it was suddenly aware of a large shadow overhead. Due to its momentary lapse of concentration the hawk's strike was poor and it failed to secure a hold on the pigeon. It veered away as the pigeon tumbled towards the ground, leaving a cloud of feathers behind, but the large shadow above was still following the hawk. It made a dive to the left in the nick of time as the talons of a large buzzard missed it by inches. The hawk sped off, weaving back and forth, with the more cumbersome buzzard giving chase. At the same time, the pigeon, hurtling towards the snow-covered ground, managed to right itself and regain its balance just several feet from earth so that it was able to continue its flight. Although it now kept low and followed the contours of the ground, skimming just above the tops of the leafless trees.

Hadrian, the black-headed hound, was following the strong scent along the ridge, speeding forward over the hard frozen ground towards the unsuspecting horse and man resting at the pond. The faintest glimpse of movement caught Aurthora's eye, and he had almost drawn his sword from its sheath on his saddle when his horse also sensed a presence and turned to see the wolflike creature in the process of springing at them. The horse's spontaneous reaction was to turn and rear on its hind legs, its forelegs slashing the air in the direction of the leaping dog. The sudden twist and rearing movement of the horse beneath him threw its rider off balance, and he landed heavily on the frozen ground, his drawn sword clattering amongst the stones beneath the rearing horse.

While he was still airborne, a flying hoof struck Hadrian against his shoulder with such force it knocked him sideways. When the heavy horse's hooves came down they landed on the sword that had fallen between two stones. There was a sharp crack as the ice-cold, brittle metal snapped under the force. With a quick turn and a flick of its rear hooves the horse was off in a canter back the way it had come; unexpectedly, a figure jogging along the track towards it made the frightened horse veer sharply in panic, sending it off the path and ploughing down the side of the hill through the deep snow.

Dazed from his fall, Aurthora was lying on the snow looking up into a blue clear sky when a buzzard, his bird of good fortune, glided effortlessly past his line of vision. *Oh, what I would give to be able to change places with that feathered creature now!* he thought as he slowly sat upright. He was also mesmerised by the sight of his broken sword lying amongst the rubble of stones. The sword Great King Erion had presented to him in front of all the gathered Celtic tribes and their leaders, the sword that had supposedly once belonged to the great Celtic leader Boudicca, passed down from generation to generation to the leaders of the Celtic people, now lay in two halves amongst the rubble

A dog's growl brought him to his senses. The animal had suffered no broken bones and was back on its feet, bounding over the few paces that separated it from the man whose scent it had been given earlier that day. Delving deep in its memory it recalled that it had smelt and seen this human before. The man held no shiny object that could inflict injury or pain, and the dog could sense by the man's slow reactions that he was injured or disabled in some way. This would be an easy kill and he would not need to call the pack and wait for assistance.

As it pounced, Aurthora managed to grab its heavy studded collar with both hands, the animal's sheer weight forcing him from his sitting position back onto the ground, where it took all his strength to keep the animal's head distant enough to avoid its teeth from sinking into his neck. He could feel the strength in his arms fading as the heavy animal on top of him strained to bite, the slobber from its jaws dripping into his face. Then risking all, with a supreme effort he suddenly released his left hand from its hold on the dog's collar, swiftly hit the dog as hard as he could against the ear, then with the same free hand, reached down and drew the dagger from its sheath on his calf. As his right hand holding the collar weakened, the dog recovered from the blow and lowered its head to savage his face. Aurthora plunged the dagger into its ribs over and over again.

The great hound was so intent on attacking its victim that it was several moments before it realised it had been mortally wounded, and even though its jaws opened towards Aurthora's face, the dog did not have the strength to close them, dying where it lay, on top of him. It took Aurthora some time before he recovered enough to push the heavy animal aside, and even more before he felt he had the strength to attempt to stand. The dull throbbing in his head that had troubled him over the last days had also returned, leaving him sweating and befuddled. He slowly and painfully struggled upright and looked at the great, black-headed dog lying at his feet, his knife projecting from its ribcage and his broken sword among the stones. His horse had also bolted. He was many leagues from any dwelling, clothed in only the thinnest of garments for such extreme weather conditions and surrounded by enemies intent on killing him. His chances of survival were indeed bleak, and never before had he felt so weak, so terribly weak.

The shaft hit him square in the chest. The power of the arrow from the bow at such short range knocked him back on the ground; there he lay flat on his back, the arrow projecting upright from his body.

Maro had come onto the scene just as Aurthora pushed the leader of the pack of hounds to one side and slowly rose. He had strung the powerful bow, and taking one of the reclaimed arrows fired at the motionless, standing figure. From such a short range, even he with his limited expertise with the longbow would have found it difficult to miss such a large, still target. After the man had collapsed to the ground Maro thought first of blowing his hunting horn to call Petrov Joma and the rest of the Celts to the scene, but decided he would first search his prey. It was quite possible that a man of such high birth and position might be carrying a well-filled purse. He walked over to the twitching figure where it lay gasping for breath, spread-eagled beside the dead hound. He looked at Hadrian the dog and shook his head. It had been a clever animal and an excellent leader of the hunting pack, it would be hard to replace. He looked back at the man then bent forward and put one foot on his chest and pulled at the arrow. It came away from the tear in the tunic much too easily. Maro's eyes focused on the end of the shaft where the point should have been, but it was several moments before he realised what was on the end of the arrow. The killing barb had entered the mouth of a small drinking goblet and there it was securely wedged; the blood on the man's clothes was not from the wound inflicted by the arrow but had come from the wounds in the dog's side.

The force of the arrow hitting him in the chest had knocked Aurthora to the ground, leaving him battling for breath. Through a glazed haze he saw a figure standing over him and felt the man's foot on his chest. Slowly reaching out with his right arm his fingers grasped the handle of his broken sword, using all his remaining strength he thrust the broken weapon upwards in the direction of the figure.

Maro saw what was happening as if in slow motion. His eyes transfixed on the small goblet wedged on the point of the arrow, so that when the man moved his arm towards the broken sword he attempted to step backwards, slipping on the loose stones which sent him stumbling forward over the man and onto the jagged end of the sword. He wheeled away clutching his stomach, but even as he did so he knew the blow was fatal. He staggered backwards towards the edge of the pool still holding the arrow in one hand and trying vainly to withdraw the sword with his other. His mouth opened in a scream of pain, but no sound came. He wrenched the sword from his stomach, looked for several moments at the bloodied jagged end, then fell backwards, shattering the thin sheet of ice on the still water. After a few frantic splashes, he sank beneath the surface.

Chapter Forty Two

As Aurthora sat upright he saw the man's wild gestures as he sank, holding aloft the goblet fastened to the arrow point in one hand and the bloody broken end of his sword in the other, before they too disappeared below the surface. The ripples settled and apart from the broken ice, all was as before. Aurthora did not know how long he lay at the side of the pool, but when he eventually regained consciousness it was dusk and snow was beginning to fall, and never before in his life had he felt so cold. He found it difficult to rise, he was so stiff; his senses were reeling and he could not focus his eyes. Even in this confused state he realised he had to find shelter of some kind or he would perish before morning. The only shelter he could think of was the deep cleft in the cliff that formed a cave, the one called Ludd's Chapel. If he could reach there he would be sheltered from the worst of any bad weather, and he still had his flint and dagger. If he could light a fire he might survive until morning. Yet he felt so terribly weary, and it was so difficult to place one foot in front of another. He would have to stop, just for a few moments, just to take a brief rest, then he would carry on. Only a moment's rest, no longer…

Maddoc, the lead dog handler, was the last to come out of the great cleft in the rocks along with several of the men on foot. They were all exhausted, they had been constantly on the move since the previous evening and not had the luxury of riding a horse like Petrov Joma and his mounted followers. Instead they had to constantly struggle through the deep, energy-sapping snowdrifts, and had dropped farther and farther behind the mounted men with the pack of hounds. Below them they could see the river and the ford and a group of mounted men in the valley. They were struggling to drive the pack of hounds back along the trail and up towards the cave where he was standing. Further below, out of sight of this group but in view of Maddoc and the men on the cliff, was a horse trapped in a deep snowdrift.

He placed the hunting horn to his lips to call the hounds to him, then changed his mind. If the pack came across the stranded horse without any handler to control them they could well attack and savage the animal.

He led the men with him slowly down the steep sides of the hill, making a slight detour to collect the horse trapped in the deep snow. Maddoc could not help admiring the large, strongly muscled animal. He stroked and talked to the shivering horse, and slowly it settled down allowing them to lead it down the hill to join the rest of the mounted group making painfully slow progress upwards back along the trail.

"I see you have found the Celtic general's horse," called out Petrov Joma as the groups merged.

"Yes, Sire, it was trapped in a deep snowdrift," replied Maddoc.

"Your hounds have earned their keep today. They found the Celtic general, but all they left for us was his fancy jerkin and his satchel," Petrov Joma, laughed at his own wit, with the rest of the mounted men joining in.

Maddoc noticed that the pack leader, Hadrian, and his own assistant dog handler, Maro, were not with the group, but he kept this fact to himself. He simply did not have the energy to go scouring the surrounding hills for them; they would turn up eventually, and anyway, it was getting dark and beginning to snow again. It would be another long and weary trek before they reached the shelter and warmth of the hostel and he knew that these mounted followers of Petrov Joma would never share the contents of the heavy purse that this Celtic general would have been carrying. Neither would he receive any reward for finding the general's horse, Petrov Joma had already laid claim to that wonderful animal. So it was a very disgruntled Maddoc that whipped in the hounds as the group continued along the trail that would lead them back to the hostel.

It was Disaylann who went to the pigeon loft at noon that day to feed and give water to the birds. At times he even felt inferior to these feathered creatures that seemed to be able to communicate with one another more than he could with his own kind. He shivered despite the thick woollen cloak he was wearing over two jerkins and two pairs of trews. It had been a bitter few days with blizzard conditions and icy east winds that swept through the narrow streets of the town. He was glad he had persuaded the old physician to purchase a good store of cut logs and some of the sacks of black rock that burnt slowly but gave off more heat than the wood. He had maintained a good fire in the kitchen, so that one room in the house was always warm and comfortable. After all, Emilia was heavy with her baby and it would not be wise for her to catch a chill so close to giving birth.

Disaylann closed the loft door and was making his way back through the thick snow towards the partially open door and the welcoming warmth of the house when he stopped. He had forgotten to check the section for returning birds, even though he was sure no bird would be flying in these conditions. He hesitated, then went back to check that section of the loft. At first he saw nothing, but then a slight movement in the far corner caught his eye and he was surprised to see that there was a pigeon. He reached in and withdrew the bird, his heart missing a beat as he saw the rolled message fastened to the pigeon's leg.

Within two hours of Disaylann finding the message, Ethellro had organised the heavy cavalry. He had found mounts for Roderick Tristan the master bowman, who knew the area they would be travelling through well, and for a score of his best archers. He also sent a messager to Cimbonda Gilberto to request that he follow with the mounted warriors of the Cornovii tribe as soon as possible.

So that afternoon a large detachment of the Celtic heavy cavalry left the High Town of Buxonana with a contingent of archers, led by a grim-faced Ethellro. All the men with Ethellro had volunteered, it had been explained to them that they would be travelling over large tracts of exposed country with no shelter available. If the blizzards returned, there was a possibility that they might lose their way and freeze to death on the exposed moors. No one changed his mind, and everyone to a man stepped forward to follow Ethellro in his search for their much loved commander Aurthora, determined to wreak havoc on anyone who was holding him or had taken his life.

Such a large body of men leaving the town could not go unnoticed; as well as the families of the mounted men, there were many bystanders who stood in the cold to wave them off.

Amongst those watching the men leave was Voltigern of the Celtic Council, and beside him stood Elemar, the Great King's daughter. Also watching the large force ride by from an isolated group of buildings a fair distance from the walls of the town was the high priest Zanton, and beside him the novice who had brought him the news of the mounted expedition.

The force was several hours into its journey when dusk began to fall. Scouts chosen for their knowledge of the area had been sent to ride well in advance to seek the easiest route for the group to follow, and they had just stopped to light the oil lanterns they would carry on tall poles to light the way for the rest of the force, when two riders galloped past the column and came to a stop in front of Ethellro.

Their horses were panting and covered in lather even though the temperature was swiftly falling to below freezing. "We have a message from the Celtic Round Council and Great King Erion to Ethellro, the leader of this unlawful force," shouted the leader of the two riders. "You are to return to the High Town of Buxonana at once and explain before the Celtic Round

Council and Great King Erion why you have mobilised such a large force when you have no authority to do so. If you continue with this venture, your action will be viewed as treason," continued the messenger.

Ethellro was livid and could feel his blood boiling. He would have ridden the men down and cut them to pieces with his battleaxe were it not for the restraining hands of Aurthora's bodyguards, Darius and Cynfelin Facilus. Ethellro took several deep breaths and allowed his temper to cool slightly. "Go back to your masters and tell them we all act voluntarily and in the interests of the Celtic Alliance, for if we lose Aurthora our general, there will be no need for the Celtic Round Council, since there will be no Celtic Alliance to govern. Now out of my way! We have a long journey ahead of us." Ethellro rode his horse forward past the two stunned messengers, who turned their horses and galloped off in the direction they had come.

Ethellro and his column travelled all that night and the following day, following the trail the scouts had chosen around the deepest of the snowdrifts. They only stopped to rest for a few hours the following night in an exposed village high on the moor, which had grown there due to the prized blue stone, lead and silver that were mined nearby. They had rubbed down, fed and watered their animals, managing to get a few hours' sleep themselves before they were awakened to once again set out following the scouts' oil lamps as they continued to seek the best possible route through the deep snow.

At noon the following day the scouts came to report to Ethellro that they were close to the village of Swythaily, located at the end of a deep river. They also reported the many large boats that were tied up at the small jetty and the banks alongside.

Ethellro only knew one course of action: a frontal charge that would take everything along with it by sheer weight of numbers. He sent Roderick and the archers on ahead, while himself and the rest of the men dismounted and led their horses down a slope and through a wood that had protected the ground within it from the drifting snow. As they came to the far edge of the wood he saw a narrow bridge spanning the river. The bridge marked the furthest point the boats could go, for beyond the bridge the river was too shallow for these large sea-going vessels. Smoke was coming from the centre openings of all the thatched cottages in the village. *The men from the boats are lodged in the cottages*, thought Ethellro. *These Anglo-Saxons will come out and fight, they won't be trapped in the cottages and risk being burnt alive if we fire the dwellings.*

Going over to where Roderick was standing he outlined his plan to the master bowman. He would split his cavalry into two sections, he would lead the first charge, and then the second section would follow shortly after.

Roderick slipped off across the shallow part of the river, followed by his archers. Once on the far side, the bowmen spread out and from a series of small fires started with dry bracken taken from the wood, they sent fire arrows into the edge of the roofing thatch of the cottages nearest to the bridge.

At first it seemed as if the fire arrows had been extinguished by the snow on the thatch, but slowly the dry thatch underneath caught fire and panic-stricken shouts of alarm could be heard from the inhabitants as clouds of dark acrid smoke drifted through the dwellings and over the bottom part of the village and the bridge spanning the river. Under the cover of this smoke Ethellro moved his heavy cavalry three abreast over the narrow bridge. Once on the other side the mounted men lined up eight across and four deep across the main track that ran through the group of dwellings.

The panic-stricken shouting had brought the rest of the occupants of the village out of their dwellings, on seeing the smoke coming from the lower part of the village they rushed down the main street to help extinguish the flames. All the cottages in the village were crammed with Anglo-Saxons brought in on the boats along with the rest of Petrov Joma's Celtic renegade supporters. Petrov Joma had sent his messengers to summon them from the outlying farms and properties where they had been billeted, but they had been delayed by the deep snowdrifts, so as soon as Petrov Joma thought he had sufficient men for the task in hand he impatiently set off for the monastery, leaving the many latecomers to find whatever shelter and accommodation they could in the already overcrowded village.

As the Anglo-Saxons and renegade Celts rushed through the village with a varied collection of buckets and utensils capable of holding water to fight the fires, charging out of the billowing smoke coming towards them they were met with the charge of the Celtic heavy cavalry, their long spears pointing menacingly in their direction. Many of the potential fire fighters were unarmed, as they came to a sudden stop at the sight of the charging cavalry, their comrades rushing down the slope behind them collided into their backs.

It was utter confusion. Many of the Anglo-Saxons and their Celtic renegade allies tried to escape down the narrow passageways between the buildings, but were met by a fusillade of arrows from Roderick and his bowmen, who were positioned along the rear of the cottages. The Celtic cavalry swept through the heavily bunched, mainly unarmed body of men, first using the long spears and then thrusting and slashing with their swords. When the cavalry reached the top of the village they regrouped, preparing to sweep back down the slope and through the village again.

The enemy foot soldiers were now organising themselves; more of them were emerging from the buildings armed with their swords and axes, ready to do battle. They quickly formed a barricade across the village street of several small carts and various pieces of household furniture, waiting in readiness for the return cavalry charge from the top of the village. But the expected charge did not materialise. Instead the other half of the Celti cavalry charged through the smoke and trapped the foot soldiers against their own defences; at the same time Ethellro charged down the slope and threw his men into the fray from that direction. The sailors of the large seagoing vessels that had brought the many Anglo-Saxon soldiers to the end of the river and to the village were billeted in cottages nearby or sleeping on their boats; seeing the conflict taking place in the village they cut the moorings on four of the six vessels and were beginning to drift down the river.

It was at this point that Cimbonda Gilberto arrived with his mounted warriors of the Cornovii tribe. Quickly reading the situation, he dispatched a quarter of his force onto the far side of the river and the other quarter he'd follow the boats from his side. They were under instructions to target the crews on the boats with their bows at every opportunity, and force them to beach their vessels before they reached the wider part of the river.

He then led the other half of his mounted warriors to the support of Ethellro and his men who were still fighting in the village.

The added impact of more Celtic troops to the conflict determined the battle in Ethellro's favour. Seeing they had no possibility of winning and escape was out of the question, the Anglo-Saxons threw down their weapons and surrendered, preferring a life of slavery to death. However, this was not the case with the renegade Celts: they knew they would be shown no mercy, and so they either died fighting or committed suicide rather than be taken alive.

While Ethellro and Cimbonda surveyed the carnage in the main street of the village and the enemy lying two deep in the narrow passageways between the buildings, their men searched and cleared the village cottages and outbuildings. It was shortly after the Anglo-Saxons had been fastened together and led down to the bridge at the bottom of the village that one of the scouts came running down from the top end of the village. "A group of men, some on horseback and some on foot, are approaching the village," he gasped.

Ethellro mounted his horse and shouted to Roderick, "Take your archers, Roderick, in a large circle and cut off their retreat while Cimbonda and I go and meet these visitors."

Petrov Joma and his party eventually reached the hostel in the early hours of the morning. The snow that had been threatening had kept off and they had been blessed with a clear sky plus a full moon to light their journey. Both men and horses were at the end of their endurance. After seeing to their animals, the men stumbled into the main building and simply fell anywhere they could to lie down and sleep.

Brother Gildas, the old monk, heard them return as he knew they would; he had hidden behind the woodpile after Aurthora had charged out of the barn, and witnessed the heroic stand made by his colleague Camaro with his longbow, and the men and hounds chasing after Aurthora. He had also heard Septimius searching for and eventually finding the small hoard of coins, ransacking all the rooms in the process.

He had waited a good while after he thought Septimius had left, eventually he had managed to drag the mutilated body of Camaro, his brave colleague, to a nearby small cave where they kept cheeses and game as the temperature was always cool. Brushing away the marks in the snow, he had pulled brushwood behind him to hide the cave entrance. He felt safer there than hiding in the house or barns. He heard the men return in the early hours of the morning, then dozed fitfully until the sun was just rising on the horizon. He was awakened from his half sleep by the howling of several of the hounds outside the cave entrance.

Gildas was trembling with fear as he looked through the foliage he had dragged over the entrance of the small cave. He could see the one with the scarred face whom they called Petrov sitting on the large horse that Aurthora had ridden away on the day before. Several more mounted men were grouped around him while the men on foot were dragging brushwood and piling it at the entrance to the cave.

One came with two oil lanterns and threw the contents onto the pile of timber. Gildas crawled to the back of the cave and began to make his peace with his God. He knew envy was a sin, but how he wished he had touched the sacred drinking goblet as Camaro, his dead companion, said he had, and who now lay cold and still beside him. The smoke was now making him cough and his eyes were watering. The last thing he heard before he lapsed into unconsciousness was the loud harsh laughter of the one they called Petrov Joma.

It was late afternoon by the time Petrov Joma led his small party to within sight of the village of Swythaily. They had seen the smoke rising from a distance away and a mounted scout had been sent to check on the situation. "Well man, what's the problem?" demanded Petrov Joma as the rider came to a stop in front of him.

"The thatch on a roof of a cottage at the bottom of the village is alight," the man gasped, regained his breath and then continued, "the village is full of smoke."

Petrov Joma cursed. It was a regular occurrence during the winter when fires were built too high during cold spells and the roofing thatch caught fire. Unless quickly brought under control the fire could easily spread to the adjoining dwellings, threatening the whole village. He drove his heels into the flanks of the horse, driving the animal forward into a fast trot, quickly followed by the rest of his party.

As he entered the track that led down through the village, he could see below figures moving about in the thick smoke that had engulfed the bottom half of the village. Turning to the rest of his men behind him he called out, "Hurry and join those idiots and put out that fire. And be quick about it if you want a roof over your heads tonight."

As he and his men quickened their pace down the paved road that sloped through the village they came to an abrupt halt. Suddenly, out of the smoke emerged a mass of mounted men wearing chain mail armour and bearing long spears and heart-shaped shields. There was nowhere for Petrov Joma to go: he pulled his horse to a slithering halt and was buffeted and nearly unseated by the horsemen following behind him. He turned to curse the rider but the man, who was in the process of drawing his sword, fell from his horse with an arrow projecting from his chest. Several of the foot soldiers tried to escape by running down the side passageways between the cottages, but here they were met by fatal, well-placed arrows from Roderick's archers. Riding his great black stallion and leading the Celtic cavalry charge, Petrov Joma recognised the tall figure of Ethellro, the horse breeder.

A brave renegade Celt rode past Petrov Joma, and waving his sword attempted to unhorse Ethellro, but the big man's lance lifted the man off his horse and dumped him on the snow-covered ground. Ethellro saw that Petrov Joma was riding Aurthora's horse, and unhooking his great battleaxe he gave a bellow of rage and drove his stallion at the stationary renegade leader. As Ethellro drew level, Petrov Joma swung his sword in a wide arc. It smashed into Ethellro's heart-shaped shield with such force that it cut through the metal and penetrated Ethellro's forearm, but he did not feel any pain as he swung his great battleaxe. The blade penetrated just above Petrov Joma's chest, sinking so deeply into the man's body that the shaft was snatched out of Ethellro's grasp. Petrov Joma's mount galloped off down through the village, the body of its rider lolling from side to side with the shaft of the axe projecting at an acute angle until eventually Petrov Joma fell from the saddle to join the rest of the dead Anglo-Saxons and renegade

Celts that littered the bloodied snow of the smoke-filled village.

Only one of the renegades survived the battle that followed: it was the badly injured Celt that Aurthora had cut down in the courtyard of the hostel, and the reason this man had not bled to death was that it was so cold his wound had congealed. It was from him that the story of the last days unfolded before he too eventually died of his wounds.

As dusk came, so did the snow, and it was several days before the heavy falls subsided and the full picture revealed itself. The local inhabitants had been kept prisoners and used as slaves in their own village; no one had been allowed to leave on pain of death to themselves, and all their family. The pack of hounds was used to hunt down anyone trying to leave the village also travellers and merchants travelling through the area who might inform the Celtic authorities of the Anglo-Saxon and Celtic renegade occupation of the village.

With the help of Petrov Joma and the rest of his traitorous band, the Anglo-Saxons were building up a large force behind the Celtic defences. Supplied from the sea by the great ships, when ready they planned to attack the Celtic army from the rear as well as simultaneously advancing in force from the lands they already occupied in the north of the country.

Only one of the great ships had managed to evade Cimbonda Gilberto's mounted archers, the others had been forced into the riverbank through the lack of able seamen to man the ships because so many had been injured or killed by the accuracy of the Cornovii long-bowmen who were following the boats along the riverbanks.

Several days later the bodies of the two monks were discovered in the cave, and on the orders of Ethellro the entrance was sealed and became the tomb for the Christian friars. The body of Septimius – who the renegades had thought was Aurthora – was found, and even though the man's face was unrecognisable, all those that knew Aurthora well, knew it was not him from the stature of the man. Though Ethellro's men searched for many days, Aurthora's body was never found. Even when they received a message from Myridyn to search the high ridge of hills, all they found was a dead hound and the broken end of Aurthora's sword. As a lasting monument to his lifelong comrade Ethellro decided he would have several images of his friend's face wearing his Celtic battle helmet carved into large stones in the area. To remind people in the years to come of the general of the Celtic army, who had defeated his country's invaders, then disappeared without a trace.

By the time Ethellro and his men returned to the High Town of

Buxonana, word had already gone ahead of their great victory and the capture of the Saxon warships. They were met by cheering townsfolk and treated as victorious heroes. No more was ever said to Ethellro about disobeying the Celtic Council's direct order to return with his men or the charge of treason.

He was offered the position of Captain of the Town Guard, but he declined since the threat from the Anglo-Saxon invaders had been broken. He had lost so many close friends of late and was so disillusioned with the politics and the officials of the Celtic Council that he decided all he wanted to do was go back to his farm and breed horses as his father and grandfather had done before him. His sister Katrina moved into the monks' hostel near the village of Swythaily, which Emilia purchased from some of the proceeds of the satchel that Ethellro had taken from Aurthora's horse. She later gave birth to a son, and several months later Katrina gave birth to a daughter from her union with Aurthora.

Both women were attended by the old physician Myridyn, who eventually left his lodgings in the High Town, and with his faithful helper Disaylann took up permanent residence in the lodging house run by the two women. Here he rented some outbuildings and carried on gathering his herbs and treating the sick with his ointments and potions. The two women ran the hostel for the travellers and merchants who passed that way along the old salt trail, also for the many people who came to be treated by the old physician.

Katrina spent all her free time searching the surrounding hills for some sign of the final resting place of her lover Aurthora, the father of her daughter. But it was to no avail: she too died only months afterwards from internal complications she sustained in giving birth to her daughter, although many said it was really of a broken heart. Emilia, her son and Katrina's daughter continued to run the hostel for many years.

As Great King Erion weakened further and his mind failed, Voltigern married Elemar the Great King's daughter and was appointed leader of the Celtic Council and ruler of the Kingdom of Elmet. But there was much bickering in the Council and Voltigern did not have the personality or the wisdom to give the Council and the Celtic Alliance a sense of purpose or direction. Neither did he maintain the army-training programme that King Erion had instigated and encouraged. Fearing the strength of the Town Guard and the Celtic heavy and light cavalry, whose combined forces had savaged the Anglo-Saxon invaders so brutally, he manipulated the situation so that they were eventually disbanded.

The gold and silver from the mines that had previously been used to maintain a strong Celtic army, was instead used to bribe the Anglo-Saxons to keep to their boundaries. But eventually even that was not enough, and under the leadership of Gwandelk, the nephew of the Old Saxon King Ælle, the Anglo-Saxon army moved in force into the lands occupied by the Celts and drove all before them. Several of the Celtic tribes fought bravely against the invaders, including Ethellro, who formed a company of the old, heavy Celtic cavalry and offered his services to the Celtic Council, but they were not used effectively. The council appointed Voltigern as general. There was neither the organisation nor the army discipline that there had been under Aurthora's leadership.

On his retreat with a few of the surviving cavalry, Ethellro collected Emilia, her son and his neice, escorting them back into the far mountains. The Anglo-Saxons, under the leadership of Gwandelk and future Saxon kings, eventually colonised the lands they had conquered and took over all that had previously been the Celtic Kingdom of Elmet. As had happened once before when the Roman legions had invaded the island, the Celts were driven back into the mountains and the more inhospitable parts of their island. During these troubled times many of the skills for which they were so famous were lost and never regained.

Centuries passed and the lands that had once been the Celtic Kingdom of Elmet saw further changes. They were once again invaded, this time by fierce warriors who came in great long boats, while marauding warlike tribes from the far north of the island were a constant threat. Eventually the occupying Anglo-Saxons were in turn overrun by an army of armoured horsemen supported by great numbers of archers, as had happened once before in their history. These men came from the old Kingdom of Gaul and laid claim to the country in the name of William their king. They were viciously cruel in the administration of their newly conquered lands and its inhabitants.

Chapter Forty Three.

In the year 1940, the country was again in the throes of a great war. The countryside had altered since the Celts and the Anglo-Saxons had fought over the Kingdom of Elmet. Gone were the great forests of oak, beech, elm and ash; in their place were fields and green pastures interlaced with dry stone walls and hedges. New towns and large villages had sprung up where before there had only been small, scattered hamlets and settlements. All these new communities were linked by roads. The Celtic village that had once been called Swythaily was still there, but its name had changed many times over the years and it was now known as Wincle. But the public house in the village is still called 'The Ship Inn'.

A large parcel of land covering many thousands of acres and owned for many generations by the Brocklehurst family was still called Swythamley Estate, taking its name from the old Celtic settlement.

The son of the owner of this estate, an officer in the army, had made available a deep pool in an isolated area on top of range of hills overlooking the valley. It was being used to carry out Royal Navy secret tests for a new method of deep water diving. An old family friend from the Admiralty was also taking a keen interest in the results of these tests.

"What depth is this water, Captain Brocklehurst?" inquired the gentleman from the Admiralty as he turned up the collar of his long overcoat against the low damp and misty cloud that every now and then enveloped the small party of men.

"We stopped testing the depth at sixty five yards Sir, which is over thirty fathoms – the depth they required. But it would indeed be interesting to know what depth Doxey Pool really is."

"Doxey Pool. Do you know how it came by such a name, Captain?"

"I believe the name is Celtic in origin, Sir. There are many local stories and legends associated with this water."

"Well, I must say Captain, you have certainly found an isolated spot. Ideal for these secret tests", commented the Admiralty man as he looked around at the cold and desolate surroundings.

Further conversation was cut short by a shout from one of the sailors standing at the side of the pool. "Petty Officer Robinson is surfacing now Sir," as he proceeded to slowly draw up a lifeline and lay it in neat loops at his feet.

Both men came closer to the edge of the pool, watching as the neat coil of rope grew into a deep pile. Clouds of bubbles preluded a man's head breaking the surface of the water. He slowly made his way towards them and eased himself on to the bank. He was dressed in a close fitting rubber suit with large facemask. A mouthpiece was connected to two long slim cylinders fastened to his back. This was very different from the other divers of that time in their cumbersome suits, weighted boots, and large bronze helmets attached to an air pipeline.

A navy officer came over to the two observers, saluted and gave his report. "On first observations the test seems to be satisfactory, Petty Officer Robinson is quite coherent and alert. The new mixture has allowed him to go much deeper than was possible before and without any negative effects. He also found these items that had come to rest on a ledge, but I don't think they have been there that long since they look quite new." He handed the items to Captain Brocklehurst, saluted once more and returned to his men at the side of the pool.

Captain Brocklehurst looked in fascination at the objects in his hands. One was a sword with a beautifully engraved silver hilt shaped in the form of a large bird of prey with spread wings. The blade was broken eighteen inches or so from the handle. The other object was a small goblet, apparently made from a mixture of alloys given its unusual colour.

"I think the navy officer may be mistaken, this sword handle has the most intricate workmanship. I'd say it was very old indeed. I've heard before that the presence of certain minerals in water preserves metals and prevents them from deteriorating. It will be interesting to have it inspected by a specialist," he said as he held the sword up to the light.

"This goblet has writing engraved on the base, and if I'm not mistaken, there's also what looks like an arrowhead wedged tightly inside its cup," commented the gentleman from the Admiralty, inspecting the small drinking vessel. "It also feels warm to the touch, a most peculiar sensation."

"Will you take it as a souvenir, Sir, of this successful experiment, and as a memento of your visit to the Swythamley Estate?" asked the captain.

The older gentleman thought for a moment then replied with a smile, "I accept your gift with great pleasure, Captain Brocklehurst, you are most kind."

A shout from one of the sailors standing on look-out at the higher outcrop of rock attracted their attention. "There's a runner coming from the Hall, Sir," the sailor shouted to the naval officer.

"Can you make out who it is, Mullins?" the officer shouted back.

"It looks like Able Seaman Hughes, Sir,"

"If Hughes is running it must be urgent. Right men, pack up this equipment," the Captain ordered. "Let's be ready to leave as soon as possible."

Able Seaman Hughes came jogging along the path gasping for breath, wishing he hadn't given way to temptation and drunk that extra pint of Stone Waller's best bitter at The Ship Inn the night before. He stopped in front of his officer and saluted. "Telephone message from the secretary, Sir." He stopped, gasping for breath.

"The secretary? Secretary to whom, man?" snapped the officer.

"The man struggled to get his breath and then blurted: "The Secretary to the First Lord of the Admiralty, Sir, to Mr. W... The sailor stopped in mid sentence biting his lip before continuing. "The VIP gentleman sir. The message is 'Can the VIP gentleman phone his secretary as soon as possible,' Sir." Able seaman Hughes couldn't understand what all the secrecy about the gentleman's name was all about. In the local village and the pub it was common knowledge who he was.

The hurried ride back to the Hall on the small Shetland pony was most ungainly for the rather portly gentleman. The bailiff who was leading the pony had to stop on several occasions and retrace his steps back up the narrow track to retrieve the city gentleman's hat, dislodged due to the severe bobbing motion of the passenger straddled side saddle across the pony's back.

On arriving back at the Hall, the Brocklehursts' guest was directed to the library where he could make his phone call in private. It was several minutes before he reappeared, shouting for his valet to run a hot bath to ease his bruised rear, also to pack their bags as they were leaving for London at once.

As Sawyers, the valet, ran the bath as instructed he could hear his employer pacing the floor in his bedroom; he was obviously very agitated, doubtless something to do with the telephone conversation. His employers secretary had seemed very excited when Sawyers had spoken to him earlier. When Sawyers had suggested waiting until the party returned to the Hall for afternoon tea, the secretary had replied very tersely that that would not do at all, insisting that he be informed immediately. He tested the temperature of the bath water with his fingers, ran a little more cold, then tested it again. That's near enough, he muttered to himself. "Your bath is ready, Sir," he called as he knocked on the bedroom door.

The portly gentleman entered the bathroom and handed his bathrobe to his valet. Sawyers took the bathrobe and hung it on the rear of the bathroom door, then left to get some towels from the nearby cylinder cupboard. *The birthmark on his shoulder is more prominent today,* he mused, *but then it seemed to do that whenever the First Sea Lord was agitated or excited.*

He was interrupted by the arrival of Captain Brocklehurst.

"Ah, Sawyers, I've been in touch with the Chief Constable, the five-forty-five from Manchester to London will be held at Macclesfield until our guest arrives at the railway station. A car with a police escort is waiting outside; they're ready to leave as soon as your employer is ready. "I will pass the message on at once, Captain Brocklehurst". The valet answered, giving a slight bow.

It was six o'clock and Captain Brocklehurst had begun to pace irritably up and down the hallway at the bottom of the stairs. It was a good half hour's drive to the Macclesfield railway station, and the train had already been delayed at least fifteen minutes. Sawyer appeared at the top of the stairs.

"The cases are ready for taking down to the car Captain Brocklehurst," he said to the Captain's strained, upturned face.

Several minutes later the gentleman himself arrived at the top of the stairs. "Everything is loaded and we are ready to leave now, Sir," the Captain called up to him.

"One moment, Captain, I've left something behind in my room," he replied as he turned and made his way back down the corridor. The Captain groaned inwardly.

Once in his bedroom he crossed to the dressing table and took from its highly polished surface the small goblet with the arrow head embedded in its opening. As he looked at the cup a strange feeling overcame him. "I will keep you as a good luck charm," he said aloud as he slipped it into his overcoat pocket, turned, and quickly made his way back down the stairs to the waiting transport. It was several hours later as the Captain was passing the guests bedroom. He overheard the chambermaid complaining to her companion that it would be days before they could clear the stale smell of cigar smoke from this part of the hall...

The rest is history.

Endnote

Visitors to this area of the Peak National Park where the River Dane forms the boundary between Cheshire, Derbyshire and Staffordshire can, if they wish, see the outline of Aurthora's face and chest shaped by the distant hills. The legend is that Katrina is still looking for the resting place of her Celtic Prince, and descends to earth riding a rainbow, still hoping to find his body. This legend also goes on to say that if the rainbow ever touches his lips, this giant of a man will rise again to join his beloved.

Directions

Take the A54 from Congleton to Buxton. At the crossroad turn right (just past the Four Ways Motel), and follow the sign for Wincle (Barlow Hill). Take the first turn right into narrow Top House Lane, a public road serving several farms. Pass Wood Cottage Farm (the first farm on the left) then stop and look east (to your left) at the outline of the far range of hills, and notice the shape of a man lying horizontally. You have just seen the last resting place of Aurthora Ambrosius Aurelianus, a giant of a man in the eyes and legends of his people, the Celts. And if the day is clear and you are very, very lucky, you may also see a buzzard floating on the high thermals above this range of hills. Continue along the tarmac lane through two gates, (don't forget to close them behind you), pass Wincle Grange (the old monastery) on your right and continue on to the end of the lane. Turn right at the road and after several hundred yards you'll see The Ship Inn on your left. On your right a hundred paces further on, you can purchase a specialist bottled beer named Aurthora from the local brewery: The Wincle Beer Company.

If you feel energetic you can put on your walking boots and walk the few miles along the footpath that takes you to the hills above Wincle. Here you will find Lud's Church and a little further on, Doxey Pool.

Cheers!